HIGHEST PRAISE FOR JOVE HOMESPUN ROMANCES:

"In all of the Homespuns I've read and reviewed I've been very taken with the loving renderings of colorful small-town people doing small-town things and bringing 5 STAR and GOLD 5 STAR rankings to readers. This series should be selling off the bookshelves within hours! Never have I given a series an overall review, but I feel this one, thus far, deserves it! Continue the excellent choices in authors and editors! It's working for this reviewer!"

—Heartland Critiques

We at Jove Books are thrilled by the enthusiastic critical acclaim that the Homespun Romances are receiving. We would like to thank you, the readers and fans of this wonderful series, for making it the success that it is. It is our pleasure to bring you the highest quality of romance writing in these breathtaking tales of love and family in the heartland of America.

And now, sit back and enjoy this delightful new Homespun Romance . . .

TOWN SOCIAL

Trana Mae Simmons

TOWN SOCIAL

Trana Mae Simmons

JOVE BOOKS, NEW YORK

TOWN SOCIAL

A Jove Book / published by arrangement with
the author

PRINTING HISTORY
Jove edition / October 1996

For information address: The Berkley Publishing Group,
200 Madison Avenue, New York, New York 10016.

The Putnam Berkley World Wide Web site address is
http://www.berkley.com/berkley

ISBN: 0-515-11971-7

A JOVE BOOK®
Jove Books are published by The Berkley Publishing Group,
200 Madison Avenue, New York, New York 10016.
JOVE and the "J" design are trademarks
belonging to Jove Publications, Inc.

PRINTED IN THE UNITED STATES OF AMERICA

10 9 8 7 6 5 4 3 2 1

To my Twysted Sisters.
Thanks for dragging me through the lows
and helping me celebrate the highs!

and

to Aunt 'Cille and Uncle Keith,
my favorite visitors!
I think you'll like this one.

TOWN SOCIAL

Liberty Flats, Texas
July 1879

In the early-morning light, Jake scanned the dusty street from one end of town to the other. Silent. Peaceful. Just as he liked it. So what if those two elderly women had grumbled yesterday within his hearing about the town being so quiet they could hear the spiders spin their webs?

He took another sip of coffee and got a mouthful of grounds for his trouble. Grimacing, he flicked the remainder of the liquid into the street, then set the cup on the jailhouse windowsill and pulled the rickety straight-back chair closer to the edge of the walkway. It creaked alarmingly when he settled his large body on it and propped his feet on the railing along the walkway.

Maybe today he'd find the energy to at least add a supporting slat to the bottom of the chair. And maybe not. Why mar the tranquility of the lazy day with work? If the town would hire its own sheriff or Austin would finally succeed in getting a marshal assigned here, the new man could fix his own damned chair. Tipping his hat down to shade his eyes from the rising sun, he crossed his arms and reconciled himself to spending another boring day in Liberty Flats, Texas.

Heel taps clicked smartly down the walkway, and Jake instinctively tuned in to the sound, not bothering to lift his hat and look. Definitely a woman. None of the men in town were small enough to make that little bit of noise, and the children went barefoot in the summertime. A young woman, since her gait was more sprightly than that of any of the elderly ladies in town. Might be one of Ginny's girls, but he couldn't imagine any of them up this early after a late night.

Her gait faltered, and he heard a smothered gasp. Uh-oh. She'd probably encountered one of the unsteady boards on the walkway. Hell, she must be new in town. Every other woman knew exactly where those semi-rotten boards were—and bitched pretty vocally to the store keepers, who claimed lack of money to repair them. He didn't recall any recent arrivals, but then, he hadn't seen any need to interrupt his poker game when the stage came in late yesterday.

The clicking taps drew closer, and he stifled a sigh, still not bothering to raise his hat and look up.

"Marshal."

Yep, definitely a new woman in town. He would have remembered that throaty, feminine voice from anywhere. And someone should tell her Liberty Flats didn't have a marshal. Maybe someone would.

"Marshal!"

A tapping-toe sound accompanied the voice this time, and Jake grunted under his breath in irritation. Yeah, she was addressing him, but why didn't she just get on with it and explain what she wanted? He lifted his index finger in acknowledgment, that brief movement his only response.

The tapping noise continued, accompanied by an indignant huff of breath. "Lazy small-town officials," she muttered.

Suddenly his hat went flying. Only the rigid discipline he'd honed over the years kept him in place without a muscle moving for a good, long ten seconds. During that time the tapping toe faltered, then ceased the annoying clicking noise.

He slit his eyes open first. The faint scent beside him had to be hers—the dust and horse manure in the street didn't smell like a mixture of fresh lemons and wild roses. He uncrossed his ankles and slowly lowered his feet from the railing. Her skirts rustled—sounded as though she wore at least half a dozen starched petticoats—and she evidently backed away a step or two. Wonder how long she would continue to wear all those underclothes in the Texas heat? Most of the women in town settled for one limp petticoat under their dresses, even though it left some of their more enticing curves open to appreciative male regard as they walked around, especially during the frequent gusts of dusty wind.

The chair creaked as he rose. He caught a glimpse of her from the corner of his eye—a flash of bright yellow that was her dress—but he ignored her in favor of looking around for his hat. Damn, it had landed in the street, right in the puddle of drying mud where he'd dumped his shaving water a while ago. Shrugging his shoulders in displeasure, he climbed down the two steps and picked it up, turning it over to survey the damage.

Mud stained the sweatband inside the rim. He ran a finger around it, then wiped it on his less-than-immaculate denims. He'd meant to stop by the laundry yesterday and pick up his fresh clothes, but the poker game at Ginny's had interfered. Besides, he'd had one more pair of clean socks left. And it didn't bother him to put on his denims without underwear this morning—much.

Well, the damned hat would have to dry before he could

wear it. He slapped it against his thigh, swearing under his breath in exasperation when it swept through mud he'd wiped on his pants. Drawing in a breath, he held it for a second, then let it whoosh out through puffed cheeks. This was not starting out to be one of those peaceful, lazy days that he had disciplined this town to since he'd drawn the assignment of taming the place so the citizens could walk the streets without fear of being struck by a stray gunshot.

Carrying his hat with him, he climbed back up the steps and headed for the jailhouse door.

"Marshal! I need to speak with you!"

He stopped, shook his head, then continued on his way. "I'm not the marshal," he tossed back over his shoulder. Usually he left the door open in order to enjoy the early-morning air, but this time he closed it behind him with a backward kick of his booted heel.

It flew open again before he could get to the dilapidated desk.

"Then what are you doing occupying the marshal's office and wearing a star on your chest?" the woman demanded. "I've read enough descriptions in dime novels to know what a Western peace officer looks like!"

Jake clenched his fists at his side, then forced himself to continue on to the desk. Tossing his hat aside, he picked up a pile of Wanted posters waiting for his attention and shuffled through them as he said, "Have you read enough descriptions to know what the inside of a jail cell looks like? You're right on the verge of finding out."

"For what?" Her voice rose indignantly. "I haven't done a darned thing to deserve being tossed into jail—except insist that you talk to me, since I'm now a citizen of this town and will be assisting in paying your salary."

Jake dropped the posters and held his hand up to tick off on his fingers the reasons she was flirting with being locked up. "Assault on a peace officer. Damaging another person's property. Disturbing the peace."

"You call my knocking your hat off your head because you were ignoring me an assault? Why, you overbearing, ignorant lout! You try to haul me into court for something like that, and all I'll have to do is stand there beside your big, lanky body and let the jury look at us. They'll laugh you out of town as a coward for daring to admit I got the better of you. As for disturbing the peace, all I did was disturb your lazy morning nap, when you should have been on duty anyway!"

That did it. She'd definitely managed to spoil the entire day. He damn sure wasn't going to let a cantankerous female make a fool out of him in front of the town he'd risked his life to tame. She was obviously one of those spoiled, sassy women who didn't realize she could end up with her butt in a whole world of trouble if she antagonized the male population, which ultimately protected the women in the West.

She was evidently— He whirled on her with practiced smoothness, a glower settling on his face.

She was evidently the prettiest thing ever to hit Liberty Flats since the town was born. Maybe even the entire state of Texas. Blond hair brought the Texas sunshine into the office, curling and cascading in a riot as it escaped the yellow ribbon she'd tried to tame it with and wisping around her heart-shaped face. Above an elfin nose and insolently pursed lips, eyes the color of spring bluebonnets met his glower with impudent defiance. She drew herself up to at least a full five feet, tipping her chin until he could see her entire smooth neck.

Hell, the men in town wouldn't need to imagine her curves. The tight bodice of that yellow dress outlined every one of them, nullifying the fact that her petticoats blurred the shape of her bottom and legs. Even the skimpy attire that Ginny's girls wore wouldn't allow them to compete with her. For some reason, the yards of material on her were more alluring than if she'd bared as much as the saloon women did.

He took a step backward, settling his rear on the edge of the desk and recrossing his arms defensively. The involuntary protective gesture was too late to counteract the feeling that a fist had just slammed into his stomach.

"Then spit out what you want and let me get on about my business," he halfway snarled at her.

Having his full attention at last didn't appear to defuse her indignation one iota. She matched him glare for scowl.

"I fail to understand how you can consider sleeping on a chair in front of your office doing your business," she spat.

He briefly closed his eyes and shook his head. No sense even attempting to dispute that stupid comment. There were some things people like Little Miss Greenhorn had to learn on their own.

"What do you want?" he prodded again.

"I wish to lodge a complaint." She started that danged toe-tapping again. "And from what I understand, this town has no government officials—not even a mayor, let alone a town council. You seem to be the closest thing to an authority figure available, so I came here. Perhaps I've miscalculated, however."

"Well, I reckon that depends on what your complaint is. If it's got something to do with a law being broken, I might be able to help you out. If not . . ." He shrugged in disregard, although his fingers tightened on his upper arms. No one messed with a woman in his town, whether she be a lady or a doxy.

"It's the streets," she said resolutely, surprising the hell out of him and quelling his incipient empathy as effectively as if she'd thrown a bucket of ice water on him.

"They are in a deplorable condition," she continued as he gritted his teeth to keep from telling her that he didn't give a damn about the town's *streets*.

"Yesterday I almost ruined one of my best traveling gowns," she went on in that prissy voice, "and that was just taking the three steps from where the stage stopped to the walkway. Surely there are some resolutions on this town's books about street maintenance. If not, there certainly should be! Since Liberty Flats is now my home for a while, I wish to be able to traverse the streets without worrying about ruining my attire each time I venture out."

"The streets," Jake repeated in a dumbfounded voice. "You want me to have the streets paved. It's not even six o'clock in the morning, and you want me to start going around telling everyone we have to pave the streets."

"Don't be ridiculous, Marshal. I'm well aware that it would be a major undertaking for a town like this to pay for enough bricks to pave its streets. However, it should be a simple enough matter for the store owners all to contribute toward paying for someone to periodically go up and down the streets and clean up after the animals. In fact, although it's necessary for the horses to be allowed access to the streets—after all, they provide transportation for the stores' customers—I see no reason why the streets should be a depository for all sorts of other refuse."

She lifted her index finger, admonishing him as though he were a child. "For instance, I watched you dump a basin of dirty water in the street a little earlier, and also the dregs of your coffee." Her chastisement accomplished, she still wasn't done. "Furthermore, there's no reason why other animals—besides the horses, that is—should be allowed to roam freely in town. Why, it can't be healthy for the children, not one of whom I've seen in a pair of shoes!"

Good God Almighty. Where did this woman come from? Every other female in town was probably still sleeping—or at the most, stoking the kitchen stove so the coffee would be ready by the time her man rose. And here she stood, primped and outfitted as though attending a social, radiating the kind of energy that should only be apparent after at least a full pot of coffee. She made him tired just looking at her.

He made the mistake of stifling a yawn.

She drew in a deep breath, preparatory, he was sure, to lambasting him for his rudeness.

"Look," he said quickly, "perhaps we could at least introduce ourselves before we continue this argu . . . uh . . . discussion. I'm Jake Cameron. And you?"

Her eyes narrowed ominously. "I thought all *responsible* law officials kept track of any new people in their town. Since I've been here well over twelve hours, I would think by now it would behoove you as marshal to know me—or at least, know *of* me."

"Look, lady," Jake replied, his lassitude quickly disintegrating, along with his struggle for patience. He dropped his arms and straightened up. "It's too damned early in the morning to be playing word games with you. And for your information, I'm not this town's marshal. This town doesn't have a marshal. I work for the Texas Rangers, and I take my orders from them, not the citizens of Liberty Flats. Perhaps those dime novels you're so proud of having read explained to you just what type of organization the Rangers is. We furnish our own horses, as well as our own guns. And one of the other requirements is that we damned well know how to use our firearms accurately."

She flicked a smirk of disregard at the low-hanging brace of pistols on his hips. "The Texas Rangers," she mused haghtily. "Ah, yes, I do believe I remember reading about a rogue band of Rangers that held the town of Brownsville hostage fifteen years or so ago. And the work that needs done in this town is not work that can be accomplished at the end of a gun. I suppose I'll just have to see what I can do about it myself." With a flounce of yellow skirts, she stormed out of the office.

Jake leaned back against the desk once more, the rigidity slowly easing from his body. Who the hell did she think she was, bringing up that blot on the Rangers' history? She couldn't even have been old enough to read when that happened.

Good God, he was glad to get rid of her. Wasn't he? His head swiveled slowly as he took in the contrast of the drab office to her brief, vital presence. One other shabby chair sat in the corner, and tattered pull-down shades covered the dust-smeared front windows. The only wall decorations were curled and faded Wanted posters tacked up here and there. How long had it been since he'd even checked them against the periodic updates he got over the wire on recent captures?

He mentally examined the two jail cells behind him. It had been more than a month since he stripped the bunks and took the linens to the laundry. But, hell, he'd only had a couple of drunks sleeping it off during that time. And he'd made the one who puked all over the cell clean up his own mess before he turned him loose the next morning. The drunk did a halfway decent job before Jake got tired of listening to his hangover moans and shoved him out the door.

Besides the occasional drunk, the only other person in town he didn't really get along with was Saul Cravens. So far, though, the biggest problem he'd had with Cravens was the man's seeming lack of respect for Jake's badge. But as far as Jake knew, Cravens didn't carry that lack of respect far enough to allow any crooked games in his saloon. He knew damned well that Jake continued to keep an eye on him.

And even Cravens' saloon was a tad more cheerful than the jailhouse. Jake had never paid much attention before to how dismal his office surroundings were; the town expected him to be visible on the streets, not holed up in the jailhouse office. His active presence made sure people like Cravens didn't get completely out of hand.

What the town didn't expect was an outspoken woman sticking her nose into matters she had no business prying into. His lips curled in amusement. It might be fun watching her butt heads with the merchants. There hadn't been any entertainment in town since that medicine show put on a performance a couple of months ago while the blacksmith repaired its wagon.

He'd just get back out there and claim his usual seat to observe, though it would be an hour or so yet before the town started stirring. His friend Charlie Duckworth would probably be by soon for his usual morning visit and cup of rank coffee.

Sauntering over to the pegs lining the wall beside the door, he took down his extra hat. Though he'd never bothered to have the bullet hole in the crown repaired, it would do until the mud dried on his other one and he could brush it clean.

Right before he walked out the door, a fleeting movement caught his eye. He glanced at the upper corner of the ceiling, where a huge brown spider was industriously repairing a web already hanging full of insect body husks. He didn't much care for spiders, but at least they kept the rest of the bug population down.

He turned away, then quickly looked back. Nah, there

was no way he could actually be hearing that spider spin its airy concoction. The tiny rasping noise must be his own breathing.

Liberty Flats woke up slightly earlier than usual that morning. Sunny Fannin made sure of that. She couldn't seem to muster the fortitude to rouse her Aunt Cassie after she lost patience with that hardheaded Texas Ranger and returned to the white clapboard house on the edge of town. Considering the lukewarm reception she had received from her aunt yesterday afternoon, it might be best to prepare the morning tea and biscuits herself, and keep something back for Aunt Cassie to eat when she rose.

The only thing was, she couldn't find anything but coffee in the cupboards. She despised that bitter brew, and besides, just because she found herself in the wilds of the West didn't mean she couldn't maintain some semblance of civility.

But did she have time to run back to the general store and pick up some tea before the biscuits baked, or should she wait until she got back before she made them? The town wasn't at all that large, as she'd been able to determine when she arrived yesterday at the stable and stage stop catty-corner and a little west across the street from her aunt's house. It didn't look like there were more than a dozen and a half buildings total, evenly divided on either side of the street.

She'd had to cross the street and pass the stable this morning in order to talk to that darned Ranger, and she'd passed only a couple other buildings before she came to the jailhouse. She had noticed the general store on the opposite side of the street, however, the same side as her aunt's house sat on. There was an intersecting street between the house and the main street of the town, but she should have plenty of time to get to the store and back if she walked swiftly.

Just then, her stomach growled, making the decision for her. She hurriedly mixed the biscuits and popped them in the oven. Leaving the house once again, she headed for the general store.

As she neared the store, she could hear a wagon coming down the street behind her. The only other sign of life, except for the mangy hound raising its leg next to one of the hitching rails, was that Texas Ranger lazing in front of the jailhouse again. He definitely wasn't asleep, although she had no idea how she could be aware of him watching her when he was that far away. Her stomach clenched as she recalled how far back she'd had to crane her neck to meet those whiskey-hued eyes when he finally deigned to look at her a while ago. Had he been standing in the street, with the sun at his back, she would have been completely engulfed by the shadow of those broad shoulders.

His narrow hips had seemed barely wide enough to hold up the gunbelt with two deadly-looking pistols riding low on his thighs. But, when he had nonchalantly strolled down into the street to retrieve his hat, she'd realized the bulk of the weight rested on a well-formed rear. The skintight denims outlined every curve, hugging the long expanse of his legs and fitting like an extra layer of leather over his boot tops.

Chastising herself for even the memory of that outlandish sight—and her extremely unladylike reaction to it—she could barely keep from waving a hand in front of her flushed cheeks. Land sakes, it was hot in this town, even on the shaded boardwalk. She should have picked up her parasol before she left the house. Then she could have shifted it sideways to block the gaze from the other side of the street.

He'd used those whiskey-brown eyes to try to intimidate her in his office, but she'd been distracted by the shining blackness of his hair and the rugged planes of his face. It should be against the law for a man that good-looking to have such an obnoxious personality. But then, he *was* the only law available here, from what her aunt said.

And to be honest—which she prided herself on being—part of her indignation had been because of his rude attitude, fostered by his apparent indifference toward her. Why, from what she'd read, she expected Western men to exhibit a more reverent manner toward women. She was no slouch in the looks department, and she'd certainly had her share of beaus back in St. Louis. However, Jake Cameron had stared down at her as though she were a pesky fly buzzing around that run-down office.

Just then, he raised his hand and very deliberately tilted his hat up just a tad. Land sakes, had he put that muddy hat back on over his clean hair? Didn't the man have any pride? Oh, he must have another hat, because that one was a couple of shades darker than the one she'd knocked off his head.

An older man emerged from the doorway behind the Ranger, blowing on the rim of a cup in his hand. The Ranger kept his gaze on her, though, instead of turning away to speak to his companion. She guessed he was practicing ignoring people once again. She very deliberately lifted her nose a trifle and stared straight ahead, telling her mind to concentrate on tea, not whiskey-colored eyes.

The wagon reached the general store at the same time she did, and the woman driving it pulled to a stop. Sunny nodded a brief greeting, then tugged on the door of the store. It refused to budge, and she stepped back a pace, frowning at the closed sign in the window.

"Fred doesn't usually open for another hour yet," the woman in the wagon called to her. "But I'm fixing to pick up some supplies I ordered, so I can let him know you're down here. He lives above the store."

Sunny stifled a horrified gasp as the woman climbed down from the wagon. She wore . . . pants. And they were every bit as skin-tight as those denims on the Ranger. Embarrassed, she quickly focused her gaze on the woman's face, feeling a surge of pity for her that was not entirely due to her plainness.

She couldn't have been more than ten years older than Sunny. The sun had frizzed her dark-brown locks, and lighter streaks filtered through them. She'd cut her hair so short that it barely swung down to her shoulders. A man's hat hung down her back, probably more often there than on her head.

Tiny wrinkle lines had already settled in the outer corners of her brown eyes. And such sad eyes. Shadows filled them for an instant before the woman visibly straightened her shoulders with an effort and spoke again.

"I'm Mary Lassiter."

"Sunny Fannin," Sunny responded. "And I suppose I could wait until the owner decides to open, but my aunt appears to be out of tea. I wanted to have breakfast ready for her when she woke."

"Tea?" Mary chuckled wryly. "I doubt you'll find any tea in Fred's store. You can ask him to order some, but since his new order just came in, you'll probably have to wait a month or two."

"Oh, for pity's sake. I could get it quicker by writing to one of my friends back East and having her mail it to me."

"That would be faster," Mary agreed. "Well, it was nice meeting you. But I need to get my supplies and hurry back to the ranch. We're de-horning the yearlings today, and cas . . . uh . . . taking care of that other nasty job with them."

"Other job?" Sunny unfortunately asked.

"Um . . . you know." A brief flash of amusement lit

Mary's eyes. "Making them into steers instead of bulls, so they're not so randy they fight with each other all the time when they should be grazing and putting on weight."

"Oh!" When she understood the meaning of Mary's words, a giggle erupted from Sunny's mouth. She tried to smother it with a hand over her lips, but Mary laughed too, and Sunny immediately forgot her embarrassment and joined her.

"I don't suppose that works on human males," Sunny found herself daring to say when she could speak. "At least not your Western males. Why, every one of them I've seen since I left St. Louis has carried a gun and just bristled with the urge to draw it and protect himself."

She wrinkled her nose and cast a disparaging look across the street. "Well, at least *almost* every one. That Ranger over there acts like it would be an effort to flick a fly off his nose."

"Never underestimate Jake," Mary said in a warning voice. "He's the reason I can come into town alone, without wearing my own pistol and having to bring half my crew with me. I still carry my rifle under the wagon seat, but it's more habit than because I really need it."

"You . . . you wear a pistol?"

"I can hit what I aim at, too," Mary informed her. "And with the rifle. Nowadays, though, I usually only shoot a rattlesnake once in a while. Or a coyote that thinks my henhouse holds a free meal."

"Hmm," Sunny mused. "Since I'm going to be a Western woman, at least for a while, maybe I should learn how to shoot a gun."

"Tell you what. Give me a week or so to get the cattle taken care of, then ride on out to my ranch and I'll give you a lesson. I've got a stash of tea, too. I still had plenty left, so I didn't order any this time, or I'd give you some before I leave. But if you get desperate for a pot, maybe I could send one of my hands into town in a couple days."

"That's so nice of you," Sunny said, beaming to herself at the stir of beginning friendship she felt for this plain woman. "Please don't bother, though. And I'd love to come visit you, but it will depend on whether I can rent a buggy at the stables. Besides never having shot a gun, I've never learned to ride a horse either."

"My, my," Mary said with a gentle smile, which made Sunny completely disregard her ordinary features. "We've got lots to do to turn you into a Western woman."

A flash of movement drew Sunny's attention across the street as the Ranger surged to his feet.

"Mary!" he shouted. "Ring the fire bell! Miss Foster's house is on fire!"

Sunny froze for a second as Mary whirled away. Miss Foster's house? Her aunt's house was on fire?

Heart pounding, Sunny whirled and stared back down the walkway, but she could only see the front of her aunt's house from her position. Picking up her skirts, she raced out into the street where she would have a better view, like the Ranger had from the other side.

Oh, my Lord!

Smoke drifted from the rear of the house!

BURNED-BISCUIT SMELL permeated the interior of Aunt Cassie's house. Sunny waited just inside the front door while her aunt thanked the townspeople and sent them on their way, explaining that there had been no fire—only a pan of biscuits left uncared for in the oven by Sunny. By the time Jake had arrived, the odor had already awoken Cassie, who had taken care of the matter. The other townspeople who came in response to the fire bell were also unneeded.

Sunny would have bet her newest ball gown—the one she had yet to wear—that Aunt Cassie abhorred having to face the entire town dressed in her nightclothes, with her gray hair rolled up in those rag scraps. But how the heck was Sunny supposed to know her aunt's stove cooked faster than the one she and her mother had used in St. Louis?

Aunt Cassie stepped inside and closed the door very deliberately behind her. Her pale blue eyes scanned Sunny, centering on her niece's hands, which were clasped in front of her. Sunny unclenched her fingers, smoothing her palms against her skirt.

"I'm sorry, Aunt Cassie. I was just trying to do my share. I thought I get breakfast ready for you."

"It's a poor cook who doesn't watch her dishes," Cassie said with a sniff of disdain. "Samantha should have taught you better."

Sunny immediately bristled. "Let's leave my mother out of this! *I* burned the biscuits, and I'll take care of cleaning up the mess."

Cassie shrugged and headed for her bedroom. "The smell's already set into the kitchen curtains. They'll need to be hung out to air as soon as possible."

The smell's already set into the kitchen curtains, Sunny mentally mocked. *They'll need to be hung out to air as soon as possible.*

Good grief, didn't she have any rights around here? Granted, Aunt Cassie obviously spent a lot of time keeping her house in such immaculate condition, but it wouldn't hurt to leave the curtains until she at least had a bite to eat. Her stomach rumbled, agreeing with her. The house belonged to her too, she reminded herself—a full half of it. After her mother's untimely death, the lawyer had made sure Sunny was fully apprised of what the estate entailed.

As always when she thought of her beautiful, loving mother and the wonderful relationship they'd shared, her eyes filled with tears. She missed her so terribly. The painful memories continued to intrude on her conscious thoughts. How suddenly her mother had been ripped from her life just over three months ago by the drunken carriage driver. Ten other people leaving the opera house were injured when the driver lost control of his horses, but only her mother—who was directly in the path of the horses' deadly hooves—had been killed.

She probably would have been right there beside her mother that evening had it not been for a slight case of sniffles. Ever protective, her mother had insisted that she sit out the opening night of the opera, to which she'd so looked forward. Did she want to risk a full-blown case of pneumonia by exposure to the night air and miss the rest of the season? Sunny recalled her mother asking. Or would she rather be healthy enough to enjoy the never-ending round of galas, which was just beginning?

Before the debilitating grief could take full hold of her, Sunny blinked away her tears and started for the kitchen. Had she made the wrong decision in coming to Liberty Flats? Aunt Cassie was her only other relative but her mother had hardly ever spoken of her sister. Since her arrival in Liberty Flats, Sunny already had more than one occasion to wish she knew more about the reason for the rift between the two sisters, but it had never seemed that important back in St. Louis. At least they'd shared Christmas letters, so she had Aunt Cassie's address.

Barely one month after her mother's death, she realized she would never be able to come to terms with her grief in St. Louis. The house echoed her mother's presence, and every building in town reminded her of shopping trips or nights out—always shared with her mother. They had been more like sisters than mother and daughter. Aching for a change and never dreaming that her aunt would be the total opposite of her mother, Sunny had made plans to travel west. She had sent only a brief telegram to warn her aunt of the impending visit.

She could always return home, she guessed as she opened the kitchen windows to allow the smell to dissipate. Rather than selling the St. Louis house, she had rented it to one of her newly married friends.

Shaking off her morose mood, she walked out onto the back porch to retrieve the metal biscuit pan Aunt Cassie said she'd thrown out the kitchen door. Halfway across the porch, she stopped in shock when a small, grubby figure sprang into view. After a split-second, frightened glance, the figure scrambled away, clasping an armful of burned biscuits to her chest.

At least Sunny assumed it was a *her*. Matted curls of

indeterminate color snarled down the child's back, and the ragged gown looked as thought it might originally have been fashioned for a little girl. Although it could be a child of either gender running around in a nightshirt, she guessed as her heart wrenched with pity.

"Wait!" she called. "Please! If you're hungry, I'll fix you some breakfast!"

The child skidded to a stop, then whirled with wide eyes. "Huh? You . . . you'd really feed me?"

"Of course," Sunny called back. "Why, it's inhuman to let a child go hungry. Where are your parents?"

"You ain't Miz Foster," the child replied warily. "You's too pretty for her. How comes you's in her house?"

"I just arrived yesterday, and Miss Foster is my aunt. Now, why don't you throw those biscuits down and leave them for the birds? I'll mix up a batch of flapjacks, and I saw some maple syrup in Aunt Cassie's pantry."

"Flapjacks?" It didn't seem possible, but the child's eyes widened even further. Sunny could make out their bright blue color from where she stood. "And . . . and syrup?"

"Butter, too," Sunny said with a nod. "And how about some buttermilk? But you'll have to agree to wash up a little first. Want to come into the kitchen and do that while I mix up the flapjack batter?"

"I be right back."

The child dashed away to the high weeds at the edge of the yard and dropped the biscuits—except for one, which Sunny saw get surreptitiously slipped into a pocket on the tattered gown. Catching a glimpse of brown and white fur when an animal's head popped up from the weeds, she realized the child was sharing the burned bounty with an animal of some kind—it looked like a dog.

Finally, the child started back toward the house, the walk a mixture of seeming nonchalance and restrained eagerness.

Sunny studied the figure as it drew closer, empathy for her slowly combining with outrage toward parents who would allow a child to fall into such a state. The child wore no shoes—but then, neither did the rest of the children in town. The torn hem of the gown fluttered just below knees covered with scabs and scratches scattered through streaks of dirt on the lower legs. On keener inspection, Sunny realized one of the spots on the face, at first taken for dirt, was instead a discolored bruise, faded now to a sickly yellow color.

She waited until the child stopped at the bottom step before she asked, "Want to tell me your name? Mine's Sunny."

The figure toed the dirt with one foot, blue eyes dropping for a minute, then gazing past Sunny to the open door leading to the kitchen. The yearning face tore at Sunny's heart.

"It's Teddy," the child finally said. "Can we go eat now?"

"It'll take me a little while to cook the food. But you'll have plenty of time to wash up while I do that. And . . . um . . . well, is Teddy a boy's name or a girl's?"

"Boy's," Teddy said. "But I got stuck with it anyway. Pa thinks it's funny to call a girl by a boy's name. When he says anythin' about it atall, anyways."

She slowly climbed the steps, and Sunny suppressed the urge to cover her nose. It would take more than a basin of water to counteract the rank odor, but she was leery of asking the child to take a complete bath. It wasn't really her place to do that. She fully intended to get to the bottom of why this child was in such a neglected condition though. Right now, it seemed like a better idea to get something in her poor little stomach besides burned biscuits.

"Come on in, Teddy." She motioned the little girl past her, and the child moved hesitantly through the door. Inside, she stopped abruptly and stared around the room. Sunny had to squeeze past her to get to the stove.

"Sure is pretty," Teddy said in a reverent voice. "Ain't never been inside a real house a'fore. Not's I 'member anyways."

"Um . . . what sort of place do you live in?" Sunny ventured as she filled the basin from the reservoir of water on the side of the stove and set it on the counter.

"Just a shack outside of town. It ain't so bad in the summer. Gots lots of places for the wind to blow through, there be any wind. This past winter, it got kinda cold sometimes."

Thinning her lips, Sunny shook her head. But it wasn't the child's fault she lived in such dreary surroundings, she reminded herself.

"Here's a washcloth and some soap," Sunny said cheerfully. "Go ahead and clean up while I get started on breakfast."

As Teddy complied, Sunny gathered flour and other supplies from the pantry, keeping an eye out to see whether Teddy had any idea of how to clean herself. Surprisingly, the child seemed to enjoy washing the dirt from her body. By the time Sunny had flapjack batter mixed and a skillet heating on the stove, Teddy had cleaned her hands, arms, and face, and had started working on her legs.

"Would you like some more hot water?" Sunny asked.

"Oh, could I? I don't wanna waste it. Our well's been 'bout dry for so long. We gets a little water from it, but then has to wait for more to come in. I was meanin' to get to the creek pretty soon, but it's a fur piece of a walk."

A hundred questions ran through Sunny's head, intermingled with her still-simmering anger over the child's condition. However, she restrained her usual forthrightness in deference to Teddy's youthfulness. She didn't want to scare the child away, although Teddy didn't appear to have any qualms about answering inquiries.

Sunny dumped the dirty water into the sink and refilled the basin. As she poured a cup of flapjack batter into the skillet, she heard Teddy sigh. The child stood with her eyes closed, running the washcloth around her neck and under her dress, across to her shoulders. Then she rather reluctantly rinsed the cloth out and resoaped it, bending once more to her legs.

"Uh . . . how old are you, Teddy?"

"Eight," she responded without hesitation.

Good grief! She was so tiny that Sunny had thought her no more than five or six. Raising her estimate of Teddy's age, however, didn't diminish her outrage at her condition one bit.

"Have you lived in Liberty Flats all your life?" Sunny questioned next.

"Huh-uh. We gots here last fall."

"Um . . . does *we* mean you and your folks?"

"Nah. Just me and Pa. Don't 'member my ma, but probably should. When Pa gets to talkin', he says she left when I was four. You'd think I'd 'member her, bein' that old, but I don't."

"Do you remember where you lived before Liberty Falls?"

"All over," Teddy said with a shrug of her slight shoulders. "Towns run together after a while. Just wherever Pa could find work, 'till he decided to drag up for one reason or another."

Sunny flipped the flapjack to the other side. "Drag up?"

"Yeah, that's what he always called it. Like it was his own idea we moved on. Sometimes I sorta got the feelin' it wasn't him quittin' on his own, tho'."

Sunny slid the flapjack onto a plate and poured another

cup of batter into the skillet. When she noticed Teddy eyeing the plate longingly, she hurriedly buttered the flapjack and added syrup. After filling a glass with buttermilk from the pitcher she'd brought in earlier from the well house, she motioned Teddy to the table.

"Go ahead and eat this one while I fix some more," she said, but Teddy was already digging into the flapjack.

Then her fork paused halfway to her mouth, dripping syrup onto the plate. "You mean, I can have more than one?" she asked in an awestruck voice.

"You can have as many as you want," Sunny said with a laugh. Thinking better of it, she qualified, "Well, as many as I think are good for you. I get the feeling you haven't had a lot to eat lately, and sometimes when people overindulge after not having eaten for a while, it's not real good for them."

"Over . . . over . . . in . . . ?" Teddy mumbled around a mouthful.

"Overindulge," Sunny repeated. "It means having too much of something, even if it's something that's good for you. And it's not proper manners to talk with your mouth full."

"Sorry." Teddy nodded and turned her attention quickly back to her plate. Before the next flapjack cooked completely, Teddy was staring at the skillet, her fork poised. She finished three more, along with two glasses of buttermilk, before Sunny decided she should caution her about overloading her stomach. Teddy leaned back in the chair with an ecstatic look on her face, patting her tummy, and Sunny put the next flapjack on her own plate.

Recalling the glimpse of brown and white fur, she scooped one more cup of mix into the skillet before she sat down.

Over her own breakfast, Sunny learned that Teddy was an

only child and that she'd never gone to one day of school. The child was perfectly candid about herself, seemingly unaware of any discrepancy in her lifestyle and the type of existence that was normal for a child of her age. Sunny's ire grew with every new piece of information, but the child in no way could be blamed, so she restrained her anger until a more appropriate time. And that time would definitely come.

Pretending she had a full stomach herself, Sunny asked Teddy if she might want to take the last flapjack along with her. Nodding eagerly, the little girl jumped from her chair and waited impatiently for Sunny to wrap the food in a piece of newspaper and hand it to her. Before she could disappear out the door, Sunny said, "If you'd like to come back for lunch, I'm sure there will be plenty."

The first glimpse of shame that Sunny had seen filled Teddy's eyes. "Pa'll be awake by then," she said, making Sunny wonder if the father could be what caused Teddy's mortification. "And I ain't supposed to leave the place. But . . . maybe I could come back in the mornin'."

"Please do," Sunny insisted. "And any other time you can. Maybe we could find time for you to take a complete bath and even wash your hair."

Teddy's hand went to the snarled mass of hair, and her eyes lit up. "Yeah, that'd be nice. Wish I had me a brush, to keep it neater. But I finger-comb it sometimes. If I don't, Pa says he's gonna cut it all off. He'd probably do it, too, if he didn't fall asleep so early in the evenin' after he samples his jug."

She glanced out the door, an apprehensive look on her face. "It's gettin' awful late. I gotta go."

She ran out the door and, ignoring the back steps, jumped off the porch. Then she whirled to face Sunny. "Oh. Forgot my manners again. Thanks for breakfast."

"You're welcome," Sunny replied with a smile.

"See you tomorrow!"

While more questions filled Sunny's thoughts, the child raced off. She must remember her mother a little, since she had at one time been taught at least a few manners. From what Sunny had learned of the father while Teddy gobbled her food, she couldn't imagine that man teaching her anything.

She laughed aloud when she saw the brown and white head poke out of the weeds at Teddy's approach. The little girl knelt and threw her arms around the dog, then rose and started skipping off, with him at her heels. As they moved away, Teddy fed him pieces of flapjack. In a moment they were out of sight, and Sunny went back into the kitchen.

Before she could pick up the dirty plates and glasses, a knock sounded at the front door. Since Aunt Cassie still hadn't appeared for breakfast, Sunny sighed and headed through the house, steeling herself to meet a townsperson who had probably already heard of her debacle with the biscuits. Well, she was just not going to be embarrassed about it. Every woman alive burned something once in a while!

When she opened the door, she found Jake Cameron standing on the other side, his fist poised to knock again. He dropped his arm, nodding at her. Craning her neck, she stared pointedly at his hat, which any other man of her acquaintance would have removed immediately in her presence. Jake only stuck his thumbs in his gunbelt.

"Miss Foster around?"

"My aunt is still dressing. Or at least I assume so, since she hasn't come out of her room yet. May I help you with something?"

"Probably. Tell her Fred said her supplies are ready, whenever she wants to come by the general store and pick them up. His boy's still laid up with that broken arm, so he can't deliver them."

"Is that one of the other duties you have in town to keep you busy?" Sunny asked in amazement. "Delivering messages for the merchants?"

"Just happened to be wandering by," Jake said with a shrug. "Fred mentioned it to me after we got back from putting out the fire here."

"There *was* no fire!" Sunny exclaimed. "You know darned well it was only a pan of burning biscuits!"

"Couldn't prove it by the word going around town." Jake's lips curved up in a bare hint of a smile. "You know how it is in a small town. Story gets started, it sort of grows."

"I've never lived in a small town, so I wouldn't know about that," Sunny said through gritted teeth. "But I hope you will correct any misconceptions people have. After all, you were here!"

Jake sniffed the air. "Sure smells like a fire."

"Ohhhh!" It took a great effort not to stamp her foot like a child and slam the door in his face. Unclenching her teeth, she stared up at him. "What is it with you, *Marshal*?" she asked, deliberately misnaming him again. "Or, more to the point, what is it about me that you don't like? You've made it very clear that I'm quite low on your list."

"Well, now, ma'am," Jake drawled. Tipping his hat up an inch with his forefinger, he gazed down at her, a suspicious twinkle in his whiskey-brown eyes. "I don't keep no lists. Keep what I know about people in my head. Have a pretty good memory, too, once someone tells me their name after I'm polite enough to give them mine. And I always remember when a man tells me what he does for a living, whether it's that he's a marshal or a Texas Ranger."

Despite her vow to remain unflustered and unembarrassed, Sunny felt a blush creeping over her cheeks. Still, she couldn't bring herself to apologize to him.

"Most men who consider themselves polite remove their hats in the presence of a lady," she spat in her defense.

"Reckon they do," Jake agreed without hesitation. "In front of women who act like ladies."

With a brief nod, he turned and walked away, leaving Sunny gaping after him in fury. Although he appeared only to saunter, he was out the gate and well on his way back to town before she could find her voice. By then, she would have had to scream to make him hear her. She almost did just that but settled for slamming the door instead.

"Good grief, child," Cassie said from behind her. "Must you make such a racket? Who was at the door?"

Sunny turned to face her, hands on hips. "The most infuriating, arrogant, ill-mannered man I have ever met. *That's* who was at the door! How on earth do the people in this town stand to have that Jake Cameron bossing them around?"

"Don't underestimate Ranger Cameron," Cassie warned. "He's not to be trifled with."

Sunny blew a wisp of hair off her forehead. "That's what Mary Lassiter said, but I'll tell you what . . ."

"What were you doing talking to that woman?" Cassie snapped. "You stay away from her!"

"Mary seemed very nice," Sunny said in surprise. "And I'm quite old enough to choose my own friends, Aunt."

"Not while you're living in my house. I won't have you associating with her."

"Aunt Cassie." Sunny tried to respond in a mild voice. "This house is half mine, and you know it. And I didn't come out here to have you tell me how to live my life. I needed to get away from St. Louis for a while and come to terms with my grief over my mother. I . . ."

"You aren't even mourning Samantha properly," Cassie cut in. "Look what you're wearing. The mourning period is a full year, and you should be wearing black during that time."

"My mother believed in life, not death," Sunny said with a tired sigh. "I explained to you yesterday, after I arrived on the stage, why I wasn't wearing black. My mother would not have wanted me to. She hated me in black."

"Perhaps you could get away with that in a large town like St. Louis," Cassie said with a sniff, "but this is a small town, and I have a reputation to keep up. Once people find out Samantha's only been dead three months, they'll frown on your wearing bright colors. I intend to honor the mourning period."

Sunny stared at Cassie's black gown. It intensified her sallow skin, although with her hair now styled, it set off the iron-gray curls. She searched for a glimpse of her mother in Cassie's face. One reason she'd decided to come to Liberty Flats was the fact that her mother's sister lived there, and she'd been hoping to find a kindred spirit in her grief.

Admittedly, she'd also been yearning to find another person as wonderful as her mother, and she'd thought her aunt might be that person, since she was her mother's blood sister. That hope had been dashed when Aunt Cassie didn't even bother to meet the stage, despite the follow-up telegram Sunny had sent at the stage stop in Dallas, on the way to Liberty Flats. She'd had to ask directions to the house and hire a man lounging on the walkway to carry her trunk.

And given her aunt's attitude toward her, she definitely couldn't talk to her about the other reason she had chosen Liberty Flats as the final destination for her journey.

"Aunt, if my presence here is so disturbing to you,

perhaps there's a boardinghouse in town where I can find a room," Sunny said at last.

"The only boardinghouse is usually full, with a waiting list," Cassie replied. "And, as you pointed out, the house is half yours. I can't afford to buy your interest and, even if I could, I'd never be able to find another place on what my share would be. Besides, I've lived here all my life. I was born in this house!"

"I have no intention of asking you to move," Sunny said in exasperation. "But I also don't intend to return to St. Louis until I feel I can handle it. Please. Can't we at least try to get along?"

Cassie sniffed again—Sunny was beginning to find that sound immensely nerve-wracking—and turned toward the kitchen. "Is there any coffee left?"

Shoulders drooping in defeat, Sunny followed her. "I'm sorry." Darn it. Why did she keep apologizing to the woman? "I don't drink coffee, Aunt Cassie, so I had buttermilk instead. But I'll make you a pot of coffee, if you wish."

"Never mind. I like my coffee made my own particular way. You'd probably make it too weak. I'll just have some biscuits while it perks."

"Uh . . . I made flapjacks instead of more biscuits. But there's still some batter left."

"Flapjacks? That's much too heavy for breakfast."

"Well, the little girl looked like . . ."

"Little girl?" Cassie stared at her. "What little girl? I'm not partial to having a pack of children hanging around my house, Miss. They do nothing but destroy things with their rowdy ways."

"She was gathering up the burned biscuits by the back porch, Aunt Cassie! And she didn't look like she'd had a decent meal in weeks. Months, maybe. What did you expect me to do? Shoo her off like a stray dog?"

"That would have been the best thing," Cassie said. "People need to be made to take responsibility for their own children."

"That's one thing you and I can agree on," Sunny said in a grim voice. "Totally."

3

"SUNNY," JAKE MUSED as he sauntered away from Pete, who was lounging in front of the stage stop, as usual. Well, he had to admit the name fit the new woman in town—at least in a physical way. Her temperament, now, was a different matter.

He headed for the telegraph office to send a wire once again reminding the Ranger headquarters office in Austin that they were supposed to be getting a marshal assigned to Liberty Flats. His feet were so itchy he could barely keep from jumping on his horse and leaving the town to fend for itself. He'd never been in one place this long in all the time he'd been a Ranger. As a matter of fact, he hadn't stayed this long anywhere for a full half of his life.

In defiance of his father's command and after lying about his age, he'd managed to get assigned to the squad of Terry's Texas Rangers for the last two years of the War between the States. Since he'd already attained his present height, the army officer didn't question him too closely when he stated his age as eighteen, rather than the true sixteen. After the war he returned to the ranch but found himself too used to the respect he'd gleaned in the army to knuckle under again to his father's orders. Besides, Douglas Cameron didn't need his help to run the vast Leaning C spread southwest of Austin. He had dozens of hands at his beck and call.

As soon as Jake pushed open the door of the telegraph office, Turley looked up with a scowl settling on his face. "Morning, Jake. You sure cleaned me out last night. Guess Lady Luck was riding your shoulder."

"Luck's got nothing to do with it, Turley. And a man shouldn't gamble money he can't afford to lose."

"Well, you never seem to lose none," Turley muttered. "You need to send a wire?"

"That's usually what a person comes into a telegraph office for," Jake replied, making a mental note to stop by Turley's house later and hand over a portion of the money he'd won off the man to Turley's wife. He could always make the excuse that Turley had been half drunk—which wouldn't be a lie—and left part of his stake on the table.

After taking care of the telegram, Jake strolled over to the stables and checked on his dun. Dusty nickered eagerly when he saw him, racing up to the corral gate.

"Sorry, old son," Jake told the horse as he scratched that special spot behind Dusty's ear and fed him the apple that had been in his shirt pocket. "Maybe we can go out for a run later this evening, when the town's asleep. It's been quiet the last few nights." He pressed his lips together and continued, "Hell, it's been quiet the last few months! If I could get one of those lazy-ass men in town to sign on at least as deputy, I could get out into the countryside now and then."

"Not much chance of that, Ranger," a voice said behind him.

Jake slid a sideways glance at John Dougherty, the stable owner, as he limped to a halt beside the fence.

"You'd be the first man I'd pick, John, if you'd show an interest. This stable doesn't take up all your time. And you're not married—don't have a wife to tell you what you can and can't do."

"Yeah, I ain't got no wife to leave behind as a widow, neither, any outlaws ride into town. And after that tussle I had with that wild bronc that broke my leg in four different places, I ain't got two good legs to stand on."

"There's nothing wrong with your arms, John. Or your gun hand."

"I'm not fast with a gun like you are, Jake. Don't have your rep, neither. A rightfully deserved rep it is, too. Hell, it only took you a month to clean the riffraff out of this town and end that feud between the Lazy J and the Bar M. And it's been a right pleasant place to live the whole three or four months ever since."

Jake sighed and shook his head as he studied the shorter man. "People need to take responsibility for their own town, John. If some other assignment comes up that's more important, the Rangers will call me in. This town's gonna have to stop depending on me and think about getting organized to protect itself."

He got the same response from John as he did from the rest of the men in town—shrugged shoulders and an evasive look in his eyes.

"Wonder where the hell Tompkins is?" John asked. "Even hungover, he's usually here by now. I'll dock his pay some, he don't show up pretty soon."

"You seen his little girl, Teddy, this morning?"

"Yeah. Saw her heading back to that shack a while ago. Called her over and gave her the sandwich you saved for her and them leftovers for the dog. She didn't gulp her food down like she usually does. Just thanked me real politely and took it."

"She have any more bruises on her?" Jake asked in a deceptively mild voice.

"None," John replied with a sardonic chuckle. "Some

scratches and stuff on her legs, but those were just the normal things young'uns get running around in the outdoors. I don't think Tompkins will lay a hand on her again, at least not while he's living in our town."

"Yeah," Jake mused. "But what happens after he leaves here? Damn it, there ought to be a law against a man mistreating his kid like that."

"Well, if you say there ain't no law against it, then I guess we can't do nothin'. Besides, I don't figure any of the old biddies in this town would take in a stray young'un, we did offer to try to find her another home."

Dusty nickered and stared over Jake's shoulder. Jake knew that welcoming whicker, so he didn't turn to greet Charlie for the second time that morning. The older man propped his arms on the railing as John walked away to tend to chores in the stable.

"Morning, cayuse," Charlie said to Dusty. "This here whippersnapper keeping you penned up again? Don't seem right, a frisky horse like you not getting out to run once in a while."

Jake reached down and pulled a stem of grass. Sticking it between his teeth, he muttered, "Yeah, Dusty. One of these mornings I'm gonna come out here and find you with your bones creaking like Charlie's, you don't start getting some exercise. Might even be the beginning of a bald patch on your head, just like his, and we'll have to make you wear a bonnet so you don't get sunburned."

Charlie sighed dramatically. "Yep, cayuse, there ain't nothing like being alone all the time to age a person or a critter. Maybe what you need is a little filly to keep you company. Why, I actually saw a spark of something besides downright boredom in this young pup's eyes earlier this morning. 'Course the filly he was eyeing was the wrong species for you. That pretty yellow color looks mighty good on one of them palominos I just had shipped in, though, and the two of you would make awfully pretty colts."

Jake scowled sideways at Charlie. "If you're so lonesome, old pard, why don't you concentrate on your own love life before you end up losing all your hair? After that happens, the women will be more interested in using your bald pate for a mirror to primp in, instead of their fingers itching to have something to hang on to when you kiss them."

Charlie didn't answer for a minute, while he dug in his shirt pocket. He pulled out a package of makings, rolled a smoke with practiced ease, and lit it before he said, "You find out anything more about that pretty little gal who burned the biscuits at Cassie's house this morning?"

"Why? She's too young for you."

Charlie flicked ashes and waited. Jake had dealt with that aspect of Charlie's personality too many times not to know his friend wouldn't bother to repeat the question or expand on his reason for asking it. As close as they were, there were areas of Charlie's life he refused to discuss with Jake. Nights around the low-burning campfires they'd shared had been the same, both during the war where they'd met and afterward when, in return for a small share in the mine, he'd joined Charlie in working his silver claim outside of Denver. Charlie told a person just exactly what he felt like telling them and not one word more.

He knew Charlie had grown up in Liberty Flats. When the mine became successful enough to pay the expenses, he left a manager in charge and returned to his childhood home to restore the family homestead and raise horses. Having no other use for his share of the profits, Jake was more than glad at the time to invest them in Charlie's ranch. Dusty was a product of Charlie's careful breeding; Jake had asked for the horse once in lieu of the annual payment for his contribution to the working capital.

As far as he knew, no one else in Liberty Flats had any idea how well off Charlie was, since his friend was careful not to, as he put it, "put on snooty airs." And Jake would never tell anyone. Despite their bantering, he cared more for the older man than even his father. In fact, Charlie had been more of a father to him than Douglas Cameron had ever tried to be.

"Well," Jake said, after he decided the silence had strung out long enough. "Her name's Sunny Fannin, and she's the niece of your old flame, Cassie Foster. Pete said he asked her how far she'd come before she got on the stage from Dallas, and she told him she'd come all the way from St. Louis. Took a riverboat to New Orleans, then a ship to Galveston. She might have got a ride on that railroad from Galveston to Houston, but my guess is she's probably been on a stage since she left the ship in Galveston."

"Probably," Charlie agreed, blowing out a stream of harsh-smelling smoke with the word. "But . . ."

"She's not much of a cook," Jake said, overriding Charlie's intention to continue before he realized the older man had meant to say more. "Not if those burned biscuits this morning are any indication of her ways in the kitchen. But I suppose someone with her background has probably never had to cook her own meals anyway."

"Don't bet a wad on that." Charlie spoke up in a firmer tone. "And Cassie ain't an old flame. Things never got that far between us."

"So why's that?" Jake asked. "Did she have a sister you found more attractive? Or is there a brother somewhere? She's gotta have one or the other, for Sunny to be her niece."

Charlie dropped his smoke stub and ground it beneath a

run-down boot heel. "Sister," he said shortly. "And that little Sunny gal is the picture of her at about the same age."

"Considering what I've seen of Miss Foster, then, I couldn't blame a man for eyeing her sister instead of her."

Charlie flicked a cold glance at him. "Son, I know for a fact you've got a few brains above your neck, but I guess you still ain't outgrowed thinking with what's between your legs. Man needs to look beneath the beautiful outside of a woman, which is what stirs his groin at first. Sometimes a plain woman's got a lot more to her."

Stung by Charlie's criticism, Jake shot back, "You sure as hell don't know me very well if you think I don't realize what a viper a beautiful woman can be. My father drank himself into a stupor in front of my mother's portrait more nights than I can count."

"You're missing the point, son," Charlie said in a softer voice. "It ain't the beauty or the lack of it. It's the woman herself you need to get to know."

Jake shook his head. "You've done fine without a woman around to worry about taking care of. If you think that's so important, why haven't you ever courted anyone since I've known you? You've got plenty to offer a woman, money to give her a fine life. Hell, you don't even have to do your own chores at your ranch in the mornings. You just leave orders for your men and ride into town to bother me."

"Maybe I'm like your pa," Charlie mused. "Maybe I figure I need a whole heart to offer a woman, and part of one just won't do."

"Say," John called from the stable door, "ain't that Teddy coming there?"

Jake followed the direction of John's gaze and saw Teddy racing toward them, bare feet flying along the dirt track leading to the shack Tompkins had taken up residence in when he hit town last fall. The brown and white dog that had adopted Teddy a few weeks ago followed at her heels. As she got closer, Jake could hear her tortured sobs. He knelt and opened his arms, and she threw herself against his chest.

"I cain't wake him," she cried between sobs. "He won't get up. And . . . and I think . . . he's stiff. And cold."

Jake pushed her away far enough to cup her face in his palms. "Who, Teddy? Your pa?"

"Y . . . yeah," Teddy said, tears streaming down her face, which for some reason Jake noted in a corner of his mind was clean. "Oh, Ranger Jake. I think . . ."

"Shush, Teddy." Jake pulled her close again, and she buried her nose against his shoulder. "Take it easy, darlin'. I'll go check on him."

"Won't . . . won't be no use," she said in a muffled voice. "I don't think he's gonna get up again. Pa's dead, I think." She wiped her nose against his shirt and leaned back in the cradle of Jake's arm. "He . . . it smelled pretty bad, even worse than usual. He throwed up."

John Dougherty walked up to join them. "Probably choked to death on his own puke," he said in a disgusted voice.

Jake threw him a quelling look, then rose with Teddy in his arms just as Sunny raced up to them, gasping for breath.

"I saw her running down the road when I was out shaking the rugs on the porch," Sunny said. "I could tell something was wrong. What's happened?"

Jake willingly transferred Teddy to Sunny when she reached for her. "It's her pa," he said in quiet voice. "We think he might have passed on during the night."

"Oh, my God," Sunny breathed. "What can I do?"

"Take care of her while I go check it out," Jake directed, covering up his prickle of amazement when Sunny gazed at him with tears in her bluebonnet eyes and actually nodded her head in obedience. "You can take her to my office if you want."

"I'll take her to my own house," Sunny said sternly. "It's a much more appropriate place. And cleaner, too."

Now that was the same women he'd been dealing with, Jake reflected. Always getting her gibes in. Right now, though, he had more important things to do than spar with her.

"Go get Doc and tell him to meet me out at Tompkins' shack, Charlie," he ordered as Sunny walked away, still carrying Teddy, the mongrel dog trailing behind. Good Lord, he hoped Sunny knew what she was doing. From the little he knew about the reclusive Cassie Foster, his office might be a better place for Teddy to wait for the verdict on her pa.

CASSIE STOOD ON the porch as Sunny approached, her back rigid and a forbidding look on her face. Without hesitation, Sunny straightened her own shoulders and marched on up the steps.

"What's happened?" Cassie asked.

"Teddy needs a place to stay for a little while." In deference to Teddy's torment, Sunny kept her voice low, but she met her aunt's gaze unflinchingly. "Something's happened to her father."

"The dog stays outside," Cassie snapped as she turned and held the door open for Sunny.

When she glanced behind her, she saw that Cassie's directive was unnecessary. The dog sat down in the yard near the bottom step. He cocked his ears and whined but made no attempt to come any closer.

She carried Teddy on into the parlor and tried to lay her down on the settee. But the little arms clung frantically to her neck, and Sunny settled for sitting down herself and cuddling Teddy on her lap. The small shoulders continued to shudder, and already the front of Sunny's dress was soaked with tears.

"Would you get her a hankie, please, Aunt?" she asked Cassie, who stood in the parlor doorway.

Cassie's mouth tightened, but she gave a curt nod and left. A few seconds later she came back and handed Sunny one of the linen towels from the kitchen.

When Sunny glanced questioningly at her, Cassie shrugged and said, "Way she's crying, she needs more than a handkerchief."

You bitter old biddy. The words flashed through Sunny's mind, but she managed to hold them back. Instead, she gently pried Teddy's hands away from her face and wiped her cheeks with the towel.

"Shhhhh, sweetheart," she soothed. "You'll make yourself sick, crying like that. Would you like a glass of milk?"

Teddy shook her head and began coughing. Doubling over, she buried her face on her knees, and Sunny gently patted her back, then ran her hand up and down it. She could feel the knobby protrusions of the spine, and when her palm brushed against the child's ribs, the lack of padding on them reminded her how she had gulped down her flapjacks as though starving.

Cassie left the room, and when Teddy stopped coughing, Sunny pulled her into her embrace once again. Rocking back and forth, she hummed a lullaby she remembered her mother singing to her. After a few long minutes, Teddy relaxed and her breathing evened out. Sunny kept humming for another moment or two, until she was sure Teddy had fallen into an exhausted sleep, then laid her gently down on the settee. Though the day was already showing promise of being as hot as when she arrived yesterday, she draped an afghan over the tiny body.

She hoped the poor child would sleep for a while. She needed to change her dress. Tearing her worried gaze away from Teddy, she turned to see Cassie again standing in the parlor doorway. Her aunt jerked her head, silently indicating for Sunny to follow her.

In the hallway, Cassie faced Sunny. "Don't get any ideas about keeping that child here permanently," she warned. "Why, it sounds like she's even sickly."

"Oh, for God's sake," Sunny spat. "What kind of woman are you, anyway?" Realizing she was having trouble keeping her voice down, Sunny reached back and closed the parlor door.

"I don't allow profanity in my house," Cassie said before Sunny could speak again.

"It's not your damned house!" Sunny marched toward her, and Cassie faltered backward a step before she caught herself and defiantly stood her ground. "That child in there—" Sunny raised a hand and pointed at the parlor door. "That tiny, newly orphaned child in there was coughing because she'd been crying her little heart out! Anyone with a decent bone in her body would realize that! But I'm beginning to think my mother inherited all the compassion in this family, leaving you a bitter, dried-up husk of a woman!"

Cassie's hand lashed out, landing forcefully on Sunny's cheek. Sunny didn't even think. She lashed out in response, and Cassie's head snapped back with an almost audible crack. A deadly silence filled the hallway as the two women stared at each other in mutual horror.

Sunny found her voice first. "I . . . I'm sorry, Aunt. I really am, this time. But don't you ever raise your hand against me again, or against that child in there as long as she stays here."

With a smothered sob, Cassie turned and fled to her

bedroom. As soon as the door closed behind her aunt, Sunny lifted one hand to her burning cheek and rubbed the stinging palm of her other hand against her roiling stomach.

"God help us," she murmured.

SUNNY OPENED THE parlor door again and quietly walked over to the settee. Teddy was sleeping restlessly and would probably wake up shortly, but then she would be caught in the horrible half-world of grief prior to the funeral and the soul-wrenching emptiness after it. With memories of her mother's funeral still so very fresh in her mind, Sunny vowed to do everything she could to be there for the tiny scrap of a girl she'd so recently taken into her heart.

But, recalling Jake's words, she realized the Ranger hadn't been sure Teddy's father was dead, despite what she had said to Cassie during their angry exchange. Perhaps there was a mistake—perhaps he was only extremely ill, or in some sort of catatonic state. She would have to wait to hear from Jake for a final resolution.

Teddy twisted on the settee, but only snuggled down again, sniffing back a sob. With tears misting her eyes, Sunny straightened the afghan before she left the parlor. In the kitchen, she filled a pan of water for the little dog waiting for Teddy out front and carried it to him. The dog's ears perked up when she descended the steps and set the bowl down, but he kept a distrustful distance.

She couldn't blame him. More than once she'd seen stray animals miserably mistreated.

Sunny sat on the bottom step, wrapped her arms around her knees and stared in the direction she'd seen Teddy running from a while ago. In a moment, she saw a figure walking back up the path, but the man was too short to be Jake, and he limped. She watched him pass the stable and cross the open space to where the boardwalk began in front of the first store on that side of the street. He glanced over at her briefly and nodded before continuing on his way.

The little dog whined, drawing Sunny's attention. Tail tucked between his legs, he cautiously crept closer to the water pan. When she murmured a sympathetic sound, he trotted on up to the pan, his tail floating out behind him, waving tentatively. After satisfying his thirst, he cocked his head and whimpered.

"Come here, boy." Sunny held her hand out, and the dog bounded up to her. Patting his head and scratching behind one ear, she said, "Guess you haven't had an easy life either, have you, boy? You've probably been yelled at and chased off, when all you were doing was trying to clean up the scraps somebody tossed out. Hmm?"

His tongue came out in a pant, and he leaned against her hand. When she withdrew it, he whined again and looked past her to the open doorway behind Sunny.

"Teddy's sleeping, boy," Sunny murmured. "Don't worry, I'll take care of her. And you, too."

Though he couldn't possibly have understood her words, her tone of voice must have soothed the dog. He collapsed at her feet, settling his muzzle on his paws. Instead of closing his eyes, though, he kept watch on the house.

A wagon pulled into the street from the narrow alley running between the stable and the stagecoach stop across the way, and Sunny clenched her teeth. The wagon was painted black, and the driver wore a severe black suit. He turned the wagon to the right, in the direction both Teddy and the limping man had come from.

Sunny bowed her head for a moment. She hadn't known Teddy's father, but there must have been some redeeming qualities in the man. After all, he'd left behind a precious, wonderful daughter. When she opened her eyes, she realized she was still wearing the yellow dress, and she became aware of the stiffness where Teddy's tears had dried in the heat. With a sigh, she stood and went back in to change.

Cassie's bedroom door remained closed, but when Sunny checked the parlor after she'd changed into a plain gingham gown, she found Teddy stirring. She could tell the moment the little girl was fully awake. Teddy's blue eyes flew open, searching the room until she saw Sunny.

"Pa?" she asked hesitantly.

Sunny crossed to the settee and sat beside Teddy, searching for the words she needed. But Teddy read the silent message, and her face crumpled. Throwing herself into Sunny's arms, she clung tightly, miserably. Far sooner than Sunny expected, she pulled away and wiped the back of her hand across her nose.

"I . . . I guess there's things I gotta do, huh?" she said in a quiet voice. "Pa . . . he'll have to be b . . . buried."

A mixture of pride and compassion swelled in Sunny's heart as she gazed at the tiny child struggling to master what had to be overpowering grief and worry about her own future. Taking the small hands in her own, Sunny squeezed gently.

"Will you let me help you, Teddy? Please? I want to be your friend."

Teddy nodded gratefully. "T . . . there's a suit Pa wears sometimes," she said, still speaking of her father in the present tense. "He'd probably like to be a-wearin' it. But how do we do that?"

Sunny heard the sound of the wagon coming back into town and quickly stood to protect Teddy from the view out the parlor window. "Let's go into the kitchen and talk, all right, Teddy? There's a person in town called an undertaker, and he'll handle everything for you. We just have to tell him what you want done."

Teddy slid off the settee and preceded Sunny into the kitchen, where she climbed into the same chair she'd used for breakfast. "Where's Miz Foster?" she asked.

"Um . . . resting in her room," Sunny explained, which seemed to satisfy Teddy. Knowing there wasn't anything else in the kitchen to offer Teddy, she poured her a glass of buttermilk, then took an apple from the bowl on the counter. While Teddy dispiritedly nibbled on the apple and drank a few sips of milk, Sunny gently talked to her about the necessary preparations for the funeral.

They were soon interrupted by a tap on the back door.

"I'm Ruth Hopkins," the gray-haired woman said, walking into the kitchen in response to Sunny's welcoming motion. Sunny introduced herself as Jake Cameron came in behind Ruth, his hat in his hand for once. Ruth set a covered dish on the table, and Jake sat down beside Teddy.

"You were right, Teddy," he said tenderly, embracing her small shoulders. "Your pa's gone. I wish I didn't have to say that to you, but it's true."

A tear rolled down Teddy's cheek. Ruth gazed kindly at her. "Teddy, I'm very sorry about your father. You've been a big help to me at times, sweeping out the store when your father would let you. I'd like you to come over and pick up a dress I have that I think will fit you. You can wear it to the services."

"But . . . but you already paid me for the last time I swept up for you, Miz Hopkins," Teddy said with a sniff.

"I know," Ruth replied. "The dress is a gift. Please accept it."

"I'll bring her over after a while," Sunny murmured.

"I'll be watching for you." Ruth stroked Teddy's matted hair, then patted Jake on the arm. "Let me know if there's anything else I can do, Ranger," she said, turning to leave. "And you too, Miss Fannin. I think a lot of little Teddy."

"I will," Sunny agreed. "Thank you so much for coming by."

As soon as Ruth was gone, Teddy swallowed her sobs and looked up at Jake. "I already knew, Ranger Jake. Miss Sunny and me have been talking about what needs to be done."

Jake glanced questioningly at Sunny. "I saw the wagon leaving town," she explained. "Will you please assure anyone who asks that I'll keep Teddy here with me for now? She'll be taken care of."

Teddy tugged on Jake's sleeve. "Ranger Jake, will I get to see Pa at least one more time?"

Sunny clapped a hand over her mouth to still her protest as Jake nodded in reply.

"If that's what you want, Teddy. I'll come get you when it's time for you to do that."

Sunny walked over to the counter and gripped the edge tightly as she listened to Teddy explain to Jake where in the shack he would find the suit her father would want to wear. A vision of her mother's body in the satin-lined coffin appeared in her mind's eye. She knew exactly how hard it would be for Teddy to see her father the same way, but she also realized she had no right to deny the child a final good-bye, no matter how young Teddy was. Instead, she tried to focus on what Jake was telling Teddy—the time of the services tomorrow would be at ten o'clock in the morning.

"I'm going over to talk to the minister now," Jake said as he rose to his feet. "I'll let him know that I've spoken with you. Is there anything special you'd like him to say at the services?"

"Guess he'll know best," Teddy said. "Me and Pa, we didn't go to church much. Only prayer I remember is the one I say 'bout laying down to sleep at night."

Jake bent and hugged Teddy, then picked up his hat. With a nod at Sunny, he walked toward the kitchen door. She forced her hands loose from the counter and went after him. When she quietly called his name, he paused on the back porch.

"I want to thank you for being so caring with her," Sunny said. "And I'll go with you to the funeral home when you take her over there. She might need me."

"She needs everyone who's willing to help her through this right now," Jake agreed. "But you look awful shaky. Are you sure you want to put yourself through what might be an ordeal at the undertaker's? I can handle it alone, if you'd rather."

Sunny clenched her hands in front of her. "My . . . my own mother died just three months ago," she revealed. "Yes, it will be hard for me, but I want to do it for Teddy. Besides, you'll be with us."

Jake stepped close to her, reaching for her hands. Gripping them gently, he gave them a compassionate squeeze. The whiskey eyes beneath his hat brim were soft with sympathy, which Sunny sensed came honestly from his heart, and she caught herself wishing desperately she had found the same understanding in her aunt upon her arrival.

"I'm sorry about your mother," Jake said. "Knowing that, I realize you deserve a lot of respect for what you're doing for Teddy." He released her hands, and they fell limply to her sides. "And yes, I'll be with you both."

He strode down the steps and around the side of the house. Sunny vaguely wondered why both he and Ruth had used the back door, but his promise to help her and Teddy get through the coming hours overrode that questioning thought. He seemed to have a depth that she had overlooked. A steady, considerate presence such as his would have been appreciated in her own grief-stricken days.

And this was definitely not the time to wonder why she could still feel his gentle touch on her hands even though he had disappeared.

THE BLACK WAGON, now holding a pine box in its bed, turned off the main street and stopped beside Cassie's house at exactly ten o'clock the next morning. As Sunny had learned from Cassie the previous evening, the church was located a few hundred yards down that street. Her aunt had declined to attend the services, however. Had Teddy not been sitting there at the time, she supposed Aunt Cassie would have grimly reminded her that the responsibility for the orphaned girl was Sunny's, not hers. Cassie did follow them out onto the porch this morning, nodding at the undertaker on the wagon seat and also at Jake when he walked over to meet them. Then she disappeared back into the house.

Teddy squeezed Sunny's hand tightly while Jake escorted them over behind the wagon. There didn't seem to be anything to say. They followed the slowly moving wagon to the church, where it turned into the graveyard gate. Several people already waited for them beside the open grave, but Sunny concentrated on Teddy instead of greeting them. The little girl's grip on her hand had become painful, but she couldn't bring herself to pull away.

She led Teddy over to the grave as the preacher and an older, balding man Sunny thought looked somewhat familiar came forward to help Jake and the undertaker with the casket. As soon as the casket was lowered into the grave and the ropes holding it removed, the preacher began the service.

Teddy's hair streamed down her back, the sunshine turning it to molten gold. Once during the brief ceremony, she unconsciously ran her free hand over the bodice of the pretty gray dress that Ruth had given her from the general store stock. Her face was still puffy and tearstained, since she had been weeping off and on for two days now.

"Ashes to ashes, and dust to dust," the preacher intoned. He scattered a handful of dirt on the pine coffin, looking at Sunny when his hand was empty.

Sunny led Teddy forward. She handed the wildflowers they had picked early that morning to Teddy, and, as she had told the child to do, Teddy dropped them into the grave. Then she turned and buried her face in Sunny's skirt.

After a final prayer, the preacher indicated the service was concluded. Sunny lifted Teddy into her arms and started walking away. She would not let the child stay to watch the dirt being shoveled into the grave. She hadn't been able to bring herself to stay at her mother's grave for that either.

Outside the gate once again, she paused to speak to the townspeople who had followed her and Teddy. She recognized the stable owner, John, who had led the change of teams out to the stagecoach when she arrived two days ago, and she knew from Jake that Teddy's father had worked for him. Ruth's husband, Fred, accompanied her, mumbling at one point about leaving the store unattended until he realized Sunny could hear him. Ruth's dig in the ribs with a not-go-gentle elbow shut him up.

Ruth had been the only one from town who called at Aunt Cassie's house yesterday. On their visit to the store, she'd also sent a picnic basket full of food back to the house with Sunny. It remained nearly untouched.

"How you doing this morning, Teddy?" Ruth asked.

Teddy responded by bending forward and hugging Ruth's neck tightly, also shyly greeting Fred.

The older, balding man who had helped with the casket had stayed behind, and Sunny saw him pick up a shovel to help the undertaker. She quickly shifted her gaze away from the sight, recalling now where she had seen the man. He was the one who'd been with Jake outside the jailhouse the previous morning.

The only other woman at the service had stood off to the side. She wore a plain brown gown and she didn't stop to offer condolences. Instead she nodded and gave Teddy a comforting smile as she passed. Her subdued bonnet failed to detract from the abundance of shining red hair. Though her face remained solemn in respect for the service she attended, no one could miss the clear green color of her eyes. Jake and John spoke a murmured hello to her, but when Fred glanced her way, Ruth gave her husband another none-too-gentle nudge in the side.

After a moment, Ruth acceded to Fred's insistent tug on her arm and started back down the road, with John trailing behind them. With a promise to the preacher to bring Teddy to church on Sunday, Sunny followed. Jake fell in beside Sunny and reached out a hand to stroke Teddy's cheek.

"How are you, darlin'?" he asked the little girl.

"Will my pa be able to get out of that hole and find his way to heaven?" Teddy asked.

A wrenching sob caught in Sunny's throat, and her eyes blurred with tears. She stumbled slightly, and Jake put a steadying arm around her waist. Gratefully, she glanced up at his face.

"Steady, Sunny," he murmured, and Sunny immediately felt a measure of comfort.

To Teddy, Jake said, "Darlin', your pa's already in heaven. That's just the body he left behind there in the grave. His soul's gone on ahead."

"I know what s soul is, but I'd forgot about that," Teddy replied. "Once in a while, when Pa would try to get off the jug, we'd go to one of them tent meetings. We used to have some good times for a while after that, but he always ended up drinkin' again."

"Try to remember the good times," Sunny told her. "Those will always be precious memories for you."

"All right," Teddy said. "But . . ."

She stared back over Sunny's shoulder, toward the graveyard. Since her arms were getting tired, Sunny put Teddy down, thus shielding her from the sight behind them. It would take the undertaker and the other man quite a while to fill the grave.

Instead of walking on, Jake stopped beside them. "What were you starting to ask, Teddy?"

When she hung her head, her tiny figure a picture of dejection, Jake tucked his index finger beneath her chin and gently lifted her face up. The contrast of that large male hand next to Teddy's piquant face left its image in Sunny's mind. It seemed impossible for such a man to act so tenderly, speak so softly. *There are inner depths to this man,* she thought to herself. *Deep ones.*

"Teddy?" Jake murmured.

She wiped her eyes with her hands, then looked up at Jake with a heartbroken expression. "What's gonna happen to me now, Ranger Jake? You . . . you think someone might give me a job in town? I gotta take care of my dog, Rowdy, you know. He ain't got no one else."

Sunny's heart broke into a million pieces. Her eyes flew

to Jake's, and she noticed a suspicious mist in his own eyes, muting the whiskey color to a lighter brown. Her tears spilled over, streaming down her cheeks, her throat clogged too tight to speak.

Jake knelt in the dirt and put his large hands on Teddy's slight shoulders. "I promise you, Teddy, you will be taken care of," he growled in an emotion-laden voice. "And Rowdy, too. I don't want you to worry about it."

"But I's the one who's *gots* to worry about it, Ranger Jake," Teddy said seriously. "You and Miss Sunny both been real nice to me, but you ain't my kin. I ain't got no kin now."

"We might not be kin," Jake assured her, "but we're your friends. And friends stand by each other when bad things happen. Friends don't leave each other to face things all alone when they have problems."

Smoothing a hand over Teddy's hair, Sunny finally found her voice. "I'm adding my promise to Ranger Jake's, Teddy. I'll see that you're taken care of. There are three bedrooms at my house, and one of them is yours for as long as you need it."

"But Miz Foster don't like me being there," Teddy reminded Sunny.

"That's my aunt's problem, not yours. The house belongs to me also, and I have my own say about who shares it with me."

"Thank you, Miss Sunny. Can I go tell Rowdy we don't have to worry about a place to live now?"

"Sure, sweetheart," Sunny agreed. "But be back in a little while. I'll worry about you if you're gone too long."

Teddy nodded, then walked away, searching for the little dog, which was never very far from her. She spotted him down the street, and her steps hastened toward him.

"We need to talk about this, you know," Jake broke into Sunny's thoughts.

"There's nothing to discuss," Sunny assured him. "She has no one else, and I'll see that she's taken care of. I won't stand for her being sent to a foundling home."

"She might have a mother somewhere."

"A mother?" Sunny gazed at him in astonishment. "If she does, that mother gave up all rights to her by walking out when Teddy was four years old! Teddy needs someone who won't leave her—who loves her enough to give her a decent life, instead of the neglected, abused life she's suffered so far. If her mother cared for her, she wouldn't have left her to that sort of life!"

"I'm sorry, Sunny. But as a law enforcement official, I have to try to track down her mother. I . . . ."

"You do whatever the hell you have to, *Ranger* Jake," Sunny spat. "But if you find her, she damned well better deserve a wonderful daughter like Teddy, or I'll fight tooth and nail against her!"

Jake let out a sigh. Instead of reacting to her anger, he surprised Sunny with a look of tenderness.

"I can totally sympathize with you, Sunny. And I entirely agree. I'm also sure you'll give Teddy a fine home, even though I don't know you that well. I've seen you with her—and seen how much Teddy's taken with you in return. But my hands are tied. I'm bound by regulations to make an attempt to find the child's mother in a situation like this."

"She's probably dead. I can't imagine a mother not checking on her daughter for four years."

"There's no proof that she's dead," Jake explained. "It's very probable that, even the way Tompkins moved around, word of his wife's death would have caught up with him. If for no other reason than that the town that had to bury her would try to find out if he could pay back some of the expenses."

"That's a wicked reason to try to find someone."

"Yes, but it's also a fact of life. Look, Sunny . . ."

"When did you stir yourself to find out my name?" Sunny blurted, shocked at herself the minute the words were out of her mouth. It didn't matter one iota to her that Jake Cameron finally knew her name. Did it? Or that the sound of her name sort of stole through her each time he said it. Just after a funeral was not the time to be thinking thoughts like that!

He smiled down at her, the gesture transforming his face from ruggedness to almost heart-stopping handsomeness. Well, she'd already been honest enough with herself to admit he was the best-looking man she'd ever laid eyes on, but that didn't excuse his obnoxious personality.

He hadn't seemed at all obnoxious with Teddy, however. It amazed her, now that she thought back on it, how much his quiet presence beside her during the funeral service had helped her bear Teddy's heartbreak. He'd kept his promise, and she owed him for that.

This morning before the service, he had escorted her and Teddy to the funeral home so Teddy could say a last good-bye to her father before the pine coffin was closed. Sunny's eyes filled with tears again as she recalled Jake holding Teddy up so she could see into the coffin and Teddy reaching down to give her father a final pat on the cheek. The man in the coffin—no, the body, Sunny reminded herself—didn't look like a person who would abuse or neglect a child. Instead, he looked tired and dissipated, despite the rather worn suit and tie.

"Hey, you all right?" A calloused finger slipped under Sunny's chin and tilted her face up, as it had Teddy's moments before. His thumb brushed away the tear slipping out of her eye. She sniffed and pulled her handkerchief from her sleeve, succumbing when he took it from her to wipe her cheek.

"You were off in some faraway place. I was telling you that I was following up on what you consider one of my failings—not knowing the background of new arrivals in town," Jake said in a teasing voice. "I was just doing my duty, ma'am."

"Well, I wish you didn't consider it your duty to try to track down a woman who abandoned a little girl," Sunny replied, taking the handkerchief back. Her tears had miraculously dried, perhaps partially because of his soothing hand.

"I have to keep an open mind about this, Sunny. We don't know the background of the split between Tompkins and his wife. Only Teddy knows that, and I'll have to question her at some point." When Sunny glared at him again, he raised a cautionary hand. "I said at *some* point, Sunny. There's no hurry about it. She's going to have enough to handle right now with her new situation."

"I fully intend to ensure that her *new situation* is a much better one than she had before," Sunny said determinedly. "My mother and I had a perfectly wonderful life together—the two of us. She left me with enough funds to care for myself for a while. And Teddy, too."

Suddenly she frowned. "You don't suppose there will be a problem with the other women in town about me taking Teddy, do you? I'm new here, and they might resent my stepping in. But I haven't seen anybody else come forward and offer help, except the general store owner's wife, Ruth. And she seems much too elderly to take on raising a small child."

Her forehead creased deeper, and she added, "Well, there was that other woman at the funeral service. She appeared to be not much older than me, but . . ."

Jake choked so hard she was tempted to thump him on the

back. When she looked at him, she couldn't tell whether the glint in his eyes came from laughter or his fight for breath. She drew herself up defensively, just in case she decided he was laughing at her.

"Uh . . . Ginny McAllister was the other woman at the funeral, and I don't think you have to worry about her fighting you over taking Teddy in," he finally assured her, avoiding her gaze. He settled his hat on his head and said, "Look, if you need anything—any help with Teddy—I think an awful lot of that little girl. Let me know if I can do anything."

"Humph," Sunny couldn't stop herself from saying. "Seems to me you could have helped Teddy earlier—when she was living in those deplorable conditions. Did you know I first saw her when she was scrounging for those burned biscuits behind my house?"

"No, I didn't know that." Jake released a long-suffering sigh. "And I'm not going to get into the vagaries of the law about what it takes to remove a child from a parent with you. Just remember what I said—I care about her too. Good day, Miss Fannin."

He strode away before Sunny could voice any of the bristling comments crowding her mind. Lord, it appeared impossible for him to move so quickly in that seemingly easygoing, sauntering gait, but he was out of earshot in a blink. Sunny wrenched her eyes away from the long legs and frock coat hanging down over that gunbelt and went to find Teddy.

IN HIS OFFICE, Jake picked up the stack of letters he'd found in Tompkins' shack. Only the one on the bottom of the pile had been opened. They all carried the same postmark, each mailed from Kansas City, Missouri, but sent to Tompkins at various towns, the locations of which traced an east-to-west path across the United States.

After slitting the envelopes open with his pocketknife, he found that each one contained another letter, which had been mailed on unopened. Instead of being addressed to Tompkins, however, those envelopes carried Teddy's name.

Jake tapped one of the letters against his chin while he pondered the situation. The letters belonged to Teddy, no doubt about that. And he'd be willing to bet his last dollar that they were written by her missing mother. Did he have any right to withhold them from Teddy for a while? He had no idea what would be in those letters, and Teddy might not be in any shape right now to handle whatever was.

On the other hand, it would probably be a sound decision to let Sunny Fannin know about the possibility of other relatives in the picture, before she got any more attached to the little ragtag. His most pressing task at the moment, however, was to get a telegram off to the law enforcement officials in Kansas City.

He didn't know how much success they would have in tracing the letters. Beyond the Kansas City postmark and mailing addresses, there were no other identifying names on the envelopes.

"WHY, OF COURSE Liberty Flats has a schoolteacher, my dear," Ruth said three days later as she set a plate of cookies and glasses of lukewarm lemonade in front of Sunny and Teddy. "But she's off visiting her family for the summer. She'll be back in a couple of months."

"Do you think she'd mind if I borrowed a few school-books, so I could start Teddy on some lessons myself?" Sunny asked. "She has some catching up to do to get to where the other children of her age are. I'd be willing to contribute to the school, to pay for borrowing the books."

"As a matter of fact, my husband is on the school board," Ruth informed her. "If I ask him to, he'll be more than glad to grant you the use of the books. After all, Fred and I both firmly believe in education for children, even though our son is long out of school."

"Wonderful," Sunny said. Just then she noticed Teddy surreptitiously trying to slip a cookie into her dress pocket and frowned in warning.

Ruth caught the byplay and chuckled aloud. "Teddy, dear, you are more than welcome to take a cookie with you for later. But it's polite to ask for it first."

"It weren't for me, Miz Ruth," Teddy said, ducking her head in embarrassment.

"It *wasn't* for you," Sunny corrected. "And I assume you wanted the cookie for Rowdy. Still, you need to ask permission."

Teddy brightened. "Can I have a cookie for my dog, Miz Ruth? Please?"

The two women glanced at each other with understanding. "Yes, you *may*," Ruth replied. She smiled in approval when Teddy murmured a mannerly thank-you.

As Teddy munched away on her cookie, Sunny exchanged chitchat with Ruth, realizing as they spoke just how much she had missed having another woman with whom to converse. Aunt Cassie had remained tight-lipped and uncommunicative since their altercation in the hallway. Although she didn't close herself up in her room, she barely acknowledged Sunny's presence in the house when they shared a meal or sat in the parlor in the evenings.

The only other woman Sunny had spoken to at any length since her arrival in Liberty Flats was Mary Lassiter. She'd been thinking seriously of hiring a buggy to visit Mary's ranch, just to break the boredom of the long, hot days. In St. Louis, she would have made rounds to her friends' houses or participated in some of the meetings of the various social committees on which her mother served.

Here in Liberty Flats, though, no one visited Cassie's house, and Sunny was loathe to approach the few women in town who barely nodded at her when they passed on the boardwalk. Today, she had used the excuse of returning Ruth's picnic basket and dishes to see if the elderly woman might invite her in for a visit. She was almost embarrassed at the gratitude she felt when Ruth's face lit up and she waved her into the living quarters above the store.

She gazed around the neat-as-a-pin kitchen as she and Ruth talked. It was every bit as clean as Cassie's house, yet it had such a different atmosphere—homey, much like Ruth's own friendly personality. A pie cooled on the windowsill, and the spicy smell lingered in the kitchen. Beside the pie, a pot of geraniums bloomed riotously, with some cuttings taking root in a clear glass jar next to the pot. The pine floorboards gleamed with a coat of wax, and the handmade rag rugs were interwoven with the same red color of the geraniums. Sunny couldn't help but think how much brighter and more comforting Cassie's house would be if a little color were added to the decor.

Noticing that Teddy was squirming on her seat, Sunny said, "Would you like to play outside until Ruth and I get done visiting, honey?"

"Could I go see Ranger Jake while I wait for you?" Teddy asked hopefully. "I ain't seen him since the other day."

Sunny carefully masked the frown that was trying to crease her face. After all, Jake Cameron was Teddy's friend, and in a town as small as this they couldn't avoid him. Besides, Jake had been the one person she could count on to help get Teddy through the funeral.

"I guess that would be all right," she said after a second's hesitation. "But remember, we're going to look for a few more pieces of clothing for you in Ruth's store. I'll come get you when it's time for us to do that. Do you also remember what I told you about using 'ain't'?"

"Yes, ma'am," Teddy said with a long-suffering sigh. "You said it ain't a word. I'll try to 'member that."

Ruth turned her head quickly, but Sunny caught the smile on her friend's face and shook her head tolerantly as Teddy jumped to her feet and fairly raced to the door, pausing just briefly when she remembered to thank Ruth for the lemonade and cookies. Ruth chuckled as they heard her clattering down the steps, calling for her dog.

"She seems to be overcoming her grief," Ruth said. "But children always do bounce back more quickly than adults."

"She still wakes up crying at night," Sunny said quietly. "I probably shouldn't do it, but I take her into bed with me when that happens. She's so tiny, and thinking of her lying there in the dark in that room all by herself just tears me apart."

"It's not spoiling a child to give her comfort," Ruth assured her. "Time will eventually help her overcome her nightmares."

Sunny bit her lip for a second, wondering if her tentative friendship with Ruth would allow her to ask some of the questions she'd been pondering the last few days. After all, this town was Ruth's home, and she appeared to be well contented with her life. Granted, the town was extremely peaceful, but . . . well, darn it, the town was also extremely boring. What on earth did the women do with themselves day in and out?

"Ruth," Sunny ventured, "ah . . . back in St. Louis I was involved with my mother on a few committees in town. I've been wondering if there might be something here I could perform a service for. Teddy hardly takes up all my time, and I'd be more than willing to contribute. I'd thought I would introduce myself to some of the ladies at church tomorrow. Perhaps you could give me a hint as to what might be the best way to approach them."

Ruth clapped her hands together, her eyes gleaming excitedly. "Sunny Fannin, you're a woman after my own heart! As bad as this town was before Ranger Cameron ran off the outlaw element, at least there was a measure of excitement from day to day. But you'll be sorely disappointed if you think you'll find any activities already set up in town. What this town needs is a woman to get the other women organized—a female leader. I don't have the time to pursue what needs to be done, since I have to help Fred out in the store. And the bookwork keeps me busy other times."

Sunny pressed her lips together in disappointment, ignoring Ruth's enthusiasm. "Ruth, none of the other women in town have even tried to become acquainted with me. Given that, I fail to see how I could ever attempt to *lead* them at anything."

Ruth leaned forward, propping her arms on the table. "The problem's not you, Sunny. It's Cassie."

When Sunny raised an inquiring eyebrow, Ruth took a deep breath. "Oh, she didn't used to be like that, Cassie didn't. At one time we were fairly close friends, even though she's ten years younger than me. I don't know what happened, but Cassie turned into a different person after your mother left town. I tried for a while to keep our friendship going, but it became more and more apparent that Cassie didn't want anyone to be close to her any longer."

"Did you know my mother?" Sunny asked eagerly. Right now, she wasn't the least bit interested in why her aunt was such an embittered and reclusive woman. She wanted to discuss her beloved mother with someone who might share her own feelings.

"Of course," Ruth replied. "Samantha was a wonderful child, and she turned into one of the belles of the county. It was such a shock to all of us when she up and left, saying she was going to St. Louis to stay with a friend she'd met at finishing school. Cassie wouldn't say much about her after that, beyond the fact that she'd gotten married to a man named Fannin and they'd had a baby daughter."

"Did she tell you my mother was killed in an accident just three months ago?" Sunny murmured, choking on her words.

Ruth face registered her sympathy. "Oh, I'm so sorry, Sunny. No, Cassie didn't tell *anyone*. I would have known if she'd even told one person, since absolutely everyone comes into the store fairly regularly. And Samantha's husband? Your father?

"I never knew him," Sunny said evasively. "He died before I was born."

Something didn't gibe here. Sunny's brow creased in puzzlement as Ruth murmured some of the same compassionate phrases she had heard at her mother's funeral. Why wouldn't Cassie have at least informed the townspeople of her mother's death? As Cassie had insinuated after her arrival, no one in Liberty Flats knew of her mother's death.

Also, the one bone of contention between her and her mother had been her mother's adamant refusal to discuss the man she had married, beyond saying he was dead. Somehow, though, Sunny had had the impression that her mother had been married *before* she came to St. Louis. If she had married while she lived in St. Louis, surely some of her friends would have remembered the wedding. The tentative inquiries Sunny had made now and then had all fostered the conclusion that Samantha had been a widow before her arrival in St. Louis.

Cautiously, remembering the other reason for her trip to Liberty Falls and the mystery she was determined to solve, she probed Ruth's memory of her mother a little more.

"Who else was my mother friends with, Ruth? It sounds like neither she nor my aunt was reclusive while they were growing up. And my mother continued to be very active and outgoing her entire life. She had scads of friends back home in St. Louis. I wonder what could have changed my aunt so much."

"Didn't you talk to your mother about her life back here, child?"

"No." Sunny sighed deeply. "You know how it is. We were busy and happy, and I thought I had all the time in the world with her. Once in a while, around Christmas time when she'd get a card from my aunt, she'd mention maybe taking a trip back here someday. But she did tell me that her own mother and father had died a few months before she came to St. Louis, so there was only her sister, Cassie, back here as far as any family went. Since Aunt Cassie had never married, I had no cousins or anything like that here."

Ruth dropped her gaze, then rather hastily shoved her chair back and stood. "Oh, my. Look at me sitting here and leaving you with an empty glass. Let me get you some more lemonade."

Taking Sunny's glass, she bustled over to the counter and refilled it to the brim from the pitcher. When she picked up the glass, some of the lemonade sloshed onto the countertop. Ruth grabbed a rag from the sink to wipe up the spill, which seemed to take an inordinately long time. She polished the counter with the cloth over and over for several long seconds, after the spilled lemonade had clearly been cleaned up. Glancing up at the window, she finally tossed the rag back into the sink and turned to carry the lemonade over to Sunny.

"My geranium cuttings are about ready to plant," she said as she set the glass down. "I've got too many plants already. Would you like to take some with you and use them around the porch on Cassie's house? They would brighten the place up quite a bit. Cassie and your grandmother used to love working with flowers and keeping their yard up, but your mother wasn't much for gardening. Funny how different the sisters were. Here, I'll get some more cookies too. There's plenty left I'll wrap some up for you to take home for Teddy."

Sunny captured Ruth's hand when she reached for the cookie plate. "Ruth, please. Please. Sit down and tell me what you're trying to hide from me. What did I say to bring on this sudden case of jitters?"

"Sunny, child, maybe you should talk to Cassie."

"I've tried, Ruth. Really, I have. About all I've been able to glean is that something caused a rift between my mother and her sister. And I gathered that more from my aunt's attitude, not anything at all she will tell me in words."

When Ruth still hesitated, though she did sit down again, Sunny pleaded, "Don't I have a right to know if there's some reason my aunt resents my coming here, Ruth? I can't think of a thing I could have done to her to make her hate me, since I'd never even met her until a few days ago."

"Oh, Sunny, dear. I wouldn't call it hatred. And I doubt very much that it's you personally. It might just be some of the memories you bring back to Cassie. You look an awful lot like your mother, you know."

"What memories?" Sunny insisted.

Ruth's brow furrowed, and she clasped her hands on the table. "It's . . ." She took a deep breath. "Sunny, you have to realize that I don't know a thing for sure. There was speculation back then, but I don't hold with that sort of stuff. Rumors are only that—rumors. Small towns are rife with things like that, and I hear all of them at one point or another in the store. But as many of them turn out false as true."

"At least tell me what the speculation was, Ruth. Please. I have my reasons for wanting to know."

Ruth leaned back in her chair and studied Sunny for a long moment. "All right," she said at last. "But you keep in mind what I said about all this being speculation."

"I will. I promise."

"Well, as you already know, your grandparents died not

long before your mother went to St. Louis. Both Cassie and Samantha took their deaths hard, especially since they lost them both within a few days of each other in an influenza epidemic. Did you know how they had died?"

"Yes. Yes, I knew about that. I'm sure it was very hard on both of the girls."

"Well, Cassie had planned to be married the week after their deaths. Of course, she canceled her wedding until she'd gone through a mourning period. Cassie's very strict on maintaining convention."

"I've found that out already about her," Sunny agreed. "Who was she betrothed to?"

"A man named Ian Lassiter. I heard around town that Ian was pretty upset about the wedding being postponed, and some of us even wondered if that would give Charlie a chance to pursue his own suit with Cassie. We all really felt Charlie was a better choice, but Cassie was all starry-eyed over Ian. She fell for him hook, line, and sinker within a few days of when he came to town. And he was a mighty fine-looking man, although I didn't much care for his overbearing, selfish attitude."

"Who's Charlie?" Sunny asked. The name nagged at her, but she'd known several men named Charles in her life. "And why did the wedding never come off?"

"Charlie is Charlie Duckworth," Ruth explained. "He was a friend of both Cassie's and Samantha's while they grew up. They were quite a threesome, and you usually saw them together. Cassie even called him 'Duckie' now and then, and Charlie had a few set-tos with some of the other boys over that nickname. Charlie was at Mr. Tompkins' funeral, but I guess no one introduced you to him. He was helping the undertaker fill in the grave as we left."

"I remember seeing him. I also saw him with Jake the other morning."

"Yes, he and Jake met somewhere along the way after Charlie left Liberty Flats, I guess. They're very close friends."

Sunny's impatience with Ruth's meandering tale grew, but she forced herself to remain quiet. Ruth could just as easily clam up and leave her without the information she needed. The bits and pieces still weren't making a bit of sense to Sunny, but she hoped her patience would result in some clarification.

"As you know," Ruth said into the silence, "the wedding never came off. That's where all the speculation comes in. Charlie, being a close family friend, spent a lot of time with both Cassie and Samantha after their parents died. Then one day . . ."

"What?" Sunny couldn't keep from prodding.

"One day Samantha announced she was going to St. Louis to stay with a friend she'd met while she was away at finishing school. And she went, just like that. The very next day she got on a weekly stage. Why, I can't imagine that she even had much time to pack."

"I don't understand," Sunny said. "My mother probably just wanted to get away for a while and come to terms with her grief over her parents' deaths. That's why I came to Liberty Flats, you know. It was somewhere to get away from all the memories of my mother for a while."

"Yes, but . . . but . . ."

"But what, Ruth? Please. Please go on."

"Charlie disappeared, too," Ruth said in a musing voice. "The very next day, his mother told me she'd found a note in his bedroom saying just that he was going away for a while. That he'd be in touch. Then we heard that Cassie had completely broken her betrothment to Ian. It looked like . . ."

"It looked like Charlie and my mother had run away together, didn't it?" Sunny supplied. "That maybe Cassie had realized she really cared more for Charlie, but by then it was too late because Charlie had eloped with my mother. And Aunt Cassie broke her engagement because she knew she didn't love Mr. Lassiter. But that can't be true, because my mother married someone else."

"I know, dear. That's why I say everything is speculation and rumor. Now, truly, let's talk about something else. Why, there are so many opportunities for improvements in Liberty Flats, now that Jake has brought law and order to the town."

Ruth's voice faded into the tumbling thoughts in Sunny's head. It still didn't make a bit of sense. Had her mother met her father, William Fannin, somewhere during her journey to St. Louis? Had they had a whirlwind courtship and already been married when they settled there? But why wouldn't her mother have settled in whatever town she met her husband in? It seemed way too much of a coincidence for her to have met a man already from St. Louis on her very journey to that city. However, she supposed it could have happened—there could have been a chance meeting with someone returning home to St. Louis from a trip out of town.

Why hadn't she at least checked the marriage records before she left St. Louis? But she'd had no reason to doubt her mother's story at that point, at least based on the little bit of information she had. And why did the name Charlie Duckworth seem so familiar? It was a strange enough name that it would have stuck in her mind.

"Despite your recent bereavement, everyone will be pleased to know you don't intend to shut yourself away from life like Cassie does," Sunny became aware of Ruth saying. "I'd be awfully pleased if you and Teddy would attend church with Fred and me tomorrow. It would give me the opportunity to introduce you to the townspeople afterward. Church is one place that Cassie always goes, however, so she may expect you to walk with her."

"I doubt that. I . . . you might as well know, I guess. I'm not having much success at being friends with my aunt. If there were any other place in town for me to live, I do believe I might move out. The strained atmosphere isn't really conducive to a child's high spirits, and I hate to subject Teddy to that. But Aunt Cassie tells me the boardinghouse is full."

"She told you right about that. As far as I know, there's only one empty building in the entire town, and that's right next to Ginny McAllister's place. It's hardly a suitable place to live in, either. I'm not of the same mind as some in town are about Ginny, since she runs a sedate, honest business—not like that Saul Gravens' place. And Ginny pays her bills on time, instead of waving them off like her father did until I had to threaten to cut off his credit. It's not her fault she got stuck with such an inappropriate lifestyle for a woman."

"Ruth!" Sunny held up her hands in surrender. "You forget, I've hardly met anyone in this town beyond you, Fred, and the undertaker and preacher. Well, and Ranger Cameron. I have no idea who all these other people are you're talking about."

"Ah, yes, Ranger Cameron," Ruth mused, her face taking on a glow. "Why, if my Fred wasn't such a wonderful man and if I were a few years younger . . ."

The glass of lemonade Sunny was lifting to her mouth wobbled dangerously in her hand, and she quickly sat it down. Ruth's words and tone of voice had conjured up that rugged face and whiskey-colored gaze again, and she dropped her eyes, rubbing the image away with her fingers, endeavoring to erase it. The crash of breaking glass brought her surging to her feet, grabbing at the chair behind her before it could topple over.

"Heavens, Ruth! I'm s . . . sorry," she sputtered, seeing the broken glass amid spatters of sticky lemonade marring the shining floor. "How clumsy of me! I must have set the glass too close to the table edge. Don't worry, I'll clean it up."

Kneeling beside the shattered glass, she reached for one jagged piece as Ruth hurried around the table, admonishing her to wait for her help. In her chagrin, Sunny misjudged the position of the glass and it pierced her finger deeply. Instinctively, she uttered a sharp cry of pain and drew her hand back. She stuck her finger in her mouth, the salty tang of blood and the sting of the wound bringing a sheen of tears to her eyes.

"Sunny, dear," Ruth murmured as she knelt beside her, "I told you to please wait and let me help. Now you've gone and hurt your finger."

Sunny rose and backed away a step, watching Ruth gather the shards of glass into a towel, then carry them to a trash can. Ruth returned with a broom and dustpan and efficiently swept up the remaining mess. Glancing down at her finger, Sunny wrapped her other hand around it when she saw the deep-red blood welling out of the cut and running down her palm.

Ruth led Sunny over to her sink and attempted to pry her hand loose to examine the cut. "Sunny, dear," she said when Sunny stared at her in bewilderment, "you've got to let me look at it. Why, it seems to be bleeding quite profusely. You must have cut it severely."

Sunny's knees wobbled under her, forcing her to loosen her hold on the wound and grab the edge of the sink.

"I . . . I . . . don't much care for the sight of blood," she managed between gritted teeth.

"Then close your eyes," Ruth said in a logical voice. "Blood doesn't bother me that much."

Sunny started to comply, then recalled that her eyes being closed was what had brought about her mishap in the first place. Instead, she turned her head, offering her hand to Ruth to examine. The elderly woman murmured soothingly as she held Sunny's hand under the pump spout and worked the handle until a gush of water ran out. The pain eased beneath the cool stream of water, and when she felt Ruth wrap a piece of cloth around the wound, she chanced a glance.

Unfortunately, she also glanced at her other hand, which was smeared with blood from holding on to the wound. Her vision swam, and her stomach surged. She swallowed desperately against the bitter taste of lemonade rising in the back of her throat. When she swayed, Ruth grabbed her around the waist and steered her back to the chair.

"Here, dear," Ruth said. "Put your head down. And for pity's sake, don't look at yourself until I get you cleaned up."

"I'm so sorry," Sunny mumbled, her voice muffled in her skirt. "I'm not usually so clumsy. I . . ."

"Pooh, my dear. There's not a person alive who doesn't have problems facing one thing or another. Your failing just happens to be blood. Now you just relax and let me take care of you."

Feeling her stomach calm somewhat, Sunny turned her head aside, but kept her cheek pillowed on her knees while she responded to Ruth's tug on her arm. She clenched the towel in her right hand while Ruth gently washed the other one. Vaguely, she heard clumping footsteps and straightened in her chair as she realized they were climbing the stairs outside Ruth's living quarters.

"Someone's coming, Ruth."

"Probably Jake," Ruth replied nonchalantly. "He usually stops by around this time for a spot of coffee. He'll just have to wait a minute today."

Sunny groaned and Ruth mistook the sound for pain, instead of an innate response to the flash of resentment crowding Sunny's mind. After all, if she hadn't been thinking of that darned Ranger, she wouldn't have set the glass too close to the edge of the table and cut her finger in the resulting mess. As Ruth turned away, assuring Sunny that she would get some salve for the cut, Sunny fretted in disgust at herself for having such a childish thought. She surely was too mature to blame her own clumsiness on someone who hadn't even been in the room at the time of the mishap.

Jake walked into the kitchen without knocking, Teddy trailing at his heels. Both their faces creased in concern when they saw Sunny holding her towel-wrapped hand to her chest, and she again chided herself for her infantile deliberations, although she was the only one aware of them.

Teddy hurried over to her. "Miss Sunny! Have you hurt yourself? Oh, you done gone and got blood all over your pretty dress."

At the word "blood," Sunny's head fell back to her knees so quickly that the *thunk* of her skull hitting knee bone resounded through the kitchen. Now she had added pain in her head to contend with, as shooting stars swirled behind her closed eyes. With an unstifled wail of dismay, she lurched to her feet and barely made it to Ruth's sink before the lemonade spewed from her mouth, along with the breakfast she'd eaten a couple hours earlier.

When her shoulders stopped heaving, someone wiped her face with a cool cloth, and Sunny gratefully leaned against Ruth. Only it didn't feel like Ruth's comforting bosom—unless the other woman had grown several inches and firmed up quite a bit in the last few minutes. A large, steadying hand clasped her about the waist, and a hard object pressed against her hip on her other side, where Ruth's leg should be. It felt suspiciously like a gun, and when Sunny realized the Ranger had her in his embrace, she willed herself to pull away. Her body ignored her mind's command, though, and she sagged even closer to him, her cheek nestling against the open V of his shirt.

Somewhere beyond the sensual circle in which she stood, Sunny could hear Ruth shushing Teddy and assuring the child it wasn't her fault that Sunny had been overcome by an upset stomach. Primarily, however, she tried to fathom the rumble under her ear, which suddenly sounded suspiciously like laughter—or at the very least, suppressed chuckling.

With an effort, she pulled back and tilted her face up in time to catch Jake transforming the slight grin on his lips to a straight line of concern. He couldn't mask the twinkle in his eyes quite as quickly, though, and her cheeks heated with both resentment at his amusement and humiliation that he had witnessed her shame. When she tried to pull away from him, he tightened his grasp and held on to her.

"Easy, Sunny," he said, in the same tone he had used at the funeral. "Let's make sure you're not gonna upchuck again before you sit back down. Don't worry. I'll stay right here with you."

"That's the problem," Sunny said before she thought. Jake's brows lifted in what could have been inquiry or surprise, but she wasn't about to explain that stupid statement to him. Instead, she sidled away from him, digging her elbow into his stomach to silently emphasize her determination for him to release her. Her elbow felt as though it were pressing ineffectively against a thick board. However, with another muffled chuckle, he removed his arm.

As she attempted to steady her trembling legs, he strode over and picked up the chair, which had toppled completely over. Within seconds he had it beside the sink and gently pushed her into it. With a sigh, she complied, then almost jumped up again when he knelt in front of her.

"Whoa," Jake said, reaching out to hold her in place. "You're as skittish as a new-broke mare. Just hold on for a minute, and I'll help Ruth get you taken care of. We need to see where all that blood's coming from."

"If you'd all just quite using that word," Sunny said through clenched teeth, "I could handle this entire situation a whole lot better!"

"What word? Oh," Jake continued with more understanding after she shot him a lethal glance. "That *b* word. Well, you just close your eyes, and let me look at your hand."

"I'm not going to close my darned eyes again," Sunny fairly snarled. She shoved her towel-wrapped hand at him. "Just do whatever you have to do."

"Probably a good idea, not closing your eyes," Jake mused as he wrapped his fingers around hers. "You might not get that one back open again for a while."

"What do you mean?" With a horrified gasp, Sunny lifted her free hand to her face, then felt along her forehead until she encountered the puffiness above her right eye. "Oh, no! I must have hit my head on my knee harder than I thought."

"You hit it a pretty good clunk," Jake agreed. "It's already turning a real pretty purple color. Better let me put a cold cloth on it."

"I'd prefer you let Ruth do it."

Just then a pounding sounded beneath her feet, and Ruth

said, "That's Fred. He hits the ceiling with a broom handle when he needs my help in the store. I really need to go, Sunny. I'll take Teddy with me. You'll be in good hands with Jake."

Before Sunny could protest, Ruth took Teddy's hand and the two of them swept out of the kitchen. Rather than going through the door leading to the outside staircase, however, they went deeper into Ruth's living quarters.

"Ruth has another staircase down into the store," Jake explained in answer to Sunny's unasked question. "That way she can go back and forth without getting wet if it happens to be raining outside."

"This country is so dry, I doubt she'd have to worry about that very often," Sunny said with a huff.

"You'd be surprised. Spring and fall are when we get most of our rain. Problem is, the rain comes with some pretty terrific thunderstorms at times, along with tornadoes."

"Tornadoes?"

"Yep. It's so flat around here, I watched one boil around out there for fifteen minutes one day, before it finally went back up into the clouds. There. You're all fixed up, except for putting a cloth on that eye. I don't think your finger will need any stitches, if you're careful with it for the next few days. But you can check with the doctor if you want."

Sunny stared down at her hand and saw that a neat bandage covered her wound. As Jake held a dishtowel under the pump spout, she realized he'd kept her distracted with conversation while he doctored her finger. A second later, he held the cool cloth to her forehead, and she covered his hand with her own.

"Uh . . . I can hold it there myself," she said when he made no attempt to remove his hand.

"I'm sure you can," Jake conceded. "And I'll let you do that, as soon as you lift your hand enough for me to pull mine out from under it without hurting your bruise."

Sunny sent a baleful, one-eyed glance at his amused face and raised her hand. After he removed his, she caught the cloth before it dropped, then clamped it back over her sore forehead. Carefully, she elevated her bandaged finger, to keep it from getting soaked from the wet cloth.

Jake walked over to the stove and looked back over his shoulder. "You want a cup of coffee?"

"No, thank you," Sunny murmured primly. She couldn't decide whether to get up and leave or continue sitting there. She felt ridiculous, alone here in Ruth's kitchen with Jake, nursing both a sore finger and a sore head. When she lifted her free hand to catch a lock of hair falling over her ear, the heel of her palm touched her dress bodice, brushing the stiffness of drying blood. The gorge rose in her throat, and her face felt strange, as though it had tightened and paled.

"Uh-oh," Jake muttered. Slamming his coffee cup onto the table, he grabbed another dishtowel and strode back to the sink. A second later, Sunny's eyes flew open when she felt him rubbing at her breast.

"Stop that!" she demanded. "What on earth do you think you're doing?"

Jake shoved her hand aside. "I'm washing this stuff I'm not supposed to mention off your dress," he said, "before you upchuck again."

Sunny could feel her breast tips crinkling against the front of her dress, and she swatted at him again. "Quit it! I'll . . . I'll do it. Give me the cloth!"

"Sure, and have you pass out on me," Jake said, pushing her hand down into her lap. "I'm almost done, except for this little bit right here. You must have had your finger in your mouth."

Sunny's mouth dropped open when he shifted the dishtowel and wiped at the corner of her lips. His arm skimmed her breast, and a queer little shiver ran down through her stomach, centering in the exact spot where her bottom pressed against the chair seat. Her eyes widened and her mouth rounded, her breath caught in her throat and her gaze unerringly drifted to the whiskey depths so near her own face.

Jake's fingers froze, and his gaze locked with hers. The color in his eyes deepened to a dark walnut, and she caught the scent of coffee as his breath feathered across her face, mixing with her whoosh of released air. Feeling as paralyzed as a rabbit caught in a corner of a cage as a snake slithered closer and closer, she watched his tongue flick out and run across his bottom lip.

It didn't look like a snake's tongue. Instead, she found herself wondering which was softer—his tongue or the lip it caressed. Powerless to resist the urge, she imitated his action, only she traced her tongue across her upper lip.

"Damn!" Jake backed away from her, rubbing his forearm, where it had come in contact with her breast. For some reason, his action accelerated the dwindling sensation in her bottom again. She shifted, as though trying to scratch the itch the sensation fostered.

"Quit that, damn it!" Jake growled.

"Huh?" Her head snapped up, and she cried out in pain when her teeth inadvertently clamped down on the edge of her tongue. "Ouch!" Her fingers flew up to probe her stinging tongue. When Jake reached out toward her, she heartily slapped his hand aside.

"Get away from me! If you don't leave me alone, I'll end up a mass of bruises from one end to the other!"

Jake withdrew and stared at her skeptically. "I fail to see

how you can blame me for your various injuries. I wasn't even here when you cut your finger, and you managed to get that knock on your head and bite your tongue completely by yourself. Hell, all I've been trying to do ever since I got here is get you fixed up. As far as what else just happened . . ."

Sunny bounded out of the chair. "*Nothing* just happened! And nothing else *will* happen if you'll get out of here!" She pointed emphatically toward the door. "Go! Now!"

Jake ambled over to the table and sat down, pulling his coffee cup back from the edge. "Well, now," he drawled, "since this is Ruth's place, not yours, I guess she'd have to be the one to order me to leave. And I think I'll just sit here for a minute and try to figure out which one of those statements you just made is true. And which one's not."

"Which . . . what . . . You're not making sense," Sunny sputtered. "I have no idea what you're talking about."

"Don't seem to know what you're talking about yourself," Jake mused. "At first you say nothing happened. But then you say nothing *else* will happen. Sure is an enigma, how nothing else can happen if nothing happened at first. Now . . ."

"Ohhhhh!" Realizing she still held the cloth over one eye, Sunny flung it into the sink. When she peered back at him, she couldn't see him one iota better. She gingerly reached up and touched the swelling over her right eye, finding herself barely able to open the eye.

That did it. Her finger throbbed, her tongue burned, and her eye was swollen and probably so discolored she wouldn't be able to show her face for days on end. She could imagine the pitying looks of the women she had anticipated meeting at church the next day when she tried to explain what had happened.

"They'll probably believe I hit my head on my knee about as much as they'd believe I ran into a door in the dark," she muttered aloud. "Just like they'd believe any other woman who tries to cover up that she's been hit by a fist."

"Now, wait a minute," Jake said as he got to his feet. "Nobody hit you with a fist. You can't be thinking of . . ."

"What I'm thinking of is none of your business!" Peering cautiously ahead of her, Sunny stiffened her back and headed for the kitchen doorway. "I'm going home before I end up flat on my back over at the doctor's office with more than a gashed finger, a black-and-blue eye, and a sore tongue!"

"Your sore tongue appears to be working fine, at least."

She heard him start after her, but she managed to slip out the door and head downstairs. His steps paused at the top of the steps, and she bunched her skirt higher, hanging on to the railing with her other hand to ensure that she didn't make a further fool of herself by tripping and tumbling. At the bottom of the steps, she didn't even glance back. As fast as she cautiously could, she ran onto the boardwalk and turned toward Cassie's house.

It wasn't until she was almost home that she realized she'd left Teddy at the store with Ruth. With a groan of dismay, she stopped in her tracks. Turning, she was able to make out the tall figure standing on the walkway in front of the store. She would have to pass him to get to Teddy.

Well, Teddy knew the way home. Surely she'd return when Sunny didn't come for her. But recalling her promise to help Teddy pick out some new clothes, she knew she had to go back. Still, she stared at the store for a long moment before she forced her legs to move.

After a few steps, she saw Jake head for the jailhouse across the street. Breathing a sigh of relief, she hurried on. Just before she reached the store, the door flew open and Ruth came out.

"Jake!" Ruth called across the street. Glancing that way,

Sunny saw the Ranger had reclaimed what she was coming to believe was his favorite spot—the tilted chair beside the railing, with his boots resting on the crosspost.

"Jake," Ruth called again. "Where's Sunny? She and I need to talk to you. Or did she already ask you?"

6

As SHE PICKED through the bolts of cloth on a shelf, Sunny resolutely ignored Jake, who was sipping another cup of coffee at Ruth's counter. After choosing three cottony materials, she laid them on the cutting table, murmuring to Ruth to measure off the appropriate lengths for dresses for Teddy. Then she moved over to a rack of ready-made dresses.

"Evaline makes up a few dresses now and then for sale," Ruth explained as Sunny perused the other selections. "Most of the women still make their own children's clothing, but sometimes there's a call for something in a hurry. I think you'll find that blue one, and maybe the pink one, of a size to fit Teddy."

Sunny added the blue and pink dresses to the bolts of fabric. "I may ask Evaline to make up a couple of Teddy's dresses, although I'll have Teddy help me with one herself," she told Ruth. "Teddy needs to know how to sew. But Evaline does nice work, and although I'm no slouch with a needle, sewing's not one of my favorite chores."

"Evaline will be glad to get the business. Now, how much of this one do you want?"

Sunny stared at the fourth bolt of material as Ruth rolled it out on the cutting table. She had been surprised at finding such a fine silk in Ruth's store. The delicate blue shade had an almost watery tinge to it—but it was not the kind of fabric to wear in this town. It would be much more appropriate for the opera house back in St. Louis. She didn't remember putting that bolt on the cutting table.

"Ah . . . well . . ."

"I assume you want this for yourself, since it's not the type of stuff for a child's dress," Ruth went on, draping several yards of the material to the side and picking up her scissors. "This should be about the right amount."

Before Sunny could protest, she snipped the length of material, folded it, and added it to the other pile. With a sigh of resignation, Sunny turned away to scan the store for Teddy. She found her standing before a shelf of dolls with porcelain faces, a look of awe on her face.

"Teddy," she said to get her attention. "We need to choose a few other things for you."

Teddy reluctantly walked away from the shelf, and they spent the next fifteen minutes or so selecting underclothing and several pairs of stockings. Her vision had adjusted to her one-eyed gaze somewhat, but Sunny noticed that at times she would reach for something, only to find it an inch or so to the side of where her fingers fell. When she got back to the house, she intended to use cold cloths on her eye until the swelling receded.

She finally couldn't put off approaching the counter to pay for her selections any longer. She concentrated on Ruth's chatter as she totaled the purchases, until she heard a gasp from Teddy. Turning, she saw Teddy holding one of the dolls, a delighted grin on her face.

"Thank you, thank you, thank you, Ranger Jake," Teddy chanted. "I ain't . . . I never had a doll before. She's sooooo pretty!"

"I chose that one because her face reminds me of you,"

Jake said. "See? She's got blue eyes and blond hair, just like yours."

"Oh, but I'm not that pretty, Ranger Jake," Teddy said with a giggle. "She looks more like Miss Sunny."

Jake glanced over at her, and Sunny felt every inch of the slow scan he made of her body. When he finally dropped his gaze to the doll again, she released a breath she hadn't even realized she was holding.

"Could be," she heard Jake murmur to Teddy. "Let's say she looks like both of you. And you know what?"

"What?" Teddy asked eagerly.

"You can make some dresses for your doll from the material left over from your own dresses, if you ask Evaline to save the scraps for you."

"Oh! Then we'd be twins." Teddy nodded her head earnestly, a few tendrils of hair escaping from the pigtails Sunny had braided that morning. "I thought it was just gonna be work to learn how to sew, like Miss Sunny said she was gonna teach me to do. But if I can learn how to make dresses for my dolly too, then it won't be so bad."

Jake slipped Sunny a wink, which went unnoticed by either Ruth or Teddy but which zapped through Sunny with startling intensity. She caught herself wondering how Jake could know just what to say to get Teddy enthusiastic about learning a new task; she herself had encountered only disinterest when she mentioned sewing to Teddy. He seemed to have had plenty of practice with children.

Heavens, was he perhaps married himself? She hadn't seen any sign of a wife—or children, for that matter. Possibly, though, he had a family to get back to somewhere. After all, from what she knew about the Texas Rangers, they were a mobile unit of trained men sent to various areas of trouble in the state. And Ruth had said something about Jake's coming to town and running out an outlaw element.

Could he just be biding his time until he was released from this assignment and sent elsewhere? Or maybe back to his family?

If he had a wife waiting somewhere, she darned sure had no business getting all flustered and shaky whenever she got within two feet of him! She would definitely keep her distance from now on.

"So," Ruth said, drawing her attention. "Fred's about done unpacking the supplies in the storage room, and I have a little free time now. I could take Teddy over to Evaline's, which would free you and Jake to talk to Ginny."

"Uh . . . Ginny? I'm sorry, Ruth. You lost me somewhere."

"Well, we didn't get to finish our discussion a while ago," Ruth said. "But I've been thinking about it, and we'll need a meeting place. Also, somewhere to put on some performances, if we can talk people into coming to our out-of-the-way little town. I've got several ideas, Sunny. Why, I've heard that Dallas has no dearth of performers for their Cultural Center, and I've got a friend I correspond with there. I can get the tour schedules from her, and with the right incentive, I'll bet we can get some of them to stop off here before they travel on to Denver or other points west."

"What the devil are you talking about, Ruth?" Jake asked. His voice came from right beside her, and Sunny hurriedly took a step away from the counter. "And what's Ginny got to do with this?"

"She's got the only empty building in town," Ruth said in exasperation. "Haven't you been listening to me? And Sunny will need someone to escort her over to talk to Ginny. I mean, it's not as if Sunny would have to go into a place like Saul Cravens', but I'd feel better if you went with her to Ginny's."

"What sort of business does Ginny run?" Sunny asked with no little trepidation.

"Oh, it's a saloon, like that Cravens man has," Ruth said. "But *not* like it that much either."

"A saloon?" Sunny said with unfeigned interest. "You mean, with drinks and gambling and women who . . ." Remembering Teddy, she glanced around to see where she was; she was just sitting at the other end of the counter trying to braid the doll's hair. She lowered her voice, her curiosity about actually getting to see the inside of a saloon making her forget Jake beside her. "And women who . . . uh . . . cater to men?"

Jake's laughter rumbled in his chest, and her cheeks flushed. However, she resolutely ignored him once more.

"Ginny's girls don't do that," Ruth denied stoutly. "At least, not since her father got killed in the shoot-out with that cheating cardsharp last year and Ginny took over. She has to sell drinks and allow gambling in order to pay her bills, but her place is more of a . . . well, a training school for her girls."

Ruth emphatically nodded her head, shooting Jake a venomous look when he choked back a laugh. "Not *that* sort of training Jake Cameron, and you're well aware of it! But yes, that's more what I'd call it. Ginny teaches her girls to do bookkeeping and ordering. And she's got a couple of women who have very nice voices—I bet we could talk them into singing for us."

Jake snorted, and Sunny added her own deadly glare to Ruth's.

"Just what's so darned funny about this, Jake?" Ruth demanded.

"Sorry," he replied around a strong hint of laughter. "It's just that I can't imagine any of the various women in Liberty

Flats dressing up in their finery and heading over to hear one of Ginny's girls sing a tune."

"*You* obviously don't know how important it is for women to have some culture in their lives," Sunny spat. "If I remember right, you don't even think there's any problem with women having to drag their skirts through animal droppings to cross the street!"

Her voice rose in pitch, as she felt her resentment at his attitude deepen. She'd darn well show this man how absolutely wrong he was. She'd darn well show him that women had rights; they need not accept being relegated to the status of second-class citizens whose opinions didn't matter and who couldn't even vote.

"And since I'm responsible for Teddy's upbringing now," she continued, "I feel it's my duty to see that she's exposed to something more than training to be some man's servant."

"Most men consider women helpmates . . ." Jake tried to interrupt, but she waved a hand to silence him.

"Tell me more about the women who work with Ginny, Ruth. Would any of them perhaps have any other musical training? I would love to have Teddy take piano lessons, but Aunt Cassie's piano is totally out of tune."

"I believe Perry, Ginny's bartender, keeps her piano in tune," Ruth replied. "At least, I seem to remember Ginny mentioning how nice it was that she'd discovered Perry's other talents after she hired him when her other bartender married one of her girls and left a few months ago. I . . . um . . . don't know what Cassie would say, though, about Perry coming to her house, even to tune a piano."

"I'll worry about that later," Sunny replied. "Right now, I'd really like to go meet Ginny. Thanks so much for offering to care for Teddy while I'm gone. I'm sure your selections for dress styles for her will be just fine."

She started for the door, pausing when she didn't hear

anyone following her. "Are you coming, Ranger Cameron? If you've got other things to do, I'll just go on by myself. You *are* so busy, keeping that chair across the street warm."

Ruth choked on a giggle, but instead of the annoyance Sunny expected to see cross Jake's face at the audacity of her words, he grinned straight back at her. Grabbing his hat from the countertop, he slapped it on his head and strolled toward her.

"I wouldn't miss this for the world," he drawled.

He held the door for Sunny, and she lifted her chin as she walked past him and on down the boardwalk. He started whistling a song when he fell in beside her, and she thought she recognized the melody, though it was a recent addition to the programs in St. Louis. Thinking she must be mistaken, since she couldn't imagine that song already being a common melody this far west, she decided not to say anything about it. After passing two other buildings, one of which Sunny thought must be Evaline's dress shop, Jake took her arm and steered her toward the steps to the street.

"That's Ginny's place down there—the last one on the block," Jake told her, nodding his head. "Make sure you lift your skirts."

"Lift my . . . !" She quickly clamped her mouth shut before he could realize she'd mistaken his comment for a double entendre.

She gathered her dress skirts up and studied the building as they angled across the street. Freshly painted a clean white, it sported red trim. The sign over the door said only GINNY'S, in red letters matching the trim. Wondering why Jake started across the street so far in advance of where they needed to cross to reach Ginny's, she turned slightly. What could he be avoiding?

The batwing doors on the building directly across from Ginny's place sprang open, and a man flew through them, sliding across the walkway and into the street. A second later, another man emerged, sauntered to the edge of the boardwalk and stared down at the man groaning in the dirt. The second man wore a black suit, complete with vest, despite the heat of the day. He dusted his hands together, then snapped the cuff of each sleeve back into place. The sun glinted on the pomade slicked over his black hair.

"I've warned you about trying to mooch drinks in my place, Collins," Sunny heard him say. "You keep your ass out of here until you've got your own money to pay for the booze you wanna drink. And there's also the matter of your outstanding bar tab."

Jake tugged on Sunny's arm, and she realized she'd come to a halt, gawking at the scene. The sign over the building indicated it was another saloon, simply called SAUL'S SALOON. Under his tapered suit coat, the man who had tossed the drink moocher out the door looked adequately muscled for the task, although, from what Sunny could see of the man moaning in the street, he was thin and wiry. Before she could respond to Jake's urging to move on, the man in the suit noticed them and headed in their direction.

"Hey, Jake," he called, striding heedlessly past the man still lying in the street, "who's the pretty lady?"

Jake's fingers tightened on her arm, and he muffled an oath. He didn't appear to be rude enough to disregard the man's greeting, though, since he stood waiting.

Sunny examined the approaching man. He was shorter than Jake, and his clothing was spotless and well tailored, speaking of his close attention to his appearance. She'd always felt a stab of distaste for men who used that messy oil on their hair, but beneath that, his face was clean-shaven. He did have a faint touch of jowliness, but his arresting eyes mitigated that flaw. They were almost black and could probably be as cold as the eyes of a lizard, though now they held a hint of appreciation—appreciation clearly focused on Sunny.

When the man got close enough to make conversation without straining his voice, Jake introduced the two of them. "Saul Cravens, Sunny Fannin. Miss Fannin is Cassie Foster's niece."

"Completely delighted," Saul said in a smooth voice, reaching for Sunny's politely extended hand and carrying it to his lips. He attempted to hold her hand after he kissed the back of it, but she firmly pulled it free, fighting the urge to wipe it on her dress skirt.

"Mr. Cravens," she forced herself to respond.

"And where are you headed this beautiful day?" Saul asked.

Loathe to countermand the training in manners her mother had drilled into her, Sunny said, "We're on our way to talk to Miss McAllister."

"Why, Miss Fannin," Cravens replied, "if you have a desire to see the inside of a saloon, I'd be extremely pleased to show you my own establishment. And I can promise you I wouldn't allow another mishap to mar the loveliness of your face while you were in my company."

"Forget it, Saul," Jake snapped. "We're seeing Ginny on business, not for a tour of her place. If you'll excuse us, the middle of the street isn't the place to carry on a long conversation."

Sunny complied with the pressure of his touch this time, nodding her head briefly at Cravens before moving along with Jake. His brisk steps carried them across the street and up to the red batwing doors on Ginny's place in far less time than it had taken them to stroll the previous distance. He started through the batwings without pause, but Sunny pulled free, remembering Cravens' reference to her injured face.

"What's wrong?" Jake grumbled.

"Perhaps I should have gone by the house first and picked up a hat with a veil," she said.

"It's too danged hot to wear a veil," Jake said with a sigh of impatience. "Come on."

"Bossy know-it-all," Sunny muttered, sweeping past him with a haughty sniff. Her impaired vision caused her to misjudge the opening when she tried to avoid touching him in passing, and her shoulder grazed the side of the doorway. She gritted her teeth when her dress sleeve caught on a splinter of wood and ripped. Not pausing to examine the damage, which couldn't be remedied anyway, she walked on into the saloon. Immediately she forgot her blemished face and less-than-perfect attire, eagerly gazing around at the first gaming and drinking establishment she'd ever entered.

It looked exactly as she'd imagined from reading the dime novels her mother had never known she hid in her room. A bald man with a drooping walrus mustache ran a polishing rag across a bar on the right side of the room. A huge mirror covered the wall behind the bar, reflecting the multitude of bottles and glasses on the shelves, and at the far end of the room there was a small stage, with a piano in one corner. On her left, a staircase led up to another floor.

Spittoons were placed in scattered piles of sawdust beside the tables and along the bar, and a stale smoke smell lingered in the air. Once she had eavesdropped on two of her male acquaintances, who were talking about various saloons in the bawdier district of St. Louis. They were having a friendly argument about the attributes of the different nude women in the pictures over the bar. Somewhat hesitantly—somewhat eagerly, though she would die before admitting it to anyone—Sunny scanned the room, but she was a tad disappointed to find only some rather dismal pictures of flowers decorating the walls. One table was occupied, and she recognized the woman who had attended the funeral of Teddy's father as she eagerly came forward.

"Jake!" the woman said. "What brings you here so early in the day? Not that you're not always welcome, but there won't be a poker game going on until later."

She stopped in front of them and held out her hand to Sunny, not waiting for Jake to answer her. "I'm Ginny McAllister, Miss Fannin, and please don't be surprised that I already know who you are. This is, after all, a very small town. I'm very pleased to meet you. What on earth happened to your eye?"

Sunny flushed as she took the extended hand. Normally she didn't greet another woman with a handshake, but Ginny appeared to be easy with that type of greeting. Then she saw Ginny glance down at her bandaged finger, and the other woman released her hold before she squeezed too tightly.

"Oh, dear. You've injured your finger, also," she murmured. "Jake Cameron, I hope you didn't have anything to do with poor Miss Fannin's injuries. She looked perfectly fine when I saw her the other day at the funeral."

"Hell, no, I didn't cause her to get hurt," Jake said irritably. "Look, Sunny wants to talk to you about some harebrained idea she and Ruth have cooked up."

"Hmm," Ginny said. "Every once in a while one of your remarks does remind me how nice it is that some poor woman's not shackled to you as a wife, Jake. If it's something you consider harebrained, I'll bet I'm going to love it." Sharing a conspiratorial look, she took Sunny's arm and led her toward the table where she'd been sitting. "Would you like some tea, Miss Fannin? I'm a late riser, since the evenings here do tend to go on late, and I'm just finishing up my breakfast."

"Please, it's Sunny." Sunny's steady voice covered up quite well the strange stab of elation flashing through her. It was just the prospect of having her craving for tea satisfied, she chastised herself—not the lessened guilt feelings for finding out the man she had responded to wasn't married after all. "And I'd absolutely love some tea. If I'd known how unavailable it is out here, I'd have brought some from back East."

"Then we'll just have to share what I have," Ginny said with a nod. "Perry," she called as she motioned Sunny to take a seat, "please fix up a package of tea for Sunny to take with her when she leaves."

"Yes, ma'am," the bartender replied.

When Sunny glanced at the bar, she saw that Jake was standing there instead of joining them. He propped a booted foot on the brass rail running the length of the lower portion of the bar, leaning against the surface and speaking quietly to Perry. The bartender pulled a lever on a nearby barrel, then set the foaming glass of beer in front of Jake.

"Hmmph," Sunny said. "Isn't it rather early in the day to be imbibing?"

"Oh, Jake never gets drunk," Ginny assured her. She pushed a beautiful china cup filled with tea across the table. "Now, I can't decide which to ask you about first—the idea you and Ruth have or the reason you're sporting that black-and-blue eye. But I truly don't want to embarrass you."

Sunny giggled and shook her head. She'd begun to feel a rapport with Ginny as soon as she supported the *hare-brained idea* without even knowing what it was. She explained her bumps and bruises while Ginny finished a plate of ham and eggs.

"This tea is delightful," Sunny said after completing her tale.

"I'm glad you're enjoying it. It's also delicious with ice, so feel free to drop in anytime you need a cool drink."

"Ice? Here in this town?"

"Yes. You could use some on that eye," Ginny told her with a chuckle. "My bartender, Perry, is quite resourceful. He used to work in that new ice plant in New Orleans, and he built me a tiny model for my own use. We can even keep the ice for quite a while in the zinc-lined box he built to go with it. Saul Cravens is fit to be tied because he didn't think of the idea first. He's offered time and time again to pay Perry to make one for him. Perry intensely dislikes Saul though, because Perry found his cousin Marg working over there when he first came to town."

"Ah . . . working over there?" Sunny asked.

"Yes," Ginny said with a sigh tinged with resignation. Then she brightened somewhat. "But Perry soon heard I was in desperate need of a bartender, and he agreed to come work for me if I'd also hire Marg. He told me what a wonderful singing voice his cousin had, and he was right. Marg draws a lot of Saul's former customers to my place now, for a completely different reason."

Ginny's openness in discussing a subject that would have horrified any one of her mother's friends back in St. Louis—or any of Sunny's own friends, for that matter—brought a slight flush to Sunny's cheeks. There was quite a contradiction between Western women and Eastern women, yet she already felt a kinship with the women in Liberty Flats and a deep respect for what Ginny had done. She looked around her with new eyes, realizing the pictures on the wall were actually oil paintings. The delicate cup holding her tea and Ginny's own place setting were of the same china pattern, set on a hand-woven mat edged with lace.

"It's the women who will eventually tame the West," Ginny said, evidently noticing Sunny's appraisal of the divergent furnishings in the room. "My paintings are some I bought on the only trip I ever made to France, which I practically had to beg my father to let me take when I graduated from finishing school. I went with my aunt, who lives in Boston and whom I stayed with while I went to school. The piano's a Chickering; my aunt gave it to me when she got it into her head to order one of those silly Fourneaux player pianos she saw at the Philadelphia Centennial Exposition in 1876."

"I took lessons on a Chickering," Sunny said. "But I've never had a musical aptitude myself. I do love to listen to music, however. Your aunt must think a lot of you."

"She did. She would never even have thought of coming out here to see her brother, but my father did let me visit Boston. And when my aunt died last year, a few weeks before my father was killed, her will directed that I get her things."

"You never thought of going back there to live?"

"Heavens, no!" Ginny laughed gaily. "That life's much too stodgy for me, since I was raised out here. But it did make me appreciate a few of the finer things in life, and I enjoy having them around me. Even though I do have to take into consideration my male clientele and their disgusting habit of needing spittoons, not one of my customers would dare miss the mark when he spits. If they're a little tipsy and do, they clean up the sawdust and spread more under the spittoons themselves. I don't mind providing a masculine atmosphere for them to do their drinking and gambling, but they know better than to walk close to my piano with a lit cigar and take a chance of dropping a burning ash on it."

She leaned back in her chair, a pleased smirk on her lips. "Now, satisfy my curiosity and tell me of what possible use the infamous owner of Ginny's could be to you and Ruth."

"I think the infamous owner of Ginny's is exactly the person Ruth and I need," Sunny said with a determined nod.

"JAKE CAMERON, IF all you're going to do is make negative remarks about this building, Sunny and I will finish exploring and discuss possibilities ourselves!" Ginny tossed her red-gold curls in frustration and propped her hands on her slim hips. "We've got eyes. And even if we're women, we can recognize that this place will need some remodeling to suit our purposes."

"Remodeling?" Jake peered through the dim light in the empty building next to Ginny's saloon. "Hell, it's gonna need a major overhaul. The roof's even been leaking. Look over here."

Ginny tromped toward him, and Jake slipped an arm around her waist to help her past a pile of rubble on the floor. Sunny started to follow but paused when Ginny reached up and patted Jake's cheek, cooing coquettishly, "Oh, my, my. It's so nice of such a big, strong man to help poor little female me keep from stumbling and falling on her face. I just don't know how I've managed to walk all by myself for so many years."

"Damn it, Ginny. You and your outlandish ideas that a man's overstepping his bounds when he's trying to be a gentleman. I suppose you expect me to apologize for taking liberties with your person!"

"Why, Jake, honey," Ginny drawled. "You take all the liberties you want. It's such an honor for poor little me to have a brawny protector looking out for me. But you really should watch your language. You don't want to hurt my delicate ears, now do you, honey?"

Jake snorted in skepticism, and Sunny felt a different stab of emotion this time—jealousy, maybe—when Ginny giggled and ruffled Jake's hair. The easy camaraderie between the two of them spoke of either long acquaintance or perhaps something deeper. She turned away, focusing on the building around her in an effort to blot out the sound of Ginny's teasing banter and Jake's chuckled responses, though she had no earthly idea why they should bother her.

Ginny had said the two buildings were part of the deal when her father bought the saloon. He had anticipated expanding the saloon, but it never came about. The two front windows were covered with dirt so thick that barely any light filtered through. A few broken tables and chairs littered the floor, probably the result of some barroom brawls from next door. Perhaps they could be salvaged for furnishings. She didn't know much about carpentry, but maybe Ruth's husband could advise them.

The place would never even begin to compare to the opera house in St. Louis, but she could envision a few nicely placed tables, covered with snowy cloths and vases of flowers. They wouldn't even need to build a stage at first, since the length of the room appeared sufficient to have the performer at the far end.

She decided that a lot of the work would be basic cleanup. A broom and mop bucket would work wonders, along with a ladder to reach the spiderwebs draping the rafters and corners. Given her own unexplained clumsiness lately, however, she made up her mind right then and there not to be the person on the top of the ladder.

Something touched the back of her head, and Sunny brushed at it, expecting to pull her hand back full of distasteful spiderwebs. Swiping only at air, she turned to find a rope hanging down from the ceiling. Evidently someone had built an upper floor partially over the rafters—the rope was attached to an iron loop on what looked like a trapdoor.

Hmm, she mused, reaching for the dangling rope. *That might make a good storage area.*

She tugged, expecting the hinges on the trapdoor to be rusty from disuse and hard to open. Jake's shout startled her so badly that she jumped, thankfully, to one side. A jointed ladder tumbled down through the trapdoor, landing on the floor with a resounding crash and missing her by only inches.

"Damn it!" Jake grabbed her and dragged her further away from the ladder. "Don't you have any better sense than to stand right under that thing and risk it falling on you? Where the hell are your brains, woman? I'm starting to think you're just an accident looking for a place to happen!"

She stared in wide-eyed horror at the ladder for a second, then glanced at Jake's face. Rather than the outrage she anticipated, she saw a deep concern that belied his angry words. A sniff escaped her, and his face blurred when tears misted her eyes. Suddenly her finger stung, her swollen eye throbbed, and even her tongue hurt again. Burying her face in his shoulder, she flung her arms around his neck, unable to choke back the sobs breaking through the fear that clouded her mind.

"Aw. Aw, shoot, Sunny," he murmured, gathering her closer. "I didn't mean to yell at you. Dang it, it scared the living daylights out of me when I saw you reaching for that rope."

"And in typical male fashion," Sunny heard Ginny say,

"you hollered and cursed at her, instead of realizing she'd just had the wits scared out of her! Here, give her to me."

Sunny sought to turn toward the comfort Ginny offered, but Jake refused to release her. Sweeping her into his arms, he started walking.

"I'll take her to your office, Gin," he said. "She can rest there a minute, and we can make sure she wasn't injured."

"I'm not hurt," Sunny assured him, wiping one hand across her eyes and holding on to his neck with her other arm. "I can walk. Please, put me down."

"Nope," Jake said. "Not until we get out of this darn mess and have a safe place to put you down. I swear, Sunny, you need a keeper to look after you."

She tried to muster up some indignation at his words, but traces of her fright lingered. Had that ladder landed on her, she would have had a lot more severe injuries than she'd already suffered. Right now, having a keeper didn't sound half bad, especially one with such a nice, broad chest to cuddle against and muscular arms to hold her.

She sighed lazily, dropping her head on his shoulder and letting her eyes drift shut. All too soon she felt him lowering her and looked up at him from a reclining position on a soft settee in a strange room.

"You're in Ginny's office," Jake explained. He hovered over her, concern still shadowing his whiskey eyes as he reached to brush a lock of hair back from her forehead. "Feeling better?"

"Yes," she admitted. "I . . . I don't understand why I'm so awkward lately. I thought I outgrew that after my first couple of years as an adolescent."

"You're definitely not an adolescent any longer, Sunny."

His appreciative gaze ran over her, and all at once she became aware of her disheveled condition—the way her dress skirt was twisted under her and how tightly her bodice was pulled across her breasts. The darkening in Jake's eyes assured her that he was totally aware of it also.

At a slight noise, she shifted her attention toward Ginny, who stood at the foot of the settee with a glass in her hand and a contemplative look on her face. The redhead quickly smiled at her and handed Jake the glass.

"I'll be back in a minute," she said. "Something needs my attention in the bar."

Before Jake could stop her, Ginny hurried out of the room and Sunny sat up. "Heavens, I need to go check on Teddy."

"You're not going anywhere for a minute or two," Jake ordered, extending the glass toward her. "You wait until you're a little less shaky. Teddy's fine with Ruth for a little while longer."

"Ginny's right," Sunny blurted. "About your typical male attitude. I don't appreciate your bossiness one iota!"

"And in typical female fashion," Jake responded, "you can't tell the difference between bossiness and consideration. Drink this darned glass of water!"

He shoved the glass at her, and Sunny grabbed it. The coolness felt wonderful, and she immediately decided it would taste better going down her throat than it would look spattered on his stern face. She drank half of it before she lifted the glass to her forehead and ran it back and forth, flicking out her tongue to catch a drop of water spilling from the corner of her mouth.

"Ummmm. Oh, that's just what I needed. I wonder if Ginny would consider making some ice for us to use at the performances. We could have iced drinks—an additional attraction."

Glancing once again at Jake, she saw him staring fixedly at her. A dribble of water she'd missed slithered down her chin and dropped to the bare skin above her dress collar, Jake's eyes dropping with it. The water droplet traced a path on downward, beneath her collar, and Jake sighed with what could have been disappointment. Her skin flushed so hot she almost expected steam to rise from the droplet's route.

"I really need to get over there and check on Teddy," she repeated.

She jumped to her feet, thrusting the glass at him, and swept past him while he juggled the glass in his hand. Back in the saloon, she reluctantly stopped when Ginny called to her.

Holding out a pitcher and a brown paper bag, Ginny said, "Take this ice with you and put it on your eye when you get home. And don't forget your tea. Let me know what you decide about using the building. I'd love to be able to tell you that I'd let you have it for free, but I've been a businesswoman too many years. We can work it out, though. Repairs for rent for a while, then maybe a percentage of your draw or something. How does that sound?"

"Uh . . . sounds perfect to me," Sunny said, too anxious to get away to prolong their discussion. Any minute Jake would appear to make sure she could cross the street without getting trampled. "That way we won't have to come up with a lot of money at first, other than what we'll need for supplies for repairs."

"Get the merchants to contribute things you need like paint and lumber," Ginny suggested. "And the men to do the labor."

"Good idea. I'll let you know when our first planning meeting will be, so you can get credit for all your help."

Sunny edged toward the door, while Ginny threw back her head with laughter.

"I'll be there. Most definitely," Ginny called as Sunny pushed open the red batwing doors.

Pausing briefly halfway through the doors, Sunny called back, "Thanks for the ice." Past Ginny she saw Jake lounging in the office door, thumbs hooked in his pants pockets and hat low over his eyes. As clearly as if he'd spoken, she knew he was waiting for his own thanks for keeping her from being injured by the falling ladder. The best she could do was nod her head at him.

TEDDY PROPPED HER doll on the table that evening while Sunny spread the flower-printed material for her dress on the kitchen table.

"We gots to watch close, Dolly," Teddy said. "So's we'll know how to make you a dress when Miss Sunny's done."

"We *have* to watch close," Sunny corrected her, nodding encouragement when Teddy repeated her words. "Is that what you've decided to name your doll? Dolly?"

"I think so. We talked about it for a long time today, 'cause a name's a real important thing. Dolly's a happy name, and I want her to be happy, like I'm starting to be."

"We? Oh, you mean you and your doll talked about it? I see. I had a doll I used to talk to like that, and we had some really interesting conversations from time to time. Even when my mother was busy, she was always there to listen to me. I'm awfully glad you're starting to feel happy again, Teddy."

"Can Dolly sleep with me tonight?" Teddy asked.

"I don't see why not. However, if talking to her when you wake up at night doesn't help, you can still bring her with you and come into my bed."

Teddy swung her legs back and forth, propping her chin on her palm as Sunny laid one of the other dresses on the material for a pattern.

"I still miss Pa in the day," she admitted in a quiet voice. "But nights are worse. Did you miss your pa when he was gone, Miss Sunny?"

"I never knew my father," Sunny said, picking up the

scissors rather awkwardly because of her injured finger. "But I miss my mother terribly yet."

"How come you didn't know your pa? Did he die before you was born?"

"To be truthful, Teddy, I don't really know. You see, my mother would never talk about him. He evidently provided for us, since my mother didn't have to work and we always had adequate money to get by on. We weren't by any stretch of the imagination rich, though. My mother was a widow, which means my father's dead, but that's really about all I know. I don't know if he died before I was born or when I was too young to remember him."

"Gee, it's sorta like me, 'cept it's my mama I don't know."

"Well, maybe when you get older, Teddy, we can see what we can find out about her."

"Is that part of why you came back here?" Teddy asked astutely. "'Cause you're old enough now to try to find out somethin' 'bout your pa? Was he from here?"

"Again, I don't know, Teddy . . ."

A crash sounded in the hallway outside the kitchen door. Startled, Sunny snipped an inch too far with the scissors. The tip of them cut into one of the sleeves on the pattern dress, and she uttered a muffled "darn it," before tossing the scissors aside and starting out of the kitchen to investigate.

In the hallway, she found Cassie bending down to pick up the metal tray she'd used to carry her supper to her room. The plate and cup lay shattered on the floor.

"Let me help, Aunt," Sunny said. "I'll get a broom. I already found out today how easy it is to get cut on broken dishes."

Cassie straightened, peering at Sunny with a strange look on her face.

"Are you all right, Aunt?" Sunny asked. "You didn't hurt yourself, did you?"

"No, I don't seem to be quite as clumsy as you," Cassie said in an even voice. "I overheard you and the child earlier today, speaking of your accidents. You must be more careful, you know." Turning away, she started back toward her room. "I'll appreciate your cleaning that up, Miss."

The words to tell her aunt that both she and "the child" had names got mixed up with her indignation at her aunt's gall in ordering her to clean up the broken dishes. Not that she hadn't already offered—but only to help. The bedroom door closed before she could think of an appropriately impertinent comment to fling after Cassie, and her shoulders slumped. Sighing in defeat, she went to fetch the broom.

Teddy followed her back to the hallway and held the dustpan for her. The little girl carefully carried the almost overflowing dustpan to the trash can in the kitchen, and Sunny heard her giggle.

"What's so funny, young one?" Sunny asked.

"Just was thinkin' that you and Miz Foster both sure break a lot of dishes," Teddy said, dumping the shards into the trash can and sneaking a look over her shoulder. "Maybe you oughta get tin dishes, like me and Pa used."

Sunny joined her laughter, nodding her head. "Maybe we should," she agreed. "At the very least, we need to start being more careful."

Sunny left the broom on the back porch, returned to the table, and picked up the scissors. She didn't know what had startled her aunt and made her drop the tray of dishes, but it couldn't possibly have been the same thing that had caused her to break the glass at Ruth's. She couldn't comment about that to Teddy, though. She couldn't imagine Aunt Cassie being distracted by thoughts of blatant masculinity to the point that she injured herself.

At least the ice had taken care of the swelling on her eye. The purple had faded to a sickly greenish-yellow, and she could try to cover up the bruise with powder before she went to church in the morning. And if that Ranger also happened to be in church, she'd make darn sure she sat in the opposite section of the pews from him, as far away as she could get. She had to protect herself against this unexplainable clumsiness around him!

"Miss Sunny?"

"What, Teddy?"

"Is you just gonna stand there looking at the material? Or is you gonna cut some more on it?"

"Are you," Sunny corrected. "Uh . . . I was just looking at the cut I made by mistake, when the noise from the hallway startled me. I think it can be sewn up easily enough and not even be noticeable."

She glanced toward the kitchen door, a slight frown on her face. What on earth *could* have startled Cassie into dropping the tray of dishes? Surely her aunt would have mentioned it if she'd seen a mouse or something in the hallway.

Teddy stifled a huge yawn, and Sunny laid down the scissors. "It's past bedtime for you, Teddy. I lost track of time while we were working on your dress. Why don't you get changed into your nightgown, and I'll come tuck you in."

"Aw, it's not even dark yet," Teddy pleaded. "I used to stay up lots later than this."

Sunny bit back a smile, remembering how many times she'd begged her own mother to let her stay up later. Her mother had never actually ordered her to bed, but she now realized she had used her own method of discipline.

"Well, Dolly looks awfully sleepy," she told Teddy. "And Rowdy's already curled up on his rug on the back porch.

You'll all have lots more energy to play together tomorrow, if everyone gets a good night's sleep."

"Guess you're right," Teddy agreed around another yawn. "'Sides, I's got that pretty nightgown to wear tonight."

"I *have* that pretty nightgown," Sunny corrected.

Teddy giggled at her as she slid from her chair. "Nope, it's *my* nightgown. It's too little for you."

With a saucy glance at Sunny, clearly denoting that Teddy was well aware she'd won that word game, the little girl tucked her doll under her arm and skipped out of the kitchen. Sunny shook her head tolerantly, then walked over to the sink to get Teddy her ritual glass of bedtime water. The child was so bright, she was going to be a joy to teach.

She carried the glass into Teddy's room and set it on the bedside table. Sunny settled in the rocking chair with the storybook she'd been reading to the little girl the previous evening and waited until Teddy finished her prayers. After Teddy climbed into bed and snuggled under the light, summer-weight blanket, with Dolly on the pillow beside her, Sunny began to read. But Teddy slipped into sleep before Sunny had completed even three pages of the continuing story.

When she returned to the quiet kitchen, she was too restless to work on the dress again. She should go on to bed, since the church service would begin early in the morning. Yet she would only toss and turn. She would almost welcome even Aunt Cassie's company right now—almost. At least she could ask her aunt what had startled her in the hallway.

She wandered toward the front door and out onto the porch. The cooler night air flowed over her, and she thought of the pitcher in the kitchen, now holding only melted ice cubes. Wouldn't it cause a stir if she went to Ginny's to return the pitcher and ask for a cold drink?

She peered down the street. The lights from both the saloons at the far end of town twinkled in the distance. She would no more go there at this time of night than she would undress and walk down the street at high noon, she admitted to herself with a smile. But she bet the people there were having fun with each other, rather than prowling around a lonely house with a sleeping child in one bedroom and a cantankerous, embittered woman holed up in another.

It was so beautiful out, it seemed a shame to close things up and go to bed. The sky—the Texas sky—spread over her in a wide, endless black swath dusted with sprinkles and clusters of stars. She wrapped her arms around a porch post, laying her cheek against the cool wood and looking up at the sky. That was the Big Dipper over there, but she'd never studied constellations enough to recognize anything else.

Off in the distance, a coyote howled. A horse nickered, and she glanced toward the stable, catty-corner across the street. As though he'd sensed her gaze on him, one of the men standing by the corral fence straightened and turned toward her. Even from this distance, she recognized that physique. Well, surely she was far enough away from Jake to be safe from the fumbles. He hadn't even been in Ruth's kitchen at first this morning, though. To be safe, she left the post and sat down on the porch step. She wasn't going to let him run her off from this beautiful night.

The shorter man beside Jake glanced over his shoulder toward the house, then concentrated again on the horse inside the fence. When the other man removed his hat for a minute and wiped his forearm across his head, a glint of light from the low-hanging moon shone on his partial baldness.

Charlie Duckworth, she thought. Such a memorable name. Where on earth . . . ? Of course. Duckie! She'd heard her mother say that name a time or two when talking about her childhood with friends. Or was it just her childhood? Had her mother ever mentioned Charlie Duckworth in connection with their life in St. Louis?

Sunny drew in a shocked breath. *Could* the rumors be true? *Had* Charlie eloped with her mother, then abandoned her? Did he even know there had been a child . . . Sunny?

Where there's smoke . . .

If it were true, it would have been very logical for her mother to change her name to something else noteworthy than Duckworth, especially if she was so ashamed of being abandoned that she wanted to pass herself off as a widow. Being a widow was acceptable—unlike being an abandoned wife. Evidently the man had made financial arrangements for his wife and daughter, but that darned sure didn't make up for the fact that he'd deserted them, leaving her mother to raise their child on her own! And leaving Sunny without a father's love!

For a moment she wondered if she should even pursue the identity of her own father—whether it would be worth the pain that discovery might bring. Just as quickly, though, she realized she definitely wanted a chance to confront the man—to lambast him for his desertion and show him that she had turned into a fine person despite his lack of interest in her life.

Revenge is sweet. She'd never really believed that saying before, but she had every right in the world to know who her father was. And it further diminished her opinion of Jake Cameron to think he might count a deserting husband and father as his friend. Ruth had said the two of them were extremely close.

Birds of a feather flock together.

The inane adages kept intruding on her thoughts. Maybe she should confront Charlie Duckworth directly. But he could easily deny her accusations. What if she had irrefutable proof? And what better place to find out about a man than from the man's good friend?

The good friend ambled away from the corral, heading in her direction. Charlie mounted another horse tied to the corral, turning it down the road leading out of town. By the time Jake arrived at the porch, Charlie had all but disappeared into the night.

"Evening."

"Ranger," Sunny replied.

"Nice night."

"Ummmm."

"How's your eye? And finger?"

"Healing."

"Well, sounds like you want to enjoy the night alone. I'll get on with my rounds." Jake started to move away.

"Ah . . ." Sunny bit her lip. She wouldn't get any information out of him if she didn't talk to him, for pete's sake. "Ah . . . if your rounds take you by Ginny's, maybe you could return her pitcher for me."

Jake pushed his hat brim up to peer at her. The moon gave enough light for her to see the mixture of emotions on his face. She stifled a giggle as the impact of what she'd asked him to do hit her. Such a sight that would be—Jake Cameron carrying a glass pitcher into Ginny's saloon!

"I guess I could," he said. "Problem is, I like to keep my hands free when I'm making rounds. Wouldn't want to smash the pitcher if I had to drop it to break up a fight or something."

"That's all right. I understand. I can take it back tomorrow. Um . . . it's still rather humid out. I drew a cool bucket of water from the well right before I put Teddy to bed. Do you need a drink? Or would you rather wait until you get to Ginny's and get something colder?"

"Drink of water would sit real good about now. But I don't want to put you to any bother."

"No bother." Sunny rose to her feet. "I'll be right back."

She managed to go into the kitchen, pour a glass of water, and carry it back to him without spilling a drop or fumbling even once—until she handed him the glass. Her fingers bumped his and she jerked her hand back. Jake smoothly caught the glass, then drained it in one long gulp. Chuckling under his breath when he started to give it back to her, he reached for one of her hands and carefully closed her fingers around the glass.

She pressed her lips together and bit back the comment forming in her mind about how she got clumsy only around him. Instead, she said, "The friend you were just with will have a warm ride this time of night. I should have offered him a drink before he left."

"Charlie? He filled his canteen from the pump at the stable. Besides, he only has a short ride. He lives off a road that comes into the main road about half a mile from town."

"I saw him at the funeral. And Ruth mentioned he's a close friend of yours." She paused, not having had time enough to really formulate which questions would get the best information out of him.

"Yeah," was all she got right now.

"Ruth . . . uh . . . said your friend Charlie grew up in Liberty Flats. That he knew my mother."

Jake stuck his fingers in his back pockets, the stance drawing his denims even tighter across his thighs. She mentally cautioned herself to keep her eyes on his face and hold on to that darned glass, as he continued, "I met Charlie during the war. Men form pretty strong friendships in times like that—those who make it through it, anyway."

While she puzzled over how to come up with something to keep him talking, the horse Jake had just left in the corral kicked up its heels. It raced around the circle of fence posts and threw up a cloud of dust that partially obscured it. Jake turned sideways to watch, and she was treated to a different view of him.

"Is that your horse?" she asked at last.

"Yep. Got him from Charlie. I call him Dusty, and he needs some exercise."

Ah. An opening for her to question him. "Charlie raises horses, then?"

"You seem awfully darned interested in Charlie. Are you hinting for an introduction to him? He's a little old for you."

"No!" Too emphatic, she realized, calming her voice and saying, "You know how it is in a small town. At least that's what Aunt Cassie tells me. Everyone knows everyone else, and all their history. Or what they think is everyone else's history."

Jake let the silence stretch for quite a while. He took his fingers out of his pockets and stared at her. She kept looking at the horse over in the corral, but she was aware of his every movement and sensed a tenseness in him. Had she gone too far? She hadn't even really asked him anything at all.

"Rumors in small towns are just like those in big towns," Jake finally said in a flat voice. "They're usually half lies and speculation."

She met his wary gaze defiantly. "Only half lies?"

He jerked his hat brim down. "Thanks for the water. Have a good evening."

His lithe, deceptively slow saunter carried him out the gate. He passed through a pool of moonlight, which glinted off the polished cylinder of one gun hanging on his hard thigh. Sunny barely managed to grab the glass when it slipped through her fingers. At least she caught it this time, before it shattered on the porch floor and drew his attention back to her.

Gritting her teeth in vexation, she whirled, then glared at the doorway. It was perfectly wide enough to walk through without tearing her skirt, but she nevertheless gathered it around her with her free hand before she walked into the dark house. Smiling in satisfaction when she reached the kitchen without further mishap, she put the glass in the sink to wait for the morning dishes.

If Jake Cameron didn't want to talk to her about his friend Charlie, there were plenty of other people in town who would.

JAKE PULLED HIS hat down another inch over his eyes irritably, shutting out the sight of the activity at the other end of the street. Short of sticking his fingers in his ears, he couldn't block out the sounds of hammers and saws. After propping his booted feet on the railing, he shoved his thumbs in his gunbelt, allowed his fingers to dangle and his chin to fall to his chest as he sighed in displeasure.

Funny how the noise from the building repairs—the new Cultural Center, he reminded himself—cut right to the bone. Horses and wagons passing on the street had never bothered him. He could usually tell who was going by without even opening his eyes. Some of the wagons had a distinctive pattern of squeaks to their wheels, and a few of the horses even had distinctive gaits. His own dun could hardly ever be held down to a sedate walk, prancing with bridled power when restrained to anything less than a full gallop.

Damn, he wanted to take Dusty out for a run. And not just because the horse needed exercise. If he sat on this damned chair much longer, his own muscles would start to atrophy and his brain would follow right behind them. He needed more activity—for both his body's health and his mind's. Walking up and down the peaceful streets of Liberty Flats several times a day was not his idea of action.

Hell, he could get all the exercise he needed if he went over and helped with the building repairs, but that wasn't what he'd been sent here to do. Besides, the last time he'd picked up a hammer had been to repair a fence at the Leaning C, and he'd resented every inch he'd pounded there. He'd ridden out of the ranch barely half a day after he flung the hammer down in disgust. He'd had no intentions of spending the rest of his life nursemaiding a bunch of crazy cows or repairing fences to protect the stupid beasts. And the last thing he wanted to do now was pick up a hammer and help a town build a Cultural Center.

Besides, there were enough men helping out to make sure Miss Sunny Fannin didn't end up with any further injuries to that curvaceous body of hers. After just one meeting of the women in town, their men knew they'd never have any rest until that Cultural Center was up and running. They'd been working over there all week, and the only time anything had happened was when Fred fell off that rickety ladder Ginny provided. Fred's cursing as he tromped up the walkway to get a new ladder from his own store had proved the only thing hurt was his dignity.

"Ranger Jake!"

Jake opened his eyes to see Teddy skipping across the street. His sour mood lightened and a smile curved his lips as he dropped his feet and removed his thumbs from his gunbelt.

Teddy presented a far different picture today than the little ragamuffin who had prowled the streets barely two weeks ago. Two cute golden pigtails flopped against her back, and the knee-length skirt on her spotless pink dress fluttered around her legs when she skipped. Rowdy followed her, as usual, his brown and white coat gleaming in the sunlight as though it had just been washed and brushed. And it probably had been.

It hit Jake that the only thing he truly regretted about his plan for the future was that it didn't include children. He couldn't quite hold back the thought of how nice it would be to have a child of his own, perhaps a perky daughter like Teddy. But children meant a wife and a wife meant settling down in one place—and Jake Cameron already knew from being forced to spend boring weeks and months in this lifeless town that staying in one place for too long was beyond his capabilities. His toes curled in his boots against the itch on the bottom of his feet.

Teddy bobbed up the steps, and he shifted on the chair to greet her. "What you got there, Teddy?"

"Telegram for you, Ranger Jake. Mr. Turley asked me iffen I'd bring it over to you. Whoops. I mean *if* I'd bring it over to you. Miz Sunny says 'iffen' 's not a word, like 'ain't' ain't."

Jake chuckled at her chattering, then scanned the yellow piece of paper quickly. He couldn't believe that he'd get an answer from Kansas City about Teddy's background this soon, barely a week since he'd sent the first inquiry. Given the scant information he'd been able to provide them, it would surely take the law officials longer to investigate.

And he was right. It was just a weekly report from Austin, telling him once again that the headquarters office hadn't been successful in getting a marshal assigned to the Liberty Flats area. He shoved it into his shirt pocket in disgust, then wiped the frown off his face when he looked back at Teddy.

"Sounds to me like you're learning a lot from Sunny," he said, focusing on what Teddy had been saying. "I'll tell you a secret. I never let anyone know it, but I liked school when I was growing up."

"You did?" Teddy's blue eyes widened. "All the kids I've been talkin' to said they hated school, and I was sorta worried about having to go when the teacher gets back to town. But I'm havin' lots of fun when me and Miss Sunny have our lesson time in the mornings after breakfast, before she comes down here to work in the afternoons. The words under the pictures in the books are pretty easy to read, when you've got the picture right there to tell you what's goin' on."

"Well, the right teacher makes a difference. Sounds to me like Sunny's one of those teachers who enjoys making it fun for you to learn, Teddy. And I've met Miss Harding, the teacher here in town. She's a lot like Sunny, so you'll probably have fun learning with her, too."

"Couldn't be more fun than with Miss Sunny," Teddy said loyally. "Why, I bet when she has kids of her own, they'll know how to read and write even before they start to school. Miss Sunny says kids don't usually go to school 'til they're six or so, and she already knew how to read and write by the time she was four. And she could add and s'tract, too."

A stab of something Jake couldn't for the life of him identify went through him at the thought of Sunny Fannin with a passel of tiny little children of her own gathered around her skirts. Though Teddy was far too young to know the whys and wherefores of how children came about, he had a flash of Sunny's face in the throes of ecstasy, her slender legs around some man's hips and the tip of one of those pert breasts lost within the warm male mouth. His groin stirred in reaction, especially when he recalled how her nipple had pebbled against her bodice when he had been cleaning the blood off the material.

"Uh . . ." Jake rose, grabbing the chair when it threatened to topple behind him. "I need to go over and send an answer back to headquarters, so they'll know I got their telegram," he told Teddy. "Want to walk back with me?"

"Sure. I gotta go back and help out at the Cul . . .

Cultural Center." She nodded in satisfaction at her pronunciation of those big words. Taking Jake's hand, she hopped down the steps beside him, chattering away as to how many jobs she could actually do to help out at the center.

". . . hand Mr. Fred nails when he comes over to help out between customers. And I even fetch drinks for people when they get thirsty," she concluded about the time they climbed the steps on the other side of the dirt street. "Why, Miz Caroline even lets me watch her baby sometimes while she sews on the curtains and tablecloths. Some of the boys keep sneakin' off to play marbles out back, but Mr. Fred puts them to work loadin' wood scraps in the wagon when he catches them. It's fun gettin' to know everybody in town. Why aren't you over there helpin' out, Ranger Jake?"

"Well, Teddy"—Jake glanced down the street toward the repair noises—"you see, I've got my own job to do in town. The Rangers are pretty strict about us taking care of our duties."

"But you ain't . . . don't have no duties these days. No one's doing anything bad that you gotta arrest them for. I'm havin' lots of fun with all the people. Bet you would too, and bet it would at least be lots more fun than sittin' in front of the jail all day long."

"I do a little more than that," Jake grumbled guiltily. "Remember, I'm on duty at night too, when all the rest of the town's sleeping."

"Yeah, I forgot about that. Does you sleep at the jail too, Ranger Jake?"

Jake grimaced in distaste at the thought of the tiny room off the jailhouse office, which was barely big enough for the lumpy cot the town provided. Hell, he'd slept in worse places. He much preferred the open sky for a roof, but at times he even found himself longing for his sparsely furnished but comfortable bedroom at the Leaning C.

"Yeah Teddy, they provide me a bed at the jailhouse . . ."

"Jake!" Ruth strode down the walkway toward him. "You're just who I need to see. Have you got a minute?"

"Plenty of time," Jake replied cynically. "What's up?"

"We need someone to escort Sunny out to Mary Lassiter's ranch. We've decided to have a social for a fundraiser to pay for the rest of the supplies we need for the Cultural Center. And everyone else is so busy, we thought we'd ask you to do that for us."

"Can I go too, Ranger Jake?" Teddy put in eagerly. "I saw Suzie at church Sunday, and she told me if I ever got to come visit her, I could ride her pony."

"Just wait a minute, Teddy." Jake concentrated on Ruth with a frown on his face. "What's Mary got to do with your fundraiser?"

"Jake Cameron, if you'd pay attention to what's going on around you, you'd know." Ruth sniffed in exasperation, then slowly explained, "We've decided to have a fundraiser . . ."

"You already said that once, Ruth."

"You just said you had plenty of *minutes* available, Jake." The smirk in Ruth's voice made Jake clench his teeth, but he stuck his fingers in his back pockets and waited.

"So it's not going to ruin your schedule one bit to listen to what I have to say twice," Ruth continued. "Our fundraiser will be a town social, and Mary always furnishes a steer for us to barbecue when we have our Fourth of July celebrations. She has ever since her husband died, anyway. I'm sure she'll be willing to do the same for our social, but we need to go out and ask her right now, since we're planning on having the social next Saturday."

Jake groaned under his breath. "And I suppose you're planning on getting the word out to everyone within a hundred miles, so they'll come and spend their money."

"Of course! Really, Jake, the purpose of a fundraiser is to

raise funds. And it's payday for the ranches next week, so everyone should have a little extra money to spend."

"Yeah," Jake growled. "Every piece of riffraff will have a pocket full of cash and just be looking for a place to cut loose and get rid of it. And by evening, half of them will be drunk and probably dangerous."

"Well, what on earth do we have you in town for," Ruth asked, "if not to make sure the riffraff abides by the law so the decent citizens can enjoy themselves? Really, Jake. If you don't want to help us out, just say so. I guess I could pull one of the men off the repair work and ask him to go. John's already said Sunny can use one of the buggies from his stable."

"I'll go," Jake said with a defeated sigh. "My horse needs some exercise anyway. And given her propensity for bumbling, Sunny would probably get lost within sight of town."

"Sunny is one of the most capable women I've ever known," Ruth huffed indignantly.

"Couldn't prove it by me." Jake held up his hands to forestall Ruth's rebuff. "I said I'd go. But if anything happens in town while I'm gone, don't blame me."

"What could possibly happen in just a couple of hours? That's all it should take you to go out to Mary's and back, even if you spend a while there letting Teddy ride Suzie's pony."

"If you'd like to go ahead and let your horse run for a while," Sunny said, glancing admiringly at Jake's dun, "feel free. He looks like he's getting tired of you holding him in."

"Well, if you're sure." Jake looked down the rutted trail. "All you have to do is stay on this track. It leads right to Mary's—only about another fifteen minutes' drive. But I'll be coming back as soon as Dusty gets the friskiness out of him, in case you have any problems."

"I learned to drive a buggy years ago," Sunny informed him. "And I can assure you that I know how to follow a road. Or a trail, for that matter. Mother and I periodically visited friends in the countryside around St. Louis."

"Yeah, but they don't have coyotes or rattlesnakes on the roads there. And out here, those aren't always of the animal variety."

"We had *beasts* like that where I grew up too," Sunny advised him with a disdainful sniff. "I never had any trouble handling them."

Jake studied her for a second, then shrugged. Loosening his reins, he settled his hat more firmly on his head and hied Dusty into an immediate gallop.

The nearly flat country stretched out endlessly ahead of them. Sunny watched his receding figure as the powerful dun's legs stirred up a cloud of dust. The heat waves rising from the arid ground encompassed horse and rider in a shimmering haze when they approached the horizon. Only the fading sound of pounding hooves disturbed the surreal image, and Sunny sighed in admiration of the dynamic picture they made, contrasted against the dry and dusty land.

"Ranger Jake sure rides good, don't he?" Teddy asked. "Bet I won't never learn to ride like that."

"Ladies ride a lot more sedately than men," Sunny explained. Then she nodded her head in agreement. "But I'll admit, they do make a handsome sight."

"You think Ranger Jake's handsome, Miss Sunny? I do. I was thinkin' 'bout marrying Ranger Jake when I grew up, but I figured he'd be way too old for me by then. Don't you think?"

A flush heated Sunny's cheeks, but she couldn't think of a suitable excuse for voicing a thought she was afraid Teddy might inappropriately pass on to Jake. Of course the man *was* handsome—he was just about the most ruggedly handsome man she'd ever laid eyes on. She'd already admitted that to herself days ago, when she first encountered him. And he had an admirable soft spot for children. His consideration had extended to her also, when necessary, but she darned sure wasn't going to start thinking about those crazy dreams she'd been having ever since he'd carried her in his arms.

There was no getting around it. The man was just plain lazy. Every other man in town had pitched in to help with the building repairs. Jake Cameron, however, spent his mornings either walking around town or sitting on that chair in front of the jailhouse, visiting now and then with his friend Charlie. More than one afternoon, she'd found him at a card table in the saloon when she'd gone over there to have a cold drink with Ginny. At times he'd be playing some sort of game alone, laying the cards on the table in front of him. Other times, one or two of the men on their work crew would make an excuse to disappear, and she'd find them at that table with Jake.

The men always glanced at her guiltily, but she'd restrained herself from tattling to their wives about their slothfulness. After all, everyone was volunteering their time. She also reminded herself that Ginny depended upon her customers to make a profit in her saloon, and without Ginny there would be no building for the Cultural Center to use.

Some structures appeared in the distant haze, as well as the image of Jake astride his dun, returning to escort them. The dun trotted more slowly now, though he still tossed his head and pranced. Sweat had darkened his withers from coffee-with-milk to a dark chocolate, and Jake's shirt clung to his chest and stomach. He pulled the red bandanna off his neck and wiped his face.

"Yep," Teddy said, "he sure is handsome."

"Uh . . . Teddy. Listen, we shouldn't tell a man when we think he's handsome. Ladies don't do that."

"Why not? How's they gonna know we like them if we don't tell them?"

"Can we talk about this when it's just us girls?" Sunny asked hurriedly, noting that Jake was almost in hearing distance. "Maybe this evening?"

"Sure," Teddy agreed in a lilting voice. "I like it when we have our girl talks."

"Girl talks?" Jake dropped his reins for a second, controlling the dun with his knees while he retied the bandanna around his neck. "Am I interrupting the two of you having a girl talk?"

Vaguely aware of Teddy's voice answering Jake, Sunny contemplated the length of his fingers and the strength of his hands. He'd opened a couple of buttons on his shirt, and hair of the same raven shade as that on his head was visible on his chest. The sweat had curled it into tight whorls, much as a woman's fingernail might do.

Teddy's voice broke into her thoughts. "Aren't you gonna answer me, Ranger Jake? What you lookin' at?"

Sunny quickly lifted her eyes and, for just an instant, met Jake's gaze. He just as quickly shuttered his eyes and shoved the bandanna knot to the side of his neck, reaching for his shirt buttons.

"Sorry," he murmured. "I forgot I'd unbuttoned them. Now, what were you saying, Teddy?"

He turned the dun and rode beside the buggy as Sunny urged the horse back into a trot. She sure hoped Mary had something cool to drink. The buggy roof had provided adequate shade so far, with a nice little breeze flowing by them as the horse trotted along, but the temperature must have climbed drastically in the last few minutes. Holding the reins in one hand, she reached up and jerked her hatpin free, then removed her hat. When she waved the straw hat to cool her face, she heard a smothered chuckle beside her.

"Yep," Jake said in a nonchalant voice, evidently continuing his conversation with Teddy. "There's lots of difference between boys and girls. When they get older though, sometimes they have the same feelings about certain things."

Before Teddy could question him further, he raised a hand to wave at someone he'd spotted in the ranch yard and urged the dun forward. Sunny glared after him. Surely he wasn't alluding to the feelings she'd experienced while studying what she could see through the open V of his shirt, was he? She narrowed her eyes in contemplation. If so, he'd as much as admitted that he'd been having some feelings of his own.

She would definitely have to make sure nothing like that happened again. Why, he might get the idea she was interested in him! She had completely different plans for her future than becoming involved with a man whom she'd constantly have to light a stick of dynamite under to get any action!

9

THE WOMAN WAITING on the ranch house porch definitely wasn't Mary Lassiter. Jake already had his dun tied to a hitching rail, and he approached the buggy to help Sunny to the ground. Teddy scrambled out on her own, looking around eagerly, but Sunny didn't see a sign of Mary's daughter either.

Jake swung her down and released her a little too quickly. She stumbled a step, then swatted his hand away when he held it out to her. Darn the man, anyway. Didn't he even know how to help a lady down from a buggy? Grimacing at him, she turned her back and walked to the porch.

"I am Theresa," the beautiful Spanish woman on the porch said when Sunny approached. Her deep brown eyes flickered past Sunny to Jake for just an instant. "I am Miss Mary's housekeeper. She and the children are in the barn with a new colt. Shall I go get her?"

"I'll go," Teddy said earnestly. "Can I, Miss Sunny?"

"Why don't we all go?" Sunny responded. "I'd like to see the colt too."

"I will prepare some cool drinks for when you return." Theresa turned back to the house.

A bright-red structure shining in the sun, the barn was set quite a ways from the house. Corrals of split-rail fencing painted white circled both sides, and a spirited horse with a shining black coat pranced around in one of them, while the other one was empty.

"I've never seen a red barn before," Sunny mused. "But isn't it pretty?"

"Pretty?" Jake replied. "Guess you could call it that. Only a woman like Mary would paint her barn red."

"Spoken like a true bigot," Sunny muttered, shooting him a disgruntled look. "I understand from the other women in town that Mary Lassiter has had to run this ranch alone for five years, ever since her husband died. And the ranch has prospered a lot more than it ever did with him in charge. I would think she has a right to dress as she wishes and paint her barn any darned color she wants!"

"Whoa!" Jake raised his hands. "I meant that in an admiring way."

"That's not how it came out."

"Or maybe that's just the way you took it."

"Perhaps if I saw in you a little admiration for what women can accomplish—for instance, like what we're getting done in town—I might revise my opinion of your character."

Before Jake could reply, they entered the barn and Sunny hurried away from him into the dimness. The shaded interior was a relief from the heat outside, and as soon as her eyes adjusted, she saw Mary motioning to them from a stall a few steps away. She once again wore her britches, although she had worn a pretty gray dress to church last Sunday.

"Shhhh," Mary whispered as they reached her. "The colt's only an hour or so old, and the mare had a rough time. This was her first birth, and she foaled a few days early. My foreman, Chuck, knows more about helping in difficult births than I do, but he's out on the far range, checking fences. I wouldn't have sent him out if I'd had any idea the mare was ready to foal."

As Mary spoke, Sunny looked into the stall, where a chestnut mare stood with her head hanging wearily. But, the spotted calf at her flank nursed enthusiastically, its coat still wet in places from the birth fluids.

"It's beautiful," Sunny said in awe. "And so active and hungry for only being an hour old."

The colt wobbled and fell, then scrambled back to its feet, sticking its head beneath the mare's flank again and butting against her. The noisy slurps hung in the air, the only sound other than the muffled giggles of the women and Teddy as they watched. When Sunny glanced behind her to see what Jake's reaction was, since he was so quiet, she slam-banged straight into his whiskey gaze.

"I'll wait up at the house," he said, abruptly turning away.

"I need to mix a pail of mash for the mare," Mary said, ignoring Jake's sudden exit. "If you'd like to wait up at the house too, I'll be along shortly. I don't usually entertain guests in my barn."

"Oh, this is fine," Sunny said. "And very interesting. If you don't mind, Teddy and I would like to stay."

"Of course. But maybe Teddy would like to see the new kittens in the loft. That's where Suzie and Chester are." She pointed to a ladder across the way. Teddy bobbed her head and took off, hiking her skirts to climb the ladder, her pigtails bouncing on her back.

Lowering her voice for just Sunny's ears as she walked away out of the stall, Mary continued, "Suzie would have been perfectly happy staying with me during the birth, but Chester got green around the gills. They came down to see the colt after it was born, then went back up to the loft. At eight years old, Suzie's quite the little tomboy, but of course Chester's two years younger. I'm sure he'll come around."

"I'm looking forward to meeting your Suzie and Chester," Sunny said as Mary pushed open the door on a room that held tools and supplies. "I was so busy with all the other ladies at church Sunday that I missed your children. I . . ."

A muffled scream cut off Sunny's words. At first Mary looked at the loft, but they both realized at the same instant that the scream had come from the direction of the house. When a curly-mopped little girl peeked over the edge of the loft, Mary ordered, "You young'uns stay up there until we tell you to come down!" Grabbing a pitchfork from inside the storage area, she took off at a dead run. Sunny lifted her skirts and raced after her.

Mary headed toward the back of her house, and Sunny hiked her skirts even higher, trying to keep up. By the time she rounded the corner of the house, Mary was standing to one side, watching Jake pound the daylights out of a man Sunny didn't recognize—a man who probably outweighed Jake by at least fifty pounds. Theresa huddled on the back step with her hands over her face.

Jake's fist thudded into the other man's face and he crumpled to the ground. Jake dragged him to his feet again, then drew his fist back and drove it deep into the man's stomach. The man flew backward several feet. Jake walked toward him, flexing his shoulders and clenching his fists at his sides. The man groaned and rolled away, shakily regaining his feet and backing away from Jake, his hands outspread in defeat.

"Get out, Miller," Mary snarled, raising the pitchfork to emphasize her demand. "You're fired! You've got exactly one minute to get your gear and clear my property. If I see you even close to my land again, I'll shoot you the same as I would a fox raiding my henhouse!"

"She's been askin' for it . . ." Miller started to whine.

When Jake took a step toward him, he flinched and shut his mouth.

"You can press charges against him," Jake told Mary. "Or at least, Theresa can."

"Please just make him leave," Theresa spoke up from the steps. "I do not wish to have the whole town know he attacked me."

Jake glanced at Mary, and Mary nodded. "Get going, Miller," she snarled. "And remember what I said."

Stumbling and holding his stomach in pain, Miller grabbed the reins of a sorrel horse nearby and heaved himself into the saddle. He rode over to a building Sunny assumed was the bunkhouse, dismounted, and went inside. No one spoke again until Miller came out and remounted his sorrel, reining it toward the front of the house. As he cut a wide swath around the group watching him, Sunny noticed that Jake had his hand on the butt of the gun in his right holster.

Her staunchly held opinion of Jake Cameron's laziness started pulverizing into the same dry dust that littered the Texas landscape. No man could handle himself as Jake had with muscles grown lax from inactivity. The coiled power she'd witnessed in his shoulders and fists had her swallowing back a stab of fear, given all the times she'd unwittingly baited him with her own wayward tongue.

His face still bore the residue of his anger. His normally whiskey-colored eyes had darkened to walnut and narrowed to bare slits. His jaw was clenched, and his lips thinned in a straight line.

Catching a glimpse of movement, Sunny's eyes fell once again to the right holster on his tense thigh. His forefinger and thumb rubbed together next to the gun butt, twitching back and forth as though any second he would draw and fill the air with a blaze of bullets.

All at once she knew explicitly what Mary, Ruth, and her aunt had meant about not underestimating Jake Cameron, the Texas Ranger in Liberty Flats. Gulping against the apprehensive lump in her throat, she cautiously edged toward Mary and her pitchfork.

As soon as Miller disappeared, Jake turned to Theresa. The young Spanish woman looked at him, then surged off the steps and into his arms. Jake's face changed instantly as he gathered her close and stroked her back, murmuring soothingly to her. Unexpectedly, Sunny felt a violent stab of jealousy, but she quickly chastised herself. Theresa had just had to fight off a man's attack, and she had a right to their comfort and concern. However, when Jake laid his cheek against Theresa's silky black hair, Sunny abruptly turned her back.

"I'll go check on the children," she said to Mary. "They're probably worried about what's happening."

Mary nodded agreement, then moved toward Jake and Theresa. As she walked away, Sunny could hear Mary's voice added to Jake's, offering her own consolations to her housekeeper. She hurried her steps, but turned back to see Mary and Jake leading a still-sobbing Theresa into the house.

In the barn she found all three children waiting at the foot of the loft ladder, worried expressions on their little faces. The curly-headed moppet who was Mary's daughter, Suzie, spoke first. "Is my mama all right?"

"She's fine, Suzie," Sunny assured her. "There was a problem with one of the hired hands, but your mother fired him and sent him away."

"Must have been that Miller," Suzie replied. "He's a no good if I ever saw one."

"Yeah," the little boy whined. "But what if he comes back and tries to hurt us?"

"Oh, shut up, Chester!" Suzie exclaimed. "Mama will take care of us, and Chuck will be back soon. Miller won't mess with Chuck, and I'll bet Miller's as sorry as the flea-bitten hound he is that he messed with Mama and got his rear end fired."

Sunny's mouth dropped open further and further as more colorful language spewed from Suzie's cute, bow-shaped lips. She and her brother were dressed almost identical, both in denims and checkered shirts, but Suzie's tousled curls and pixie face left no doubt as to her gender. Her language, though . . .

"What did that dirty dog do to make Mama finally fire him?" Suzie asked her.

"Uh . . . he . . . uh . . . I'll let your mother explain that," Sunny stammered, glancing at Teddy, who had a look of rapt admiration on her face as she listened to her new friend. Already Teddy's skirt sported a long rip, and Sunny shook her head. Instead of it bothering her, though, she made up her mind right then and there to buy Teddy a couple of pair of denims to wear when she visited Suzie. And wouldn't pants be much easier to work in while the Cultural Center was undergoing repairs? That, however, might be going just a tad too far, she realized with a reluctant sigh.

"Would you children like to come on up to the house now?" she asked.

"I promised Teddy she could ride my pony," Suzie replied. "If that's all right with you, that is, Miss Fannin. I can have him saddled in a jiffy shake, and we'll only ride around the corral this time."

Feeling certain that Teddy would be in capable hands with the self-assured Suzie, Sunny gave her permission. Though Suzie tried to insist that Chester go on to the house, the little boy stuck out his lower lip stubbornly and refused.

A smile curving her lips, Sunny left the children to work out their own differences.

A BEAUTIFUL TEXAS sunset lit the western sky as the buggy horse trotted back toward Liberty Flats in the cooler evening air. Fiery streaks of vermilion shaded to deep purple on the horizon when the sun sank out of sight. Sunny couldn't ever remember seeing such a wondrous sunset. Perhaps her appreciation of the magnificence came partially from her own contended feelings, she admitted to herself.

Teddy curled up at Sunny's side, and from the sounds of the stifled yawns she heard, Sunny figured the little girl would be sound asleep by the time they reached town. They'd lingered at Mary's even after Teddy had her first riding lesson, then agreed to share a meal of stew and Theresa's fresh-baked bread before undertaking the trip back. Despite Theresa's reddened eyes, she had insisted she was perfectly able to serve the meal and had sat with the family at the table. Sunny's praise at how delicious everything was had been sincere, and she'd left with a recipe for Theresa's bread in her pocket.

Teddy shifted sideways and laid her head on Sunny's leg. A moment later, her even breathing told Sunny that she slept.

Jake kneed his stallion closer to the buggy. "If you want," he said quietly, "I can tie Dusty to the back of the buggy and drive for you. Then you can rest too."

Sunny mentally measured the width of the buggy seat and knew instantly how crowded it would be with Jake's large body sharing the space. "Oh, no. No, that's not necessary," she hastily hedged. "Uh . . . Teddy's sleeping on the seat, and I don't want to disturb her. And I'm not tired at all. It was a wonderful day."

She caught herself frowning. "Well, most of it anyway,

after that horrible man left the ranch. Mary's son was worried that Miller might come back. You don't think he will, do you, Jake?"

"I very much doubt he wants to tangle with me again," Jake assured her. "That's part of what my presence is for around here—to keep crime down. And despite what I'll admit were a couple of blots on Ranger history, it's not just me personally who scares the sh . . . uh . . . who scares the outlaw element in the area into giving Liberty Flats a wide berth. Outlaws know that if they harm a Ranger, they'll have every other Ranger in Texas after their lawbreaking hides until they're caught and punished."

"I see," Sunny mused.

And she did see, although she didn't completely agree with his assessment of its not being him personally who instilled the fear of reprisal in the bad guys—not after seeing him at work today. She'd sure as heck hate to be the bad guy a Texas Ranger was after, if the rest of them were anything like Jake. She shivered just a little as she recalled his furious face and tensed, ready-for-action stance as he watched Miller ride away from Mary's ranch.

But she still didn't understand why he couldn't at least help a little with the repair work. After all, he would be visible to practically everyone in town if he would join in. In fact, he'd be about the most visible man there, given his height and the breadth of his shoulders. He certainly had the muscles for the hard labor it took to saw the timbers, lift them into place, and hold them until they were secured. After all, he'd had no trouble punching the devil out of Miller, a man who outweighed him significantly.

That funny little sensation she noticed once in a while when she was near him tickled in her belly, and she unconsciously pressed one palm against the stirring. She realized what she'd done only when the sensation trickled downward—and upward, into her beasts. Suppressing a gasp of dismay, she jerked her hand back to the reins . . . *where you should have stayed to begin with*, she silently admonished her errant appendage.

Lights shone in some of the town's buildings as they approached the house she shared with her aunt. She couldn't quite call it home yet. She was still contemplating whether she should return to St. Louis—taking Teddy with her, of course. She still hadn't discovered the solution to the other mystery either—the identity of her father. She was about ready to start making some pointed inquiries, since her vague attempts at questioning the other townspeople hadn't borne fruit.

Most of the stores on the main street should have been closed by now, except for the saloons, but Sunny saw a light in the doctor's office and even Ruth's store appeared to be open yet. Perhaps Ruth had a late customer. She couldn't see any of the other residences in town from here, since they were scattered here and there behind the businesses. She'd recently come to realize that the few townspeople who hadn't built living quarters into their stores, as Ruth had, maintained houses elsewhere. She'd visited a couple of the houses this past week, once to have tea with the twittery banker's wife, Cathy Percival. For some reason Sunny had been designated the spokesperson to talk some sense into Cathy, who was horrified that the other women in town had accepted Ginny McAllister into their newly formed Women for Cultural Advancement group.

Sunny chuckled when she recalled the way Cathy's haughty dignity had crumbled when Sunny shrugged her shoulders and told her that she truly hoped Cathy didn't pine away with loneliness while the other women in town were so busy. Now, although Cathy and Ginny would never be bosom friends, Cathy had become an avid supporter of their plans. She'd even offered her husband to subscribe to several of the weekly newspapers from Dallas and further east, so they could scan them for mention of performers they might entice to Liberty Flats.

Twilight lingered yet as she pulled the buggy horse to a halt at her house, and Jake dismounted. Leaving his own stallion's reins trailing, he tied the buggy horse's lead rope to the fence around the front yard. Approaching the side of the buggy, he held up his arms. Sunny lifted Teddy down to him.

"If you'll carry her in, I'll be right behind you," she told him.

Jake regarded her for an instant, one corner of his mouth uptilted, but he shrugged and carried the sleeping Teddy toward the house. Sunny wrapped her skirts to the side and managed to get one leg on the buggy step. Then she made the mistake of glancing after Jake. His powerful thighs flexed in his close-fitting denims, and the material tightened across his rump as he climbed the steps to the porch. Her foot slipped, and Sunny tumbled from the buggy, cursing in a very unladylike manner under her breath and thankful Jake didn't hear her skirt rip as she fell. Sprawled on the ground, she saw he'd gone on into the house.

Why the *hell* couldn't that man wear looser clothing?!

10

BY THE TIME Sunny got to Teddy's room, Jake was gently helping a groggy Teddy into her nightgown. He looked up as Teddy stuck her head through the neck of the gown.

"Figured this was her room," he said softly. "One door was closed, and the other room looked like it was yours. Besides, this one had the doll in it."

Sunny flushed when she recalled she'd left a few of her underthings strewn around her room that day. She wasn't the neatest person anyway and, thanks to Teddy's insistence that they finish the book they were reading this morning, lessons had run long. She'd barely had time to fix lunch and get to the Cultural Center at the agreed-upon time.

"It's her room," she managed, pushing the vision of those whiskey eyes scanning her private underthings out of her mind. "Are you going to want a cup of coffee?"

"If it's not too much bother. I've still got a long evening ahead of me."

"I'll see if Aunt Cassie left any. If not, I'll start a fresh pot."

On the way to the kitchen she firmly closed the door to her room. The stove was still warm. Stirring up the embers, she added a couple of pieces of wood, then checked the coffeepot. Having become somewhat familiar with Cassie's habits, she wasn't surprised to find it still half full. She put it on a burner to warm as Jake entered the kitchen.

"Teddy's back to sleep," he said. "I didn't know if you usually heard her prayers in the evenings, but she was so tired I didn't think I ought to wake her completely."

Cassie appeared behind Jake, a fierce scowl on her face. "I find it highly improper for you to be entertaining a man alone in my house at this hour of the night," she said, ignoring Jake. "And where have you been all afternoon?"

Unwilling to start a spat with her aunt in front of Jake but unable to quench the desire to defend herself, Sunny said with a huge sigh, "I'm not *entertaining* Jake. He was kind enough to escort me on an errand for our women's group, and I'm just offering him a cup of coffee. Besides, we're not alone with you in the house."

"Harumph. Well, you might consider leaving word as to your goings-on. Ruth came by here a while ago looking for you. She seemed agitated about something, and I would have thought she'd have known where you were. *If* your absence had, as you say, something to do with that silly group you and she formed."

"I don't appreciate your insinuation that I'm lying," Sunny responded with gritted teeth, sending Jake an apologetic look. Then Cassie's words sank in. "What do you mean, Ruth was agitated? Did something happen?"

Cassie sniffed disdainfully. "I didn't ask. I was already perturbed with her for dragging me over to that building this morning when I went into her store for a few things."

Sunny shoved the coffeepot to the back of the stove, releasing it quickly when she realized the handle was already almost hot enough to burn her palm.

"Teddy's asleep," she tossed at her aunt as she hurried out

of the kitchen. "I'll be back after I find out what Ruth wanted."

Cassie muttered something she couldn't quite make out, but Sunny kept going. A second later she heard Jake's footsteps behind her. He took her arm, forcing her to slow her steps.

"It's getting dark," he said. "Be careful, or you'll fall again."

"I didn't think you saw me tumble out of the buggy," Sunny admitted.

"Figured your petticoats had cushioned you. And how's your hand? Or does it just not take you long to look at a coffeepot?"

Sunny couldn't stifle her giggle, and she shook her head. "You don't miss much, do you?"

Jake pulled her to a halt. "As long as we're being honest with each other . . ." He tugged her deeper into the shadows beneath the walkway overhang. "I'm finding out that every one of my senses is completely attuned to any little move you make, Sunny Fannin. What the hell are you doing to me?"

"I'm not . . . uh . . . Ruth . . ."

His lips cut off her stammering. Gently he nibbled at her, and she clenched her fists on his shirt. She'd been kissed before, but never like this. He coaxed, teased, and nibbled, barely brushing her lips with his and making her yearn with all her might for him to deepen the kiss—the kisses. Her swimming senses had already lost count of how many times he feathered his mouth against hers.

Even with her eyes closed she knew when he started to pull away. Maybe she missed the feel of his breath on her cheek. Gripping his shirt tighter, she raised herself on tiptoe and silently demanded that he continue.

Jake complied. This time he took her mouth fully, wrapping one large hand behind her head to hold it in place. He needn't have bothered, since she had absolutely no desire to end the embrace. Desire gained a totally different meaning right then. It sang through her, making each and every inch where their bodies pressed together long to get closer.

A soft brush against the back of her hand made her realize her arms were around his neck, her fingers close enough to find out whether his black hair was as silky as she'd imagined. It was. She threaded her fingers through it, feeling his fingers respond and weave into her hair.

A deep groan escaped his throat, rumbling from his mouth to hers, catching and mixing with the whimper emerging from within her. She flicked her tongue to try to capture the elusive sound, and instead felt the erotic slide of Jake's tongue against hers. For a bare instant, Jake cupped her hip with his free hand and pulled her against him. Before the craving in her center had more than a chance to realize this was what it had been yearning for, he pushed her away, forehead against hers.

"Jesus God, Sunny," he growled. "I've never before in my life wanted a woman as bad as I want you right now!"

She pulled back an inch or so. "As long as we're being honest with each other . . ."

"Don't say it!" he demanded. "Don't you dare! Hell, I'm gonna have to go over to the stable and jump in a horse trough now before I can face Ruth and see what's going on!"

"A horse trough?" Sunny asked with a frown. "Full of water?"

"Yeah," he replied with sardonic chuckle. "And after this hot day, I doubt very much the water will be cold enough to do me any good."

"Good for what?"

"If I showed you for what right now, Miss Innocence, we'd both be on one of those cots in the jailhouse within the next five seconds." He reached up and caressed her cheek. "You do know what would happen on that cot, don't you?"

Sunny stepped away from him. "Oh! Oh, I didn't mean . . . I mean, I've been kissed before, but . . . well, I've never had anything like this happen. And I have no intention of going with you to the jailhouse. And I'm sorry if you misread something. I didn't realize . . ."

Jake clamped his hand over her mouth, stilling her babbling. "I've been kissed before, too," he whispered. "And I've done a lot more than that—which is exactly what I'd like to do with you right now."

Sunny's entire body began sagging as though some sort of weight was pulling at her. The only time she could remember having any similar feeling was when she'd fallen into the pond and had to stumble to shore, her sodden clothing dripping with water and dragging against her. Her breast tips prickled, as though responding to the chill of the water, but she knew her bodice was completely dry.

"Uh . . ." She licked her still-moist lips, trying to ignore the lingering taste of him, and mentally ordered her body to straighten itself. "Ruth. We need to go see what Ruth wanted."

"And it's a damned good thing we do have to do that," Jake said with a grunt as he squared his shoulders. "Let's get the hell going."

He started off ahead of her, and Sunny hastened after him. Her shoe heel caught in a crack, and she tried to stifle her gasp as she stumbled. She heard him sigh, and a second later, he came back and slipped an arm around her waist. Sunny immediately shook free.

"I only need your arm to hang on to," she said primly. When she heard the tone of her voice, she mentally shook her head. Sure, *now* she turned prudish! A minute ago, she was holding on to every part of him she could reach! And enjoying every hard, masculine inch she touched.

Realizing she was standing there dumbfounded while these thoughts raced through her head, she slipped a look through her eyelashes at Jake. The shadow from his hat brim partially concealed the grin on his face, but she knew immediately that he wasn't accepting this prissy turnabout on her part as an undisputed fact. With a suppressed chuckle, he held out his arm.

"Well, as you said, it's rather dark out here," she said in an effort to prick the circle of silence that seemed to surround only the two of them.

"Yeah. And dark places can be dangerous. I wouldn't want you to get hurt."

Hurt, she mused silently as she caught the double entendre. Tucking her hand in the crook of his arm, she started on down the walkway beside him. Yes, there could be a world of hurt waiting for her in the darkness if she allowed herself to be alone there with Jake Cameron. Look what had happened this time—the very first time she'd been with him without prying eyes to chaperon them.

Despite the fact that her body appeared to feel differently, she knew he wasn't her type at all. Could her body actually have separate feelings from what her rational mind told it to feel?

It evidently could, because her rational mind told her Jake Cameron was a rambler, a man who couldn't wait to get on to his next risky assignment. Hadn't she heard from Wanda Turley that Jake got as surly as a hungry alligator after his weekly telegrams from Austin, which continued to order him to remain in Liberty Flats? And he claimed as his best friend a man Sunny thought truly detestable, should her suspicions prove true.

But her body was wondering just what would have happened on the jailhouse cot. Wondering if the sensations she felt were building up to something even sweeter and more thrilling than what she had been feeling in the dark shadows of the walkway.

Jake held the door of the general store open, and she went in, calling for Ruth. When no one answered, she glanced at Jake with a frown.

"There weren't any lights on in their living quarters upstairs," Jake said. "And I don't like the fact that the store's unlocked this late with no one here. I doubt most people in town would walk in and help themselves, but you never know what might happen if someone with a few drinks in him and clouded judgment wandered by."

"Could they be in the storeroom?" Sunny forced out. "Injured or . . . or worse?"

"I doubt it," Jake assured her. "Your aunt said Ruth was upset earlier, so whatever's going on happened while we were on our way back to town from Mary's. I think we should check with Doc Butler."

"The doctor? Oh Lord! Let's go!"

He caught her as she passed, slowing her down and tucking her hand back beneath his arm. "Doc might not have time for another patient tonight."

Too worried about Ruth to give his gibe much thought, she clenched her fingers on his arm and tugged, urging him to hurry. Familiar with the town now, she headed down the walkway steps and across the street to Doc Butler's office beside the jailhouse. She resolutely angled her path to take her directly up the steps in front of the doctor's office, instead of past the jail with those cots inside.

Ruth stood talking to the portly doctor when they entered the office, and she turned tear-streaked, red-rimmed eyes to Sunny. Sunny flew across the room to enfold her.

"Oh, Ruth! Ruth, what's happened?"

Sniffing, Ruth drew back. "Didn't Cassie tell you?"

"No. She only said you were agitated about something."

"Agitated?" Ruth shook her head and curled her lips in disgust. "I just don't understand why Cassie's gotten like she has. Why . . ."

"Ruth," Sunny interrupted. "Don't worry about my aunt right now. What's happened?"

"Fred," Ruth said on a choked sob. "The ladder step broke, and he fell. There . . . there was a chair there, and he hit it. His arm's broken, and besides that, one of the pieces that splintered on the chair stabbed into his shoulder."

"My God!" Sunny's eyes flew to the doctor.

"He's going to be fine," Doc Butler said. "Well, as long as no infection sets into the wound on his shoulder. I'm pretty sure I got all the splinters out, though it took me quite a while."

"Can I see him?" Sunny asked. "I need to tell him how sorry I am about this."

Doc shook his head. "Won't do you any good right now. He's sleeping off the ether I gave him so I could set his arm and pick out those splinters."

"I wanted to take him home," Ruth said in a forlorn voice. "But Doc said it would be better for him to sleep here tonight. And I just don't know how I'm going to handle everything. Our son, Brad, is still healing from that broken arm he got himself, but I guess I could ask him to come back and at least handle the light lifting."

"I'll help, too, Ruth," Sunny said adamantly. "After all, with Fred getting hurt in our building, I feel responsible."

"No, no," Ruth assured her. "This project is just as much mine as yours, Sunny. But I will accept a little help from you around the store if you have time. And Teddy can come with you. She's such a little joy to have around."

"You can take Fred home in the morning," Doc told Ruth. "Right now, you need to go on home yourself and rest. You're gonna have your hands full nursing Fred and running the store."

"I'll go with you and get you settled," Sunny said. "I'd stay with you, but Teddy might wake up during the night."

"Yeah," Jake said, "and I wouldn't count on that aunt of yours taking care of Teddy if she does wake up. When we were leaving, she muttered something about not being a nursemaid."

"I just don't understand Cassie anymore," Ruth repeated, shaking her head. "I really expected her to offer a little comfort when I told her about Fred. But instead she just stiffened and said she hadn't known you weren't going to be at the center all afternoon, Sunny. And she shut the door in my face!"

"The witch," Sunny muttered. "And she told me a bald-faced lie when she said she didn't know why you were upset! I really better get back to Teddy, Ruth. But I'll see you home first."

Wrapping an arm around Ruth's waist, she led her out of the doctor's office. Jake followed them, and once on the walkway, he reached for Ruth.

"I'll take her home," he told Sunny. "And I can watch you until you reach your own house, too. Go straight there."

"Well, I'd planned to," Sunny said with a huff. "But I can do that just as well after I get Ruth settled."

"Go home now, Sunny." Jake nodded his head down the street, where a drunken cowboy who had just come out of

Saul's Saloon was singing an off-key tune and trying to climb on his horse. "This time of evening isn't a good hour for ladies to be wandering around on the streets alone. Like I said, I'll keep an eye on you until you get to your house."

"I'll be fine with Jake, Sunny," Ruth confirmed. "He's right. You go on home and take care of Teddy if she wakes up. I remember you telling me she still has nightmares once in a while."

"All right."

Sunny hugged Ruth, then nodded good night to Jake. Picking up her skirts, she hurried across the street ahead of them. At the end of the walkway on the opposite side of the street, where she had stood in the shadows with Jake, her steps faltered and she glanced back. Jake stood at the doorway to the general store, his large body throwing an elongated shadow into the street. He had a clear view of her the rest of the way to the house, and her back tingled as she scurried across the distance from the walkway to the porch and climbed the steps.

Hand on the doorknob, she looked back once again. In the light shining through the general store windows, she saw he'd kept his promise. Reaching up, he caught his hat brim between his fingers in a polite gesture before he entered the store. She stood there until the lights were extinguished in the lower part of the store, turning the doorknob only after she realized the drunken cowboy was riding his horse toward her end of the street.

The doorknob refused to budge, and Sunny gripped it harder, wrenching and shaking. Surely her aunt hadn't locked the door. She'd never found it locked once since her arrival, and she hadn't thought to ask for a key. The darkness beneath the porch overhang deepened as a cloud scuttled over the moon, falling across her shoulder with nearly discernible pressure.

The cowboy drew closer. Sunny rapped on the door.

"Aunt Cassie!" she called without much hope that her aunt would hear, since her bedroom was on the far end of the house. "Aunt Cassie! The door seems to be stuck!"

"Can I help ya', li'l lady?"

Sunny whirled. The cowboy sat on his horse, swaying back and forth in the saddle in extreme slow motion.

"No!" Sunny cautiously lowered her voice. "Ah . . . I'll be fine. I think the door's just stuck."

The cowboy ever so carefully dismounted, staggering a step and grabbing his saddle horn for balance.

"Whoops," he said with a laugh. "Hol' still there, horse."

After a second he pushed away from the horse and started for Sunny. "Wouldn't be p'lite for me to leave you standin' there in the dark. Lemme see if I can help."

Sunny held her hands out and backed away from the door, mentally measuring the distance around the side of the house to the back door. But what if it was locked also?

"Please don't bother," she said. "My aunt will come let me in."

"Who? Ol' Cassie?" The cowboy climbed the steps. "Why, she'd prob'ly let you sleep on the porch and not miss a wink a' sleep herself."

Rowdy rounded the side of the house, a low growl in his throat. Sunny breathed a sigh of relief, but the cowboy saw the dog and clicked his fingers.

"Rowdy, boy," he drawled. "Ain't seen you 'round for a while."

Rowdy's tail wagged, and he sat down with a whine, lifting a paw. The cowboy chuckled and knelt, wobbling on his knee and catching himself with one hand. Still slightly unsteady, he scratched Rowdy behind one ear, muttering some slurred words about him being a good dog.

Sunny surreptitiously picked up her skirts, but before she

could take a step toward the side of the house the cowboy lurched to his feet. Staggering awkwardly, he reached for the closest support. His hands landed on Sunny's shoulders, and his alcohol-laden breath hit her full in the face. Instinctively she reacted, curling her fingers into claws.

11

"WHOOPS!" THE COWBOY repeated, regaining his balance and staggering back. "Sorry, Miss Fannin. Man, I gotta start rememberin' what my limit is. I show up with a hangover tomorrow morning, Mary's gonna crack me up 'long side the head with a skillet. Got to talkin' to Saul, catchin' up on things, and guess I lost count of the drinks I had. Sure do apologize, Miss Fannin."

"You're one of Mary Lassiter's men?" Sunny asked.

"Name's Chuck," the cowboy said. "Mary's foreman. I came back to the ranch while y'all were eatin' supper, so I didn't get to meet you. Heard what had happened from Theresa when I stopped by the ranch house and came on into town to make sure Miller wasn't hangin' 'round, but I should've known he wouldn't mess with Jake. Sure was glad you had Cameron with you when you came out there. I been tellin' Mary we needed to send Miller packin', but she was waitin' 'til after the spring calves were took care of."

"It's all right," Sunny assured him, relaxing her hands a little. "Please give Mary my regards. Hadn't you better be on your way?"

"Should be," Chuck agreed. "But lemme see 'bout that door first."

Somewhat steadier now, he walked to the door. Grabbing the knob, he twisted. It opened easily, and Sunny's mouth dropped open in surprise.

"There you go," Chuck said, sweeping out a hand. "You must've been turnin' it the wrong way."

"I wasn't," Sunny said with a frown. "Or at least, I don't think so."

"Easy to get confused in the dark. Say, both Mary and Saul told me you've taken little Teddy in. Want to say I think that's real nice of you, Miss Fannin. I used to stop by that shack once in a while to check on her—and that Rowdy dog after he took up with her."

Hearing his name, Rowdy whined once more, his tail thumping the porch, and Chuck reached down to pat him. "Mary sent some things in now and then for me to leave with Tompkins for both of them. But I started takin' the stuff directly to Teddy when Saul said he'd heard John Dougherty say Tomkins throwed the dress Suzie outgrew in the trash instead of givin' it to Teddy."

"Mr. Cravens appears to know a lot about what happens in town," Sunny mused.

"Yeah, most of it gets talked about in his saloon at one time or another. Saul knows 'bout everyone around, since he's been runnin' his saloon for long as I can remember. And I grew up here myself."

"He doesn't look that old."

Chuck threw back his head and laughed, then seemed to remember what time of night it was. Leaning forward, he placed a finger near his lips, his breath causing Sunny's stomach to lurch as he whispered, "It's that black stuff he uses on his hair, and even on his mustache when he takes it in mind to grow one." He gave Sunny a conspiratorial wink. "But don't never mention it to him. He don't think none of us know 'bout it."

He straightened a second before Sunny felt she was going to have to embarrass him by clamping a hand over her nose. He tipped his hat to her. "Best say good night and get on my way, Miss Fannin. You ever need anything, like another door unstuck or whatever, you just holler. And me and the boys are sure lookin' forward to gettin' some shows to go to in town. You can bet we'll be there with our spurs a'jinglin' when you get that theater open."

"It's not a theater . . ." Sunny began, but Chuck was already wobbling down the steps to his horse. The animal snorted and sashayed away when he staggered against the saddle, and Sunny giggled as Chuck stuck his hands on his hips and glared at the horse.

"Now listen, horse," he said.

She hurried down the steps and took the horse's bridle. "I'll hold him for you," she said with another smothered laugh. "But I'm afraid you'll have to get into the saddle yourself."

"Thank you," Chuck said in a totally serious voice. His first attempt to put his foot in the stirrup missed, but he managed to stick his boot toe in the loop on the second try. Grabbing the saddle horn, he reeled into the saddle and fell across the horse's neck. The animal blew through its nose, and Sunny could have almost sworn the sound was exasperation at its rider's antics.

Chuck pushed himself upright, and Sunny handed him the reins. He nodded in drunken elegance, gathered the reins, and turned the horse. Before he'd ridden more than a few yards, he broke out into a ditty about some gal named Sal, and Sunny had to muffle her laughter again as she headed into the house.

She broke off at the door, studying the lock and feeling it with her hands in the darkness. She found only an empty keyhole, which took a skeleton key. There was no sliding lock to be set in place from inside the house. Shrugging, she decided Chuck must have been right. She'd just been turning the doorknob the wrong way.

As she made her way through the house to check on Teddy before retiring, she recalled Chuck's words about the cowboys looking forward to the shows at the Cultural Center.

"Oh, Lord," she murmured. "I wonder if we should set up a place for the cowboys to hang their spurs in our hat checkroom." Spurs a'jinglin' cowboys weren't exactly what she'd had in mind as patrons of the center, but she guessed their money would be as good as anyone else's.

Jake didn't wear spurs. He handled his powerful dun stallion with perfect expertise without them. He probably handled his women in the same way—with a masterful confidence, to which the women were completely willing to submit. She most certainly hadn't resisted him, but she darned sure would from now on.

She entered Teddy's room and pulled the sheet up to cover the tiny figure on the bed. With a smile she also tucked the sheet around the doll on the pillow. Yawning, she left the room.

She was beginning to enjoy portions of her life in Liberty Flats and appreciate the friendships she was forming, she mused as she undressed in her own room. But the strained atmosphere here at the house hadn't changed. Each day she realized more and more that she should have stayed in St. Louis, leaving Cassie to her own brooding style of living. Of course, then she wouldn't have Teddy, but Teddy might be better off back East herself if her missing, neglectful mother happened to show up.

And tonight she found another avenue she could pursue

to try to find the answer to the one other question that had brought her to Liberty Flats. According to Chuck, Saul Cravens knew everything there was to know about the town.

JAKE SCRATCHED A match on his denim-clad thigh and lit the lantern he'd brought with him from the jailhouse. The sounds from Ginny's saloon next door were a lot more muted than the noises he could hear, even all the way over here, from Saul's place across the street. Rather than risking a fire by throwing the dead match on the sawdust-scattered floor, he slid it into his back pocket. Lifting the lantern, he looked around for the ladder from which Fred had fallen.

He saw it immediately, still lying on the floor amid the splintered chair pieces. He set the lantern on a nearby table and righted the ladder, also noticing the blood spattered on the floor beside it and staining a piece of the chair.

He'd seen Fred carry that ladder down the street just a few days ago. Unless it had been improperly constructed, it should have held up for years. And his suspicions panned out. A barely discernible cut approximately an inch long had been made across the board on the broken step partway up the ladder. A person not looking for it would have missed the evidence of the ladder's being tampered with.

A slight noise alerted Jake, and he whirled in one smooth movement, his gun appearing in his hand as though it had been there all along. His motion left him beyond the lantern light, and he squinted at the doorway.

"Don't take another step," he ordered.

"Whoa! Hey, it's me, Jake." The shadow in the doorway held his hands out to the side, clearly showing Jake that he held no weapon. Recognizing Saul Cravens' voice, Jake slowly thumbed the hammer on his pistol back into place.

"What the hell are you doing over here in the dark, Cravens?" he snarled.

"Saw the light and was just doing my civic duty," Saul replied. "Thought somebody might be prowling around in here, and after what happened today figured I'd better check it out. Just in case you were playing cards at Ginny's or something and didn't know what was going on."

"Well, you can see I'm *not* playing cards. So you can go on about your own business now."

"Some sort of problem about the accident today?" Cravens asked. "It *was* an accident, wasn't it?"

"Why do you ask?"

"Just wondering." Jake couldn't see Saul's face, but he moved closer as Saul continued, "Guess finding you here looking things over this time of night makes me think there might be something fishy going on. You find anything suspicious?"

"What could be suspicious about a fellow being clumsy and falling off a ladder?"

"You're good, Cameron," Saul said with a chuckle. "You haven't answered one thing I've asked. Instead you come back with another question each time."

"My investigations aren't open for discussion with private citizens. If there's ever anything people need to know, I'll be the one to decide what and when to tell them."

"Hope you remember to do that." Saul turned away. "After all, we wouldn't want the citizens of this town to think you weren't doing your job, now would we?"

Jake didn't bother to respond. Sliding his pistol into his holster, he listened for Saul's footsteps to recede. Instead the saloon owner returned to the doorway.

"You know, Cameron, you really shouldn't let the ladies in town depend on a cowboy who's just left my place after one too many drinks to see them inside their homes, either."

"What's that supposed to mean?"

"I saw the Lassiter spread's foreman over at the Foster

house a few minutes ago. From what I could make out, Sunny seemed to be having some problem getting in her door. But don't worry. I watched until I saw Chuck leave and Sunny go inside. Didn't seem to be any trouble between them. Fact is, he and Sunny looked like they were having a high old time laughing about something. Might have been the difficulty Chuck was having trying to get back in the saddle again. I swear, that was a sight. I thought poor Sunny was gonna have to push on Chuck's ass to help him mount back up."

"Get outta here, Saul." Jake kept his voice flat, a definite contrast to his smoldering thoughts.

Saul shrugged and left again. Jake moved on over to the doorway, assuring himself that Saul crossed the street this time. Before he went through the batwing doors, however, Saul turned and lifted one finger to his hat brim in a salute to Jake. Then he threw back his head, laughing, and ducked into the saloon.

Jake's lips curled in derision, and he stomped back over to the ladder, booting aside one of the chair pieces with a kick that bounced it against the far wall. Trying to focus once again on the cut in the ladder step, he fingered it. Instead of reasoning out the cause of the vandalism, his mind formed a picture of Sunny Fannin's smooth hands. Less than an hour ago, they had been buried in his hair, but now he visualized them reaching toward Chuck's ass to help him on his horse. Hell, he might think Saul was just trying to get a rise out of him if he hadn't seen Chuck riding out of town half drunk. With a muffled curse he flung the ladder aside and strode next door to Ginny's.

"Whiskey," he ordered from Perry, propping his elbows on the bar.

"Huh?" Perry responded.

When Jake gave him his best murderous glare, Perry

hastily grabbed a bottle from the shelf behind him and a shot glass from the clean ones lining the sink. He set them both in front of Jake and started to pour the shot glass full.

Jake grabbed the bottle away from him. "Just leave it," he growled.

"Sure, sure, Jake," Perry soothed. "You just surprised me, was all. You usually pretty much stick to beer."

"Tonight I'm drinking whiskey."

"What bug bit you?" Perry made the mistake of asking.

"Go to hell!"

He poured the shot glass full, slammed the bottle onto the bar, and threw the whiskey down his throat. Picking up the bottle, he jerked around and scanned the room. The only empty table was back in one corner, and that suited him just fine. Scowling at anyone who made the blunder of greeting him, he threaded his way back to the table and sat down. Only Ginny had the guts to approach him, and she swept across the room with her full blue-silk skirts rustling and a warning gleam in her green eyes.

"If you're planning on getting drunk, Jake," she said, slipping into the chair across from him, "I'd rather you took that bottle with you and did it somewhere else."

"Why?" Jake muttered. "This is a saloon, isn't it? Men drink in saloons."

Ginny sighed in resignation. "Why, he asks. Because Jake Cameron drunk in my place might just be a little too much for even both Perry and me to handle, that's why. And you know I've got a limit on how many drinks any customer can have. Once I see somebody getting plastered, it's cutoff time."

"I'll take my bottle to the jailhouse."

Jake reached for the whiskey, but Ginny grabbed his arm.

"What's wrong, Jake? I thought we were friends. I'd come to you if I needed to talk."

Jake slowly withdrew his arm, then picked up the bottle and poured another shot. After he downed it, he glanced at Ginny and said, "That's only my second one."

"I'm counting," Ginny assured him.

Jake slouched back in his chair, slipping his thumbs into his gunbelt. He stared at the scarred tabletop for a while, then looked into Ginny's concerned eyes. "Friends don't repeat stuff a friend asks them to keep confidential, right?"

"Right," Ginny agreed. "If you want to talk, it's just between us."

Jake allowed another long minute to pass before he said, "Did you ever think you had your life all planned out, then have something happen that kicked you in your gut and turned everything upside down?"

"Not really," Ginny said. "I guess the worst thing that ever happened to me was when my father got killed right in front of my eyes. But nothing changed much in my life after that. I'm still trying to make a living out of running a saloon."

"You ever wanna do anything else, Gin?"

"Sure. Lots of things. I have done some of them, and I'll do some more someday. With my father not squandering all the profits, I've been able to put money aside the last few months."

"Well, I never did— Wanna do anything else, I mean." When Ginny raised an eyebrow at him, Jake continued, "All I ever saw when I looked ahead was my still being a Ranger. I like my job and the men I work with. I like knowing I'm making a difference—making places safer for people with families."

"What about a family of your own?"

"Never wanted one," he denied. "Hell, I know what I do is dangerous. Wouldn't be right to leave behind someone who'd be depending on me."

"Any particular someone you're thinking about when you say that?" Ginny raised one perfect eyebrow even higher. "Like maybe a pretty blonde with eyes the color of bluebonnets in the Texas spring?"

"No, dammit!" Jake reached for the bottle and refilled his glass again. But instead of picking up the drink, he rubbed his eyes with his index finger and thumb. "Look, Gin, I'll admit Sunny's a woman a man could build reality out of dreams with. But I'm damned sure not the man to do that with her. Hell, yeah, I'm attracted to her—I'll admit that just between us. But it's probably only because I need to forget my own principles and go visit one of Saul's girls."

Ginny's full lips curled into a sneer. "If that's what you think you need, you won't find it in my place," she reminded him.

"I'm sorry, Gin." He pushed his chair back. "Maybe you're right. I better get out of here." Before he rose, a thought flashed through his mind, and he sipped his drink, pondering the idea. Propping her elbow on the table, Ginny cupped her chin in her hand, waiting patiently for him to speak again.

"Gin," he mused at last, "you get men here in your place that drink at Saul's also, don't you?"

"In a town of this size, yeah, Saul and I share some of the same customers. But it's usually the other way around. They come here first, then go over to his place after I cut them off. Or when they need to forget their *principles*."

"I'm sorry, Gin. I didn't mean it like that. But you can't sit in judgment of the women who work over at Saul's. Not everyone offers women a chance like you do—to get some training in things like handling books and managing the place, which lets them eventually move on."

"I don't sit in judgment of them, Jake." Ginny picked up his glass and drank part of it. She carefully replaced it in the same exact spot, tracing the rim with her index finger and staring at the glass. "Not every woman's as lucky as someone like Sunny. She was left pretty much alone in the world, except for that parsimonious aunt of hers, but her mother appears to have provided for her. At least she's not desperately looking for some man to help keep her from starving to death, and she doesn't have to be willing to do just about anything it takes to stay alive."

Ginny's words jogged Jake's memory of Sunny's questioning him about Charlie. Yeah, Sunny appeared to have financial security, but she didn't seem to appreciate her lot in life. He'd heard those rumors about Samantha Foster and Charlie himself and knew his old friend would never have walked out on Samantha if they had been married. He shook off the growing suspicion in his mind that Sunny Fannin might possibly be just a gold digger who had learned from her aunt of Charlie's concealed wealth.

Concentrating once again on the subject at hand, he said, "That's what I mean. Those women at Saul's don't have any other choice."

"They should have a choice," Ginny insisted. "And they would have if they would stand up for themselves. Saul's even worse than my father was when he made the women in this place whore in order to earn a living. Saul keeps the money the men pay him for the women's services and only pays the women a share of the drinks they sell."

"How do you know that? Gin!" Lowering his voice, Jake leaned toward her. "Gin, you haven't been interfering in Saul's business, have you? Damn it, you stir those girls up in a revolt and Saul will have your ass—and I don't mean between a set of satin sheets!"

Ginny's solid gaze didn't waver when she raised her narrowed green eyes to his. "I hear enough gutter talk around here, Jake. I don't need it from my friends."

Blowing out an exasperated breath and shaking his head, Jake grabbed the shot glass. Downing the whiskey remaining in it, he shoved back his chair, stood, and picked up the bottle. He dug a coin from his pocket and dropped it on the table, the clink hardly audible above the noise in the room.

"Hope you know what you're doing, Gin. I was going to ask you if there were any problems between you and Saul. Whether he might be pissed because you might draw off even more of his customers when this center that Ruth and Sunny are determined to open gets going. Since you're right next door, your place will have first crack at the men leaving those performances. But I guess I don't need to know the answer to that any longer."

He started to move away, and Ginny rose, laying a hand on his arm. "I hope you know what you're doing, too, Jake," she said. "Choosing to walk away from the possibility of a full life and family with a woman like Sunny. I hope your memories of everything you've done for other people will be enough to keep you company when you're old and gray."

"That's the problem," Jake replied with a sardonic chuckle. "I may never make it to old and gray." He covered her hand with his. "Still friends, Gin?"

"Still friends," she agreed, but Perry's shout from the bar drowned her response.

"Hey, I smell smoke!"

12

"Miss Sunny! Miss Sunny, wake up!"

"Hmm? Teddy, crawl in here with me and go back to sleep." Though she couldn't quite recall what it was about, Sunny struggled to hold on to the remnants of her dream. The sensation lingered, however—the cozy lethargy, the feel of a slightly bewhiskered cheek beneath her palm. And wedding bells ringing. Such beautiful wedding bells.

"Um, bells," she murmured, snuggling her cheek into the pillow and hugging it closer.

"Miss Sunny!" Teddy shook her shoulder. "Miss Sunny, that's the fire bell! Me and Dolly are scared."

Sunny shot up in bed. "What? Fire bell?" The sound ceased, leaving just a resonant echo in Sunny's ears. She threw back the comforter and swung her legs over the side of the bed. Grabbing Teddy's shoulders, she asked, "Are you sure, Teddy? The fire bell?"

Teddy sniffed and wiped her nose with the back of her hand. "I heard it once before, the day you fed me and Rowdy that first time. When you burned the biscuits."

Sunny leapt out of bed and grabbed her robe.

"Please don't leave me here alone, Miss Sunny," Teddy said with a sob.

"No, no, I won't," Sunny told the frightened little girl.

"We don't know where the fire is, and I want you with me. Go get your own robe on. Hurry now."

Teddy flew out of the room, and Sunny raced to the front door. Flinging it open, she ran onto the porch and peered down the street. A crowd was gathered in front of the Cultural Center and she could see flames inside the building reflected in the windows.

The fire was all too real this time—nothing as innocuous as a pan of burning biscuits. She clasped a hand over her mouth in horror as Teddy ran onto the porch.

"It's your building, Miss Sunny. Oh, no! We better go help put it out."

Teddy started past her, but Sunny pulled her back. "I have to wake Aunt Cassie, Teddy. You wait right here on the porch. Do you hear me?"

"Yes, ma'am."

Spying Rowdy on the steps, Sunny hastily pushed Teddy down to sit beside him. "Promise me you won't move, Teddy."

"I won't. I promise."

Racing back inside and down the hallway, she threw open Cassie's bedroom door without knocking. A lantern turned low burned dimly on Cassie's bedside table, and her aunt sat on the side of the bed, wearing her wrapper and with her head in her hands.

"Aunt, there's a fire in town!"

Cassie's head popped up. "I heard the fire bell."

"It's down at the other end of the street in the Cultural Center building. I need to go. I don't think the fire could possibly spread, but I wanted to make sure you were awake, just in case."

Cassie's eyes widened in panic. "No, no, it couldn't spread," she said. "It shouldn't spread."

"Just stay alert, Aunt. I'm taking Teddy with me."

She flew back down the hallway and within seconds, she and Teddy were racing down the street, Rowdy at their heels. A bucket brigade had already formed, running from a town pump on the other side of Ginny's place to the Cultural Center. Both windows on the building were now shattered and smoke poured out, thicker beneath the walkway overhang and drifting down the street.

While still several yards away, Sunny pulled Teddy to a halt, hugging her and turning her face against her when the child began to cough. Her own eyes teared and stung, but she kept her gaze trained on the building. Just then three men with bandannas over their lower faces emerged onto the walkway, waving the crowd back.

"I think it's out," one of the men called. "Let's let the smoke clear."

Though muffled by the bandanna, the voice was recognizably Jake's. She started forward but thought better of it as the crowd fell back into the street, the workers in the brigade setting their buckets down in a line in case they might still be needed. Releasing Teddy for a moment, she wiped her stinging eyes. Her vision cleared and she saw Jake striding toward her, the bandanna now around his neck and the crowd parting for his approach.

"I don't think there's too much damage," he said, reaching out to stroke her upper arms soothingly.

Her knees wobbled and she swayed forward. Jake caught her, and she buried her face in his strong shoulder for an instant. Between them Teddy squirmed, struggling to free herself, and Sunny hurriedly stepped back.

"Gee, Miss Sunny. You 'most smothered me," Teddy said in a injured voice. She glanced up. "Hi, Ranger Jake. You get the fire out?"

"It's out, Teddy," he replied.

"How'd a fire start in Miss Sunny's building?" she asked.

"It's nighttime. There's not supposed to be no one in there at night."

Wanting the answer to the same question, Sunny carefully studied Jake's grim face. Frown lines furrowing his brow, he stared across the street in the direction of Saul Cravens' saloon, and she turned. Outlined by the light inside, Saul stood in front of his batwing doors, thumbs hooked in his vest pockets. He nodded and started walking toward them.

As Saul stepped down into the street, Ginny rushed up, elbowing Jake aside and taking Sunny's hands in her own. "Come in off the street, Sunny," she said. "You and Teddy both, if you don't mind her coming into my place. Goodness, neither one of you has on any shoes."

Knowing Cassie would full well have a fit when she heard about it didn't make Sunny rethink her quick decision. "Would you mind just taking Teddy with you for now, Ginny? I'd like to examine the fire damage."

"You can't go in there barefoot," Ginny insisted. "There's broken glass all over the walkway. But I'll settle Teddy in my office and bring you out a pair of my shoes. Come on, darling."

She took Teddy's hand, and Teddy gave her a wide grin. "I'm really gonna get to see inside your s'loon, Miss Ginny? Gee, the other kids are gonna be so jealous. A couple of the boys have peeked under the door, but that's all they ever had the nerve to do."

"It's just a business, sweetheart," Ginny assured her. "We sell drinks instead of goods like the general store does. I'm afraid you'll be awfully disappointed if you expect to see anything decadent."

"What's 'de . . . decadent' mean, Miss Ginny?"

Jake stiffened and Saul Cravens' voice overrode whatever answer Ginny made to Teddy. "I'm real sorry about the fire, Sunny," he said.

Saul took one of her hands between his. Up until now it hadn't bothered her at all that she was wearing only her gown and robe in front of half the town. Saul politely kept his gaze on her face, but her toes curled in the dirt as embarrassment at her inappropriate attire flushed her cheeks.

"Thank you, Mr. Cravens."

"Saul, please, Sunny. And since I haven't made a donation to your new endeavor, I want you to know that I'll have one ready for you in the morning. Perhaps it will help defray some of the expense of repairing the fire damage."

"Why, that's wonderful, Saul." She withdrew her hand and threw Jake a brilliant smile. "Isn't that wonderful, Jake?"

"Yeah," Jake snarled. "Just wonderful. By the way, Cravens, since you spend a fair amount of time keeping an eye on the goings-on in town, you didn't happen to see anything suspicious over here right before the fire, did you?"

"Come to think of it, Cameron," Saul mused, "I did notice something after you and I talked, a few minutes before the fire. After I came back here and you went on over to Ginny's, I saw you'd left your lantern behind. If you'll recall, seeing the lantern light was what drew me over there in the first place."

"That lantern was on a table," Jake said, a warning growl in his voice. "It couldn't have fallen off on its own."

Saul shrugged. "You asked, Cameron. We've got plenty of stray animals roaming around town. Could be one of them got in there, knocked against the table and caused the lantern to tip over. I sure don't leave any burning lanterns in my place after I close up at night. Hell, I . . . uh, excuse me, Sunny. Shoot, I heard a noise one morning and came downstairs with my gun in hand. Found a pig wandering around. He'd tipped over every darned spittoon in the place."

Sunny gasped, a slow dread stealing through her. "What were you both doing in the center in the first place? At that time of night? Did you close the door when you left, Jake?"

Jake took her arm, gently pushing her away. "We'll talk about this in a minute, Sunny. Go on over to Ginny's and wait for me."

Sunny jerked free. "I will not! I demand to know what's going on here. Now. Right this instant!"

Saul chuckled under his breath. "Jake knows as much as I do now, Sunny, so I'll leave you two to discuss it. Don't forget to stop by tomorrow for my donation."

"I'll remember, Saul. Good night." Sunny continued to glare at Jake as Saul sauntered away, his subdued laughter lingering behind.

"Did you close the door when you left the center, Jake?" she repeated.

"I'm the one authorized to ask questions right now," Jake informed her. "But for your information, the door was closed when I went over to check out the smoke odor. Now, get over to Ginny's and wait for me while I try to figure out how the fire started."

"I'm going with you. You'll need another lantern, and you can get one from Ginny while I put on the shoes she offered to loan me."

Sunny heard a snicker and moved to one side to glance around Jake. He turned at the same moment, waving his hand at several townspeople who were standing nearby, listening to their conversation.

"Go on home," he ordered. "Thanks for your help, but the fire's out now and I'll handle things from here on."

"Looks like there's still some fire burning out here in the street," one man said with a snort of laughter.

Jake advanced a step, and the man hurriedly threw an arm around the shoulder of another man next to him. "Come on,

Shorty. The excitement's over for a while. I'll buy you a drink so's we can clear the smoke out of our throats."

The crowd broke up, part of them heading across the street to Saul's, others walking back to gather the buckets of water. Sunny determinedly marched toward Ginny's, pausing when she reached a man picking up a water bucket.

"Sir, would you pass the word to everyone who helped put out the fire that there will be a free ticket to our first performance in the center for them?"

"Yes, ma'am, Miss Fannin."

Sunny continued into the saloon, meeting Ginny just inside the doors.

"Here you go," Ginny said, handing her a pair of black shoes and a buttonhook.

Ginny pulled a chair out from a nearby table, and Sunny sat. Jake passed on by and as she slipped on the shoes, Sunny heard him ask the bartender to hand him one of the lanterns hanging on a nail at the end of the bar.

"Is Teddy all right?" she asked Ginny.

"She's sipping a glass of iced sarsaparilla and talking to Marg while she gets ready to sing. I asked Marg to do an extra show tonight, as sort of a reward for the men who helped with the fire."

Sunny efficiently popped the last shoe button in place and stood. "Has Marg changed her mind about doing a show for our center? She has such a beautiful voice."

"I'm working on her. I received a new batch of sheet music in the mail the other day, and there's a couple of songs in it that would be perfect for her. But she's afraid the other women in town would turn up their noses, since she's only sung in saloons."

The lantern swinging in his hand, Jake passed her without a glance. "Tell her what a great chance it would be for her," Sunny said. "Once the women hear her they'll be enjoying themselves way too much to remember where she got her training."

Gathering her robe around her and tightening the belt, she stalked after Jake. The smoke smell lingered in the air, and her shoe soles crunched on the shattered glass as she approached the doorway of the center. Inside the door she halted. The tears misting her eyes came as much from the destruction inside as the smoke-laden air.

Jake had hung the lantern from a ceiling rafter, and it threw beams even beyond the golden pool of light beneath it. Soot smeared the newly painted walls. Cinders and flying ash pitted burns on the recently refinished tabletops, and someone had left the doors open on the side cupboard, where they stored the tablecloths. Everything would have to be scrubbed again.

Jake was concentrating his attention on one corner of the room, kneeling beside the spot where a half-burned table lay on its side next to the ladder. She moved closer, finally able to see the lantern base amid the rubble. Saul Cravens had been right. The lantern Jake left behind had been the cause of the fire.

Allowing her fury full rein, Sunny flared, "How could you be so incompetent? Even a child Teddy's age knows better than to leave a burning lantern unattended! I suppose your card game was more important to you than your responsibility to the citizens of this town!"

Jake didn't respond, and she took another step forward. When he grabbed a table leg and wrenched it loose, she hastily backed up. But instead of threatening her with the table leg, he prodded at the pile of ashes in front of him. A few sparks flew up from the rubble and Jake rose, stamping out the embers before they could blaze into new flames.

"Probably ought to pour some more water on this," Jake muttered. Brushing past her, he went out the door.

Sunny wrapped her arms across her breasts and stared at the room. Only a few feet from the area of the fire, Fred and John Dougherty had set up two sawhorses to cut boards for the small stage the women had decided to go ahead and build at the back of the room. Piles of sawdust lay beneath the sawhorses. If the lantern had landed in them rather than where it did, the entire building would have been a roaring inferno in seconds. The nearby stack of paint cans and turpentine-soaked rags the men used to clean their hands would have furnished enough other fuel to assure a rapid spread of the fire.

Jake strode over and poured a pail of water on the rubble he'd been examining, then picked up the table leg and poked it around again.

"Do you need any more water?" Sunny asked. "I'll be glad to go get it."

"This ought to do it."

He tossed the half-burned table to one side, throwing the leg after it. Pulling another table over to the same area, he removed his bandanna and used it to protect his hand while he set the lantern base in the exact center of the unburned table. He kicked the leg once, then again, harder. The table wobbled but didn't tip, and the lantern base only moved an inch.

Grabbing the edge of the table, Jake tipped it on its side. The lantern base skidded across the surface, landing in the rubble with a solid thunk when it hit the ladder rim.

Realization downed on Sunny. "Are you trying to prove that an animal couldn't have tipped over that table?"

Jake picked up the lantern base once more. "This type of lantern has a very heavy bottom. It's designed to minimize the chance of it tumbling over if it *is* jostled."

He tossed the lantern down, then picked up the end of the

ladder, positioning the burned side pieces on either side of the lantern base.

"And the first thing I noticed after I got the fire out was that it looked like the ladder had been on top of the lantern when it started to burn. I can't be sure about that, but I do know I'd left that ladder propped against the wall. It's pretty damned suspicious that the ladder fell right after the table got knocked over—and the ladder landed just in the right spot to send the evidence of it being tampered with up in flames."

13

"TAMPERED WITH?" SUNNY hurried to his side. "What are you talking about? Do you mean someone wanted Fred to fall from that ladder?"

"Fred, or you, or whoever happened to be climbing it when the step that was cut part way in two broke. The same step that's now completely burned up. The same step that just happened to land right on top of the flames, so it *would* be the first part of the ladder to burn."

"My God," Sunny breathed. "Who would do something like that?"

"That's what I have to find out. And until I do, I'm going to have to order you to forget about working on this place."

"I will not!" Sunny fumed. "Our plans are too far along, and we've already got a commitment from Grace Adams' manager for her to do a show here for us after her engagement in Dallas in two weeks. We've planned that for our opening. With having to repair this fire damage now, we'll barely be ready in time as it is!"

"You may never open at all, if you don't listen to me." Jake took her arms, shaking her slightly. "Pay attention to me, Sunny. Neither Fred's fall nor this fire was an accident. They were deliberate attempts to cause someone to get hurt and then cover up the evidence."

Sunny tilted her head defiantly. "You don't know they were directed at the center! There could be a grudge between other people in town. We'll just have to be more careful; if necessary, I'll post a guard in the building at night. The entire town is joining in to make this project happen, and I refuse to let some disgruntled person sabotage us."

"I'll guard your damned building, Sunny, because that's part of my job. As for being careful, you bet your ass you will be. But right now's not the time to let on that we're aware of the sabotage."

"Why not?"

"Because . . ."

Jake moved his hands to her back, tangling his fingers in her unbound hair and sweeping his thumbs back and forth, very close to the sides of her breasts. Her knees weakened, and she gripped his shirt for support.

"W . . . why not?" she managed to repeat.

"Because if whoever's doing this realizes we're onto him," Jake murmured, "he might make a more determined attempt than he has so far. And I couldn't live with myself if you ended up on the wrong side of that attempt."

"Why not?" Sunny asked again, for a different reason.

Inch by inch, he slowly lowered his head. "Because."

He breathed the word more than spoke it, his breath tingling on her lips. He paused before his mouth met hers, and she waited only a second before she stood on tiptoe and wrapped her arms around his neck. His lips were warm and firm, tasting of the smoke that had filtered through his bandanna. And tasting of Jake, the only man she'd ever kissed who could send her senses reeling with his touch.

With a muffled groan, he drew her closer. Deserting her lips, he kissed her cheek, then slid the tip of his tongue across her earlobe, into her ear. Shivers of delight crawled over her body, and her breast tips pressed against the front of her gown and robe.

Oh, God. For the second time that night she was kissing this man as though she wanted to throw caution to the bowels of hell—and join it there. And this time she was a lot more appropriately attired to join him on one of those cots at the jailhouse.

"Beautiful, so very beautiful," he murmured.

The resulting uproar his words caused in her body scared the bejesus out of Sunny, and she twisted free, clapping her hands over her mouth and staggering back. Eyes wide and straining, she stared at him. The whiskey depths of his eyes held a feral gleam and met her gaze unflinchingly, but she jerked her eyes free with extreme effort. Only—her gaze caught again on his lower lip, protruding as though in a pout.

He raised his hand. "Sunny," he said around a groan.

She shook her head wildly, and his hand dropped to his side, drawing her scrutiny with it. Beneath the gunbelt buckle, the button holes on the front of his denims stretched to near bursting. The two low-hanging pistols lay against his muscular thighs, the gun butts in line with the bottom button—the one most nearly ready to tear loose. It was a more erotic sight than she had ever imagined, even in the suggestive dreams that had been disturbing her sleep lately.

Muttering a vile oath, he turned his back on her. Shoulders rigid and fists clenched beside his guns, he snarled, "Get the hell out of here while I've still got sense enough to let you go!"

She stood stunned for what seemed like forever, unable to even force her breath to leave her lungs. Suddenly a sob tore free. Fumbling for her robe, she stumbled toward the doorway, eyes too misted with tears to see her way.

"Sunny, wait!" Jake called in a tortured voice.

Her knees hit the side of a chair and she fell forward. Arms outstretched, she landed on the chair seat, her breath whooshing out with the impact. Before she could feel any pain, he swept her up and cradled her against his chest. He sat—probably in the same darned chair that had blocked her path—and she found enough breath somewhere to shriek her rage at him.

"Let me go!" She pounded on his chest, and when he only tightened his hold, she let fly with one fist in an uppercut, as she'd seen a boxer do once in St. Louis. Jake's head snapped back and he muffled a grunt, instinctively lifting one hand to his face. She grabbed the index finger on the hand still holding her and bent it back until he groaned in pain and freed her.

Scrambling off his lap, she tossed her tangled hair behind her shoulders and glared at him. "How dare you?" she snarled.

"What the hell do you mean?" He cradled his injured finger with his other hand, staring at her as though she'd just appeared from the bowels of the same hell she'd contemplated a few minutes ago. "I wasn't daring a damned thing that you weren't willing for me to do!"

She inched her chin forward and propped her fists on her hips. "I'll tell you what you dared to do, you . . . you scum! You used every trick in the book—every part of you from those damned whiskey eyes to that . . . that . . . you know what I'm talking about. You made me lose my mind and forget my morals. You had me thinking you were the most special man I'd ever had the pleasure of kissing—of letting touch me."

She ignored the dark scowl gathering on his face, waving one hand in the air. "And then you turned your back on me! As though I were some tart you'd picked up to have a little fun with for a few minutes and . . ."

Jake surged out of the chair, jerking her against him. She squealed in protest and tried to batter his chest again, but he caught her hands and pulled them behind her. Securing her wrists in one of his hands, he cupped her hip to hold her and glared down at her.

"And just how many other men have you had the pleasure of letting kiss and touch you?"

The murderous glower on his face made her mouth go dry, and she closed her eyes to block out the sight. Shaking her head, she tried to force words out, but they couldn't get past the panic in her throat. What had she done? The Jake who held her now was the same one she'd seen unleashed at Mary's ranch. And her goading had liberated the caged tiger beneath his civilized facade.

Along with her panic, however, came another thought. She cracked an eyelid to examine his face yet again. One corner of her mouth curved all on its own, and she opened her eyes fully, tilting her head far enough back to stare directly at him.

"Why, Ranger Cameron," she mused, "I do believe your eyes are jealous green now. And they used to be such a lovely whiskey brown."

Jake held his glower for a slow count to five, but he pulled his bottom lip between his teeth and clenched it tightly. His chest heaved once with what could have been a suppressed chuckle. The next heave definitely preceded a loud guffaw, and he dropped her wrists. Pulling her to him, he buried his face in her neck, shoulders shaking with laughter under the arms she wrapped around him.

"There, there," she murmured, patting his back. "We all have those spasms of jealousy now and then."

A squeak of dismay cut off her chuckles as he sat down and gathered her onto his lap again. Tongue in the side of her cheek and finger on her lips as she waited to see what he would say next, she studied him worriedly. He shook his head, a curl of black silk falling across his forehead, and she tentatively reached up to push it back in place.

"You're way too wise for your age, Sunny," he said, catching her hand and enfolding it in his. "How'd you know I was so jealous at the thought of another man touching you that I was ready to kill him?"

"I . . . I was only hoping, Jake. Taking a chance. My mother taught me to be honest, and a few minutes ago I honestly thought there was something more happening between us than just lust. But if you'd laughed in my face, it would have devastated me."

"Let me assure you, Sunny, that lust is definitely a part of it." Her face started to crumple, but Jake tipped his chin up with the back of his hand. "I said part of it, darling. A part I'm starting to think could culminate in the type of mind-shattering passion a man and woman only dream of having."

"And what's the rest of it?" she whispered.

"The rest of it is the problem," he admitted, his flat voice making her heart sink. "I could never make love to a woman like you and walk away from it unscathed, Sunny. You're a woman a man builds his dreams with—not one he loves and leaves."

She nodded her head slowly. "And I guess you're a man without dreams."

"That's right. Or at least not the type of dreams that include being tied down with a wife and family."

Pursing her lips, Sunny continued nodding her head. "I understand completely, Jake." She scooted off his lap and stood. As she readjusted her robe, she said, "That's all I'll ever ask of you, Jake. To be completely honest with me. We'll only be friends, all right? I mean, after all, we'll be running into each other practically all the time in a town this size, and it would be hard not to talk to each other now and then. So since there's no future in it, you can forget all about your jealousy and any more kissing between us."

Sticking out her hand, she said, "I'm glad we had this discussion. Let's shake on it."

"Shake on it?" he growled, raising a raven brow.

"Yes." She firmly shoved her hand forward another inch. "Isn't that what two mature people do after they've come to a mature decision about something? We've just admitted there's an attraction between us, but there's no future in that attraction. You're only killing time here until you can move on, and I need to be careful of my reputation—not only for myself but for Teddy's sake. Now that we both understand the situation, it should be a fairly simple matter for us just to be friends—to realize it's just an attraction with no prospect to it."

Jake gave her hand a quick shake. Inadvertently, she supposed, his fingertips brushed her palm when he withdrew and her shoulders jerked in reaction to the pleasurable sensation. She rubbed her hand against her thigh, quickly stopping when his eyes centered on the movement.

"Well," she croaked. Clearing her throat, she went on, "Well, I need to get Teddy home. You'll let me know if you find out anything else about who could have set the fire, won't you?"

"Yes."

"All right. I . . . I better go get Teddy."

"You've already said that. Go get her, and I'll meet you out front to escort you home."

"All right. I'm glad we've made this mature decision."

"Yeah."

"Um . . . uh . . . just how old are you, Jake? You never said."

"I'm thirty-two," he growled.

"Oh, my," she murmured. "Fourteen years older than I

am. Yes, we've definitely made the right decision. You're probably set in your ways by now and have no desire to change."

"Go get Teddy!" he snarled.

She whirled and ran. She made it safely clear of the building this time, skidding to a halt beside the doors to Ginny's. Leaning against the wall, she drew several deep breaths and waited for her racing heart to calm, feeling as though she'd made a narrow escape from an extremely dangerous predicament.

She had unleashed the tiger in him again, and managed to avoid being trapped by being foolish enough to think the animal wasn't dangerous— that she might have a chance to tame him. People in town had warned her; well, she wouldn't forget to be wary again.

She straightened and brushed back her tangled hair. Pushing open the batwings, she scanned the saloon for Ginny. Knowing the other woman probably had Teddy in her office at the back, she walked on through the room. The men inside quieted as she passed, and she glanced in the mirror over the bar, realizing what a wreck she was—soot-stained clothing and flyaway hair. Even smudges of ash on her face, except—she peered a little closer at her reflection—except around her extremely clean mouth, which pouted as though yearning for something. Or perhaps it pouted in satisfaction at being sufficiently kissed.

A man nearby muttered something about fire, and she distractedly answered him. "The fire's completely out."

He threw back his head and guffawed loudly. Sunny tossed him an exasperated glare, recalling the idiot in the street a while ago who had insinuated there was a different sort of flame still burning—one between her and Jake. This was a different man, and he helped once in a while with the repairs on the center, so she didn't want to alienate him. She sniffed haughtily, however, as she deliberately bypassed him without deigning to speak again.

He didn't know she and Jake had effectively quenched any flames between them just now. He'd find out soon enough, and the town would settle for some other gossip on which to chew.

After almost silently escorting Sunny and Teddy home and seeing them safely inside, Jake strode over to the stable. Grabbing his tack from the storage room, he headed for the corral to saddle Dusty. The stallion caught his tension, prancing and sidling around until Jake swore at him in exasperation and tied him to a rail. After he jerked the belly cinch tight, he left the horse to settle down and stalked over to John Dougherty's small house behind the stable. He pounded on the door until John opened it, peering at Jake in annoyance.

"I'm not giving you any choice this time, John," Jake ordered. "I've got to leave town for a couple of hours, and I want you to get your ass dressed and watch over things while I'm gone! You can wait in the jailhouse if you want, but I expect to find you awake when I get back."

"Damn it, Jake," John whined. "I was down there helping put out that fire with everyone else. I'm tired . . ."

"The next damned fire might be at your stable!" Jake spat. "Get your clothes on!"

"That fire wasn't an accident?" John asked.

"You keep that information to yourself for now. If you need me, I'll be out at Charlie's place. But I won't be gone long."

Barely waiting for John's nod of agreement, he stomped away and headed back to the corral. A few seconds later he gave Dusty his head, and the powerful stallion flew down the road, hooves pounding a rhythm to his racing thoughts.

The cool night air flowing past him failed utterly to chill his overheated body, and he leaned into the brisk wind. A strand of Dusty's long, coarse mane brushed his cheek and he slapped at it, recalling how much silkier the blond curls had felt against his cheek a few moments earlier.

He had to rein Dusty to a slow lope to enter the road to Charlie's ranch, and the stallion protested, shaking his head and snorting annoyance. Though Jake made sure he considered the bit in Dusty's tender mouth in his hold on the reins, he took a sullen satisfaction in maintaining control. His thighs and arms transmitted his power and command, and Dusty yielded to his domination, albeit reluctantly.

At least he still had supremacy over one area of his life, Jake scoffed to himself. His horse knew who was boss and didn't give him any sass. His horse didn't stand there and look him in the eye, tell him he could ignore the bond between them and treat him just like any other man who forked his saddle.

But that was exactly what he wanted, wasn't it? Dusty valued the freedom they had every bit as much as Jake did. The horse fought the confining corral, making his displeasure well known. Without Jake's contrary directive, the stallion would have raced through the night, stretching his long-awaited release from the restraint of the corral to the maximum.

Aw, shit. And his horse didn't have bluebonnet eyes and sunshine hair. Curves that felt like satin beneath the strokes he yearned to use to possess her loveliness. Strokes that on the stallion would be meant to calm and soothe, but on the woman would be meant to stir.

And Dusty didn't tell him that he was too old and set in his ways for him!

Outlined by beams of moonlight, the large family home Charlie now occupied alone loomed at the end of the road.

His parents had accepted Charlie's offer of financing a dream they had long held—moving to Dallas to live their remaining days in comfort while their son fulfilled his own desire to raise his blooded palominos and dusky duns on the ranch. The last time Jake had asked Charlie about them, they were still active and healthy, enjoying their lives immensely.

The glow of a cigarette tip from the shadowed veranda alerted Jake that Charlie was still up and about despite the late hour. Jake was already swinging out of the saddle by the time he halted Dusty at the hitching post, and Charlie strolled over to the edge of the veranda to meet him.

"You just letting that horse run a few kinks out, or you got some other reason for riding hell-bent for leather this time of night?" Charlie asked. "I heard you coming all the way from the main road."

"I need some answers," Jake returned in a flat voice.

"And you think I've got 'em for you?"

"I don't know," Jake admitted. "I don't know if anyone has."

"Well, we ain't gonna find out if we talk in riddles," Charlie stated. "Come on in and we'll have us a snort. Might calm you down enough to start making some sense."

Jake followed Charlie into the house and down the hallway to the library, which Charlie used for an office. Flinging himself into a leather-covered chair, he impatiently watched Charlie fill two glasses from a bottle of fine bourbon he took from a shelf. He accepted the glass Charlie held out to him and swallowed half of it by the time Charlie settled in the chair behind his desk.

Charlie studied him for a second, then lifted his own glass in a toast before he took a swallow and set it on the desk. "That's fine bourbon," he said. "Ought to be savored a little."

"Brandy's for savoring," Jake responded. "Bourbon's for . . ."

"For what?" Charlie prodded when Jake fell silent.

"Hell, I don't know." Jake took another long swallow from the glass before resting his head against the chair back. "But it sure feels better in my belly than it does in a glass in my hand."

The clock on the fireplace mantel chimed once. When no other sound followed, Jake slit an eyelid to check if it was chiming a half hour. The hands indicated one o'clock—even later than he had thought. He sat up, swirling the bourbon once, then drinking half of the remainder.

"You're up awful late," he pointed out to Charlie. "I can remember when you thought anything past nine at night was sleeping time."

Charlie only shrugged and reached for his glass. He leaned back in his chair, cradling one hand in the other. Jake suddenly noticed the dark shadows beneath his friend's eyes. Glancing down at Charlie's desk, he saw a bankbook scattered amid some other papers.

"You worried about finances?" he asked his friend.

"Hell, no," Charlie said. "In fact, I just got a letter yesterday from the mine manager. They hit another large vein of silver, even richer than the last one. It's on that part of the claim we used your name to stake out, so your share's gonna be a lot bigger next year."

"I don't need any more money, Charlie. Put it into the ranch."

"I've got all I can handle right now, unless I wanted to buy more land. And I've got no use for that."

Jake looked around the office. The curtains were tattered in places, and the windows needed a good washing. The desk Charlie sat behind looked like it had been through a battle in the war, and he felt a spring poking him from the leather chair. Mrs. Duckworth had taken a lot of the furnishings with her when she moved to Dallas, and the last time Jake had visited here, he'd noticed Charlie still hadn't seen fit to replace them.

"Well, you could hire yourself a housekeeper and get someone to help you fix up the inside of this house," he said. "You keep everything outside in good shape, but I don't think your mother would appreciate how you've let things go in here."

"Ain't no reason to worry about that. I don't do any entertaining, and I eat my meals out at the bunkhouse. Every once in a while I borrow Theresa from Mary Lassiter and let her give the house a swipe or two. Dust just settles back, though."

"Yeah, I guess you're right," Jake agreed. "Not having a woman around means a man doesn't have to worry about all the trappings they seem to think makes a house into a home. Hell, all I need's a bedroll and my gun and tack. Even Dusty would rather be staked out on the range than penned up in a corral or a stall, even with a feed trough full of grain."

"It's different with a horse, though," Charlie reminded him. "They ain't interested in a filly unless it's just that certain time when the filly's breeding. Once that's taken care of, that old stallion loses interest."

"Works for me." Jake finished the bourbon and stood to walk over to the shelf and replenish his glass.

"Does it?"

Charlie's question drew Jake up short when he reached for the bottle. Pretending a nonchalance over Charlie's query that he was far from feeling, he shrugged one shoulder and then forced himself to fill his glass. Returning to the chair, he faced Charlie rather than sitting back down.

"Look," Jake growled, "I came out here tonight to talk to

you about something. I've been mulling over whether or not to say anything about it to you for a week now."

"Something between you and that pretty little Sunny gal?"

Fixing Charlie with a sharp look, Jake replied, "It's got to do with her, but not anything between her and me. It's . . ."

"Could've fooled me," Charlie interrupted. "Hell, you pay so much attention to that house she lives in you don't hear half what I say when we're talking."

"Damn it, Charlie! Shut up and let me finish!"

Gesturing acquiescence with his glass, Charlie took another sip and waited for Jake to continue.

"Look, Charlie, part of my job is keeping my ears open. And I learned a long time ago that people like to talk. Well," he qualified, "most people. You don't say much except what it damn well pleases you to say. But soon as I got to town a few months ago, folks knew you and I were friends. One of the first things I heard about when they talked about you was that you used to be real close to the Foster family."

He paused, expecting a comment, and Charlie complied. "Nothing secret about that. I suppose they even told you that Ian Lassiter beat my time with Cassie and she ended up planning on marrying that bastard."

"Yeah, I heard that part. But the thing that's been bothering me is that they said the *three* of you were real close—you, Cassie, and her sister, Samantha. Yet I haven't seen you make one move at all toward Sunny since she arrived in town. Seems to me you'd want to get to know her, what with Sunny being the daughter of this close friend you used to have. Maybe even just to be polite—to tell Sunny you're sorry she lost her mother."

"You're right about one thing."

Charlie lifted his glass again, and Jake could have sworn he saw the liquid inside shaking, which meant Charlie's hand was trembling. But the older man threw the dregs of the bourbon down his throat and rose from his chair, crossing to the liquor bottle. When he poured his glass full again, his hand was steady.

"What am I right about?" Jake prompted as Charlie reseated himself.

"That I don't talk about things unless I'm of a mind to," Charlie said. "And I've had my fill of what those people in Liberty Flats *thought* they knew about what happened nineteen years ago. Nothing that's said now would make things any different. And I don't intend to pay any attention to their speculating on it again after all this time, just because Samantha's daughter came to town."

Jake sensed a much deeper well of emotions in Charlie than he let on about. You couldn't live with a man for years, practically on top of each other when you were trying to stay warm around a campfire or wintering in a small log cabin, and not know a little about each other's inner workings. If that closeness fostered friendship rather than enmity, however, it also fostered respect for each other's privacy. Still, loyalty to his friend left him with at least one more thing to say.

"Glad you reminded me that I ain't paid my respects to that there Sunny gal," Charlie said before Jake could speak again. "And I'll take care of it. She don't know me from Adam, though, and I don't reckon it will mean much to her."

"She darned sure *wants* to know you," Jake said, stepping into the opportunity Charlie himself offered.

Charlie leveled his gaze at Jake, waiting for him to go on.

"She's been asking me questions about you," Jake admitted. "Hell, Charlie, I don't really know how to say this."

"Just spit it out," Charlie demanded.

"All right, dammit. Are you Sunny's father?"

The glass of bourbon spilled on the desk, but Charlie

ignored it, never once taking his eyes off Jake's. He slowly lifted one hand, which was spattered with bourbon, and wiped it on his pantleg beneath the desktop. Somehow Jake became aware that Charlie's eyes were not focused on him—that the other man was concentrating inward, reliving his own exclusive thoughts. He also knew the exact second when Charlie saw him sitting there in front of him again.

"You worried about that little gal's bloodline in case you decide to hitch up with her?" Charlie asked with a smile that creased his lips but didn't chase any of the shadows from his eyes. "You know, we can pick and choose what mare we mate with what stud, but there's a little more to that when it comes down to human beings."

Annoyed at Charlie's evasiveness, Jake said impatiently, "Sunny and I have already come to the conclusion that neither one of us is right for the other. She . . ."

Charlie interrupted, "Well, now, that's another thing you don't seem to understand. People don't pick their mates like we pick them for our horses. We . . ."

"Dammit, Charlie! Are you going to answer my question or not?"

"No."

The flat word could have meant two different things—no, he wasn't Sunny's father or no, he wasn't going to answer Jake's question. Jake gave up in exasperation. Pushing harder might make his friend's temper flare and cause a breach in their relationship. As it was, Charlie was making some insinuations of his own that needed to be nipped in the bud before he got the wrong idea.

"Well, it's your business, Charlie." Jake said. "But don't go getting any ideas that there's something between me and Sunny. We talked after we got the fire out tonight and agreed we were about as mismatched as a polecat and a house cat. We're just friends."

"Which one did you decide was the polecat?" Charlie said with a chuckle. "As if I didn't know. And what's this about another fire?"

Disregarding Charlie's gibe, Jake said, "This fire was real this time—not just a pan of burned biscuits. I think someone set it deliberately, to cover up evidence."

14

CHARLIE WAITED THREE days, chewing over his thoughts and losing sleep. Daytimes weren't so bad, even though he skipped his usual morning ride into town to exercise his primary stud. Instead he rode over the ranch checking fences, disregarding the fact that his hands made those rounds themselves at least weekly. The third morning he found himself at the old swimming hole, remembering the childish shrieks of laughter from the two girls who had been like sisters to him when they swung out over the water on the old vine and dropped with enormous splashes. Then he knew he had to face some things or continue subsisting on a couple hours sleep at night—way too little at his ripe old age of forty-one.

He started out over the blue water of the pond, ruffled just a bit in the middle by a lazy morning breeze. Blue eyes that used to sparkle with excited laughter mocked him, and he dropped his chin on his chest, kicking at a stone and sending it plummeting into the water with a loud *kerthunk.* The resulting eddies spread over the surface, disturbing the placid water nearer the shore. The concentric circles of an unexpected splash like that shifted things around in real life, too, he mused. Sometimes it seemed like fate took advantage of an unforeseen disturbance and turned things upside down. Things never were the same afterward, though they might seem to be, on the surface.

He didn't remember exactly when his brotherly feelings had changed toward one of the sisters. Hell, if you wanted to look at it that way, she wasn't even the prettier of the two. Yet his father had always taught him to look deeper, beyond the first eye-catching glimpse that drew a person's interest. In horses it meant taking into consideration not just the physical conformities, but also how the spirit of the dam and sire would blend in the offspring. He hadn't realized it at first, but that reasoning had carried over into his maturing years.

He'd seen plenty of his friends captivated by a pretty face and sashaying hips; he'd also seen their hangdog expressions when the pretty gals dumped them for men with broader shoulders or better smiles. When he and his father discussed it, they'd concluded that some females—and males too—fed a rather selfish ego trait by showing off the best-looking person they could attract on their arms.

He'd been willing to wait until his own choice for his attentions outgrew those rather immature ideas, but he'd waited too long. He'd waited until her own heart had been shattered, seemingly irreparably, after her misguided choice. He should have killed the bastard, like he'd wanted to. But that would have brought the whole situation to light, and it would have been even worse on her. He couldn't have done that to her.

He'd even thought for a long time that his own heart was broken beyond mending. His visits home had been brief, just long enough for the memories to overtake him and send him on his way again. But he'd handled the recollections pretty well the last few years, after he decided not to let the past override his yearning to fulfill the dream he'd always had of taking over from his father.

Then that little Sunny gal had come to town—bringing it all back.

The stallion snorted and Charlie stiffened his stance. With firm strides, instead of the lollygagging, indecisive steps he'd been taking lately, he went over to the horse and mounted.

GRUBBY AND SWEATY, Sunny stared around the interior of the Cultural Center with pride. They'd accomplished so very much in the last three days. After learning about the fire, even the owners of some of the surrounding ranches had sent in hands they could spare to help out. She glanced in amusement at the curved hooks inside the front door, where she had very nicely demanded the cowboys hang their jingling spurs.

All the fire damage was repaired, the linens washed, and the odor gone. They still needed to repaint, but no merchant had offered to donate that. Fred could only give so much, he'd explained, but he'd be willing to sell them what they needed at his own price. He'd already ordered it, and they could pay with funds raised at the Saturday social.

Oh, land's sakes! Being so busy the last few days, she'd completely forgotten Saul Cravens' offer of a donation. He probably thought she wasn't interested. She had to get over to the store and help Ruth for a while, and tomorrow she'd be baking and preparing food for the social most of the day. But she had a few minutes right now. Hurrying out to the boardwalk, she decided to clean up a little at Ginny's rather than making the trek back to her own house. Though none of the women would even consider entering Ginny's in the evening, many of them went in and out during the day to have a cool drink or wash the grit and grime away. So no one even thought it unusual now when she came through the batwing doors.

She paused a moment, listening to Perry's cousin, Marg, practice one of the new songs she had recently added to her repertoire. Cathy Percival, the banker's wife, was actually standing at the bar sipping a glass of lemonade and nodding her head as the haunting notes of the ballad filled the room. Sunny waved at Cathy, then went on to the washroom off Ginny's office. A few minutes later she reemerged to find Cathy gone. Feeling refreshed, she headed over to Saul's saloon.

Halfway across the street, she swerved to avoid dragging her skirts in a pile of horse droppings, which reminded her that as soon as she got the Cultural Center up and running, there was another goal on her agenda. One way or another she was going to force the town to pay attention to street upkeep! She swung her gaze toward the jailhouse up the way. Jake was sitting on that darned chair, which almost seemed a part of his backside. She giggled under her breath when she thought of demanding that he patrol the streets for garbage rather than human lawbreakers. Those whiskey eyes would spit scorn and cantankerousness at her so fast she'd have trouble ducking the flood.

He rose to his feet and she stumbled on a rut. Gosh darn it, anyway! She hadn't had a bout of clumsiness since the night of the fire. She'd been so pleased with the civility she managed whenever he stopped by to check on their progress at the Cultural Center. Now all he'd done was stand up from halfway down the street and her feet faltered!

She hesitated at the other set of batwing doors, calming the flutters in her stomach, which she assured herself were caused by her audacity in entering this shady establishment.

They didn't have a thing to do with the recollection of her dreams—dreams of what something other than friendship would be like with Jake Cameron—dreams that had absolutely no future, as they had both agreed.

Even out here on the boardwalk she could smell the interior of Saul's place, and she wrinkled her nose. Mixed with some yeasty aroma, the same odors of cigar smoke and sawdust that at Ginny's seemed part of the atmosphere smelled different here. She finally recognized the yeasty smell as the same one she'd smelled in a glass of warm beer a cowboy had left half finished on Ginny's bar.

Saul Cravens peered over the batwings and smiled at her. Throwing open one side of the doors, he said, "Sunny! I thought you'd forgotten all about me. You needn't come inside if you don't wish. I understand that a lady of your sensibilities might be offended in here."

"I wouldn't think of insulting you like that, Mr. Cravens," Sunny replied. "This is your place of business and we have some business to discuss."

"Saul, please," he reminded her. "Please do come in, then."

He held the door for her, and she entered. Although she knew Aunt Cassie would have a fit when she learned her niece had been seen going into this saloon, she gazed around eagerly, unable to disguise her interest. Aunt Cassie had already had a hissy fit when Teddy had unfortunately chattered away about their having iced sarsaparilla at Ginny's yesterday. This place was everything she had expected to find at Ginny's and didn't. The interior was stark and plain, the tables set on a warped pine floor, and wall decorations were nonexistent—except for one area that was covered by brightly colored women's garters. Feeling sure the answer would embarrass her, she bit back inclination to ask Saul about the significance of the garters.

Saul put a guiding hand on her back, murmuring for her to come with him to his office in the rear of the room. As they passed the bar on her right, she peered at it inquisitively. Unlike the highly polished mahogany bar at Ginny's, deep nicks and scratches marred Saul's bar. It even looked like a couple of the craters on the front might be bullet holes.

And, yes, there it was. Over the bar hung a picture of a very full-bodied nude woman! She reclined on a fainting couch, a flirtatious smile on her lips and a come-hither expression in her eyes. One hand lay strategically across the apex of her thighs and the other one cupped her . . . breast!

Oh, my!

Saul evidently caught the direction of her gaze and made a disconcerted sound. Stepping around her, he blocked her view and urged her quickly through the door to his office, closing it firmly behind them.

"Uh . . . please have a seat, Sunny." He held the top of a straight-back chair politely, but Sunny turned and reopened the door part way. Cravens flushed slightly.

"Sorry," he muttered."I'm not used to having a lady in my office. I only closed the door from force of habit."

Since the entire town knew of the soiled doves who worked in Saul's saloon, Sunny assumed he *had* had other women in his office, but she held that thought in abeyance. After all, the man was offering a donation for the cause of culture in the town.

She seated herself, and he took his place behind a plain desk. Removing a ring of keys from his vest pocket, he avoided her eyes and unlocked a desk drawer. "I assume you've come for my donation," he said as he placed a cash box on the desk. "I think you'll find it appropriate, but if you need more, please don't hesitate to ask."

"I do have one comment," Sunny said. "Since we'll be in competition for customers, I find it extremely generous of you to help subsidize our center."

"Quite the contrary," Saul said with a wry chuckle. "In case you haven't noticed, my dear, business in this town has picked up considerably since you ladies announced your plans. And I anticipate an even bigger draw when you finally get the center open."

Sunny's brows rose in inquiry, and he continued. "It's not that much further for the cowboys who work the ranches around here to ride on west to Abilene on payday instead of into Liberty Flats. Abilene's on the path of the cattle drives and still a wide-open town, which makes it a rather dangerous place. Some of the youngsters who want to sow their wild oats will make that trek, but the customers I cater to in this town are a fairly steady clientele."

"I guess I don't understand," Sunny mused. "We'll still be competing, won't we?"

"Not at all." Saul leaned back in his chair. "Your center will offer entertainment earlier in the evening. In fact, it will draw people into town even more often. Granted, some of the men leaving the performances will stop at my competitor's establishment across the street, but others will want a less . . . uh . . . refined atmosphere in which to indulge themselves. And they'll be even more ready for what my place offers after an evening of abstaining in the company of the ladies."

His eyes wandered upward, toward the second floor of his building, where Sunny assumed the "indulgence" to which he referred took place. A hot flush of indignation stole over her. She would just bet the men would be ready to break their evening's abstinence! Saul was insinuating that the men would not only be thirsty for drink but also be randy after being in close proximity with their untouchable feminine companions for several hours and then taking them home.

She gritted her teeth in vexation, trying to think of a suitable chastisement—one that would let him know she had seen beneath his supposedly innocuous comments without humiliating herself by blurting out her understanding. But Saul leaned forward. He removed a bag of coins from the cashbox and pushed them across the desk toward her.

"My initial donation is one hundred dollars, Sunny. I consider it an investment in the town and in my own business."

"You . . . ah . . . appear to be a very astute businessman," Sunny admitted with a defeated sigh. She accepted the donation, placing it in her reticule, but she made no move to leave the office. This was the perfect opportunity for her to pursue the avenue for the information that Mary's foreman had inadvertently led her to thinking about.

"I understand you've lived in town your entire life," she mused, "so it makes sense that you want to operate a long-term business here. And you must have known my mother, Samantha Foster."

An interested gleam appeared in Cravens' eye. "Yes, yes, I did. We went to school together, of course, although she was a few classes behind me, as was your aunt. I graduated from what Liberty Flats had to offer back then and after that I spent the only time away from here in my life. While Samantha and Cassie completed school, I attended a business college back East for four years."

"Both my mother and my aunt went to a ladies' finishing school in St. Louis, then returned here," Sunny said. "In fact, I attended the same school as my mother for two years."

"It must be a fine school. I'd already sold my father's ranch and opened this place by the time Samantha returned from her stint at the St. Louis finishing school. Instead of the rather tomboyish creature she'd been previously, she was a lady grown by then. Why, she and Cassie had the men of the county beating a path to their doorstep."

Sunny shook her head. "It's hard to imagine my aunt as a belle with lots of beaus chasing after her," she admitted. "Now she's so . . . well, different."

"Yes, quite," Cravens agreed.

"Everyone seems puzzled by the change in my aunt," Sunny prodded. "All I've been able to find out is pure speculation. It might make things easier between us if I understood my aunt a little better."

Saul steepled his fingers against his mouth for a moment, then dropped his hands. "I only know what you've probably already heard yourself, my dear. Pure speculation. Have you asked your aunt?"

"She isn't at all willing to talk to me," Sunny admitted. "She seems to be very resentful of my presence here. I just thought that if I knew why, maybe we could work things out."

"If Cassie won't talk to you, there's only one other person who might know the full details of what happened here nineteen years ago."

"Charlie Duckworth?" Sunny questioned.

"I see you already have your suspicions about that," Cravens said with a nod. "Charlie's as tight-lipped as Cassie, though. But I can tell you a couple of things you may not know."

"What? Please."

"After Charlie came back to town and settled at his family homestead again, he received periodic letters with St. Louis postmarks on them. Ruth Hopkins' son, Brad, helps his mother sort the mail at the post office window in the Hopkins general store, and he comes in here now and then. On one occasion the telegraph operator, Turley, told me that Charlie received a wire from a St. Louis bank about . . . oh, three months before you arrived in town."

Inwardly chastising herself for her curiosity about information that Ruth's son and the telegraph operator should have kept confidential, Sunny nevertheless leaned forward. "That was around the time of my mother's death. Did he say what information the wire had?"

"Well, yes. It was late one night, and Turley was the last man in here at the time. He knows he's not supposed to pass on the information in those wires to anyone else, but he'd had a couple of drinks too many. I, of course, kept the information to myself, but I thought it peculiar that Charlie didn't notify anyone else in town—even your aunt. If he had, surely the word would have spread in this small town."

"Please," Sunny urged, "tell me what the wire said."

"Well, since you've already pretty much guessed it, I'll just confirm it. It was notification that your mother had been killed in an accident."

Sunny furrowed her brow. "My mother's attorney notified Aunt Cassie, because I was much too upset to handle it myself. But he informed me that he wrote her a letter, so it would have taken a lot longer to get the news to my aunt. I never heard a word back from her or anyone else in this town. It seems extremely odd that neither Mr. Duckworth nor my aunt would have realized my mother had other friends here in town who should have been notified."

"Extremely odd," Saul agreed with a shrug. "But only the two of them would be able to explain their actions."

"And since my aunt won't talk to me . . ."

Sunny rose, slipping her reticule over her arm. "Thank you for your donation, Saul. It's too bad we don't have a newspaper and a printing press in town. I've sent the details for our opening night programs off by mail to Dallas, and I listed all the donations on the back of them. It's too late now to add your name, but I intend to have a poster in the window of the center listing all the contributors to our endeavor. I'll make sure you're noted on that."

Saul waved a negligent hand. "As I mentioned, this is an investment toward my own profits. But I admit it gives me a sense of satisfaction to know the townspeople will see my name on that list of contributors. And it will indeed be a good bit of advertising for me."

"That it will," Sunny said with a laugh.

"Let me escort you to wherever you're headed, Sunny."

"Oh, that's not necessary."

"My pleasure, my dear."

He stepped around the desk and extended his arm. Sunny hesitated a second, but at the thought of crossing through the saloon to the boardwalk she slipped her fingers around his forearm and started out the door.

As Cravens and Sunny exited Saul's office, Jake narrowed his eyes under his hat brim. He'd meant to come in here and drag Miss Sunny Fannin's cute little ass out of Cravens' saloon, telling her in no uncertain terms never to come in here again—with or without an escort. Not that he had any right to order her around, he reminded himself, but that hadn't made him hesitate at all.

By the time he'd entered the saloon, however, caution prevailed. If he stormed into Saul's office and dragged Sunny out of there—or tried to—he might end up a hell of a lot more embarrassed then she would. If she defied him, his only alternative would be to pick her up and carry her out. The thought of having her spitting and snarling in his arms was appealing, but he'd rather have that happen in a private spot, not in front of the avid eyes of the early drinkers in the seedy saloon.

And Miss Sunny Fannin had made it perfectly clear that she had absolutely no desire ever again to seek out a private spot with him!

Yet he wasn't about to leave as long as Sunny remained in that unsuitable place, so he bought a beer as an excuse to hang around. His choice of seating had been intentional, and if Sunny hadn't opened the door herself, he would have found some excuse to go into Saul's office.

He remembered telling Charlie the other night that part of his job was keeping his ears open. He hadn't really meant snooping, which his eavesdropping just now could be construed as, but he'd sure come by some interesting information. Sunny and Saul disappeared out the batwings, and Jake leaned forward to pick up his lukewarm beer. He swished a mouthful around before swallowing it.

So Cravens wasn't at all perturbed about competition from Ginny or the Cultural Center. Either that, or the man was a damned good liar. Yet Cravens' justifications made sense. More traffic in town meant he would get his own share of those customers, both for the liquor he sold and for the services he provided on the second floor. If Cravens was telling the truth about how he felt, he had no rationale for sabotaging the opening of the Cultural Center.

That meant someone else had his own reasons for the vandalism.

The other information he'd overheard was just as confusing. Damn, he wished Charlie would open up to him. Didn't his friend realize he wouldn't judge him? He knew Charlie well enough that he figured there must have been a hell of a good reason for him to leave Samantha Fannin on her own to raise a child. Charlie's own child—or the child of some other man?

He waved away any problem with Samantha's using a different name. Hell, half the men he'd arrested used aliases, and plenty of the women he'd run across in his life admitted to not wanting their true names known. The men's reasons were straightforward—attempts to avoid capture. The women had various other motivations. Some were fleeing abusive relationships; others didn't want their families to know what had become of them. Some just didn't like the name they were born with and picked one they were happier using.

For a brief second he contemplated sending a couple of wires to St. Louis. But he'd just heard how confidential Turley kept the information that went through his office. Charlie would have a kickass fit if he found out Jake was digging into his past—and Jake would be on the receiving end of the ass kicking.

He supposed he could ride to Abilene and use that telegraph office, but that would take at least a day, then another day to go back and pick up the answers. And it would be just his luck to run into a Ranger patrol—maybe General John B. Jones himself, who constantly led his company up and down the frontier area from Rio Grande City to the Red River. Damn being tied to this town under strict orders not to leave until a replacement came!

Since he had to obey orders or face expulsion from the Rangers, maybe he should stay a little closer to Sunny. Just to keep abreast of what she was finding out, he assured himself. He owed Charlie that much at least, even though he'd pretty much lost his suspicion of Sunny being some sort of gold digger since he'd gotten to know her better. But she might yet cause his friend Charlie a whole lot of embarrassment by pursuing this nonsense about him being her father. Or was it nonsense, he wondered.

Shoving back his chair, he left half of his beer on the table. For some reason he found himself whistling a rather jaunty tune as he headed out to find the perky blonde, even though he knew he should be concerned about his friend.

15

INSTEAD OF STABLING his horse as he usually did when he planned to be in town for a while, Charlie rode the palomino right up to the picket fence surrounding Cassie's house. He was tired of avoiding her—tired of a brief tip of his hat if he happened to be in town and meet her when she made one of her rare excursions out. Besides, he could see that the town was pretty much deserted this afternoon. Everyone was at the church for the much-touted fundraising social. If anyone saw him here . . . well, he was also tired of pretending to have no interest in Cassie Foster's life.

After tying his reins to the fence, he strode through the gate and up the porch steps. Memories assailed him—times when he wouldn't even have bothered to knock. Times when he wouldn't have bothered with the front door, instead going charging around the back and straight into the welcoming kitchen, not worrying about whether he had a hole in his pants knee or his hands were washed.

Now he paused for a moment on the porch, running his palm across his face for the twentieth time to make sure he hadn't missed a whisker when he shaved so carefully this morning. His good suit still fit, though it was a tad snug in the waist. Theresa had fixed it up real proper when he took it over there yesterday, and she also washed and ironed his white shirt into snowy brightness. Felt like she had put some starch in the collar, though. He ran his finger under it, trying to loosen the black string tie.

Removing his hat, he pulled his handkerchief out of his back pocket and wiped his balding head. He caught a whiff of the bay rum he'd used this morning—for the first time in too many years. The Texas summer heat usually sucked that right off a feller's skin, but he'd taken that into consideration and been extra liberal with it.

Dang, maybe he should take time for a smoke first. He stuffed the handkerchief back in his pocket, then felt inside his coat for his makings. Changing his mind when he realized he was dillydallying around and putting off the inevitable, he knocked firmly on the door. Dropping his head, he waited—but no one answered.

Hell, maybe she'd gone to the social. No, he doubted that. He banged on the door louder, then caught a glimpse of a curtain moving at the front parlor window. So that was the way she wanted to play it?

He tested the doorknob and found it unlocked. With only one deep breath for courage, he shoved the door back and strode inside, going directly into the well-remembered parlor.

Cassie stood in front of the window, her hand clasped at her throat. For just a brief instant he thought he saw a flash of the young Cassie in the blue eyes that used to welcome him. Just as quickly it was gone, replaced by the dimness and paler color he'd seen over the past years. That brief flash, however, gave him some fortitude.

"Hello, Cassie."

"Please leave," she murmured. "I didn't invite you here."

"Never used to need an invite," he replied. "And I ain't gonna leave. Not until we have us a talk that's long overdue."

Her back rigid, she started past him to the door. He

snaked his arm in front of her and swung her around to face him—close, very close. They'd both been the same height when they stopped growing, and her eyes were on the same level as his. She stared at him in increasing fright, then clamped her eyes shut.

"Please," she repeated. "We don't have anything to talk about. And even if we did, you can't force me to talk to you."

"Then you just sit down and listen, Cassie, sweetheart."

The endearment had the desired effect, and she opened her eyes. "I'm not your . . . I don't want . . . oh, please, Duckie. Leave me alone!"

"No one's called me Duckie in years," he said with a half smile.

She stepped back and he let her go, as long as she didn't start for the door again.

"You beat up anyone else who tried to call you that, except Sammie and me," she blurted.

"Yeah, I remember. And I remember lots of other things, including some big mistakes I made. Sammie's daughter coming to town made me do a lot of thinking."

Cassie whirled and strode to the settee. "That girl! She never should have come here! She doesn't have any idea what she's done!"

"That's the problem," Charlie said, walking over and gently pushing her down onto the settee. Sitting beside her, he took her hands in his. "She doesn't know. And I think we should tell her."

"No!" Cassie gripped his hands in a fiercesome hold. "Please, Duckie, you can't! It's over and done with and it's stayed buried all these years. It was hard enough going through it the first time. I can't bear it all over again!"

"Cassie, I've come to the conclusion over the past few years that we've done our bearing of the situation entirely wrong. We've acted like the guilty ones, instead of holding our heads up without shame. It wasn't our fault, you know."

"It was!" Cassie shook her head, clenching her teeth and swallowing before she continued. "If I had been . . . if he hadn't . . . if Sammie . . ."

"Damn it, listen to me! Remember how young we all were. Maybe if we'd gone to my parents, like I suggested, things would have turned out different. Your folks had just died. You didn't have anyone to turn to."

"It still would have been just as bad. Even worse on Sammie, after what we saw later on. The best thing to do is let it lie. Send Sunny back to St. Louis where she belongs, before she succeeds in . . ."

"Jake came out to the ranch the other night," he interrupted. "He asked me flat out if I was Sunny's father."

"Oh, my God!" Cassie pulled her hands free and put them on his forearms. He covered one of her hands with his palm, allowing himself at least that much.

"What did you say?" she asked in an anxious voice.

"I dodged answering him. Let him know it was none of his business. But Sunny's got a right to know, Cassie. And we're the only ones who can tell her."

"No! No, no, no! What gives her more rights than I have? I've suffered through this for nineteen years, Duckie! I'm begging you. If you have any feelings left at all for me, for the friendship we once had, please don't let all of this come out again."

"It's not me that's digging into it," he said with a tired sigh. "And if I recollect right, bulldog persistence is a trait you and Sammie both had, so you can bet your niece has it too. Remember that time you were bound and determined you were gonna catch that old carp that lived in the swimming hole? You fished every day for two weeks. You even learned to put your own worms on the hook, after I wouldn't do it for you any longer."

"I caught him too, didn't I?" Cassie's face creased with a smile, making her look more like the younger Cassie he had known. "But I put him back. *You* thought we should eat him!"

"The swimming hole is still there. I was out there a couple of days ago. It was awful lonesome there by myself, though. It's been awful lonesome for a great many years now."

Cassie faced him rebelliously. "I don't care how many times you bring up the past, you're not going to talk me into it. It's past, and we can't change what happened. I guess I can't stop you from doing whatever you want to, but if you do I'll be forced to leave town. And I have nowhere else to go. Please don't do that to me, Duckie."

Charlie stood. Jamming his hands into his pants pockets, he strolled over to the parlor window. He knew she was stubborn. Hell, he probably knew her better than she knew herself. She wasn't easy to manipulate, but he'd done some developing himself over the years. And his father had always said the best way to handle the stubborn mares without breaking their spirit was to let them think that whatever you wanted them to do was their own idea all along.

"All right, I'll keep quiet for now," he agreed as he turned back to her. "But you need to quit blaming yourself, Cassie. You need to stop hiding in this house and start holding your head up again. Haven't you punished yourself enough for something you didn't have any control over?"

Cassie chewed her bottom lip in a remarkably girlish manner. He remembered her doing that whenever she was trying to decide if she wanted to go along with some suggestion he and Sammie had made for the day or force them to submit to her own idea for fun. Nine times out of ten, Cassie's plan had won out.

She was even the one who came up with what needed to be done nineteen years ago, he reminded himself. Sammie and he had both leaned on her, neither of them realizing how shattered her own emotions must have been. He'd seen that only later, during that first visit home from St. Louis.

Cassie rose, scanning Charlie's clothing as though noticing it for the first time. She glanced down at her own plain black gown, a frown furrowing her forehead.

"I never did look good in black. Sammie could wear it, but she didn't much care for it. Her blond hair was set off by it, though, while mine used to have more brown in it. Black washed it out even further."

"Your hair used to sparkle with gold in the sunlight," Charlie told her. "But I like that pretty color you have now, too."

"It's gray," Cassie sneered. "Seems like it turned gray overnight. Mama grayed early on, too."

"It's a nice soft white, like your mama's was," Charlie said. "You remember what I told you I once heard my dad say to my mother one winter night when I snuck out of bed? Just because there's snow on the roof . . ."

". . . doesn't mean there isn't a fire in the furnace," Cassie finished, then clapped a hand over her mouth and giggled. Dropping her arm, she released a deep sigh. "But there's too many cinders in the furnace now. It's too late to do anything about them."

Charlie's hopefulness faded as Cassie took a step toward the parlor door. "It was nice seeing you again, Duckie. And thank you for agreeing to keep quiet about everything. You'll soon realize it's the only way to handle this."

"Maybe I've changed my mind," Charlie said truculently.

Cassie gasped, and her eyes widened as she whirled to face him again. "You promised!"

"Yeah, well, maybe I lied." He jammed his hands into his pockets to keep from reaching for her. He wanted to assure her that he would never do anything to hurt her. But sometimes, his father used to say, you had to hurt a person for the person's own good. "Maybe I'm tired of letting you push me around and always have your own way. Maybe I should have done something about that nineteen years ago."

"I did what I thought was best for us! All of us, you and Sammie included."

"What *you* thought was best," Charlie repeated, the emphasis he gave the words at odds with her own meaning. "Now, I'm gonna do what *I* think is best."

"And what would that be?" Cassie asked cautiously.

"I find I'm all dressed up with nowhere to go," Charlie mused. "And just down the street is a nice town social. I find I'm wanting to go to that social, but I don't wanna wander around all alone."

"You know everyone at that social."

"Well, I guess then it's more important to me who's not at that social. And I intend to see that she is there. Go change your dress, Cassie, sweetheart. Put on something blue, like your eyes."

Cassie glared at him. "I . . . you can't force me to go with you!"

"Don't bet on it," Charlie said sternly. "And there's something else I expect you to do for me, if you want me to keep quiet."

"Are you trying to blackmail me, Charlie Duckworth?"

"If I am, what are you gonna do about it? Have me arrested, so I can let Jake force me into telling him what hold I have over you? Why, Jake might even bring me to trial if I plead not guilty. Then the whole town would be there to listen when I broke down and admitted what I was guilty of."

"You wouldn't!"

"Don't bet on it," Charlie repeated.

"You've changed, Duckie," Cassie said, shaking her head.

"No . . . well, yes, maybe I have," he admitted. "Or maybe you're just seeing the real me. Charlie instead of Duckie."

Cassie's shoulders slumped in defeat. "What do you want me to do?"

Charlie took his hands out of his pocket and crossed his arms over his chest. When Cassie glanced at him again, he could have sworn he saw a little respect in her eyes. He cupped his chin in his palm, stroking a finger on his clean cheek.

"Seems like I've got a house that needs a woman's touch. My mother took most of the stuff with her to Dallas, and I ain't got around to fixing things up again. There's a few things up in the attic at the homestead, but I wouldn't know what would fit. Or reckon I could just order new stuff through some of them catalogs over at Fred's store, if I got someone to give me advice on what would look nice."

"You've been living out there in an unfurnished house ever since your mother moved to Dallas four years ago?" Cassie asked in astonishment. "You should be ashamed of yourself."

"No more ashamed than you should be for spending almost all your time inside these walls, even if they do have somewhere to set or lay down in them."

"I'll help you pick out some furniture, Duck . . . Charlie," Cassie said.

"Well, I figure I'm gonna need some little doodads to put around here and there, too," Charlie mused. "Things like what might be on sale at that social. Things some of the women in town might've made up for people to decorate their homes with. I find myself wanting my old place to be a home again, not just a house."

Digging in his inside coat pocket, he walked over to the settee and sat. "I'll just wait here and have a smoke while you change, Cassie. Bring me an ashtray, would you? Unless you want me to flip the ashes in the fireplace."

"You'd end up dropping them on my rug!" Cassie fumed.

He raised an eyebrow at her, and she stomped over to a lamp table beside the window. Picking up a cut-glass bowl, she came back and shoved it at him. "I don't have any ashtrays. And when did you start smoking? I don't like the smell of those things."

"Well, now." Charlie took the bowl and set it on the end table. "Reckon if I had someone it was important enough to, I might give up my smokes." He concentrated on rolling the tobacco inside the paper as he went on. "But it would have to be somebody pretty danged important. Not just anybody can make a man give up something as serious as his smokes."

Charlie knew she was inwardly smoldering when she propped her fists on hips that were not much fuller than they had been nineteen years ago. Lifting his leg, he laid his boot on his knees and struck a matchstick on the sole. He lit up, drew in the smoke, and let it out—directly into her face. She coughed and backed away, turning toward the door.

"Don't forget," he called after her. "I like you best in blue. Blue's a serious, important color in my mind."

She shot him a venomous look, reminiscent of his young Cassie when he had—rarely—managed to thwart her, and stormed from the room. When she came back ten minutes later, she wore a summer-sky blue gown, but it didn't quite match the summer-storm color of her eyes.

"Does this suit your majesty?" she snarled.

He nodded his head and rose. "It suits me fine. And you, too," he said softly. "Just fine. And I've sorta grown used to you calling me Duckie for the past forty years. Don't much care for 'your majesty.' "

She sniffed, tilting her nose up. "I feel every one of those forty years and then some, especially recently. I've had a nosy niece move into my house, asking questions she has no right to ask. Within a day of that, she brought a noisy little child to stay here and ruined my peace and quiet. Now you come back into my life, ordering me around with threats of blackmail. Don't think that just because I knuckled under to you, I'll forget what you've done."

"Ah, Cassie, sweetheart." Charlie moved over to her and tucked her hand in his arm. "I'm going to make sure you don't forget me. Not for the *next* forty years."

With a wink, he placed his hat on his head and led her from the parlor.

SUNNY WIPED HER sweaty brow with the back of her hand. Shoot, she wasn't even sure which one of the ladies on the fundraising committee had left the note for her at the house about needing "desert mushrooms" for some sort of contest at the social. Whoever it was evidently realized how hot this trek would be and sloughed the job off on her. She'd been directed to the field behind the church and informed to make sure she found the driest and flattest mushrooms available.

Heck, everything out here was dry—seared by the hot Texas sun and the lack of rain. The little grass that there was crackled beneath her shoes, and the baked rocks reflected even more heat into the air. She'd only seen cactus in books up until today, but plenty of the ones she recognized as the low-growing prickly pear flourished in this area, ready to snag an unwary dress hem with their harmless-appearing but far-from-innocuous clumps of feathery prickles.

She rubbed the side of her arm, which had brushed up against some of those prickles when she bent to drive her small spade under a flat, brownish mushroom and drop it in her bucket. She thought she'd managed to get all the tiny barbs out by pulling them with her fingernails, but the area was still reddened and swollen.

Lordy, lordy, it was hot. Her chip straw bonnet shaded her face somewhat, but not enough to keep her nose from feeling warm and on the verge of sunburn. She should have brought a parasol.

She hadn't even realized how much she missed real trees until she found herself longing for a little shade. The only thing even close to a tree out here was the scrubby brush she'd learned was called mesquite. One of the men had been cutting that a while ago, saying something about using it to flavor the steer that Mary's foreman, Chuck, had brought in yesterday. The steer was cooking over a pit back beside the church, and the man had left long ago, dragging his cache of wood behind him.

That darned mesquite had thorns, too, she recalled. Long, sharp thorns, one of which had pierced the man's heavy gloves. She felt sure his response to the pain would have featured even more colorful language had he not looked up to see her watching him, her attention drawn by his first yelp.

"Miss Sunny, over here's one!" Teddy called.

Picking up her tin bucket, Sunny trudged in the little girl's direction. Her back ached from bending over, and a hot knot flared between her shoulder blades. This mushroom would fill her bucket, and if that weren't enough for whatever crazy contest the note writer had in mind, that person could gather more herself!

Just as she reached Teddy, the little girl's eyes widened in horror and she froze in place. Sunny immediately identified the sound reaching her ears, and her heart pounded in terror. Eyes searching the rocks around Teddy, she saw the wavering tail of the rattlesnake—a huge tail, covered with a dozen layers of vibrating scales. The sound escalated when she gasped and dropped her bucket.

"Teddy!" she whispered harshly. "Don't move!"

Teddy's eyes rolled sideways at her, but she obeyed. The terror she saw on Teddy's face matched her own dread. Oh, God! Where was Rowdy? If the dog should try to protect Teddy . . .

She cautiously turned her head but didn't see the small brown and white dog. Maybe if they stood still enough, the snake would slither away. Her own knees threatened to buckle, though, and she didn't know how long Teddy could face the snake without breaking and running. If she did, she didn't have a chance of escaping the snake's strike.

She tensed her body, prepared to lunge forward and fling herself between Teddy and the snake if necessary.

The snake's triangular head came into view, mouth slightly open to show deadly white fangs and a black forked tongue flickering in and out. Sunny began to pray.

A loud explosion sounded, and the snake's head disappeared in a gory flash. Sunny leapt for Teddy, catching her in her arms and dragging her several feet away. Sobbing, Teddy buried her face in Sunny's skirts and Sunny clutched her frantically. Scattering pebbles and small rocks, the snake's headless body writhed and tumbled. It was at least six feet long and as big around as Sunny's upper arm.

The scream that had been caught in her throat finally

broke free and shattered the air. Jerking Teddy into her arms, she stumbled backward, carrying the child with her.

"Easy, Sunny."

She hit the solid wall of Jake's chest and his soothing voice cut through her terror. Turning and shoving Teddy into his arms, she clung to both of them, her body shaking with receding panic as Jake gathered them close.

"Thank God," she murmured. "Thank God. How did you know?"

She felt him lay his cheek against the top of her head. "I was looking for you," he said. "I spotted Rowdy and headed this way. The dog suddenly froze and started growling low in his throat, or I would have just kept right on walking and pushed that snake into striking when I appeared."

"That wonderful, wonderful dog," Sunny said.

Teddy wiggled between them. "I want to see Rowdy. Where is he?"

Sunny stepped back, but Jake kept a firm arm around her waist, drawing her to his side while he held Teddy in his other arm. Teddy shifted around, and they saw Rowdy crouched close to the snake's still trembling body, growling low and viciously, his ears flat against his head.

"Rowdy," Teddy called around a sob. "Rowdy, come here."

The little dog looked at her, then back at the snake. His lips drew back in another snarl, baring his white teeth. It reminded Sunny way too much of the vicious fangs that had been so close to Teddy only a moment ago, and she tossed Jake a pleading look.

"The snake can't harm him," Jake assured her. "The bullet smashed its head."

"I know, Ranger Jake," Teddy said. "But I need to tell Rowdy how thankful we are. And I ain't gonna go near that snake to do that."

"I understand." Jake raised his voice. "Rowdy! Here, Rowdy. Come!"

The little dog whined once deep in his throat, then scrambled to his feet and bounced over to them, tail wagging and tongue hanging out. Jake let Teddy down and she knelt at their feet, grabbing Rowdy in a fierce hug and burying her face in the ruff of fur on the brown and white neck.

"You's a wonderful dog, Rowdy," she said. "Just the bestest dog in the whole world."

Sunny bent down to pat the dog's head, receiving a slurpy tongue in her face in return for her own thanks. She cupped Rowdy's face and stared into his deep brown eyes.

"Teddy's right, Rowdy. You are the bestest dog I've ever known. And you're going to have your very own plate of food at the picnic this afternoon."

Teddy raised her head and giggled. With the resilience of a child, she was already recovering from her fright. "You gonna let him eat off one of our good plates, too, Miss Sunny?" she asked.

Sunny returned her smile and said, "I'd like it a lot if you'd start just calling me Sunny from now on, darling. And Rowdy can eat off whatever he wants and have as much as he wants. Until his tummy is so full we have to carry him home."

"Me, too, Sunny?" Teddy asked with a shrewd grin. "I seen lots of goodies on the dessert table. Can I just eat off that table?"

"You, young lady," Sunny admonished, waving her index finger, "can . . ." Her voice faltered and tears misted her eyes. She grabbed Teddy in another tight hug. "You are so precious to me, Teddy. Have I told you today how much I love you?"

Teddy patted her on the back. "Nope, not today. And I'm

all right, Sunny. You don't have to cry. Thanks to Rowdy and Ranger Jake, we's both all right now. But I love you back just as much, too."

Sunny sniffed and rose to her feet. "Promise me you'll never come out here alone, Teddy. I shouldn't have brought you with me today. I wouldn't have done it if I'd had any idea how dangerous it was."

"I promise, Sunny. Now, can I go on back to the social? Suzie oughta be there by now, and her and me thought up a way at church last Sunday to make some money for your Cu . . . Cultural Center. We're gonna charge the town kids who don't have ponies of their own a penny apiece to ride Suzie's pony."

"That's a very good idea, Teddy. But we'll all go back together," she said firmly. "I don't want you walking through these rocks alone."

"All right. I'll get the bucket of cow patties."

She raced over to the bucket and picked it up, then started skipping back toward the church in the distance. When Jake proffered his arm, Sunny gratefully accepted it, and they strolled after Teddy and Rowdy.

"I don't know what to say," she said, gazing into the whiskey eyes beneath the shadowing hat brim. "If you hadn't come . . . that shot . . . you saved Teddy's life. That snake was large enough to have enough venom to kill Teddy."

"It looked to me like you were the one who probably would have been bit," Jake answered. "You were ready to fling yourself between Teddy and the snake. And I've never been so damned glad in my life that I'm a good shot."

Looking ahead to assure herself Teddy hadn't gotten too far away, Sunny squeezed his arm. "Well, 'thank you' seems pretty tame for what I really want to say, but it's all I can think of right now. Thank you, Jake. Thank you so much for being there."

"I'd like to always be," she thought she heard him murmur, but when she glanced back at his face, he nodded toward Teddy.

"What the neck were the two of you doing out here digging up cow patties? They planning on having a chip-throwing contest as part of the social? And if they are, why the hell didn't one of the men come out here and get them for you? You and Teddy had no business out here alone."

"Cow patties?" Sunny's voice rose in shock. "Teddy called them that a minute ago too. But the note said they were mushrooms—desert mushrooms. Teddy didn't tell me any different when I told her what we were after."

"Mushrooms don't grow out here," Jake said. "They need wet, shady ground. Although I've seen a few toadstools manage to get an inch or so tall in a fresh pile of manure after a spring rain. Still, they had no business sending a woman out to gather that stuff."

Sunny pulled him to a halt. They were close enough to the church now to hear the sounds of revelry, and when Teddy peered back at them, she waved for the little girl to go on. Teddy and Rowdy took off at a galloping run.

Sunny pressed her lips together. Even before she asked, she knew she wasn't going to like the answer. "Tell me what cow patties are," she said grimly.

Jake slipped his thumbs in his gunbelt and cocked his head. "You really don't know?"

She denied it with a shake of her head.

"Well, they're cow sh . . . uh . . . manure. Or horse manure, like you were griping about being in the streets in town. It dries out in the sun and the cowboys even use it for fire fodder sometimes, because it burns pretty well. Up in the prairie states northeast of us, the sodbusters used to burn buffalo droppings back when the herds were huge."

"I've never seen anything like what I've been shoveling up out here in the Liberty Flats streets!"

"Gets trampled too fast," Jake said with a shrug. "Other horses going by, wagons running over it. It doesn't last long enough in the streets to dry out."

"Ohhhh!" Sunny untied the chin ribbons on her chip straw bonnet, dragged it off and used it to fan her flushed face. "Someone obviously set out to embarrass me! I can just imagine how the whole town would have been laughing at me if I'd carried that bucket of cow . . . cow . . . cow *stuff* into the middle of everyone and told them 'here's your mushrooms!' "

Jake choked on something and she peered at him. His jaws were clenched, and he appeared to be staring at the sky, though she had no idea how he could see up with that hat brim in the way. A funny snort escaped his nose, and her own jaws grew rigid at what she suspected was his suppressed laughter.

"Jake," she warned.

He lost it. His shoulders convulsed and a deep belly laugh roared into the air. He threw back his head, then bent forward clutching his stomach, all the while guffawing as though someone was tickling the devil out of him. Tapping her foot faster and faster, she fumed as she watched him. If she had that bucket of cow patties, she'd toss one in his face right now!

Looking for a stick or something else to beat that darn devil straight out of him, she glared at the ground. When he stood upright for an instant and wiped his eyes, she saw a smear of moisture on his cheeks and realized he was wiping away tears of laughter. When he saw her watching him, his chest shook with another chuckle, then his laughter roared free again.

Dropping her hat, she raised her fists at him. Holding out his hands defensively, he shook his head and backed away, his laughter continuing unsuppressed.

She grabbed her hat. Flinging herself at him, she battered him about the head and shoulders with the chip straw bonnet. "Quit it!" she raged. "Quit it right this minute or I'll stuff this hat down your throat to shut you up!"

Continuing to chortle, Jake raised his arm protectively and she beat on them with her bonnet. Suddenly comprehending how ineffectual her blows were, she stilled and glared at him.

The corner of her mouth flickered in a tiny tick. She thinned her lips to a firm line. A bubble burst in her chest. She crossed her arms over it. Jake tipped his hat brim up with a finger and glanced at her. She flounced around to turn her back on him, but a snort of laughter avoided her clamped teeth. Slipping a look over her shoulder, she met his mirth-filled whiskey eyes and collapsed into most unladylike snorts and guffaws of her own.

Straightening, she wiped her eyes and peered over her shoulder. His gleaming whiskey eyes met hers and he raised a raven brow. "Desert mushrooms?" he teased.

Her giggle bubbled forth again. Skirts flying, she swiveled around, beating him once more with her bonnet. "That's what . . . the note said . . . they were!" she gasped around her laughter.

He grabbed her bonnet, holding it out of her reach over his head. "Cow patties," he said with a grin.

"Give me back my bonnet," she demanded. She jumped for it but missed and landed with a wobble. Grabbing his brawny forearms for support, she stared into his face.

"Don't you dare tell anyone," she ordered, realizing her

mistake at once when an assessing look shadowed his whiskey eyes.

"Well, now," he drawled, "what's it worth to you for me to do that? I figure I ought to get something back in return for doing something as important as keeping my mouth shut. And don't forget. I killed that snake for you."

16

SUNNY JERKED HER hands off his arms as though she'd just touched the hot Texas sun overhead. Her shoe heel slid on a smooth stone, and Jake grabbed her waist to steady her.

"Easy, Sunny," he murmured.

"You sound like you're talking to your horse when you say that to me," she grumbled. But she made no move to pull away from him.

Jake chuckled under his breath. "You're a heck of a lot prettier than my horse."

When she opened her mouth to admonish him, he broke in, "I can say that to you even as a friend, can't I? I'm just being honest—telling you as one friend to another. You're not one of those fluttery females who simpers and pouts, pushing for compliments from a man. You know darned well you're pretty—beautiful even."

Contemplating his words, she stuck her bottom lip out in a pout. His gaze immediately dropped to her mouth and a grin appeared the corner of his mouth.

"Well, maybe you pout, but it sure doesn't look like a prissy pout to me," he said. "Looks more like a kissing pout."

Becoming aware of tiny spasms on her rib cage, she realized his thumbs were slowly stroking, moving back and forth, while his fingers imperceptibly tightened their hold. Such insignificant movements for the response her skin was giving. Skitters of pleasure crawled upward, even past the point where his long thumbs missed the undersides of her breasts by a good inch. Her breasts grew heavy in response, tips puckering against her bodice as though chilled, despite the blazing heat of the day.

How on earth did he do that to her? She needed to tell him to stop, but that would only call his attention to her reaction. She swallowed against the dryness in her mouth and tried to form a suitable reply to whatever it was he'd said. What on earth *had* he said? Something about a kiss.

"I . . ." She cleared her throat, which felt like a clump of those feathery cactus prickles had lodged in it. "Is that what you want in return for keeping quiet about the desert mushrooms?" she managed when she finally recalled the focus of their discussion. "Just a . . . a kiss? A *friendly* kiss?"

He tilted his head and bent down a fraction of an inch, way too little of a distance to account for the strain she felt growing between their lips. Her toes curled, resisting the urge to push her upward and close the distance between them.

"I guess I'd consider a kiss proper compensation," he said, lowering his head a fraction more. "Just between friends, you know."

She lifted her arms, settling them around his neck. The backs of her fingers brushed the silky strands of black hair, which were damp with sweat from the hot day, and one index finger sort of coiled all on its own, winding a spiral around it. Her toes uncurled to support her when she stretched up to meet him, her eyes closing with a dreamy sluggishness.

Jake dropped his head, pecked her briefly on the mouth,

and then released his hold on her waist. He stepped back and her arms fell nervelessly from his neck as her eyes flew open in shock. Traitorously, her lips remained pursed and slightly open, yearning for the fulfillment her mind had promised them.

Blazing anger filled her, way hotter than the Texas day, and she clamped her jaw closed to trap the nasty retort flashing through her mind. A friendly kiss, he'd said. And that was darned sure all he'd given her! She didn't have a reason on earth to scream at him for depriving her of what she had expected—something more along the lines of the other kisses they had shared—the other kisses that had happened before their mutual vow of friendship. Still, she clenched her teeth even harder, until her face muscles ached with the strain.

Jake reached up and raised his hat, running his other hand through his hair, then settling the hat back into place with a tug on the brim. Stunned into senseless stupidity, she could only watch his movements, her mouth gaping like a fish tossed onto a riverbank.

"We better get on back to the social," he said. "Ready?"

"No . . . no!" she sputtered. Closing her eyes to shut out the smirk on his face, she took a deep breath. She'd be damned if she'd let him get the better of her! Somehow, with an exhaustive effort, she forced her mouth into a *friendly* smile.

"I mean, yes, of course I am," she said, opening her eyes and composing her face into what she considered a serene facade. She scanned the ground and spied her bonnet several feet away. Her cheeks flushed when she recalled sailing it away with a flick of her wrist just before she reached for Jake's neck. She took a wobbly step, paused, and mentally told her unsteady legs just what she'd do to them if they betrayed her; then she swept over to the bonnet.

Calmly retrieving it from the ground, she put it on and tied the chin ribbons, getting her finger caught in the bow only once. "Coming?" she called in a sticky sweet voice as she strolled toward the church.

It was a second or two before she heard his footsteps behind her, and she started making innocent conversation the moment he came up beside her.

"I do believe everyone for miles around has come to support the social. Just look at all the people. And even the children are doing their part. Did you hear Teddy say she and Suzie were going to charge for rides on Suzie's pony?"

"Don't know why I wouldn't have heard her. I was standing right there."

"But isn't that sweet of them?"

"Yeah, sweet."

The curt tone of his voice made her look at him. He was walking with his elbows cocked behind him, fingers stuck in his back pockets. As had most of the other men in town, he had dressed up somewhat for the social, though he still wore his ever-present brace of pistols. Instead of his usual denims, he wore dark brown trousers, and his tan shirt was pulled taut against his chest by the angle of his arms.

His brown string tie hung loose, and she stopped short as soon as she spotted the fluttering ends.

"Jake, you need to knot your tie. Heavens, it's entirely improper for you to go around with it loose like that. Here, let me fix it for you."

She was extremely proud of herself when she stepped up to him and quickly knotted the tie into place. Catching her tongue between her teeth with the tip of it barely peeking between her lips, she studied her creation. She gave the bow a satisfied little pat, then turned and strolled on. They were at the edge of the activities now, and she gazed around, trying to decide which one interested her the most.

"I think I'll go check on the food preparations," she decided aloud. "Maybe I can snitch a little bite. The smell of that roasting steer is delightful, but it's making my stomach rumble. Is it the mesquite wood that's making it smell so good?"

"Probably."

"Jake, do cheer up, won't you? We worked hard to plan this social, and I want everyone to have a nice time today. You seemed in such a good mood a few minutes ago, and I can't imagine what's given you the grumps. But you go on and find something fun to do." She peered up at him and tapped his arm with her fingertips. "Go on now. And try to have fun."

Jake nodded. "Fun. Yeah, I'll go have some fun."

He sauntered away with his usual catlike stride, and she watched him go. In deference to the ladies in the crowd, some of the men wore proper suit jackets despite the horrible heat, but she didn't condemn Jake for not wearing his. Just then she noticed his trousers were pulled as tightly across his backside as those darned denims of his.

Wrenching her eyes away from the scandalous sight, she rushed toward the smell of the cooking meat. A table she swore hadn't been there just a minute ago jumped in front of her, the edge catching her in the stomach. Sunny splatted right on top of a bowl of potato salad. When she gasped and pushed herself upright, her hands squished a bowl of pickled beets on one side and a tray of deviled eggs on the other.

Moaning in dismay, she shook her hands, scattering bits of beets and gushy egg centers. Using the back of her hand to keep from smearing beet stain on her dress, she whisked at her bodice but succeeded only in rubbing the potato salad deeper into the material.

Ruth hurried to her side. "Sunny, dear. Oh, my, what happened?"

"What the heck is someone doing with potato salad sitting out here already?" Sunny snapped. "Don't they know it will spoil?"

"Dear, it's German potato salad. It's supposed to be kept warm. Here, come over to the pump beside the church. Let's get you cleaned up."

Ruth grabbed a hand towel from the offending table, and Sunny followed her to the pump. Ruth wet the towel, then wrung it out. She motioned for Sunny to hold her hands under the spigot and pumped the handle with one hand while brushing at Sunny's bodice with the towel in her other hand. All Sunny's recently acquired pleasure at her composure in Jake's presence washed away with the gobs of egg centers and dropped to the ground to lie scattered in the midst of potato pieces.

JAKE STROLLED OVER to a table sitting in the shade of a piece of canvas that stretched overhead. Fun. Yep, he'd go have some fun, but it sure wouldn't be the type of fun he wanted to have. That type of fun involved privacy, silk sheets, and a featherbed, not a crowd of people and gangs of children racing around. The heat fit in with his idea, although he'd much rather generate that himself.

A small boy around four crashed into his leg, and he bent to steady the little fellow. A woman, evidently the child's mother, rushed up to him.

"Oh, thank you," she gasped. "I wanted to enter him in the competition for the cutest in his age group, but he got away from me."

Jake peered down into the grubby face, and the little boy responded with an openmouthed smile, showing off the remnants of whatever he had recently been chewing, which still lingered in his cheeks. "Uh . . . well, good luck," he told the woman, willingly handing the child over to her firm grasp.

The mother led the child away, and he turned back to examine the wares laid out on the table. No one was tending the goods, and he indifferently picked up something and ran it through his fingers.

She hadn't even reacted to his mocking peck on her mouth. It had taken every bit of control he could muster to keep that kiss *friendly*, especially when what he really wanted to do was carry her off somewhere and examine every inch of her satiny skin to assure himself it was still as perfect as he recalled. He'd never been as scared in his life as when he saw Sunny and Teddy facing that damned rattler. He had even stared down the barrel of a gun aimed at his chest and raced through a barrage of cannon fire on a battlefield with less terror than he'd felt today.

"Why, Ranger Cameron," a voice simpered, "are you looking for a pretty hanky for a lady friend?"

Jake glanced up into Evaline's face, then finally became aware of exactly what it was spread on the table. Pieces of snow-white lace were scattered about, as well as neatly folded embroidered ladies' handkerchiefs and ribbons in a multitude of colors and widths. Evaline had donated some things from her dress shop for the fundraiser, among them the piece of delicate frothiness that he now held between his fingers. At least two inches of lace surrounded the silk square, which was embroidered with blue roses that held the lace in place.

"It's for Teddy," he quickly said. "For her birthday."

"Oh, and when is her birthday?" Evaline asked.

"I'm . . . uh . . . not sure, but I'm sure she'll have one someday."

"Well, that hanky is a little bit much for a child. Wouldn't you rather look at something else?"

"No," Jake said firmly. "I'll take this one."

Evaline nodded and told him the price. He dug a coin out of his pocket, handed it to her, and stuffed the hanky into his back pocket.

"Oh, Ranger Cameron, why don't you let me hold on to that for you? You're getting it all wrinkled."

Jake waved a negligent hand at her and sauntered on. Fun. He was supposed to have some fun. She had tapped him right there on the spot on his arm—those dainty, slender fingers dancing against his skin—and told him go to have fun. Just what you'd tell a friend to do. She'd patted that bow on his tie, with the tip of her tongue peeping through those strawberry lips to tantalize him, making him think of plenty of other things she could use that tongue and lips for. Then she'd walked away, unconcerned and unaware that he was following her on wooden legs.

Hell, yes, she was unconcerned and unaware. He'd made damned sure she couldn't see the effect on him—at least as long as she didn't look below his belt! And he'd managed to control himself for a bit, but then he'd had to remove his hat and hold it in front of his belt buckle. He'd definitely acted friendly, and now he was supposed to go have some *fun*, even though his subconscious clamored at him to find a private place and soothe his wounded ego over how badly his *friendly* kiss had backfired right in his face and shattered straight through to his senses.

He stopped and pushed his fingers into his back pockets, looking around to see which fun he should join. Over there someone was playing a fiddle, and a crowd was gathering to join the dancing. On past them, a gaggle of children pushed and jostled while they waited their turns on Suzie's pony. Teddy importantly led the pony around in a circle, while Suzie held a cigar box to collect the pennies.

On his left, Mary Lassiter stood behind another table of

sparkling jars of jams, jellies, pickles, and crusty loaves of bread. He chuckled a little when he looked over beside the roasting pit and saw another fire going, with a huge kettle of boiling water hanging over it. Half a dozen cowboys were husking baskets of corn and dropping the ears into the kettle. He'd have been willing to bet that would never have happened. It took some tall talking to get a cowboy involved in any work he couldn't do from the back of his horse.

'Course he knew one woman who could talk just about anyone into doing just about anything, and she wasn't even that tall. She could bat those bluebonnet eyes and curve those luscious lips, and a man would fall all over himself to do her bidding. Hadn't she organized an entire town into building a Cultural Center they didn't even realize they needed? And hadn't he obeyed her order to go have some fun?

He noticed his fingertips smoothing the silky handkerchief in his back pocket and pulled his hands free. His palms brushed his holsters, reminding him that he had obligations today other than having fun. He needed to make his presence known, to forestall any high-spirited revelry that might turn into rowdiness and get out of hand.

For the first time in his life, though, he resented his role as the peacekeeper, and not just because it tied him down in one place. Today, he admitted, he would be perfectly happy to join in with the families and leave the task of keeping order to someone else.

"Jake!"

Recognizing Ginny's voice, he turned to see her at yet another table. He strolled over and frowned at the contraption she had in front of her. It sure as heck looked like an ice cream churn, although he'd seen one of those only once before—up around Denver, where Charlie had his mine.

"If you want a bowl of ice cream when it's ready," Ginny

said with a smile, "you have to sign up here and pay your five cents. Then you have to take your turn cranking for at least ten minutes. You can also sign up for a bowl for a lady friend, if you want. How about it?"

"Sure," Jake said with a shrug. "Only guess I'll just sign up for me."

"Well, move over then," Charlie said from behind him. He nudged Jake aside and led Cassie up to the table. "I've got a lady friend here who I'm willing to be sure gets two bowls of ice cream for herself."

Jake's jaw fell as Cassie smiled at Charlie and dropped his arm. Charlie took off his suit jacket and handed it to her, then rolled up his sleeves. While Ginny wrote his name down, Charlie started cranking away, playing to the admiration on Cassie's face.

What the hell was happening to this town? Everyone in it seemed to be doing a complete about-face from what he had come to expect from them. Ginny McAllister now fit right in with the other ladies in town, even to the point that she had designated three of the tables in her saloon as what she termed her "ladies' corner," covering them with bright pink tablecloths and setting vases of flowers in the center. She'd even ordered some screens from a catalog at Fred's store, to divide off that corner of the room. As he watched, he noticed several of the passing ladies call greetings to Ginny and promise to bring their own men over to earn them a bowl of ice cream.

And here amid the boisterous crowd of people stood Cassie Foster, who he would have sworn would never give up her reclusive lifestyle. She looked twenty years younger, and the blue dress she wore made her look more slender than bony—as her dark clothing always did. With a look in her eyes that made Jake suspicious that she was eyeing

Charlie's bulging forearms, she watched Charlie cranking the ice-cream churn.

Cassie caught him looking at her, and her gaze slid to the star on his shirt pocket. If he hadn't known better, he would have thought it was a rather guilty look that crossed Cassie's face. He'd seen that look on a lot of men's faces when they first realized he was a Ranger and had sworn an oath to uphold the law, even at the risk of his own life. But Cassie Foster sure as hell didn't have anything to feel guilty about, unless it was her treatment of Sunny and Teddy. Did she?

He nodded at her and received a stiff jerk of her head in reply. She immediately focused once again on Charlie, but Jake noticed that she clenched her hands in front of her and began to worry her thumbs together.

Jake reached into his pocket and pulled out several coins. "Here," he said, flicking them onto the table. "I'll pay for a few bowls of ice cream for young'uns like Teddy, but since I'm on duty, I can't help you crank. Gotta keep my gun hand free."

Cassie's face went white and she stepped nearer to Charlie. Jake had little time to ponder this disturbing reaction, since at that moment he glanced up to see Sunny heading toward the table, a determined glint in her eye. Surely she wouldn't confront Charlie with her asinine questions right here in front of the entire town. Knowing her, though, he thought she would.

He cut her off before she could get close enough for Charlie to see her, sidestepping back in front of her when she attempted to swerve and avoid him.

"Hey," he said. "I've decided what sort of fun I want to have. Let's go over and watch the cow-chip-tossing contest."

"You go right ahead," she replied in a grim voice. "I've

had all I want to do with cow chips today. I want to talk to . . ."

"Oh, come on," he said, taking her arm in a firm grip and steering her away. "Whoever sent you that note will probably be watching to see if they pulled one over on the dumb city girl. You don't want to give them that satisfaction, do you?"

"Dumb city girl?" Sunny huffed indignantly, a flash of resentment in her bluebonnet eyes when she tilted her head back to peer at him from beneath her bonnet rim. "Why, this dumb city girl has created more activity and interest in this town than it's probably ever had since the first settler laid eyes on this piece of ground! I might even toss one of those chips myself!"

Jake chuckled, and she tilted her delicate nose a trifle higher.

"Well, I just might," she repeated. "Or maybe I would, if I'd brought some gloves. Uh . . . people don't really throw those things with their bare hands, do they?"

"Let's go see," Jake said with a muffled guffaw.

17

THE PARLOR WALL sconce sputtered, and Sunny jabbed her needle into the dress material, freeing her hand to rub her eyes. Glancing over at her aunt, she found her with her head bowed, asleep with her chin on her chest. The pretty white dress that Cassie was finishing up for Teddy spread over her black skirt.

She rose and quietly added some more kerosene to the glass sconce, relighting it before she crossed to the chair where Cassie sat. For a moment she stood pondering the change in the other woman since the fundraiser. Still recalcitrant and abrupt, Cassie had nevertheless offered to help with the new gowns for Teddy and Sunny to wear to the opening night of the Cultural Center. At her wits' end to make sure every detail was taken care of before tomorrow night, Sunny gratefully accepted her assistance.

Today when Sunny arrived home, Cassie had sewn the seams of Sunny's blue watered-silk gown in place, leaving Sunny with only the hem to complete. After she tucked Teddy into bed, she found Cassie in the parlor, working some embroidered pink roses into the neck of Teddy's gown. When she commented on how beautifully the gown had turned out and how pretty it would be on Teddy, Cassie shrugged and said, "She's living with us. We want her dressed appropriately, so she won't disgrace us."

Yesterday, Cassie had even insisted she needed Teddy to be at the house instead of spending her afternoon with Ruth at the store. When Teddy had seemed agreeable to the change in plans, Sunny had left her, returning to find them baking cookies in the kitchen. Dared she hope Cassie might be thawing toward the little girl? More to the point, would this change in her aunt hold firm or would she turn back into the prune-faced recluse Sunny had first met?

And just how much did Charlie Duckworth have to do with all this? She knew he'd been by the house yesterday, because Teddy had chattered away about his visit at dinner that evening. Awestruck, Teddy had raved about the beautiful horse Charlie had led with him. He'd insisted that Cassie change into riding clothing and take a short jaunt. Teddy had gotten to ride in front of Charlie on his horse, and she'd had a glorious time.

But Charlie Duckworth made sure he left before Sunny arrived home, although Teddy also imparted the important news that Charlie was taking Cassie to the opening-night gala.

Sunny nudged Cassie's shoulder, and her aunt woke with a start.

"Oh," she said, shaking her head, "I fell asleep. What time is it?"

"Almost midnight, Aunt," Sunny replied. She picked up the dress from Cassie's lap and shook it out, holding it up to examine. "It's gorgeous, Aunt. The roses are the exact touch it needed."

"Yes. Well, I'll press both the dresses tomorrow and hang them in your rooms. All you'll have to do when you get home is take your bath and get ready."

"What are you wearing, Aunt?" Sunny asked slyly. "I haven't seen your dress yet."

"It's nothing special," Cassie said. "I did look at the

Godey's catalog over at Ruth's the other day to see what the styles were now. I had a navy dress that I took a few tucks in and added some lace to. It will do fine. I refuse to wear one of those dress enhancers Ruth tried to talk me into buying."

"You mean a bustle? It's the latest, Aunt, and we do want to keep from disgracing ourselves, don't we?" Sunny teased. Instead of responding to the joshing tone of Sunny's voice, Cassie's face closed up, deepening the age lines on each side of her nose. She took the dress from Sunny.

"I believe my nap has refreshed me somewhat, and I'll have trouble falling asleep. The dress collar needs one more rose to complete it, so I'll finish that now. You need to get your own rest, or you'll be dead on your feet tomorrow night, so go on to bed. I'll lock the house up."

"All right, Aunt Cassie," Sunny murmured, fighting the urge to push Cassie into further conversation. Perhaps the slow and easy way would work better with her aunt. In any event, as soon as opening night was behind her, she would have lots more time to pursue her own goals. Who knew, she might even get a chance to corner Charlie Duckworth on opening night and make him realize with a few well-planned remarks that she knew he wasn't at all what he seemed to be.

Murmuring good night to Cassie, she left the parlor. In her bedroom, she quickly changed into her nightgown, then turned back the bedspread and the crisp sheets. The bed beckoned, but so did her nightly ritual of one hundred strokes to her hair. Sighing wearily, she took her seat at the dressing table and began pulling out the hairpins and laying them carefully in a glass dish, then picking up her silver-handled hairbrush. She counted to fifty strokes before she remembered that she'd left the watered-silk gown lying carelessly on the back of the settee. The least she could do was hang it, so Cassie would have fewer wrinkles to press out the next day.

She hurriedly finished the remaining fifty strokes, then put her brush down and stood. Her bare feet pattered soundlessly down the hallway. The sight in the parlor stopped her in her tracks before she entered the room.

Cassie stood with head bowed, her fingers brushing the embroidered roses on Teddy's gown. Tears streaked her cheeks, and the front of her gown shone with moisture. Sunny took a step toward her, but Cassie's tortured voice stopped her in midstride.

"Oh, Sammie," Cassie whispered harshly. "How could you? How could *he*? Oh, Charlie. I just can't understand it, Duckie. After all these years, I still can't understand it."

Sunny backed noiselessly away and returned to her room. Closing her door with a quiet click, she leaned against it. Sympathy for her aunt's obvious heartbreak stabbed her, though she couldn't keep from trying to interpret Cassie's words, given what she had already gleaned about the past.

Ruth had been clear that Charlie had had his eye set on Cassie, but Cassie rejected his suit in favor of another man's. Had Cassie then realized that she indeed loved Charlie—after Charlie's attention turned to her sister and they left town together? It made sense that way, but then things got murky. Taking into consideration the happenings of the last few days—Cassie's acceptance of Charlie's apparent courtship once again—had Charlie in turn realized he had left his own true love back in Liberty Flats? Left her mother to return there and worship Cassie from afar for all these years? Had Cassie decided to give their attraction another chance now that her sister had passed on?

She walked over to the mirror and studied her face. She didn't see even one quality in her features similar to what she'd noticed the few times she'd gotten close enough to

Charlie Duckworth to examine him. She looked like her mother—the same heart-shaped face and tumultuous blond hair, the slender nose, and lips she thought a tad too full for the fashion of the day.

Suddenly another pair of lips wavered in front of her gaze, and the hazy face took form in her mind. Those lips fit hers exactly so—except when he pursed them into a friendly kiss that would have been more appropriate as a peck on her cheek! Gritting her teeth at the vexation of the intruding thoughts, she flounced away from the mirror and crawled into bed. She closed her eyes tightly, willing sleep to come to her exhausted body.

A halo of light intruded, outlining the image of rugged features and ebony hair cascading in tempting silkiness. Her finger twitched, recalling, she supposed, twisting into the damp locks last week. Her eyes flew open, and she shifted onto her elbow, leaning over to blow out the lantern on the bedside table. It didn't help much, but at least the image behind her eyelids faded somewhat when she lay down on the pillow again.

Funny, though, she mused, how her dreams all took place in bright daylight, needing not one iota of artificial illumination for her to see every feature on that ruggedly handsome face.

Land sakes! Wasn't she ever going to fall asleep? She adjusted the pillow, then burrowed into it. But it wasn't until she fell deep into those whiskey eyes in her mind that darkness closed around her.

SUNNY CHEERFULLY ACCEPTED yet another dollar bill from a spiffed-up spurs'-a'jingling cowboy and directed him to hang his spurs with the others on the wall. Jake stood nearby, taking possession of any firearms the cowboys had forgotten to leave in their saddlebags. One or two grumbled about giving up their pistols, but Jake had only to mention that they could get a refund on their money if they didn't want to comply with the rules. No one wanted to miss the show tonight.

Already word had spread of the talents of Grace Adams, the opening-night singer, and a crowd had been waiting when the stagecoach pulled in that afternoon. The singer's stylish dress, golden hair, and attractive face had the men removing their hats in awe and each vowing to be first in line for tickets that evening.

Sunny had considered herself extremely lucky to get two rooms at the sole boardinghouse for Grace and her manager. Ginny had offered her suite of rooms for Grace, saying she would bunk in with one of her other employees and even move two of them into the same room so the manager could have a private room. But Sunny had learned that two of the boarders were leaving on the stage that same afternoon, and she offered the boardinghouse proprietress a little extra for the use of the rooms for the night.

During a break in the steady stream of entering customers, Sunny scanned the room. The wall sconces would be dimmed before the curtain at the end of the room was opened for the show, and the tables were already crowded with men and women. Vases of wildflowers sat in the middle of the white linen tablecloths, and Sunny giggled under her breath when she noticed the cowboys with their hands on top of the hats in their laps. None of them dared to prop an elbow on the snowy cloths.

Frilly curtains billowed at the open windows at the front of the building, yet the odors of the women's perfumes and men's bay rum mingled in the air. Pride filled Sunny, on her own behalf and for the women and men who had accomplished turning what had been a dingy room into this gleaming masterpiece, and a fit background for the women's gay finery.

Ginny sidled up to her, a frown on her face. "What's wrong?" Sunny asked. "Oh, please. Everything's been going so well."

"It's nothing to worry about," Ginny said, her mouth curling in scorn. "It's that Grace Adams. What a hoity-toity snoot she is!" Ginny lifted the back of her hand to her forehead and continued in a fake Southern drawl, "Why, Ah swan. Ah really must rest myself before the performance. Y'all won't mind if Ah partake of the opportunity to use that li'l old couch in your office, will you, Ginny, dear? It seems Ah have arrived a tiny bit early. And would you mind askin' that dahling Teddy child to bring me a glass of somethin' cool? To soothe mah delicate throat, doncha know?"

Sunny snickered, then gave Ginny a chastising look. "Some performers are quite the prima donnas, Ginny. We were extremely lucky to get Grace Adams. Why, it's almost unheard of for a performer of her stature to have a propitious break in her schedule and be able to perform in a town as small as Liberty Flats."

"Well, she sent that manager of hers over earlier, demanding to know who had been assigned to assist her in dressing! I had to send Marg back with him, and I really needed her to help serve drinks. This whole town's been bursting at the seams since this morning. I haven't had a day like this since I took over the saloon. I've even had to turn customers away and tell them maybe Saul has room for them!"

"Oh, dear," Sunny said with a chuckle. "I'll bet those were hard words for you to get out."

"Bet your bustle," Ginny said with a wink. "Why, Ah swan," she continued in a lower voice. "Looka who's a comin' in the door. I better get out of here before she sees who you're talking to."

Sunny glanced up to see her aunt and Charlie Duckworth almost at the reception desk. She grabbed Ginny's arm before she could leave. "You stay right here, Ginny McAllister," she said in an undertone.

"Aunt Cassie," she greeted. "And Mr. Duckworth, isn't it? Why, Aunt, you look so pretty tonight."

Charlie gave Cassie a fond look. "Doesn't she, though? Blue's always been Cassie's color." He looked at Sunny, staring at her for a long, silent moment. "I haven't had a chance to tell you how sorry I am about what happened to your mother, Miss Fannin. Please accept my deepest condolences."

"Thank you," Sunny replied. She didn't want to like this man—did she? He had such a nice twinkle when he looked at Cassie, though, and anyone who could bring a faint blush to her crotchety aunt's cheeks must have some redeeming quality. Still, she had pretty much made up her mind about him, and here among all these people wasn't the place to confront him.

"I was wondering," she said, "if we might talk sometime about my mother. I understand you and she were very close . . . uh . . . friends."

"We were," Charlie agreed without any hint of evasiveness that Sunny could detect, although she noticed Cassie's fingers tighten on Charlie's arm. "Just let me know when you have time to talk, Miss Fannin."

"Please call me Sunny," she told him, and he nodded his accord. "Oh, forgive my lack of manners." She turned to Ginny who had been trying without success to work her arm free of Sunny's hold. "Ginny McAllister, do you know my aunt, Cassie Foster? And Mr. Duckworth?"

"Um . . . yes. Good evening, Miss Foster," Ginny murmured. "And Charlie."

Cassie smiled at Ginny, and Ginny's brows arched in

surprise. "Teddy speaks highly of you, Miss McAllister," Cassie said. "And I understand the town owes you a lot for your contributions to this beautiful Cultural Center."

"Ah . . . thank you," Ginny replied. "Um . . . Teddy brought over some of the cookies you and she baked and they're delicious. I'd love to have your recipe. She's been preening all afternoon in the beautiful dress you made for her."

"I'll write the cookie recipe down for you," Cassie said. "Now, we'd better find a seat, don't you think, Duckie?"

"We have place cards for you and Duck . . . uh . . . Mr. Duckworth at the large table we've reserved for our committee members, Aunt," Sunny explained. "We hoped you'd join us."

Cassie inclined her head regally as Charlie pulled something out of his coat pocket and handed it to Sunny. "I've overlooked making a contribution to the center, Sunny. This draft is on my bank in Dallas. Please use it however you see fit."

He led Cassie away, and Sunny handed the bank draft to Ginny to put with the other funds she handled for the center. When Ginny gasped, she turned from watching Cassie and Charlie make their way through the crowded room. Ginny's wide green eyes sparkled, and she fanned the bank draft in front of her face.

"Oh, my! He gave us two thousand dollars!" Ginny exclaimed. "That's way over twice what we've spent already on this place! I thought those rumors of him rolling in dough were just that. Rumors!"

"Let me . . ."

Jake nudged Ginny aside, turning her toward the connecting door to her saloon. "Put that damned draft in your strongbox, Ginny," he ordered. "When the hell are you two going to get this show started? Those cowboys are getting restless, and some of them have been sitting at either Saul's or Ginny's all afternoon getting half drunk. You're fixing to have a riot on your hands if you don't get things rolling."

"Why, Jake," Ginny said, running a finger down his cheek. "We surely don't have a thing to worry about with you keeping order. Liberty Flats is safe and sound with Ranger Cameron on patrol."

Jake bent his head and whispered something in Ginny's ear, and her delighted laughter trilled out. Sunny clenched her fists until her nails dug into her palms to keep from slapping Ginny's hand away from Jake's face. When she clamped her teeth together, she caught the edge of her tongue between them and stifled a gasp of pain.

Dang it! She'd been standing within six feet of Jake for the past hour and hadn't had one clumsy mishap! Hurriedly blinking away the tears caused by her smarting tongue, she reached for the money box in front of her, taking care not to spill it as she handed it to Ginny.

"Put this away, too," she said, trying desperately not to notice how close Ginny stood to Jake. Shoot, it would be hard to get a feather between them! "I think everyone who's coming is already here."

A rhythmic clapping started on the far side of the room. "Uh-oh," Jake said as the clapping spread, and here and there boots stomped in time to it. "Get your damned prima donna singer on that stage quick!"

Sunny gazed around inanely as Ginny rushed away, and Jake flashed her an annoyed look. "Look, you've got to give these people a show right now! You've built this up for weeks. Now follow through on it."

Glaring at him, Sunny straightened. She had to raise her voice to be heard over the rising clamor. "You're supposed to keep order! Go down front and tell them to behave until Grace gets over here."

"Me? Look, you aren't dealing with a bunch of high society matrons and sissified dandies here, Sunny. If I walk up there threatening them, they're gonna show me what they think of my threats, with or without their guns on their hips!"

Sunny shot him a vicious glower and spit out, "Well, *I* know how to handle a bunch of out-of-control men if you don't!"

She grabbed the matching gloves for her water-blue silk gown from the little reception desk and pulled them on. Then she pulled one long curl over her shoulder so it hung down to brush the top of her cleavage. For good measure, and before Jake could stop her, she inched her dress bodice down even further, then picked up her fan and evaded him when he made a grab for her.

She tapped a clapping man at the nearest table on the shoulder with her fan, widening her eyes and placing her index finger on her lips to shush him. He gulped and quieted, and she batted her eyes in thanks. Proceeding toward the front of the room, she paid attention to at least one man at each table in the same way. Silence spread in her wake, and by the time she turned to face the room, it was filled with slack-jawed cowboys with quiet hands and feet. Recognizing her successful ploy at avoiding a riot instead of judging the way she managed it, the women scattered at the other tables with their husbands smiled gratefully at her.

Jake was right there at her side. "You didn't have to pull the damned dress top down," he snarled. Stepping in front of her, he aimed a look at her cleavage, which crinkled her nipples and shot a wave of heat into her core. Gathering her wits about her, she adjusted the bodice protectively. Jake stepped aside, and she cleared her throat.

"I want to thank all of you for coming tonight." She intentionally kept her voice low so the cowboys would have to strain to hear. "Miss Adams will entertain you in a moment," she said, desperately hoping that Ginny would get the singer over there immediately. "But first I think we should all take a little time to reflect on how wonderfully well we have all worked together and . . ."

SUNNY'S VOICE FADED in Jake's mind, and he tried to concentrate on the crowd of people. Instead, her lemony-rose scent filled his senses, and his eyes ached with the strain of keeping them focused straight ahead instead of on her blue-silk-clad body. Well, mostly on the unclad part! The smooth expanse of upper arm between the cap sleeves of her gown and the end of her long blue gloves. The endless creamy skin exposed by the gown's low-cut back, with long blond curls skimming back and forth across it as she moved. A tiny black mole right at the top of one shoulder blade . . .

Dammit!

When she'd pulled her bodice lower, his response had almost burst his trousers! It had taken every bit of willpower he could muster not to jerk that damned gown down even further and feast on her breasts right there in front of everyone. His fight for control left him grabbing for her a second too late, and he was unable to stop her when she flounced saucily away through the crowd of salivating cowboys, her hips swaying and her petticoats rustling. All he could do was follow in her wake, glaring his antagonism while his fingers twitched beside his low-hung holsters. The one cowboy who dared to lick his lips when Sunny passed almost ended up with a bullet hole right between his eyes.

Hell. Some man, someday, *would* feast on those breasts. She was much too beautiful and much too caring for some man not to want her for his wife. That man would have those arms around his neck, those lips available to him, those legs tight around his hips. He would take her virginity and spend the rest of his life having only to reach for her when he wanted to sheath himself in her satin welcome. He might take her quickly, with laughter and teasing. Or he might spend as long as he wanted, tasting and stroking her body, until she begged him to make her his once again.

That man would fill her belly with his children and watch them grow. He would sit on the porch with her at sunset, contentedly reminiscing about their incredible life together.

He could love her and be loved in return for all the days and nights of their lives.

Jake would be spending his nights staring at the walls of a grubby jailhouse or into the flames of a lonely campfire, remembering how her hair sparkled in the sunlight. Remembering the lemony-rose scent of her and comparing it to the smell of horse dung and wood smoke. Wondering who was holding her beneath that star-strewn sky. And wondering why the hell he hadn't realized he loved her in time to try to be that man she was spending her life with.

Sunny nudged him in the ribs and he jumped.

"Ginny just peeped out from the curtains and said Grace was waiting," she whispered. "Go on over to the table while I introduce her."

He stomped away, taking his seat on one of the two empty chairs at the table reserved on the far side of the room. Ruth and Cathy Percival rose, starting around the room to turn the wall sconces down and dim the light while Sunny spoke in glowing terms of the performance they were about to witness. A small hand crept into Jake's, and he looked down to find Teddy sitting beside him.

"What are you doing still up?" Jake asked.

"Sunny said I could stay for one song," she replied, "then I gots to go on over to Miss Ginny's and sleep in her office 'till it's time to go home. Isn't Sunny bee-you-tiful tonight, Ranger Jake?"

"Yeah," he admitted with a resigned sigh. "Beautiful."

"Did you tell her how pretty she is?" Teddy asked.

"No," he conceded.

"Why not? We women like to hear how pretty we are. Why, even that sissy Chester Lassiter had to admit I looked pretty this afternoon, and some of the other boys did too. They had to go over to the schoolhouse and stay with the older girls, so's their mommies could come hear Miss Grace sing. But I got to stay for a little while, 'cause Sunny said I worked hard."

When Jake didn't respond, his eyes glued to the vision in watered-blue silk still speaking at the front of the room, Teddy kicked him beneath the table. Hard.

"You know, Ranger Jake," she said slyly when he frowned at her and reached under the table to rub his leg. "Me and Sunny has had lots of girl talks of an evenin'. She says some men just don't listen to their hearts like women does. 'Course women don't neither, sometimes, I guess. And Sunny says a person's gotta make up a person's own mind. Can't nobody make it up for them."

"And what's that supposed to mean, little one?" Jake asked, willing to forgive her for kicking him since she appeared so determined to have such an important discussion with him.

"Well, we was talking 'bout Miss Cassie and Mr. Duckie." Teddy peeked through her lashes at him, her blue eyes solemn. "He told me I could call him that 'stead of Charlie." she said. "And I was tellin' Sunny how sad it was that Miss Cassie and Mr. Duckie spent all them years by themselves, when they could've been together."

"I think there was a little more to it than that," Jake admonished.

"Yeah, I s'pose, 'specially since that's what Sunny said, too. But I was thinkin' on it, and seems to me, bein' grown-up don't always mean you also got smart along the way." She sighed, brushing one pigtail back behind her shoulder. "Guess I don't know which would be worse. Pa and my ma got married, then found out they was happier apart, I guess, so she left. Maybe that's why some folks are scared of getting married. They figure it won't work out, so they won't take the chance."

"There are a lot of good marriages," Jake told her. "Look at Fred and Ruth."

"That's what I mean." Teddy shook her head, pigtails bobbing on her back. "I don't understand why folks don't see all the good ones, too, and try at least. Like Sunny says, listen to their hearts, 'stead of tryin' to figure out love in their heads."

The curtains opened with a flourish, and Sunny glided toward the table. Every other eye in the room centered on Grace Adams, but Jake couldn't tear his gaze away from Sunny. He rose and held her chair, settling back beside her as soon as she was seated. The table was crowded, and her full skirt brushed his thigh, although she kept her legs from touching his.

She clapped her gloved hands, welcoming Grace Adams and gazing raptly at the singer. The dim wall sconce behind them left Sunny's face in shadow, but Jake didn't need the illumination. Her every feature was burned into his memory, and a hollow, empty feeling settled into his stomach when he looked into the future he planned for himself.

Sunny poked him in the ribs. "Watch the performance," she said, never once looking at him. "This is the only chance you'll get to hear her, since she's leaving on the afternoon stage tomorrow. We were very lucky to get her for even this one time."

Jake turned his attention to Grace Adams. The sconces on the wall behind the curtain hadn't been dimmed, and the singer stood outlined in bright light, her hands clasped in front of her and her eyes closed as she sang. Her hair, though blond, wasn't nearly as bright as Sunny's. She was also at least three inches taller than Sunny, who fit just right beneath his chin if he bent his head down a little. Grace was probably also twenty pounds heavier than Sunny, part of that weight in her larger bosom and hips. Sunny likely weighed a good ninety pounds soaking wet, but you didn't really notice how tiny she was when she got on a tear about something.

He snorted under his breath in disgust when he realized he was comparing the singer to the woman beside him. And despite her Lilliputian stature, Sunny was every bit a woman. He saw the men in the room ogling Grace Adams in her low-cut gown, which barely covered her bosom when she took a deep breath and lifted her head to fill the room with her song. Hell, he guessed she had a nice enough voice, although he hadn't been paying a bit of attention to the words in her song.

The song ended, and after the applause and whistles from the cowboys died down, Grace slowly began a sweet, haunting ballad. Feeling a nudge on his other side, Jake realized Teddy was leaning against him, her head slowly dropping, then jerking back up. The little girl yawned widely, and he bent his head to whisper to Sunny.

"Teddy's almost asleep in her chair. I'll carry her on over to Ginny's office."

"Oh." Sunny shifted as though to rise. "You don't have to. You'll miss part of the performance."

Jake stayed her with a hand on her arm. "I don't mind. You go ahead and enjoy yourself."

"If you're sure. She does have a beautiful voice, doesn't she?"

"Beautiful," Jake said, knowing damned well he wasn't talking about Grace's voice. He turned and picked up Teddy, who snuggled into his arms. Rising, he carried her along the wall toward the front door, making less of a stir that way than he would if he'd carried her through the crowd to the connecting door to the saloon. In the doorway he turned and looked back at Sunny. Grace Adams' voice broke on a note, and he saw that she was watching him. But after that slight pause, the singer took a breath and went on.

Not wanting to disturb the performance further, he walked out onto the boardwalk and over to Ginny's saloon. A man he recognized as Grace's manager was the sole occupant of the saloon, except for Perry, who was polishing the bar surface.

"There's blankets already on the sofa in Ginny's office," Perry said when he caught sight of Jake. "Just put her down in there and leave the door open. I'll check on her off and on."

Jake nodded and carried the sleeping child to the waiting bed. She didn't wake when he laid her down and pulled a blanket over her. Straightening, he jammed his fingers in his back pockets and stared down at her. She had blossomed under Sunny's care, gaining some weight and getting roses in her cheeks.

He had received a telegram from Kansas City in response to his inquiry about Teddy's mother, but it said only that officials there would look into the matter. He'd left the still-sealed letters alone, reluctant to read words obviously meant only for Teddy. If the investigation in Kansas City proved fruitless, he would give the letters to Sunny and allow her to decide when it would be appropriate to let Teddy have them.

He strolled out into the saloon, leaving the office door open as Perry had said. Grace Adams' manager gestured with his beer glass.

"Join me, Ranger?"

"Yeah, I think I will," said Jake. "Pour me a beer, will you, Perry?"

The bartender filled a glass, and Jake took it from him. Before he walked over to the table, however, he opened the connecting door to the center a crack so that if anyone got out of hand over there, he would hear the noise.

Grace's manager leaned back in his chair as Jake approached. He was only a little taller than the singer, and Jake recalled just his first name—Jud something. His round bowler hat lay on the table, and he swept it to one side as Jake sat down.

"Cute kid you had there, Ranger," Jud said. "She yours?"

"I'm not married," Jake told him.

"Don't mean you don't have any kids," Jud said with a snicker, holding up a hand in defense when Jake started to push his chair back and rise. "Whoa, I apologize. And I can't even blame the beer for that stupid remark, because this is my first one. I'll watch my mouth, if you'll stay and finish your beer, Ranger. I've heard the performance going on over there so many times I could sing every word right along with her. She does have a wonderful voice, doesn't she?"

Jake settled back in the chair, taking a swallow of his beer, then wiping away the foam on his mouth. "Yeah, it's a nice voice. She's had some good training."

"She's come a long way since I found her in that dive in St. Joe, Missouri, three years ago," Jud mused. "Gotten a lot more self-confidence, too, and an independent streak. Hell, I didn't want to stop off here in Liberty Flats on our way to Denver, but she was bound and be damned she was gonna do it. Said she was tired of only singing at the hightfalutin places and wanted to entertain the common people just like her one more time."

"Well, the town's enjoying it," Jake said.

Jud downed the remainder of his beer and lifted his glass toward Perry. "Two more over here," he called.

When he belatedly looked to Jake for his agreement, Jake nodded acquiescence. Sitting here drinking beer was better than sitting over there beside Sunny Fannin and knowing she would never be his. A woman didn't marry a *friend.*

He choked on a swallow of beer, wondering which word in his thoughts had caused that suffocated feeling—"marry" or "friend"!

"Jocie was quite taken with that little girl you carried in with you a minute ago," Jud said as Perry put two more beers on the table and collected the empty glasses.

"Jocie?"

"Oh, that's her first name, but she uses Grace Adams in her performing life. It's her middle name, along with her maiden name."

"She's been married, then."

"Not to me," Jud said. "Jocie and I are strictly business partners, and we keep separate rooms in our travels. I don't have a thing against marriage, but those sparks just aren't there between Jocie and me. If I ever give up my freedom, it's gonna be for a woman who's just as beautiful to me when I wake up beside her in the morning as she is when I go to bed with her at night. Jocie, now, she knows how to cover up the problem areas with paint, but she won't be able to keep doing that for too many more years."

He shook his head and smiled. "And it takes her at least an hour every morning to do her cover-up work, then about as long again before she performs. She's not that old—only twenty-eight—but she must have had a pretty rough life before I met her."

Whoops, whistles, and hollering erupted in the next building as Grace finished another song, and Jud waved Jake back into his seat when he started to check on the commotion.

"Jocie's got another hour left," Jud said, "and she can handle the crowd. If they get out of line, she'll just stand there and not sing a note until they quiet down again."

The noise abated, and Jake reached for his beer.

"Now," Jud went on, "that pretty lady you've got your eye on will age well. She's got the bone structure and . . ."

"I'm not eyeing anyone," Jake interrupted.

"Could have fooled me." Jud shrugged and swallowed half his beer in the resulting silence. "Well," he said at last. "That makes me wish we'd planned a little longer stay in this town. Is Miss Fannin a permanent resident here? I might be able to shuffle Jocie's schedule around and get back through here soon."

Jake's hand tightened around the beer glass, and he had to make a conscious effort to loosen his grip before the glass shattered in his hand. "She lives here for now," he said abruptly.

"I understand," Jud said, making it clear to Jake that he really didn't, as he continued, "Soon as someone's lucky enough to get a ring on her finger, she'll go off with her man. Her lucky, lucky man."

The beer soured in Jake's belly, and he pushed his glass away. "I need to go check the town. With everyone at the performance, someone might think now is a good time to pull something."

He rose, and Jud stuck out his hand. "Nice talking to you, Ranger."

Jake stared at the other man's hand for a second, then

gripped it briefly and strode off. Jud's palm had been soft, not calloused like his own hand. It wouldn't abrade Sunny's delicate skin if he touched her, and the other man wouldn't make the mistake of letting Sunny think he wanted only her friendship if he paid court to her.

Hell, *if* he paid court to her! He was probably already sitting in there over his beer rearranging Grace Adams' schedule in his mind in order to get back to Liberty Flats at the earliest opportunity. Ignoring the walkway steps, Jake jumped down into the street, then swiveled and aimed a kick at the nearest hitching post. A stab of pain shot through his foot, and he bent forward, squaring back up after a second and flexing the toes inside his right boot carefully. A limp marring his usual saunter, he hobbled toward Saul Cravens' saloon. That was the likeliest place in town for him to find trouble needing taken care of.

Maybe a good fight would work the restlessness and longing out of his system.

18

"SUNNY?"

"What, darling?" When Teddy didn't reply, Sunny looked up quizzically from grading the wobbly-printed spelling paper on the kitchen table. "Teddy? What is it?"

Teddy tied a ribbon on the braid in Dolly's hair, her little face creased with a frown. "I . . ." She heaved her small shoulders. "I was wondering. Me and Ranger Jake was . . ."

"Ranger Jake and I were," Sunny corrected.

"All right. Ranger Jake and I was . . . were talkin' about love last Saturday night at the grand openin'."

"You were?" Sunny asked with a raised eyebrow. "And what conclusion did you come to about love?"

"Well, not none, really. If a con . . . conclusion means an answer to somethin'. Miss Adams began to sing, and I fell asleep. Next thing I knew, it was mornin', and I was home in my own bed. But I been thinkin' about it some more, these whole four days."

Sunny leaned her chin on her palm, setting her elbow on the tabletop to support her head. "What's been bothering you, sweetheart?"

"Gettin' married," Teddy said with a firm nod, staring directly into Sunny's face. "You know I told you how handsome I think Ranger Jake is. I thought maybe if he waited 'til I got a little bit older, I might marry him, 'cause I really love him. But then I seen that Ranger Jake loved you, so's I figured . . ."

"Whatever gave you that idea?" Sunny gasped.

"What? That Ranger Jake loves you?" Teddy asked. "Well, I wasn't sure 'til I seen Mr. Duckie with Miss Cassie. Mr. Duckie, he looks at Miss Cassie with them same goo-goo eyes that Ranger Jake has when he watches you, and lately Miss Cassie's been looking back at Mr. Duckie that same way. So's I knows Ranger Jake's in love with you, but I still don't understand it."

"Ah . . ." Sunny swallowed apprehensively, not at all sure she wanted this conversation to continue. "Teddy, I think you're mistaken. Not about Cassie and Mr. Duckworth," she hastily assured the child when Teddy rolled her eyes as though Sunny were the youngster instead of her. "But about Jake. Ranger Jake. Jake and I are only friends. Why, we even talked about it one time, and we decided—both of us decided together—that we were much too different to ever be any more than friends."

"Yeah, that's what I don't understand." Teddy picked up Dolly and hugged her tight. "I wasn't s'posed to hear, but I did. Yesterday, when I went out to Mr. Duckie's ranch with him and Miss Cassie so's Miss Cassie could look at the furniture in the house and see what Mr. Duckie needed. That's when I heard them."

"Heard what?"

"I was s'posed to be out at the corral. Mr. Duckie, he's got a pony there, and he said if you'd let me, I could have it. Can I, Sunny? I'll take care of it, and Mr. Duckie said he'd show me everythin' I needed to do."

"I don't see any reason why not," Sunny conceded, her patience at the child's meandering tale growing thin. "But

Mr. Duckie might change his mind if he finds out you were eavesdropping on a private conversation. What did you hear?"

"Oh!" Teddy rocked Dolly back and forth in her arms. "I better not tell, then, if I wasn't s'posed to hear and if Mr. Duckie might get mad at me and not give me the pony."

She slid out of her chair and Sunny caught her arm, deciding in an instant that she truly did want to extend this discussion. But how could she do that after chastising the child for eavesdropping? "Teddy, listen. Yes, you're not supposed to eavesdrop or pass on private conversations. But . . . well, maybe I can guess what was said. And . . . and if I'm right, you can tell me just by nodding yes or no."

Teddy pursed her lips in thought, then nodded.

"Well, then," Sunny said contemplatively. "My first guess, since this talk has to do with love and marriage, would be that you overheard Mr. Duckworth ask Aunt Cassie to marry him."

Teddy's eyes widened and her mouth rounded. "Oh, you're smart, Sunny. I hope I'm as smart as you when I grow up!"

"Thank you," Sunny acknowledged with a smile, which wavered as she pondered her next guess. "I might need a little hint to guess any more."

"There's not really no more to guess. That's all it was, and I didn't hear what Miss Cassie answered, 'cause she didn't speak loud enough. She prob'ly said yes, tho', them bein' in love and all."

She wrinkled her face again. "That's what I don't understand. You and Ranger Jake bein' in love, too, and decidin' just to be friends. That's what me and Ranger Jake were talkin' about Saturday night, and I was tellin' him what you'd said. 'Bout how a body oughta listen to their heart instead of their head when it comes to love, like it looks like Mr. Duckie and Miss Cassie finally figured out. Is it gonna take you and Ranger Jake all them years to decide you should've listened to your hearts tellin' you that you was in love? 'Stead of listenin' to your heads tellin' you all them there reasons why you oughta just be friends?"

As Sunny sat immobile, Teddy started for the kitchen door. After she opened it, she turned. "I don't wanna scare you none, Sunny," she said. "And I 'member you said a body can't make another person love them—that the love has to be on both sides all on its own. But when I gets a little bigger—when I gets pretty like you—I might's be beautiful enough for Ranger Jake to fall in love with me all on his own."

Teddy started forward again, then paused. "I think Miss Cassie's real lucky Mr. Duckie didn't find someone else in all those years to fall in love with." She nodded her head emphatically. "Really, really lucky."

Gripping Dolly in one arm, Teddy closed the door. Sunny heard Rowdy's excited yips as the dog welcomed Teddy. The dog seemed to have fallen into the routine of waiting on the back porch for Teddy each day, scratching a reminder on the door if the lessons ran too long.

Sunny leaned back in her chair, releasing a breath that blew the wisps of hair away from her forehead. Teddy was wrong—dead wrong. Jake Cameron didn't love her. Oh, she loved him. The barriers she'd kept around her emotions had been crumbling with every word Teddy spoke. And the honesty she prided in herself wouldn't allow her to lie even in her own thoughts.

She'd been falling in love with Jake ever since that first day—the first time he had turned around and she'd seen his face. The first time she'd gazed into the whiskey eyes and fallen straight into their depths.

Whiskey was the right color for them—the right name. She'd been drunk on sensations every time she got near him, despite never having tasted alcohol. She had called them that color herself in her own mind, without realizing the significance. She'd stumbled, fallen, gotten bloody and bruised, all on her own and without the excuse that the men who drank one too many in the saloons had. She'd been drunk on Jake—only Jake—the nearness of Jake.

Still, Jake shared that same honest trait with her. *The rest of it is the problem,* she remembered him saying after the fire, after she'd taken yet another spill in his presence, that time over a chair. *I could never make love to a woman like you and walk away from it unscathed, Sunny. You're a woman a man builds his dreams with—not one he loves and leaves.*

And I guess you're a man without dreams, she had replied.

That's right. Or at least not the type of dreams that include being tied down with a wife and family.

Or at least not with her, Sunny reminded herself. Someday Jake Cameron might meet a woman who could make him change his mind, but the woman's name wouldn't be Sunny.

Picking up her marking pencil, she bent over the list of simple spelling words again. Teddy had already advanced to the point where Sunny was thinking of teaching her to write rather than print, but the little girl needed a bit more practice on her stick letters first. The spelling was accurate, although the letters wavered up and down the lines on the paper.

On the bottom of the sheet Sunny saw that Teddy had been doodling. She smiled at the heart with Teddy and Jake's initials inside it. *T.T. luvs J.C.* She couldn't mark that misspelling, since it hadn't been a word on the test. She did make a mental note to add to the list of vocabulary words for Teddy, cringing a tad when she thought of Teddy's insistence on having the meanings of each listed word explained to her.

But Teddy already appeared to have a lot better grasp of the meaning of the word "love" than she had herself.

Gathering up the lesson supplies, she carried them into Teddy's room and shelved them until the next day. At loose ends with all the work on the building construction now complete, she decided to go over to the store early and help Ruth. Although Teddy hadn't mentioned where she was headed, their usual routine was for Sunny to catch up to the little girl at the general store, where she always found Teddy and her dolly having a midmorning snack with Ruth.

She stopped by the parlor on her way out of the house. Cassie was on the settee, her head bent over a catalog she had borrowed from the general store. "Aunt, I'm going over to see Ruth. Do you want me to take the catalog back with me?"

"No, no." Cassie waved a hand at her. "I'm not done with it, and Duckie's coming in this afternoon. I can't decide if these white curtains would work, or if I should use colored ones."

"Which room are you working on decorating now?"

Cassie flushed bright red. "Ah . . . one of the upstairs rooms."

"The bedroom, Aunt?" Sunny teased.

Cassie sniffed, turning a page in the catalog, then glancing back at the previous page. "Go on with you, child," she ordered. "I'm busy."

Shaking her head tolerantly, Sunny left her aunt to her perusing. On her way to Ruth's, she resolved to cut her day short at the store in order to catch Charlie Duckworth at the house. He'd agreed to talk to her, and since he and Cassie were making secret wedding plans, she wanted her questions answered. Honesty was always best between people, and she was determined to make him tell her whether their only relationship would be as future uncle and niece.

An empty chair sat in front of the jailhouse, and she quelled the desire to ask Ruth if she knew of the Texas Ranger's whereabouts. She could probably couch her inquiry in the guise of friendship, but Teddy's sharp ears and chattering tongue might undermine the ploy. Besides, his whereabouts were none of her concern. None at all.

Since Fred had received another shipment of stock the previous day, the next few hours flew by. Sunny, Ruth, and Teddy finally made enough of a dent in the order to take a short break for a late lunch at Ginny's.

"My treat today," Ruth said as they strolled down the walkway. "Doc said this morning that Fred can start doing more around the store in a couple of days, so I won't need your help after that, Sunny. But I do hope you'll let Teddy keep coming."

"Perhaps until school starts in two weeks," Sunny agreed. "Then she'll be in school most of the day and need time for her lessons in the evenings."

"That will be fine," Ruth said.

At Ginny's, they peeped in the door to find all three of the ladies' tables full, and Cathy Percival and her husband waiting for the first empty table.

"Oh," Teddy said with a pout. "I'm hungry. My belly's a rubbin' my backbone."

"Teddy!" Sunny censured. "Where did you hear an expression like that?"

"Mr. Fred said it the other day," Teddy said with an innocent smile. "When Miz Ruth was late gettin' his lunch."

The two women laughed, and Ginny spoke from behind them. "Well, we can't have a hungry child in here, now can we? Why don't the three of you come on back to my office and we'll have lunch there."

As she led them to her office, Ginny said, "You won't have to stand in line much longer. Have you heard the news?" When she received a negative response, Ginny explained, "Marg's sister, Rosalyn, is coming from New Orleans. She and Marg and Perry are going to open a restaurant. Perry's already bought some land over behind our main street, and I'd be willing to bet some other businesses spring up alongside the restaurant."

She waved Sunny and Ruth to the couch, then pulled another chair up to her desk for Teddy. Sticking her head out her office door, she called for Marg to bring four lunch plates to her office. After settling behind her desk, Ginny said, "I heard some complaints about there not being a hotel in town from the people who traveled all the way in from their ranches for our grand opening, and Cathy Percival's already written to her brother in Oklahoma City, telling him of the opportunity. Evaline's thinking of expanding her shop, too, with the new business she's getting from women wanting nice dresses to wear to the center's performances. Oh, and is Fred going to the meeting this evening, Ruth?"

"He's planning on it," Ruth said. "As are most of the women in town. It's about time we got some organization around here."

"Organization?" Sunny asked as Marg brought in their plates and set them on Ginny's desk. "And what meeting?"

"Oh, dear," Ruth said as Marg left the room. "We were so busy stocking at the store that I forgot to mention it to you. And I was supposed to tell you to be sure and invite Cassie and Mr. Duckworth. Some of the other ranchers are coming in, too, and they'll all be expected to approve this, since it means they'll have to bear their share of the expense."

"What?" Sunny asked again. "You still haven't told me what this is all about."

"Why, we're having a town meeting tonight," Ruth explained, "and we've decided to use the Cultural Center building, since it's not in use during the week. We want Liberty Flats to have a town council and our own sheriff. Jake's been telling us all along that's what we need done, and the men have finally started listening to him. If the Rangers call Jake in for another assignment, we'll be left without law enforcement in town, and our new growth will come to a halt. No one will want to set up a business in a town without law enforcement."

The formerly appetizing food on Sunny's plate lost its appeal, the chunks of chicken and drop dumplings suddenly looking as though they'd already been eaten once. The odor wafted upward, unsettling her stomach rather than whetting her appetite, and she laid her fork on the plate unused.

"Why don't Ranger Jake just be our sheriff?" Teddy asked logically.

"The job was offered to him, honey," Ginny said, and Sunny held her breath. "Unofficially, anyway, until we have our first town council meeting tonight. But Jake's not interested."

Sunny's hopes crashed.

"Why not?" Teddy asked.

"He didn't really say." Ginny shrugged. "But he did offer to wire the Rangers and see if any of their men were thinking of leaving that service and might be interested in taking a job here. John Dougherty's offered to be a deputy, but he doesn't want the full responsibility of the sheriff's position."

Ruth turned a beaming smile on Sunny. "See what you've

done, Sunny? Why, with only getting the Cultural Center under way, you've started a roll in this town. My son Brad's always thought about building furniture. He does beautiful work in his spare time, but there's never been enough business here for him to make a living at it, what with the cost of him getting his lumber from over in East Texas. Now, with the hotel coming and the restaurant needing tables, he's thinking seriously about it. And who knows? If things go well, he could hire a few men and expand."

Sunny managed a tight smile in return. "Yes, that would be wonderful for him. Brad should talk to Aunt Cassie too. She's agreed to help Mr. Duckworth redecorate his house, and she's been rather disappointed in what the catalogs offer."

"I'll do that," Ruth replied, turning back to Ginny to comment on the delicious food.

Sunny pushed a chunk of chicken to the other side of the plate. No, Jake wouldn't be interested in taking the sheriff's job in Liberty Flats. Everyone in town knew Jake was only biding his time until he could get out of here. He could ride over new horizons now, meet new people, new women. Maybe he'd find that special one who would have more power than she did to break through the barricades around his heart.

No, there wasn't a chance for her heart at all with Jake.

So. She should wish him happiness, shouldn't she? She should want him to be satisfied, content with his life, to find someone to share the years ahead with him. Or, if that's what he wanted, to have his freedom to live his life alone.

Her decision made, she stood, setting her plate on Ginny's desk behind a stack of papers. "Teddy, are you ready to go? I'll need to catch Mr. Duckworth before he leaves Aunt Cassie's, to let him know about the meeting."

"But Miss Ginny said there's chocolate cake for desert!" Teddy exclaimed.

"Go on," Ginny said with a laugh. "I'll bring her home in a while."

Wanting to get out of there before either Ruth or Ginny noticed her still full plate, Sunny nodded and left the saloon hurriedly, barely acknowledging the greeting from Cathy Percival when she passed her table. Determinedly, she crossed the street and headed up the walkway on the opposite side. The chair still sat empty, but perhaps he was inside the jailhouse.

John Dougherty looked up when Sunny entered. "Howdy, Miss Fannin. Can I help you with something?"

"Ah . . . no, Mr. Dougherty. I . . . was looking for Ranger Cameron. I understand there's a meeting tonight, but I forgot to find out what time it would be held." Proud of her quick thinking, Sunny stood waiting for John's response.

"It's at eight o'clock," he said. "But you might think about gettin' there early to get a good seat. By the way, when are you ladies having another hoopla over there? I sure don't want to miss it."

"A week from Saturday," Sunny told him. "We should be getting the flyers back on the afternoon stage, so we can put them up around town and get the word out. We hope soon to start having weekly performances. John, where's . . ."

"You know," John mused. "This town keeps on growing, it could use a newspaper and printing press. My cousin Wink's working for a paper in Dallas, but he's been saving his money for his own press and business. I oughta send him a letter and have him come here for a visit."

See what you've done, Sunny? Ruth's voice echoed in her head, and the emptiness inside her grew. Yes, the town would flourish, but without Jake Cameron in it. She'd given the townspeople the incentive to set up their own officials and free Jake to move on.

"I need to get home," she said, her heart feeling as though it was shattering and her thoughts mocking her. *See what you've done, Sunny?* "Thanks, John. I'll see you at the meeting."

"If you see Jake on your way, tell him there's no hurry for him to get back here, 'cause I got that old loafer Pete watching the stable for me. Jake went over to the telegraph office a while ago, and then he was going on to the stable. You might pass him on your way home."

"I'll do that, John." She hurried out the door and across the street again. As she climbed the steps to the opposite walkway once again, her pace faltered. Why was she in such a hurry to find Jake Cameron and tell him that she wished him well in his quest to find a happy life somewhere besides Liberty Flats? Somewhere without her?

But she'd decided that was just what she was going to do, and she marched on to the telegraph office. Her good wishes would put the final stamp on their *friendship*, and free her. Free her from any persistent hope that Jake might fall in love with her in return. Free her mind to tell her heart to firmly shut away the hopes of any chance for a future with Jake Cameron and look for someone else to build her own dreams with.

Her mind needed to tell her heart that the chance of Jake ever loving her was now a completely impossible, dead dream. She would rather be totally without dreams than have those whiskey eyes and rugged face shadowing her nighttime rhapsodies.

Someone cleared a throat, and she realized she'd heard the sound twice already. Giving herself a mental shake, which she expected her mind to pass on to her heart, she looked up at Mr. Turley behind the telegraph office counter.

"I have a message for Ranger Cameron," she said, wondering how long she had been standing in his office without speaking. Fortunately for her, Turley appeared to be too polite to mention her absentmindedness.

"He's already left," the man informed her. "Said something about taking his horse out for some exercise."

"Thank you," Sunny said in defeat, turning to leave.

"Wait, Miss Fannin," Turley called after her. "I ain't had the chance to tell you how much I enjoyed that there Miss Adams the other night. And my wife did, too. First time we've really had somewhere to go, the two of us together. I . . . uh . . . she . . . uh . . . we . . ."

Sunny lifted an inquiring brow, and Turley blushed an even deeper shade of red. "We . . . uh . . . found out we could still have fun together."

Sunny smiled to herself, recognizing the man didn't want to embarrass her by admitting that their fun had extended past the time spent at the performance to the rest of the evening at home.

"I'm glad you enjoyed the evening," she said.

"And the ni . . ." Turley dropped his head, shaking it. "I mean, well, if Jake stops back by here?" He managed to lift his head, but stared over her shoulder. "Anything you need me to tell him?"

"No, it's not that important."

"Well, there's ever anythin' I can do for you, Miss Fannin, you just let me know. My Wanda's been sorta lonesome out here without any of her family, but this is where my job is, so this is where we've had to stay. But her brother's one of them fancy-pants attorneys in Galveston, and he's been thinking about comin' to a smaller town to set up shop. Wanda, she really likes her sister-in-law, and she's real excited about maybe havin' them live near us."

"That would be very nice for Wanda," Sunny agreed.

"Tell her I'm looking forward to meeting her sister-in-law. Good afternoon, Mr. Turley."

"Afternoon, Miss Fannin."

She made it out the door this time and turned toward home. Ahead of her she spotted Teddy with Ginny. They must have passed while she was talking to Mr. Turley.

Recalling the conversation she'd had with Teddy that morning, she slowed her steps. Could the child be right? Could Jake have some feelings for her in return? Feelings that would wither and die once he left? Feelings that might be love he was denying, because they'd both been listening to their heads instead of their hearts?

As she glanced over at the stable she saw Jake dismount from his dun and lead the horse into the barn. Was seeing him now a sign that she should take her heart in her hands this one time and offer it to him? Tell him she hadn't been honest with him—that he intruded on her dreams and that she loved him? Make at least one attempt to see if he could ever return her feelings?

She remembered how she'd felt in his arms—an easy memory to recall since she'd relived those times over and over again at night and even in her daydreams. Would she miss out on the one true love of her life, as her aunt almost had, if she let this chance pass her by?

He might only say no. That he didn't love her in return. His whiskey eyes might fill with derision—or worse, sympathy for her. Could her pride stand that? But could her heart stand wondering through the long years ahead what would have happened if she'd taken a chance?

"Sunny! Are you waiting here at the bank to see me?" Sunny turned to see Cathy Percival and her husband approaching. "You could have waited inside, instead of out in this heat," Cathy said.

Sunny forced a smile. "It sounds silly, Cathy, but I was

standing here woolgathering. You're right, I'd better get out of the heat. I'll see you this evening."

She walked away from the bank, but as soon as she figured Cathy and her husband had gone inside, she changed her path and headed across the street to the stable.

19

AS SHE REACHED the stable, Jake led his unsaddled horse back out and over to the corral gate. He tied the dun's lead rope to the railing, then reached for the currycomb in his back pocket. For once Sunny didn't trip and fall flat on her face when she let her eyes linger on his well-formed backside. Instead she studied his entire body, burning the memory of each hardened plane into her mind.

But, she reminded herself, she hadn't gazed into those whiskey depths yet today. She'd have to be wary of losing her coordination when she did—as well as forgetting her purpose in seeking him out.

"Afternoon, Sunny," Jake said.

"How did you know it was me?" she asked as she stepped up beside the horse.

"I knew," he said quietly.

He smoothed the currycomb across the dun's back, and the horse's muscles quivered in pleasure. He tossed his head, blowing through his nostrils, and Sunny reached out to pet his face. "He's a beautiful animal."

"Yeah, he's a good horse. One of the best Charlie's ever bred."

He brushed the back flank, then across the ribs and worked on the withers. Sweat darkened them, drying somewhat in the heat as Jake stroked that area. He ducked under the horse's neck, starting on the other side.

"Did you need something, Sunny?" he asked, looking across the stallion's neck.

"Oh." She smoothed a hand down the dun-colored neck and brushed the coarse black mane with the back of her hand. She caught a hank of mane between her fingers, comparing its texture to some other black hair. "I . . . John Dougherty asked me to tell you, if I saw you, that you needn't hurry back to the office."

"That's nice of John, but I've got some paperwork to do. Soon as I get Dusty groomed, I'll have to get on it."

"I heard about the meeting tonight. I suppose you're glad the town has decided to hire a sheriff. You'll be able to le . . . leave now."

"Yeah," Jake said abruptly. He picked up Dusty's foreleg and examined the hoof, then moved to the rear hoof. As he made his way around the horse, Sunny stepped back to give him room to inspect the last hoof. Dropping the horse's leg back to the ground, he opened the gate and led the stallion into the corral, unsnapping the lead rope and setting him free.

After he closed the gate, he tipped his forefinger against his hat brim, nodding at Sunny. "Nice talking to you, Sunny. Guess I'll see you at the meeting tonight."

He started to move away, and Sunny grabbed his arm. "Jake. Jake, wait. I want to tell you something."

He froze beneath her touch, his upper arm bunching and knotting. She scanned his face, which he kept averted, staring down the street rather than looking at her. She wished desperately that she could see those whiskey eyes. A dark beard shadowed his tightly clenched granite jaw, and the muscles on his throat worked as he swallowed.

Slowly he reached around with his other hand and removed her fingers from his arm, then spoke. "What is it?"

"I'd like you to look at me while I say this," she said, barely above a whisper.

He jammed his fingers into his back pockets and turned to her. She tilted her head back, trying to read his expression, but his eyes appeared to be focused just over her head. With a small sigh of vexation, she reached up and took his hat off, bringing a slight chuckle from him as he finally looked at her.

"You seem to have had a problem with me wearing a hat ever since I first met you," he said.

"It shadows your eyes," Sunny replied. Then, summoning all her courage, she continued, "And I really love your eyes."

His face turned serious and she felt a cautious glimmer of hope.

"I love your eyes, too, honey," he said quietly. "And your hair." He took his hands out of his pockets and touched one of her curls. "It's so soft and beautiful." He traced a finger around her ear, then across her cheek. "I don't know which feels nicer, your hair or your skin." The fingertip smoothed very gently across her lips, then back again, and a tiny whimper escaped Sunny's throat.

"I was a damned fool to miss my last chance to really kiss you the other day," Jake growled.

She dropped his hat in the dirt and lifted her arms tentatively, laying her palms on his chest. "It doesn't have to be your last chance. You haven't left yet."

His whiskey eyes darkened, and he moved his hands to her waist, his touch burning through the thin fabric of her dress and bringing a gasp of pleasure from her. He bent his head, his breath feathering over her face as he warned, "It damned sure won't be a friendly kiss. It'll be a kiss a man gives a woman he wants to love him."

She tangled her fingers in his shirt. "I don't want another damned *friendly* kiss from you, Jake!"

He groaned and pulled her to him.

"Sunny!" a woman's voice screamed, and Jake released her.

She whirled, her unsteadiness causing her to wobble, and Jake caught her arms to steady her.

Cassie stood on the front porch, screaming once again, "Sunny! Come quick!"

Her aunt wheeled and raced back into the house. Sunny lifted her skirts and ran, with Jake behind her. He reached the house a few steps in front of her, holding the door open as she tore inside.

"Back here!" Cassie called, and they ran to Teddy's bedroom. When she entered the room, Cassie was sitting on the edge of the bed, and she turned a tear-streaked face toward them. Teddy lay on the bed beside Cassie, her face dirty and her left arm on a pillow. Anxiety stabbed through Sunny, and she gratefully leaned against Jake's side when he slipped an arm around her.

"I sent Duckie for the doctor," Cassie said in a choked voice. "Oh, it's all my fault. I should have been watching her closer!"

Teddy reached out with her uninjured hand and patted Cassie on the shoulder. "It weren't your fault, Miss Cassie. Rowdy was jealous 'cause I was riding the pony Mr. Duckie brought with him today and he barked at it. And it don't hurt that bad. It's not that far to the ground from the back of the pony. Not like it would be if I fell from all the way up there on Mr. Duckie's big horse."

"Oh, Teddy, darling," Cassie said, brushing the matted hair from Teddy's face. "You're such a brave little girl."

"I just don't want you to take my pony away," Teddy whispered. "You won't tell Mr. Duckie to do that, will you?"

Cassie choked on a tearful laugh and shook her head. "No. If you still want to ride the pony, it will be there. My father always said you had to get right back on the horse that threw you, or you'd never ride again. But let's wait to see what the doctor says about your arm, before we decide how soon you can ride again."

Sunny looked from her aunt to the child on the bed, unable to decide if she should rush to Teddy's side and check her arm or leave the two of them alone. Cassie glanced up at her, wiping the back of her hand across her cheek.

"Duckie brought the pony in with him today, and she was riding it in the backyard. I was . . . in the kitchen. With Duckie. I didn't see what happened, but Teddy said Rowdy barked and the pony shied, making her lose her seat. She must not have even cried out, because I only realized something was wrong when Rowdy ran into the kitchen and grabbed my skirt. He tugged me toward the back door, and I saw Teddy lying in the dirt. Oh, I was so scared!"

Sunny finally crossed the room and sat on the other side of the bed, gently running her fingers over Teddy's arm. Teddy flinched a little, but she gave Sunny a tremulous smile.

"It doesn't seem to be broken," Sunny said. "It's probably just twisted from her fall."

"Here comes Doc and Charlie," Jake said from the doorway.

He moved aside and Doc Butler came in, carrying his black bag. Charlie followed him, giving Teddy a concerned look, then he moved over to Cassie and put his arm around her shoulders.

"Why don't you all wait for me in another room?" Doc

ordered. "I've seen enough broken bones over the years that I can tell just by lookin' at that arm that it's probably just sprained. But I'll want to wrap it in case there is a small break there. Looks to me like you women are in worse shape than the young'un, from worryin' about her."

Cassie reluctantly rose, then turned a stern look on Doc Butler. "You look her over real well. If she needs anything at all, you let me know. We'll take very good care of her."

"Get out of here, Cassie," Doc said with a chuckle. "I'll give you a full report soon as I get a chance to examine her."

Sunny kissed Teddy's head, then followed Cassie and Charlie from the room. As she passed, Jake placed a comforting hand on her waist and she gave him a grateful look while the four of them walked into the kitchen.

"Sit," Cassie told them. "I'll get us some lemonade. Ginny brought a pitcher over when she saw Teddy home."

They made innocuous conversation while they waited for Doc Butler's report on Teddy's injuries. At one point, Rowdy whined in the kitchen doorway, and Cassie looked at him, pursing her lips.

"Oh, go on," she said, waving at the dog. "Go on in and be with Teddy." Rowdy bounded through the kitchen, tail wagging. In the hallway he turned in the right direction to go to Teddy's room. "Hmph," Cassie grumped. "Looks to me like he's been in the house before. He knows where to go."

Sunny chuckled and said, "Teddy bathes him every few days, Aunt. He won't dirty your house."

"Don't hurt *our* house none to look lived in," Cassie said. "That's what houses are for, after all. Living in."

"Thank you, Aunt," Sunny said softly.

Doc Butler came into the kitchen, his black bag hanging in one hand. "Just what I thought. A sprain," he told them. "I wrapped it, and you can bring her over to the office tomorrow for me to look at it again, but it'll be fine in a day or two."

Cassie rose to her feet. "I'll go check on her."

"She's tuckered out and she fell asleep, Cassie," Doc said. "Let her rest a while, won't you?"

"I'll just look in on her," Cassie said in a firm voice. She sniffed as she passed him, her stride resolute.

Shaking his head, Doc Butler grinned after her. "Sure is a different Cassie these days." Turning, he headed for the front door.

"We forgot to pay him," Sunny said, starting to rise.

"I already told him to bill me when he's done takin' care of her, Sunny," Charlie informed her. "Finish your lemonade, before it gets warm."

With a hand on her waist, Jake pulled her back into her chair, propping his arm on her chair back when she sat down. He shoved her glass of lemonade a little closer, indicating for her to obey Charlie. A somewhat uneasy silence settled over the three of them, and she drank a swallow of lemonade, proud of herself when she didn't spill a drop as Jake's finger caressed the top of her shoulder.

She raised her eyes to his, daring to hope they could finish their interrupted conversation if Charlie would only find something else to do. The tender look in Jake's eyes deepened, and he edged his hand across her shoulder to her neck, entangling his fingers in the curls tumbling free from pins.

I don't want you to leave, she thought, hoping he could read the words in her eyes. *I love you.*

His fingers tensed in her hair. Charlie cleared his throat, and Jake shot him a malicious glare. "Don't you have something you need to be doing, Charlie?" he asked.

"Yeah, I do," Charlie replied in a quiet voice. "But I'm waiting for Cassie to get back in here first."

A foreboding feeling swept over Sunny, and she stiffened when Cassie spoke from the doorway. "I'm here now, Duckie." She hesitantly walked over and took the chair beside him, bowing her head for a moment before she looked up at Sunny. Charlie laid one of his hands over Cassie's, which were clasped on the tabletop.

"We've decided you have a right to know what you've been asking about, Sunny," Cassie said. "If you want to tell everyone else, I'll understand. It will be your decision."

"Should I leave?" Jake asked.

"No! Please stay." Sunny stared frantically at him, and Jake tightened his hand on her neck, then moved it back to her shoulder.

"Easy, darling," he murmured. "I'll stay."

Forcing her gaze back to Cassie, Sunny sat rigid, even though her aunt's face showed more kindness toward her than she had since her arrival. "Are you going to finally tell me about what happened to make you hate my mother?" she asked.

Cassie's eyes filled with tears. "I wish I could tell you that you are wrong—that I didn't hate her," she said in a choked voice. "But I did, for a long time. Charlie's made me realize we've all paid dearly for that hatred, though. I can't change it now, but I can maybe try to explain it to you."

Sunny slid her gaze to Charlie. "Are you my father?"

"No." He shook his head in accompaniment to the single word, and Sunny released her breath, though she continued to steel herself for whatever else was coming.

"Your father was Ian Lassiter," Charlie went on. "Since you already know Mary, you know your father died several years ago."

Sunny felt Jake take her hand beneath the table, and she clung to it. "What? How? Suzie and Chester? They're my half-sister and brother!"

Cassie squared her shoulders, saying to Charlie, "I'll tell her about it. You've done enough over the years."

"All right, honey," Charlie agreed.

Cassie closed her eyes briefly, then began speaking. "You asked about Suzie and Chester. Yes, they're your half brother and sister. Ian and Mary were wed nine years ago, soon after Mary's parents died in a tornado. Despite Ian's contention that he wanted a wife back when he first arrived in Liberty Flats nineteen years ago, he ended up waiting all that time before he married anyone. I've always felt that the fathers of daughters of marriageable age probably had reservations about Ian. Perhaps people were unsure about just what part Ian played in the situation back then. Mary was only nineteen herself, however, and she didn't have any other relatives after her parents died. But I'm getting ahead of my story."

After taking a deep breath, she continued, "I've been the one trying to make you leave town, Sunny. And I'm so, so sorry. I was afraid you'd do exactly what you did—start asking questions and bring the secrets I'd kept hidden all these years to light."

She glanced at Jake. "I'm ready to take my punishment, Jake. I sawed the ladder step partly in two, hoping Sunny would realize it was too dangerous in that old building to keep on working. I didn't think far enough ahead to realize someone might actually get hurt badly. It was a step near the bottom, after all, and I figured someone would only fall a little ways. When I heard about Fred, I set the fire, trying to cover up what I'd done."

"It could have been Sunny on that step," Jake growled.

"I know that now, but I was so confused at the time! I wasn't thinking straight. I just wanted her to leave. I didn't even think when I set the fire that it might spread to the rest of the town. Oh, God!" She hung her head in shame.

"I paid Fred's doctor bills," Charlie said. "And Cassie's going to tell them what she did. We're not going to have any more lies and secrets."

"What about the note I found in the house?" Sunny asked.

"I wrote it," Cassie admitted. "I was trying to think of a less dangerous way to get you to leave town. I thought you'd be so embarrassed and all the women would laugh at you if you carried a pail of cow manure into the social."

"Teddy was almost bitten by a snake that day."

Cassie gasped. "You never told me!"

"But why, Aunt?" Sunny exhorted. "Why did you want me to leave? What didn't you want me to find out?"

Cassie bit her lips, then turned an imploring look to Charlie. He patted her hand, but when he started to speak, she shook her head. "No. No, I have to be the one to tell her."

She turned back to Sunny. "I know what the rumors are around town about what happened here nineteen years ago. Part of the story is true, of course. Ian came to town a month or so before our parents died, and he bought a ranch from a man whose only son had gone off to join the war and had been killed in one of the first battles. With no one to leave the ranch to, the owner had lost his desire to build the spread up.

"Ian was a handsome man, without doubt. I first saw him at church, but Samantha had always been so much prettier than me I figured he'd be more interested in her. At first he did seem to be, but Sammy was in no way ready to settle down to one man. She was having too much fun being the belle of the county, and she had a different beau each week."

"You had your share, too, Cassie," Charlie put in. "Heck, I barely managed to get two dances with you anytime there was a barn raising or a birthday party for some gal around here."

"Thank you, Duckie," Cassie said with a tiny smile. She sucked in a breath, and Sunny forced herself to remain silent as her aunt continued, "I was so shocked the first time Ian asked me to have a picnic with him after church that I almost couldn't answer him. But I managed to say yes, and from then on, I seemed to be the only one he courted."

"Seemed to be?" Sunny asked with a frown.

"It turned out I was wrong," Cassie replied, covering her face with her free hand. Then she lifted her head. "Our parents died, and Ian wanted me to marry him right away. He said one reason he wasn't interested in Sammie was because he wanted a wife right then, someone to help him build up the ranch. I couldn't. For one thing, there was Sammie. She was younger than me, and I needed to make sure she was taken care of. Ian said she could live at the ranch, too, but I just didn't feel it was right not to honor the mourning period. I told him we could become engaged, then marry at the end of a year."

She shook her head. "He was furious. He said there was no way he would wait for me for a whole year, and I accused him of not loving me. I told him that if he loved me, he'd wait for me. He . . . he laughed at me, and said that love didn't have a damned thing to do with marriage. That all a man needed was a woman to give him children, and . . . and lay with him when he needed it. That if I didn't want to be that woman, he'd find someone else."

A tear crawled down her cheek, and Cassie viciously swiped it away. "I still had my pride back then. I told him to leave, that I never wanted to see him again. He said, 'Oh, you'll see me again. No woman makes a fool out of me and gets away with it.' "

"Cassie, darling," Charlie said. "You don't have to go back over all this."

"Yes. Yes, I do," she insisted. "You need to know it all,

too, Duckie, before you decide whether or not you still want to marry me. You need to know just how foolish I was."

Charlie sighed and scooted his chair closer to Cassie. Wrapping his arm around her, he nodded for her to continue.

"I was so upset," Cassie said, "I completely closed myself off from Sammie. I forgot she was hurting too over losing our parents. I thought she was spending her days with friends, but I found out later she'd been seeing Ian. I found out when she came to me, crying and saying that she was carrying Ian's child and he had refused to marry her.

"She said at first Ian told her that he was brokenhearted over my refusing to marry him and he just wanted someone to talk to. After seeing her a few times, he started telling her that he loved her. Looking back on it, I'm sure Sammy needed someone to turn to, since I was so wrapped up in my own hurt and our parents were dead."

"She could have come to me," Charlie said. "Or my ma. Ma always thought the world of both of you." He glanced at Sunny. "I want you to remember, we're talking about young people here, about the same age as you. Young people who can make mistakes, 'cause they ain't learned the hard lessons life teaches them later on down the road."

"I'm not going to judge anyone," Sunny said in a miserable voice.

"Don't," Charlie ordered. "And Cassie's about done in. I'll tell you the rest of it, 'cause I'm the one who handled that."

He went on to tell her that her mother confronted Ian again—with him, Charlie—and had told the man that she would agree to leave Liberty Flats and pass herself off as a widow, but only if Lassiter agreed to support her and the baby. Otherwise, she'd bear the shame of telling everyone in town who the father of the baby was, then leave anyway and raise the child somewhere where its parentage wouldn't be known.

One thought kept running through Sunny's mind. *I'm a bastard. My mother was never married.*

Charlie told how Ian had agreed to Samantha's terms, because he had sunk a lot of money into the ranch and he didn't want his reputation in town ruined. Samantha decided to go to St. Louis, where she'd attended school and had a few friends. At first, she insisted on leaving alone, but the day after she left, Charlie followed her. He cared for her as much as he would have a sister, and he wanted to make sure she was settled in St. Louis. After that, he returned to Liberty Flats, but his own feelings about Cassie were in turmoil. She, in turn, refused to see him.

"I thought she was mad at me for going after Sammie," he said.

"I was," Cassie admitted. "But I was also too ashamed. I . . . I'd slept with Ian once too. I wasn't fit for you to love."

Charlie tipped her chin up. "I ain't no virgin, neither, Cassie. Does that make me unfit for you? And I do love you. I've always loved you."

Sobbing, Cassie flung herself into Charlie's arms, and his face broke out in a huge smile. Sunny knew she should leave them alone, but she had to ask one more question.

"Mary's husband . . ." She couldn't bring herself to call the man her father. "He's been dead for several years. But there were still regular deposits in my mother's account. Her lawyer told me."

Charlie shrugged, but Cassie pushed away and looked up at him. "You sent the money, didn't you, Charlie? You took care of Sammie and Sunny."

"Well," he drawled, "that there silver mine up in Denver just kept payin' off. And seemed like the more money I put into those danged horses, the more I made off them. I figure we've probably waited too long to have us any young'uns of our own, Cassie, honey, but I'm right proud I'll soon have me a niece and a little great-niece."

He turned his beaming face on Sunny. "Right proud," he repeated. "Hope you accept that."

Sunny blinked away tears and nodded, then shoved her chair back, and pulled her hand free from Jake's. "I . . . need to be alone for a while," she said.

"Sunny," Jake shoved his chair back and reached for her, but she backed away.

"Please. I really need to be alone." She rushed past him and down the hallway to her bedroom. Closing the door behind her, she leaned on it, fighting new tears.

A bastard. I'm a bastard. From the sound of it, her father had been a different kind of bastard. He'd slept with two sisters, using them against each other, then refusing to marry the one having his child—probably as revenge against Cassie.

She wondered if Mary had any idea that her daughter and son had a half sister, but she quickly realized she couldn't have. Only Cassie and Charlie knew the truth, and now she and Jake.

Jake. Oh, God, she couldn't ever tell him she loved him now. He'd never want anything to do with a woman who was born a bastard. Why had she ever come to Liberty Flats? Why had she ever wanted to know the truth of her parentage?

She thought of her mother—the same age as she was now—alone with child. Alone because she had gotten pregnant by the man her sister loved and had lost the love of her sister as a result. Three lives had been shattered by the man who had fathered her.

And her mother had never married again. Well, not

again—had never married at all. She'd allowed men to escort her to various functions. She'd danced with men at balls and never lacked for partners. But she'd never let any man get closer than a dance.

Sunny remembered romanticizing that sometimes. Thinking her mother too much in love with her husband's memory to ever love another man. Thinking the reason her mother would never talk about her father was because she couldn't bear the pain of speaking of him.

How wrong she had been. There was pain for her mother in remembering the man who fathered her child, but not the romantic pain Sunny had imagined. She wondered if the pain her mother felt could have been half as bad as what she was feeling now, with her heart ripping in two, knowing she would never have that one final chance to tell Jake she loved him. She would live with the shame of being a bastard for the rest of her life, never having the courage to take a chance on some man marrying her out of pity.

"DAMN IT, BOY, go after her," Charlie said in exasperation.

"She said she wanted some time alone," Jake replied in a low voice.

"Yeah, that's what Cassie told me nineteen years ago," Charlie said with a sneer. "That she wanted to be alone. She was lying her fool head off, just like that Sunny gal is now. You love her, don't you?"

Jake met met his eyes steadily. "With everything in me."

Cassie reached across the table and laid her fingers on his arm. "Then go to her, Jake. Tell her. Don't throw away the chance you can have together."

"She . . . I don't know how she feels," Jake said.

"Hell, ask her!" Charlie ordered. "Maybe you don't know

it, but everybody else in town can see that little gal's in love with you. Get in there and find it out for yourself."

Jake shoved his chair back and rose. He walked out of the kitchen and down the hallway, his boot heels thudding softly on the carpeted floor. At the bedroom door, he lifted his hand to knock, thought better of it and reached for the doorknob. The door opened easily, and he saw Sunny lying on her bed, eyes open as she stared at the ceiling.

"Go away," she said in a miserable voice. "Please. I don't want to talk to anyone."

"I'm not going away, Sunny," he said as he crossed the room and sat beside her. "And you do need to talk. You've had a hell of a shock just now."

"Yeah," she scoffed. "It's not every day a person finds out they were born a . . ."

Jake clapped a hand over her mouth, stilling her words. "Damn it, listen to me." She jerked his hand away and turned onto her side with her back to him.

"Go away," she repeated.

"I've already told you I won't go away. Sunny, please look at me."

She shook her head, resisting when he took her arm and tried to turn her toward him. She scooted further away, and his hand fell to the bed.

"I'd really like you to be looking at me when I say this, Sunny," he said quietly. "But if you won't, I'm still going to say it." He swallowed, then took a breath, wishing he'd asked Charlie to roll him a smoke so he'd have something to do with his hands. But, hell, he didn't even smoke. He gripped his knees, biting back a mocking grin when he realized his fingers had been trembling.

"This afternoon," he told Sunny's back, "I wasn't just exercising Dusty. I was looking over some land Charlie had told me was for sale over on the far side of his ranch.

Between him and Mary Lassiter's. It's got water to it—the same water that runs on through to Charlie's place. Comes out of those hills north of us."

He waited for a minute, hoping Sunny would at least comment and let him know she had an idea of what he was trying to say. If anything, he noticed her back get more rigid.

"There's a real pretty spot there," he finally said. "Be a good spot for a house. Man don't need as much range if he raises horses instead of cattle. I don't guess I ever told you, but I've got some invested in Charlie's ranch, too. Reckon I've got a good start of a herd with my share."

Sunny spoke at last. "I wish you luck, Jake. I hope you'll be happy there."

He heaved a huge sigh. "I won't be happy at all unless you'll share it with me, Sunny. I'm asking you to marry me. Be my wife."

She didn't even hesitate. "No."

His heart dropped down to his toes. "You won't even think it over?" he said.

"No."

He frowned at his knees, his fingers clenching until they ached. "I love you, Sunny," he said, his voice gruff with suppressed emotion.

She gasped, and from the corner of his eye he saw her pull a pillow to her chest, then bend her golden head to it. "Go away," she said in a muffled voice. "Please go away."

Even so slowly, he forced his fingers loose. Ever so slowly, he forced himself to stand. Ever so slowly, he forced himself to walk away, when he really wanted to fling himself on the bed and gather her close. Beg her to reconsider.

He closed the door quietly behind him, jammed his fingers into his back pockets, and walked down the hallway.

At the kitchen door, he paused when Cassie and Charlie looked up at him hopefully.

"I won't be needing the land, Charlie," he said. Head bowed, he left the house.

20

A WHILE AFTER Jake left, Cassie walked Charlie out into the backyard, where Charlie tied the pony's lead rope to this saddle horn.

"I wish I didn't have to leave right now, sweetheart," Charlie said. "But that mare's fixin' to foal and it's her first. I should be there."

"You go on, Duckie. I'll try to talk some sense into my niece's stubborn head when she comes out of her room."

Charlie gave her a steady look, then reached into his trouser pocket. "I was gonna wait 'til you came out to dinner tomorrow evening, but after what happened today I don't want no doubts in your mind. I want you roped and wearing my brand so everybody, including you, knows who you belong to."

Charlie handed her the small box, and Cassie took it with shaking fingers. "I . . . there's still things to settle. The fire . . ."

"I more than paid for that fire damage with the donation I made," he said. "But if there's any consequences for you, we'll handle them together. And we'll talk to Fred later. What with all the money I've spent there lately, including buying this ring from him, I think Fred will be reasonable. You'll probably just have to sit through a lecture about how foolish women are, then listen to Fred advise me how to handle you sometimes for your own good."

Cassie felt her temper flare—at the same time realizing how much she was enjoying having feelings again. She'd been dead inside for so long. Another long-forgotten emotion peeped its head into her consciousness, surprising even her when she said coquettishly, "It's so nice having a strong man to lean on, Duckie."

Charlie roared with laughter, and she flashed him a wicked smile. "Why do I have the feeling," Charlie asked, "that I've just been manipulated? And that this won't be the last time?"

"Why, Duckie, I really do mean it. I'm tired of being alone, so you better get used to having me right there by your side." She opened the box, tears misting her eyes when she saw the diamond solitaire and matching wedding band. "They're beautiful, Duckie," she said with a heartfelt sigh.

"Well, you only get one of them for now," he said gruffly. Removing the solitaire, he placed it at the tip of her ring finger. "And you don't get that 'till you give me that final yes. Will you marry me, Cassie, sweetheart?"

"Yes, Duckie," she breathed.

"And?" he asked with a raised eyebrow.

"I love you, Duckie," she replied. He started to push the ring onto her finger, but she stayed his hand. "And?" she asked.

He chuckled, and tipped her chin up. "I love you, Cassie, sweetheart." He kissed her as he slid the ring onto her finger, then stared down at their clasped hands, turning them back and forth so the ring caught the sun's rays. "This is forever, Cassie."

"Forever," she agreed. "And just so you can get used to the idea, I want to show you this." She pulled her own box out of her skirt pocket and lifted the lid. "This was my father's wedding band. It's going to be my brand on you the day we get married."

"I'll be proud to wear it, sweetheart." He kissed her gently again, then mounted his horse. "If you need me, send someone out to the ranch. Otherwise, I'll be in to pick you up tomorrow afternoon around five. I borrowed Theresa from Mary for tomorrow and she'll fix dinner for us this time. If you want, you can be looking around for a housekeeper, but I've got a hankerin' to have a meal cooked by my own wife at least now and then."

"I've got a hankerin' to cook quite a few meals for my own husband," she replied. "Soon as you get rid of that monstrosity of a stove and order one of those new ranges I showed you in the catalog."

He grinned and touched his hat brim. "Already done told Fred to order one. See how easy I am to manipulate?"

Touching his heels to his horse, he rode away, leaving Cassie standing in a cloud of love until he disappeared from sight. She turned back into the house, biting her lip as she entered the kitchen and stared at the table, where so much had happened that afternoon. Darn her silly niece. Hadn't she learned anything from listening to the airing of the mistakes Cassie had made herself?

She thought back on her relationship with her mother, recalling how she had been so determined to ignore the advice passed on to her once she reached her teen years and got so independent. She and Sammy had giggled together, knowing their own dreams would come true without fail—knowing the whole world was open to them. Raised with love and freedom, they had never doubted they could avoid the pitfalls and bad decisions the adults made.

Until their safe, happy world crashed around their ears.

Cassie knew that had her mother been alive to witness the devastation that Ian McAllister had wrought on her daughters' lives, she would have been badly hurt. Cassie knew because she had opened herself up to love again and now cared for Sunny and Teddy so dearly. Her mother would have talked herself hoarse, trying to make Cassie realize that Ian McAllister was not the man for her. Her mother had been hesitant right from the start about Ian, she recalled. But she also knew her mother would have been around to pick up the pieces and help her put her life back together, had Cassie not listened to the warnings that came with her mother's love.

Perhaps that would be all she could do for Sunny—be there to help her pick up the pieces, as Sammie would have been for her daughter.

She went to check on Teddy and found the child awake. Rowdy lay on the foot of the bed, his tail thumping and brown eyes wary as he watched her approach. "Oh, stay right there, dog," she said. "How are you feeling, Teddy?"

Teddy pursed her lips and rolled her eyes upwards. "Well," she said after a few seconds. "My arm hurts a little bit yet, and I gots a couple aches on my shoulder and backside. They's not worth talking 'bout, really, but Doc said I gots to tell every place I hurts. Mostly, tho', I'm awful hungry. Miss Ginny left some chocolate cake with the lemonade."

Cassie laughed tolerantly, aware how wonderful it felt to laugh lately. "You can have a piece of that cake after supper, Teddy. But if you want, you can have a glass of lemonade now. And if you feel like it, you can come into the kitchen and sit with me while I cook."

"I do feel like it." Teddy nodded her head emphatically, and Cassie helped her scoot off the bed. "Where's Sunny?" she asked as they headed into the kitchen.

Cassie settled the child on the chair. "Sunny's in her room," she said as she walked over to the counter and poured two glasses of lemonade. Returning to the table, she sat down on the chair next to Teddy and placed one glass in front of her. After contemplating the child for a moment, she leaned toward her conspiratorially. "Teddy, sweetheart, I have a confession to make."

"A con . . . confession? Is that like admittin' you done something wrong?"

"Yes, but I'm hoping something good will come out of what I did wrong, if it *was* wrong. You see, I know it's not polite to eavesdrop, but I overheard what you and Ranger Jake were talking about the night of the grand opening."

"Yeah, Sunny told me eavesdroppin's not polite, but I wasn't sayin' nothing to Ranger Jake that it would bother me for you to hear."

"That's nice of you to say," Cassie told her with a smile. "So, do you remember when you said being grown-up doesn't always mean you also got smart along the way?"

"Uh-huh. Seems to me grown-ups make mistakes, too."

"They do," Cassie assured her. "I've corrected one of the mistakes I made. Charlie and I are going to be married soon."

"That's wunnerful!" Teddy exclaimed. "Did you get a ring?"

Cassie chuckled and held out her hand. "Oh, it's bee-you-tiful," Teddy said.

"Do you feel up to listening to a story about a mistake our Sunny is making, Teddy?" she asked when Teddy looked up at her.

"Sure. Maybe we can figure out how to help her not make her mistake."

"That's what I was hoping, Teddy."

THE NEXT AFTERNOON, Jake read the telegram Turley handed him, then looked at the operator's worried face.

"You haven't told anyone about this, have you?" he demanded.

"No. No, Jake," Turley assured him. "And you got my word that I won't. But what are you going to do about it?"

"There's not a damned thing I can do. Except tell Sunny."

"It's gonna break her heart." Turley shook his head sadly. "That little lady's done so much for everyone else. Why do bad things have to happen to good people?"

"I don't know, Turley." Jake crumpled the telegram in his fist, then jammed it in his pocket. "I sure as hell don't know."

Shoulders slumping in dejection, he left the telegraph office. Sunny would blame him, he realized as he crossed the street to the jailhouse. And any slight hope he'd had of her changing her mind about marrying him would be gone. Hell, he'd thought maybe if he just hung around a while longer he could court her in other ways, and so he already had his resignation from the Rangers written up.

Flowers might help, but the women in Liberty Flats had scavenged the wildflowers around town and even their own gardens for the Cultural Center opening. He'd bought a box of Fred's best candy, knowing Cassie would be out at Charlie's house that evening and Sunny would be alone. He figured he could go by a little after Teddy's bedtime. He wasn't a quitter—and the remembrance of the few minutes with Sunny right before Teddy got hurt yesterday had given him some hope. He'd been positive she cared for him in return. She just had a lot on her mind right now, what with Cassie and Charlie telling her all that stuff yesterday.

And now this. He should go tell her right away. Waiting wouldn't make it any easier, and there wasn't much time left for her to get used to the idea. He stared at that damned rickety chair leaning in front of the jailhouse, recalling the day so many—so few—weeks ago, when a tiny package of willful audacity had tip-tapped down the walkway toward him, with him being completely unaware she was walking straight into his heart.

He picked up the chair and carried it inside. He'd have Brad Hopkins make the new sheriff another chair. This one belonged to him. He'd been thinking about having Brad repair the seat and add some rockers, but that wouldn't happen now. Still, he didn't want to part with it. Hell, when had he gotten so sentimental? The chair would just be a reminder of all he'd lost, but at least he could set it on the porch of his house someday and watch the sunsets with his memories for company.

He had to go talk to Sunny. Hoping he could catch Cassie before she left, so that Sunny would have another woman there for her when she got the news, he hurried out of the jailhouse. But when he glanced down the street, he saw Charlie's buggy pulling away from the house. Cassie sat close by his side, and the horse was already in a sharp trot. He'd make too much of a ruckus now if he raced to the stables and got his dun to hightail it after Charlie and have him bring Cassie back. Too many people in town would ask too many questions, and Sunny had a right to have this information first.

But he couldn't bring himself to go over there now and also upset Teddy. He needed a woman with him—someone who would be sensitive to Sunny's needs when she read the telegram. He'd sure lacked whatever it was Sunny needed yesterday, though he'd wanted to comfort her with everything in him. He'd thought time would help, but there wasn't any time left now to make this situation any easier.

Several horses stood at the hitching rail in front of the general store, as well as a wagon being loaded with supplies. Ruth would be busy inside. He headed back across the street again, toward Ginny's. Striding through the batwing doors, he spied Ginny talking to Perry at the far end of the bar. The saloon was already busy with the start of the usual Friday evening crowd as he wove his way through the tables. Ginny took one look at his face and motioned him to follow her into her office. She closed the door behind them.

"What is it?" she asked.

Jake pulled the telegram out of his pocket and handed it to her. She scanned the words, then leaned back against her desk, tears filling her green eyes. "Oh, God. She's going to be devastated."

Jake sat on the couch, propping his elbows on his knees with his head hanging down. Ginny's tears had brought a lump to his throat and he couldn't speak. Sitting beside him, Ginny put an arm around his shoulders and took off his hat.

She ran her fingers through his hair. "She'll understand it's not your fault. Sunny's not stupid."

He shook his head. "I couldn't have done anything different," he said in a choked voice. "Hell, it was my job."

Cupping his chin, Ginny forced him to face her. "You listen here, Jake Cameron. You're a good man and a hell of a good Ranger. Even if she doesn't understand at first, she will when she has time to think about it."

She dropped her hand, wiping at a spot of moisture on her dress skirt. Jake reached for his handkerchief, but when he handed it to Ginny, he saw he'd pulled out the pretty hanky with the blue roses he'd bought at the social. The sight of it, creased from being carried in his pocket, choked him up more.

Ginny nudged him in the side. "Better not blow your nose on something like that when you're sitting in the saloon drinking beer," she said, but her voice broke on her teasing gibe.

He heaved a sigh and squeezed the hanky in his fist,

resting his head back against the couch. "Will you go with me to tell her, Ginny? Please."

"Of course, Jake. But we should wait until Teddy's in bed. Sunny will want to tell Teddy herself, in her own way."

"Yeah, that's what I thought, too." He straightened and shoved the hanky back into his pocket. "You got a drink in here?"

"Sure." Ginny rose and went behind her desk. Opening the door on a cabinet, she took out a bottle of bourbon and a glass, which she poured half full. "Ice?" she asked Jake.

"No thanks."

She handed him the glass, and he took a long swallow. The bourbon burned all the way down, but the heat mocked the emptiness inside him instead of soothing it. Ginny set the bottle on the table.

"I'll take that with me to Sunny's after a while," she said. "She might need a drink, although I've never seen her taste liquor. I've got another bottle in the cabinet if you want another drink."

"No, I don't want any more." Jake set the glass, which still had a measure of bourbon in it, on her desk. "The town's gonna be busy tonight, and I need to make sure Dougherty can fill in for me while I go over to Sunny's. By the way, I sent off a wire to Cade Hunter this morning, telling him the sheriff's job here is open. Cade might not be interested in it himself, but he knows a couple of other Rangers who have been talking about getting a job where they can stay in one place. I was thinking of asking Cade, anyway, if he was interested in going into the horse-raising business with me, but that probably won't work out now."

"The town council will be glad to know they might be getting some applicants for the job," Ginny said. "I wish Sunny had come to the meeting last night. She'd be proud of what we've accomplished. And Charlie wasn't there, either, although you said you were sure he'd be willing to pay his share of the assessment for a sheriff's wages."

"Well," Jake said with a shrug, "I guess in all the commotion over Teddy getting hurt, we forgot to tell Charlie about the meeting. And I suppose Sunny wanted to stay with Teddy."

"Doc said it was just a sprain," Ginny commented. "But I can understand Sunny wanting to keep an eye on Teddy. What did you mean about it not working out for your friend Cade to help you raise horses now, Jake?"

Jake grimaced, sorry he had let that part slip while he'd been trying to change the focus of their conversation away from his apprehension over Sunny's reaction when he and Ginny brought her the news in the telegram. Ginny would keep after him until she got an answer.

"I just meant . . . well, the land I looked at might not be right for raising horses," he said evasively. "Hell, I don't want to buy the first place I look at. If it's where I'm gonna settle down and live the rest of my life, it needs to be the right place."

"Oh, Jake, my friend." Ginny took his hands, squeezing his fingers. "You asked her to marry you and she turned you down?"

A corner of his mouth turned up in a wry grin. "Yeah, she turned me down, Ginny. And after this evening, she'll never want to even see me again." Pulling his hands free, he shoved his hair into place and settled his hat on his head. "Teddy goes to bed at eight. I'll be by here a little after that to walk with you over to Sunny's."

"I'll be waiting for you," Ginny said.

TEDDY FINALLY CLOSED her eyes and fell asleep, and Sunny put the storybook on the shelf. Today she had realized how mothers with petulant children came close to losing their tempers with their little darlings. At first she'd blamed Teddy's truculence on her injuries, but she also knew her impatience with Teddy stemmed from her own roiling emotions. She hadn't slept until close to dawn, and then she woke only an hour later.

Her eyes were gritty with lack of sleep, and Teddy had wanted to have a "girl talk" instead of a story tonight. Although she had promised they would talk in the morning, refusing the child made her feel guilty. She pulled Teddy's bedroom door almost closed, sighing in relief as she thought of her waiting bed. Tonight she would surely sleep, and maybe tomorrow she would be rested enough to tell Cassie she had decided to take Teddy and return to St. Louis. Maybe by then she'd be able to tell her without breaking down in tears.

A knock sounded on the front door, and Sunny clenched her teeth. Who on earth could be calling this late in the evening? And did she even care? If she refused to answer, surely they would leave. There wasn't one person in town she wanted to talk to right now.

Except Jake. "Liar," Sunny told her mind aloud. *Liar*, her mind told her in return. "I'm not going to marry him," she whispered. *You still love him*, her heart replied. "I always will," she whispered brokenheartedly. *Stupid*, her mind said. *He loves you, too. He told you he did.*

"Shut up," Sunny whispered angrily. "He wouldn't want a bastard for a wife." *He asked you to marry him after he knew you were a bastard*, her mind said. *And he said he loved you after he already knew that, too*, her heart added.

"It was just pity," she insisted. *Ridiculous*, her mind said. *So stupid to walk away from all that love*, her heart put in.

"Sunny?" a quiet voice called. "Sunny, we're sorry it's so late, but we really need to talk to you."

We, her mind repeated. The voice was Ginny's. Could

Jake be with her? She could no more ignore the possibility than she could win the argument against both her heart and her mind. If it weren't Jake with Ginny, she would beg her friend to watch Teddy while she went to find him. Told him how much she loved him.

She hurried down the hallway to the front door, finding Ginny and Jake already waiting inside for her. "H . . . hello," she stammered, her gaze locked on Jake's solemn face. "I'm still up. I . . . was just going to have a cup of tea. Would you like some? Or some coffee?"

Ginny took her arm and steered her into the parlor. "No, Sunny. We need to talk to you. Please sit down."

Sunny sank to the settee, watching Ginny put a basket on the corner table. Her eyes went back to Jake, but he walked over to the front window and stared through the curtains. She couldn't blame him. She'd been such a bitch toward him yesterday, when he'd only wanted to comfort her. The same afternoon he'd asked her to marry him.

"Jake?" she croaked.

He turned, then walked over and sat in the end chair. "How are you this evening, Sunny?" he asked.

"Better," she told him in a firm voice. "I'm much better." Ginny handed her a glass of brown liquid and she wrinkled her nose, trying to hand the glass back to Ginny. "I don't drink whiskey," she said.

"You might tonight, Sunny, dear." Ginny offered Jake a glass, but he shook his head, and she sat down beside Sunny with the glass still in her own hands.

Fear crawled up Sunny's spine, and her heart began pounding. "What's wrong?" she asked. "I want to know right now!"

Jake dropped his head for a moment, then reached into his pocket and handed her a crumpled yellow piece of paper. Her heart thundering until she thought it would leap out of her chest, Sunny cautiously took the telegram. The words blurred before her eyes, but she blinked, then tried again.

TO: JAKE CAMERON, TEXAS RANGERS, LIBERTY FLATS, TEXAS. STOP. REFERENCE YOUR INQUIRY ABOUT LIVING RELATIVES FOR THEODORA TOMPKINS. STOP. JOCEYLN TOMPKINS MOTHER OF CHILD. STOP. WILL ARRIVE LIBERTY FLATS TOMORROW, SATURDAY. STOP. PLEASE DIRECT QUESTIONS OF DETAILS TO MOTHER. STOP. EDWARD SMITH, ATTORNEY AT LAW, KANSAS CITY, MISSOURI. STOP.

"No. Oh, my God! No!" She stared at Jake, feeling as though yesterday had been only the beginning of a spreading darkness in her world. "Please," she begged him. "When she gets here, tell her . . . tell her you were wrong. That it wasn't her daughter! Tell her it wasn't Teddy. I can't lose her!"

"If that's what you want," Jake said. "If that's what you want me to do, I'll do it. We can go to Mexico and live. We can . . ."

"Stop it, both of you!" Ginny said sternly. "Listen to yourselves. You've got no right to make that sort of decision."

Sunny whirled on her. "I've got every right! I love Teddy and her mother walked out on her. I'll never leave her like that!"

Ginny shook her head. Setting her glass on the floor beside the settee, she took a deep breath. "And what about Teddy's rights, Sunny? What if she wants to know about her mother someday? Will you deny her that knowledge? Will you lie to her and tell her that her mother's dead? Do you have that right, just because you love her?"

Angry tears coursed down Sunny's cheeks, and she stared at the parlor window, avoiding Jake's troubled gaze. Through the sheer curtains, the black night beyond made a background to reflect the scene inside the parlor. Her on the settee beside Ginny—Jake in the end chair. At least she'd learned of the pending disaster in time to do something about it.

"You're right," she told Ginny, keeping her voice steady with a great effort while her mind raced. "I'll tell Teddy in the morning." She rose, realizing she was still holding the glass of whiskey in her hand. She handed it to Ginny. "You can take this with you. I'll be fine."

"I'm not going anywhere." Ginny set the glass beside hers on the floor and leaned back on the settee, crossing her arms. "Since this is Friday night and there's two saloons full of cowboys who could start feeling their oats after a few drinks, Jake has to get back into town. But I'm staying right here."

"I'd rather be alone, Ginny," Sunny said.

"No, you wouldn't," Ginny argued. "You just think you would."

Jake stood and came over to her. "Walk with me onto the porch. Please, Sunny."

Her thoughts continuing to speed in contradiction to her outward calm, Sunny turned and preceded him onto the porch. Outside, he reached for her, and she stepped willingly into his embrace. Wrapping her arms around his neck, she met his lips, kissing him with unrestrained fervor—kissing him as though this would be the last kiss she would ever be able to bestow on the man she loved. She welcomed his tongue in her mouth—his hard body against hers—even the evidence of his need for her against her soft stomach.

When he growled low and buried his face on her shoulder, she stroked his ebony hair and said, "Tell Ginny to leave, Jake. Stay with me tonight. Make love to me."

Jake lifted his head quickly, as though shocked by her words. "No," he said, cupping her face in his palms. "I love you, Sunny, and I want you so damned bad I could lay you down right here on the porch and take you. But that wouldn't be making love, and it will either be making love with you or nothing at all. It will either be having you as my wife or spending my life alone."

He kissed her again, an urgent kiss, which claimed her for his own at the same time it left her wanting more. "I know it won't make up for Teddy, darling," he said after a moment, "but we'll have our own children. Still, if you want me to, my offer stands. We can leave here now. Take Teddy with us."

She gave him a sad smile. "And then what? Always be looking over our shoulders to see if someone has found us? Never being able to give our own children a decent life? No Jake. As much as I love Teddy, I can't do that to us."

"Repeat that part," Jake urged. "The part about there being an us." He lowered his voice. "You've never said you loved me."

She wrapped her arms around his neck again and pulled his head down for a fulfilling kiss. The sound of a gunshot down the street broke them apart.

"Goddamn it," Jake snarled.

She laughed quietly and stepped back. "You better go. John Dougherty's not as good at keeping order as you are."

Another gunshot sounded, and Jake jumped from the porch. Halfway to the gate, he turned. "I'll see you in the morning. 'Night, darlin'."

"'Night, darlin'," she called back, blowing him a kiss. He broke into a run, and she called quietly, "Good-bye, Jake. I love you."

She walked back into the parlor, cocked an eyebrow at Ginny, and said, "Where's my glass of whiskey?"

Ginny handed her the full glass and picked up the bottle

from the end table to refill her own. Replacing the bottle in the basket, she tilted her glass at Sunny. "Cheers."

"Cheers," Sunny replied. Her eyes burned with the fumes, but she managed to take a sip of whiskey. Then she began to wander around the room, keeping her glass out of Ginny's sight as she pretended to drink from it. "I'm really glad you stayed, Ginny," she lied. "I'm sorry I asked you to leave. You've been an awfully good friend to me."

She tipped a measure of whiskey into the log basket beside the fireplace as Ginny said, "I care a lot about you, Sunny. I'm so sorry this has happened. Listen, I know a good lawyer over in Abilene. If I sent him a telegram tomorrow morning, he could be here by Sunday."

Sunny shrugged, then swallowed the last little bit of whiskey in her glass as she turned toward Ginny. "Sunday might be too late, but I'd still appreciate you contacting him for me. Can I have another drink?"

"Sure." Ginny finished the inch or so in her own glass, then picked up the bottle. She poured her glass half full, then concentrated on Sunny's. When Ginny started to pull the bottle back, Sunny placed her hand over hers and held the bottle until the glass almost overflowed.

"Cheers," she said, lifting her glass for a sip. Ginny took a gulp from her own glass, and Sunny turned, roaming the room again. Behind her, she heard Ginny stifle a hiccup.

"Aunt Cassie's going to be really upset," Sunny mused. "I never would have thought it, but she's changed. She loves Teddy. She felt so guilty when Teddy fell off her pony yesterday." With her back to Ginny, she cautiously poured fully two thirds of her whiskey into a plant Cassie had sitting by the front parlor window, then lifted her arm as though taking a long drink. But she kept her mouth closed, so the whiskey only floated against her lips.

"Yeah." Ginny hiccuped again. "S'ya know, ol' Cassie ain't bad. I shorta like her."

Sunny turned and walked back toward Ginny. "She likes you, too, Ginny. She doesn't give her cookie recipes to just anyone."

"Good cookies, too," Ginny said, tipping her glass and taking another swig. A drop escaped her lips, and she wiped at it with her hand. "Whoops," she said with a giggle.

"You know what?" Sunny asked. "I'll bet this whiskey would be good mixed with your lemonade, Ginny. There's still a couple glasses of it left in the pitcher in the kitchen. Let me go fix us each a glass."

"Sounds good to me," Ginny said, handing Sunny her glass, then the bottle from the basket on the table. "But that'sh bourbon, not whiskey. Exchellent bourbon."

"Bourbon," Sunny repeated. "Got it."

She carried the bottle and glasses into the kitchen, then mixed a touch of bourbon in one glass, a touch of lemonade in the other one. When Ginny tasted her drink a moment later, she waved it at Sunny in praise. "Good drinksh. Have ta tell Perry 'bout thesh." Then she laid back against the settee. "Geesh. I'm shorta dizzy."

Sunny rushed forward and caught the glass before it dropped from Ginny's fingers. She set both glasses on the end table, then lifted Ginny's legs onto the settee. Shaking her head at her friend in mute apology, she left the parlor and went to her bedroom. She grabbed two carpetbags from the closet, stuffed a few things of her own in one, then carried the other one to Teddy's bedroom.

Hurry, hurry, she kept telling herself. She opened Teddy's dresser drawers and shoved some underthings into the bag. Quietly, she opened the armoire and added some dresses to the bag. Setting the bag at the foot of the bed, she hurried out of the bedroom and left the house.

She calmed herself on her walk to the stable. John Dougherty was in town helping Jake keep order, but when she rounded the side of the building, she could see a lantern burning in the stable. The old lounger from the stage depot, Pete, snored in a chair, his feet propped on a bale of hay. She studied the situation for a moment, then decided she had no choice but to wake the man. She needed his help both to hitch up a buggy and to give her directions.

She shook Pete's shoulder, and his eyes popped open. "Oh, sorry, Miss," Pete said. "I was just . . . uh . . . checkin' my eyelids for leaks. Yeah, that's what I was doing."

She could smell the whiskey on his breath, recognizing it was similar to the odor in Ginny's bottle, although somewhat harsher. "That's all right, Pete," she said. "I know it's late, and you probably weren't expecting anyone to come by. But you see, my Aunt Cassie is at Charlie Duckworth's, and something has come up that I really need to talk to her about. I need to rent a buggy, so I can go out there."

Pete stumbled to his feet. "Sure, Miss Fannin. I'll hitch you up a buggy right away."

Sunny waited, stifling her impatience and glancing down the street into town now and then. Whatever had been the cause of the gunshots must have been settled, because no one was on the streets. She gave a sigh of relief when Pete led a horse with a buggy rolling along behind it toward her.

"Guess you know how to drive one of these, or you wouldn't have asked to rent one," he said. "But I hitched up one of the gentler mares, just in case."

"I'm very capable with a buggy, Pete," she said. She handed him a coin she'd brought with her from the house, and he helped her into the buggy. As soon as she was settled on the seat, she said, "I've been out to Mary Lassiter's place, but I believe Mr. Duckworth lives a little closer in. Is that right?"

"Yeah, it'll be the first wide road you come to off the main road. On your left."

She forced a laugh. "I suppose if I miss it and miss Mary's, too, I'll end up in Dallas."

"Nah," Pete said with a chortle. "You'd hit Fort Worth first. Like you came through on the stage out here. But you'll know you're lost long time before that, when the sun comes up and you see the last stage stop a'tween here and there."

"Guess I wasn't paying much attention when I came through Fort Worth. I do remember there was an overnight stage stop on my trip out here, and the accommodations weren't nearly what I was used to. Well, I'll make sure I watch closely for the road to Mr. Duckworth's. Good evening."

She clucked to the horse, and it ambled out into the street. Looking over her shoulder, she saw Pete back in his chair, his hat brim pulled down to his nose. She guided the horse down the intersecting street beside Cassie's house and into the backyard. Climbing from the buggy, she tied the horse securely to a porch post before quietly making her way into the house.

She loaded the carpetbags into the buggy first, then checked to make sure Ginny was still asleep. After she turned off the wall sconces, she hurried into Teddy's room and gathered the little girl up, blanket and all. Teddy mumbled once but slept through the transfer to a bed made up on the buggy seat. When Sunny went back to close the kitchen door, Rowdy tried to squeeze through it, and she firmly pushed him back inside.

"No, Rowdy, I can't take you with me right now. You might get antsy in the buggy and wake Teddy up."

She closed the door, then stood for a long, silent moment on the porch. She had to get to St. Louis, where she had influential friends and her mother's attorney to help her fight for custody of Teddy. For an instant she allowed herself to think of the home she was leaving behind—and the man she loved.

But she had no choice. Jake was bound by his oath to let Teddy's mother claim the child she had deserted. She would ruin him if she agreed to his offer to take her and Teddy away.

She had wanted just one time in his arms—one time as a complete woman with him—and she'd been willing to chance that she would still have time to leave after he made love to her. Even his response had confirmed how she would destroy the man Jake was if she asked him to leave with her. She'd lost him the moment he heard the gunshots in town and known he was duty bound to go investigate.

She whispered her good-byes once again and headed for the buggy.

"DON'T! *DON'T WANT* none." Ginny brushed at the wetness on her face, then flopped over, throwing her arm across her head to protect herself. Vaguely she realized her head was pounding, and she burrowed deeper into her nest, welcoming the darkness and the diminished pain. Something pulled on her dress skirt, and she heard it rip.

"Quit!" She flapped a hand behind her, shoving at whatever was disturbing her and then snuggling down once more. Just as she drifted off again, something landed on her back, whooshing the breath out of her and making her head pound again. Twisting, she flung the weight off her back, then peered around the dark room, trying to figure out where she was. She wasn't in her own bedroom. The cushioning under her wasn't her own soft mattress.

Sunny's. She'd been at Sunny's, to offer her support and comfort. Now something grabbed her arm, pulling, and a low growl met her ears. Jerking her arm free, she sat up, holding her aching head in her hands and moaning.

The growl turned into sharp barks, and she focused on the dog at her feet in displeasure. "Shut up, Rowdy! Darn it, go sleep with Teddy!"

Rowdy grabbed her skirt again, pulling backwards until she rose to keep the fabric from tearing and reached to free his mouth. He jumped away, ran to the parlor doorway and barked again. It finally dawned on Ginny that the dog was trying to communicate with her. Good Lord, maybe the house was on fire! She'd heard of animals warning of things like that.

Swiftly she left the room, her nose sniffing the air. But she couldn't smell any smoke. Still, she decided she'd better wake Teddy and Sunny.

A few moments later she ran out of the house. Halfway to her saloon, she skidded to a stop. Did she even have any right to tell Jake that Sunny had taken Teddy and left? She gnawed on her lip. But it could be dangerous out there in the dark for a woman and child alone. Shouldn't she send Jake after them?

Rowdy raced by her. Darn, she must have left the door of the house open. Still debating what to do, she followed the dog.

21

THE REAR WHEEL hit a hole in the road, and the buggy shook and rattled. Sunny pulled on the reins, slowing the horse to a walk. With a nearly full moon to light up the landscape, she had thought the road would be easy to navigate. Instead, it was darker than anticipated and difficult to see. But she couldn't stop. Up ahead she noticed a break in the brush beside the road on the left, which was probably the road to Charlie Duckworth's ranch. She fervently hoped that he wouldn't be on his way to bring Cassie home. A few seconds later she passed the road and breathed a sigh of relief.

Another rattle shook the buggy, and she looked down to make sure Teddy was still secure on the seat. The little girl shifted, then pushed the blanket aside and sat up.

"Where's we at, Sunny?" she asked, rubbing her eyes. "It's dark."

"Teddy, lie down and go back to sleep. Everything's fine."

Instead of obeying, Teddy stared around her and scooted closer to Sunny. "What's we doing going visitin' this late at night, Sunny? And where's we going?"

"Teddy." Sunny sought to make her voice reassuring. "Everything is fine. Just lie back down and I'll wake you up again when we get where we're going."

"I can't, Sunny. I gots to go. I always gots to go when I wake up of a night."

"Can you wait a little while?" Sunny pleaded. "We don't have a chamber pot in the buggy, Teddy."

"Uh-uh. I really gots to go bad."

Glancing behind her, Sunny saw they were still within sight of the road to the Duckworth ranch. Ahead was a bend in the road. "Um . . . just wait one more minute," she told Teddy. "Until we get around that bend up there."

"Why? It's dark here just like there. I can just go 'longside the road."

Sunny clenched her teeth and flipped the reins on the horse's back. It moved into a canter, and she said, "I'll stop around the bend, Teddy. Hang on one more minute."

Teddy wiggled on the seat the entire distance, and Sunny released a sigh when she finally pulled the horse to a halt. Leaping from the buggy before Sunny could stop her, Teddy squatted beside the road. "Don't you go any further," Sunny ordered unnecessarily. She scooted across the seat and handed Teddy her hanky when she saw the child was finished.

A moment later Teddy scrambled back into the buggy and tossed the hanky on the floorboard. As Sunny set the horse in motion, Teddy looked up at her. "Why's you got bags with us, Sunny? I seen them in the back."

"I'll explain everything to you in the morning, Teddy. Go back to sleep now."

"You mean we're gonna be in the buggy all night?"

Shaking her head in frustration, Sunny said, "We're just going to the next stagecoach stop, then we'll catch the stage when it comes through for Dallas. We're . . . going on a trip. I thought you might like to see where I grew up in St. Louis."

Teddy dropped her head and remained silent for a while,

long enough for Sunny to hope she would finally curl up on the seat again. That hope faded when Teddy scooted over to lean against the side of the buggy, lifting her legs and curling her arms around them as she stared at Sunny.

"What's we runnin' away from, Sunny?" she asked. "Me and Pa used to leave town after dark, but that was 'cause he didn't have no money to pay folks what he owed them. I gots the money Miz Ruth paid me for workin' in the store in my piggy bank. You can have it. And if it's costin' you too much to take care of me and Rowdy . . ."

"It's not money, Teddy." Eyes misted with tears, Sunny said, "Teddy, please. Just trust me. We have to leave. You do know I love you with all my heart, don't you? I would die before I'd let anything bad happen to you."

Teddy frowned. "You mean you's leaving in the dark 'cause something bad might happen to me if we stay in Liberty Flats? What, Sunny? Tell me what might happen."

"Nothing's going to happen to you," Sunny replied firmly. "Everything's going to be just fine."

The moon haloing the back of her head, Teddy stuck out her bottom lip in a mutinous pout. "If it's got somethin' to do with me, Sunny, you oughts to tell me about it. 'Specially if it means you gots to leave and not marry Ranger Jake. I's gonna feel real, real bad about it bein' my fault you and him can't get married. Me and Miss Cassie decided you was smart enough to listen if we both told you that you was makin' a mistake, even with you bein' grown-up and all. But you would never even give us a chance to talk to you."

Defeated, Sunny pulled to a halt again and gazed over the horse's back. The landscape stretched endlessly, a stark blanket of black coated with silvery moonlight. Only the jangling harness when the horse tossed its head broke the stillness. The road extended onward—the road to freedom. Or would it be freedom? Teddy was right—they were running away. What sort of example was she setting for Teddy? But what sort of life would Teddy have if her mother took her away? How soon would the woman get tired of the child again and abandon her?

But didn't Teddy have a right to participate in a decision that would affect her life? She could almost feel Teddy's eyes on her while the little girl waited for her to speak. Looping the reins around the brake handle, she turned on the seat to face Teddy.

"Teddy, Ranger Jake got a telegram today. Your mother's alive, and she's arriving in Liberty Flats on the afternoon stage tomorrow. I was afraid she'd take you away from me, and I wanted us to go to St. Louis. I'll hire a lawyer there and ask the courts to let you live with me."

Teddy's eyes widened and her mouth rounded. "You loves me that much, Sunny?" she asked. "So much you'd leave Ranger Jake, when you love him, too?"

Sunny rubbed the backs of her hands against her cheeks, smearing the tears slipping down her face while she tried to think of a way to explain things more clearly to Teddy. The child's words had taken her by surprise. Teddy was unselfishly concerned about her feelings instead of the fact that her own life was on the verge of disruption once again. Precious Teddy. She could learn a lot from the child.

Teddy slid across the seat and wrapped an arm around Sunny's neck. "I don't know how I feel 'bout seein' my ma after all these years," she said. "But if she wants to see me, I reckon I ought to at least let her do that. That don't mean I'd have to go with her, does it?"

"Yes, Teddy," Sunny admitted. "If she wants you to go with her, she has that right according to law." She pulled Teddy into her lap, clasping her tightly. "But if you don't want to stay with her, I promise you I'll do everything I can to get you back with me. Everything!"

"That would be the best way to do it then," Teddy said with a nod. "All legal like and everythin'. I didn't like it none when me and Pa was always runnin' away. And we weren't even leavin' a real nice place and people I like who'd been good to me."

After a lengthy silence, Sunny agreed in a choked voice, "All right, Teddy. We'll go back. We'll go back to Liberty Flats."

Teddy climbed out of Sunny's lap and settled back onto the seat, pulling the blanket around her. "And you'll be going back to Ranger Jake, too," she said.

"Teddy." Sunny unwrapped the reins and turned the horse around. When the buggy was headed back the way they'd come, she said, "Teddy, just because I'm taking you back doesn't mean I'm going back to Jake. I haven't told Jake I'd marry him."

"Yeah," Teddy said around a yawn. "You's makin' one of them mistakes that even bein' grown-up don't make you smart enough not to make. You needs a good talkin'-to, like Miss Cassie says. You're a . . . a cuttin' off your nose to spite your face, that's what you're doin'."

"Teddy!" Sunny said with a gasp. "You're being impertinent!"

"Don't know what that means, but if it means I'm tellin' the truth, then that's what I'm bein'. Miss Cassie says cuttin' off your nose to spite your face means hurtin' your ownself worse than you hurt someone else."

"I'm not trying to hurt Jake," Sunny insisted.

"Well, you's sure doin' a good job of it," Teddy replied saucily. "Ranger Jake, he went out and looked over that land Mr. Duckie told him about 'cause he wanted to buy it and build a house for you and him to live in. Ranger Jake, he's not the kind of man who gives up his freedom easy, Miss Cassie says. And a woman who a man like Ranger Jake falls in love with is derned stupid to throw that kind of love away."

"Did Aunt Cassie say that too?" Sunny asked with a halfhearted chuckle.

"Nope, that was Mr. Duckie."

"I see everyone has been discussing my love life."

"'Cept the two people who oughta be discussin' it," Teddy said in a sly voice. "You and Ranger Jake. Miss Cassie, she said that part."

After a second, Teddy continued, "We weren't talkin' 'bout you and Ranger Jake mean-like, Sunny. We was talkin' 'cause we loves you and wants you to be happy, like Miss Cassie and Mr. Duckie are finally gonna be. And someday, when I grow up, I want to find a man as good as Ranger Jake to marry. It might take me a while to show him that bein' married to me is what he's s'posed to do in his life, but if I know it's right, I won't give up tryin'."

Sunny wrapped an arm around Teddy and hugged her close. Even the rough life Teddy had been through hadn't embittered her. Quite the contrary, Teddy was mature far beyond her years. The sweetness and goodness of the child sent a stab of guilt through Sunny. She'd been very selfish, she realized. She'd been thoroughly immersed in her own emotions—wallowing in self-pity.

Well, the pity party was over with. If Teddy had the courage to go back and face her mother, she herself could do no less than confront her illegitimacy and the damage she had done to the feelings of those around her who only wanted her happiness.

She would apologize to Ginny for getting her drunk so she could leave—run away—when Ginny had come only to support her. She would tell Cassie how sorry she was that she had indeed judged her rather than forgiven her.

And Jake. Jake. What she said to him would come

straight from her heart, not her mind. What she didn't know was whether she had killed his love for her by her infantile actions. He needed a strong woman by his side, a match for his own strength and goodness. She didn't feel very strong right now. She felt small and ashamed.

As soon as she heard the thunder of hooves coming toward their buggy, Sunny pulled the horse to a halt. She knew exactly who it would be. Jake.

He pulled his dun up beside the buggy. With his hat brim shadowing his face, she couldn't make out his expression. Teddy, though, had no doubt of her acceptance by him.

"Hi, Ranger Jake," she said brightly. "We was on our way back."

"I can see that, Teddy," he replied. "And it looks to me like Charlie and Cassie are coming down the road behind you there. Would you want to ride on back to town with them?"

Teddy answered by scrambling past Sunny's legs and holding her arms out to Jake. He swept her onto his horse, then said to Sunny, "I'll be right back."

"I'll wait," Sunny agreed.

He rode on down the road, and Sunny could hear murmurs of conversation as he transferred Teddy into Cassie's care. A moment later he returned to the buggy, stopping behind it and dismounting to tie his dun on the back. Charlie's buggy passed them, with Cassie calling that she would see them back at the house. Jake approached the side of the buggy, jamming his hands in his back pockets and standing there, looking at her.

She cleared her throat. "Teddy told you the truth. We were on our way back."

"Back to what?" he asked.

"What . . . what do you mean?" She tried once again to see his expression but he dropped his head, staring at his boots and not expanding on his question. "Jake," she said. "It wasn't a *what* I was coming back to. It was a *who*. Or at least I was hoping it was a *who*, if that *who* could forgive me for being . . ."

His head snapped up. "If you're gonna bring up the fact that your mother was never married to your father, you can cut that crap right now! I never want to hear another word about it! You're the same person you were the day before yesterday, before you knew about that."

"I'm also the same person who loves you with all my heart, Jake Cameron. What I was going to say was that I hoped you could forgive me for being so steeped in self-pity that I told you no when you asked me to marry you. I hoped you would give me another chance, so I could answer with what was really in my heart."

Jake pulled his hands free and said, "Say that again."

"All of it?" she asked hopefully.

"No. Just the part about loving me."

"I love you, Jake. With all my heart."

He reached for her, and she joyfully sprang toward him. Her foot slipped on the floorboard, and she tumbled into his arms, her impetus flinging him backward. His arms held her tightly as they crashed to the ground, his *oomph* when she landed on his chest blending with her cry of pain as her forehead cracked against his chin.

Holding one hand over the pain on her forehead, she propped herself up, gazing fearfully at his face. "Jake! Are you all right?"

"I'm just fine," he drawled. "I always fall down in the middle of the road when I'm happy."

Laughing and abandoning her attention to her sore forehead, she laid her hand on his cheek, turning serious. "I'll do everything I can to make sure you stay happy, Jake."

He turned his head and kissed her fingers, staring to rise.

She pushed him firmly back to the ground, then straddled him. "You're not going anywhere until you ask me to marry you again."

He stared at her, the moonlight reflecting the laughter in his whiskey eyes and his chest rumbling between her legs. "You actually want me to ask you to marry me while I'm lying here in the dirt?" he said around a chuckle.

"Uh-huh. I feel safer down here on the ground. There's not so far to fall when you make me drunk just by looking at me."

"Is that what happens?"

She nodded. "And it even happens when I just think about you. The worst times, though, are when you saunter away from me, leaving me looking at those darn denims pulled tight across your backside."

She could have sworn he blushed, but the moonlight washed the color from his face. He pulled her down to kiss her, burying his hand in her hair and claiming her for his own with a kiss that swept everything from her mind except the rightness of the moment. The rightness of the two of them together, and the future waiting for them.

When the kiss ended, he whispered, "Marry me, Sunny. Be my wife and let me build my dreams with you. Let's build some dreams together."

"Yes," she whispered. "I love you, Jake."

22

TEDDY CLUNG TO both Jake's and Sunny's hands the next afternoon as the coach pulled in at the stage stop. She wore the white dress Cassie had made her, and Cassie and Charlie stood behind the three of them, adding their silent support for the coming confrontation.

By the time Sunny and Jake had arrived at the house the previous night, Teddy had already explained to Cassie and Charlie about her mother arriving. The other couple's good wishes to the most recently betrothed pair were tempered by their worry over Teddy's future. No one in the household had slept much last night except Teddy, as the adults had discussed their strategy until nearly dawn, although their discussion had been more a list of possibilities than solid plans.

Now Sunny looked down at Teddy's face, wishing the next few moments were behind them—then wishing they were still hours away. Teddy gave her a reassuring smile before she turned back to the stage. As the driver opened the coach door, however, her tightening hold on Sunny's hand revealed that her brave pretense was wobbly at best.

To Sunny's astonishment, Grace Adams' manager, Jud, stepped out of the coach, then reached up to help the singer down. The two of them walked over to the waiting group as the coach driver shut the door and started unhitching the team. Obviously there were no other passengers, yet Sunny couldn't quite accept what she was seeing.

"Hello, Teddy," Grace said before glancing at Sunny. "Can we go somewhere private and talk, Miss Fannin?" she asked without a trace of the Southern drawl she'd had in her voice on her previous visit.

Sunny boldly faced the singer. Her eyes narrowed with determination when she grasped the fact that Grace Adams had to be the same woman as the Jocelyn Tompkins referred to in the telegram—Teddy's mother. How dare her come to town and spy on the situation before she made her true identity known.

"Easy, Sunny," she heard Jake murmur behind her as he put his hands on her waist. She had no idea how he could sense her anger without even seeing her face, although she deeply appreciated his concern. However, her ire at Grace—or Jocelyn, or whatever darn name the woman wanted to use—coupled with her protective feelings toward Teddy, overrode her other feelings.

"We can go over to the house," Sunny told the singer flatly. "I assume you want to talk about Teddy?"

"Jud's attorney, Edward Smith, sent a wire," Grace replied. Her gaze faltered, skittering over Teddy and dropping to the ground.

Sunny nodded, then led the way across the street, keeping Teddy's hand firmly clasped in hers. No one spoke and after they entered the house, Sunny walked into the parlor. She sat on one of the side chairs, pulling Teddy onto her lap, and Jake stepped behind her. He laid his hands on her shoulders while the rest of the group found a place in the room, Cassie waving Grace and her manager to the settee. She and Charlie stood inside the door.

Grace took a deep breath, her hands twisting in her lap as

she spoke to Teddy. "First, I want to tell you that I looked for you for more than three years before I finally traced your father, Teddy. I never meant to leave you behind, but when my sister and her husband came to get you the day after I'd left, Cal—your father—had already gone. I . . . had to find a job, because my sister's husband was by no means well enough off to support me, and it took me a while to save up enough to start trying to find you."

Teddy scooted off Sunny's lap, and Sunny let her go, reaching for Jake's hands on her shoulders.

"Why didn't you tell me who you were when you first came?" Teddy asked. "And you used a different name."

Grace dropped her head. "I was afraid of what you would say to me when you found out who I was," she admitted. Jud took her hand, and she swallowed hard, facing Teddy once more. "I was using my middle name and maiden name for my stage performances, but my legal name is Jocelyn Tompkins. And I thought you would probably be better off here with Miss Fannin, instead of with the life I could offer you. I'm on the move so much, I don't even have a permanent home. Just hotel rooms."

"But you came back," Teddy said.

"Yes, yes, I did. I made Jud wire Denver and reschedule my performance there. You see, you were the reason I agreed to even come to Liberty Flats. I wrote you some letters over the years . . ."

"We gave them to her last night," Jake said. "I found them unopened after her father died, and we've read them to her."

"Then you know," Grace said, "that once I found you, I kept track of you, Teddy. Even though I never got an answer back to any of my letters, which I didn't really expect Cal would let you do, I kept track of you. Jud's lawyer told me I wouldn't have a chance of taking you away from Cal, because I didn't have a permanent home to give you. And singing's all I know. It's what allows me to make a living."

"So why did you come back?" Teddy asked.

"Because I love you," Grace said. "I couldn't stop thinking about you, and I knew I couldn't live the rest of my life without knowing what was happening in your life." She rose from the settee and knelt before Teddy. "Someday when you have a little girl of your own, maybe you'll understand. Once I actually saw you again, I knew you were better off here with Miss Fannin and that she could give you a more stable life than I could offer. But I had to come back and tell you who I was. I had to at least try to be a part of your life again. And I had to know if you hated me for leaving you, or whether you might be able to understand what happened and forgive me."

Sunny spoke up, saying, "I'd like to know about that, too. What happened to make you leave your husband?"

"All right," Grace agreed. "But would you mind if I had a hug from Teddy first?"

Teddy stepped forward, hugging Grace's neck, and even Sunny had to blink back tears when the singer closed her arms around the little girl and buried her face in Teddy's neck. After a long moment, Grace released Teddy and pulled a handkerchief from her dress sleeve. Wiping her eyes, she rose and went back to the settee. Sunny held her breath, allowing it to escape only after Teddy turned and came back to her, and Grace met Sunny's eyes, her look filled with misery but acceptance.

Grace told her story in concise phrases, glancing once in a while at Sunny, who felt her respect for the other woman increase when Grace made it clear she wasn't going to put the total blame for the failure of her marriage on her husband. She allowed Teddy to keep whatever good memories she still had of her father.

Sunny read between the lines of the tale, realizing Grace had married to escape a life of drudgery as a barmaid in her father's tavern in St. Joseph, Missouri. But she had chosen poorly—a man who sounded exciting because he had traveled so many different places. She eloped with him a few days after they met. She soon realized that his wandering ways would bode ill for a secure future, but by then Teddy was on the way. When their travels took them back to St. Joseph, she told her husband the marriage was over, but he refused to face the fact.

The shadows in Grace's eyes while she told Teddy that she had been forced to go to her sister for help told Sunny that Grace's husband had probably beaten her when she confronted him—and maybe at other times. Perhaps fear of her husband had also kept Grace from approaching him when she finally tracked him down. But the woman now graciously glossed over Cal Tompkins' faults and cruelness.

Finally Grace fell silent, twisting her handkerchief in her hands. Then she said, "I didn't come back here to take you away from Miss Fannin, Teddy. As I said, the only life I can offer you is no life for a child, and I love you way too much to force you into that. And, to be honest, I've worked very hard for my career. If I give it up, I'd have even less to offer you. All I want is for you to know who I am and to write to me now and then if you will."

Sunny clenched her fists nervously while Teddy studied the woman across the room. At last Teddy nodded.

"I don't wanna keep movin' 'round like I had to do with Pa," she said, and Sunny gasped with relief. "I wanna stay with Sunny and Ranger Jake. But I'll write to you, and it'll be nice gettin' letters from you."

"I understand," Grace said. She looked around the room. "You've got a family here, and I know you'll be happy."

"I'll want legal custody," Sunny said firmly.

Grace nodded. "I just want to be able to see her when I can break away from my engagements. At least a couple of times a year."

"We'll work it out," Sunny agreed. "How long are you staying this time?"

"The stage to Denver comes back through here on Monday—the day after tomorrow," Grace said. "But Jud didn't get any rooms for us. We thought we'd check with Miss McAllister."

"We got rooms out at the ranch," Charlie spoke up. "Why don't we go on out there and get you settled in?"

"And you can see my pony," Teddy said. "I gotta let him know I'm gonna ride him again, before he thinks he got the better of me."

"I'll bring Sunny out in a little while," Jake said as the other people in the room prepared to leave.

"All right, Ranger Jake." Teddy flung her arms around Sunny's neck and hugged her tightly, then skipped out of the parlor.

Grace hung back, turning to Sunny after the room emptied of everyone except her and Jake. "I don't think I can ever tell you how I feel. I know Teddy will be better off with you, and I want her to be happy, but it's killing me to let her go."

"She'll be fine," Sunny promised. "And you're doing what's best for her—what she wants too. It would be different if you weren't sure she'd have a good life with me, but you know she will. Jake and I are getting married, and Teddy will be just like our own daughter."

"You're being very gracious about this."

"No," Sunny denied honestly. "You're the one being gracious. You could have turned Teddy's life upside down, but you're putting her welfare and feelings ahead of yours. It's not your fault you and Teddy were torn apart, and you could have rightfully blamed your husband for what happened. As Teddy gets older, she'll appreciate what you're doing a lot more than she does now, and I can assure you that I'll accommodate you in our lives any way possible."

Grace nodded and left the parlor. As soon as she was gone, Jake stepped around the chair and pulled Sunny into his arms. "Looks like we've already got us a family. How soon do you think we could start working on a little sister or brother for Teddy?"

"Just as soon as we can get married," Sunny said, throwing her arms around his neck. "Oh, Jake, I feel so stupid!"

"Huh," he muttered. "If marrying me makes you feel like that, you better get used to feeling stupid. Because if you try to leave me again, I'll just chase you down one more time."

"It's not that," she denied. When she looked into his whiskey eyes, she saw the twinkle intermingled with his concern. "You're trying to cheer me up, aren't you? I could have ruined everything by running away last night. And what sort of influence was I on Teddy? Why, she had more sense than me. She was the one who insisted that we come home."

"Yet you're the one who made the decision to do just that." Prodding gently, Jake moved her to the settee. With a lithe movement, he slipped around her and sat down, pulling her onto his lap. "You came back—to your life here and to me."

"I did, didn't I?" Sunny drew back and traced a finger around his lips. "We're very lucky we're not wasting a lot of years like my aunt and Charlie did."

"Remember what Charlie said—they were young when all that happened. They've finally forgiven themselves and I think you need to do that too. Teddy's not going to remember the mistake you *almost* made—she's going to remember that you chose her happiness and to be a good example to her. That you chose to bring her back here and give her a good life."

"I hope you're right . . . Jake! What are you doing?"

Jake unhooked another button on her bodice, then another one, despite her attempt to restrain his fingers. When she grabbed his hand with both of hers and froze his movements, he dropped his head and captured her lips. He kissed her gently at first, then deepened the pressure as he laid her against the settee, shifting his weight to slide free and lie over her.

He nudged his tongue against her lips and she welcomed it inside her mouth. Wrapping her arms around his neck, she buried her fingers in his hair, then gasped with longing when he abandoned her mouth. An instant later she realized her bodice was completely open when his mouth found one of her breasts.

"Jake!" she said around another gasp. "What . . . ?"

He raised his head and fixed her with his whiskey gaze. "I'm making damned sure you never think of me as a *friend* again," he growled. "I want you to always remember that I'm a man and I want you as my woman, my wife and lover, not my *friend*."

She giggled, but only for a moment. He meant what he said. The next time she lifted her sluggish gaze far enough to see his expression, she hovered only a split second before she fell drunkenly into his eyes. But this time his arms caught her and she delighted in the sensations.

"I love you," she murmured. "I'll love you forever."

Suddenly she heard an ominous creak, and Jake's head flew up. He lunged to his feet, barely managing to pull her into his arms before the settee settled into a lopsided heap when one rear leg gave way. Had she still been lying there, her weight would have tumbled her and the settee backward.

She giggled, hurriedly buried her face against Jake's neck to muffle her laugher, and broke into loud mirth when his chest rumbled against her breasts as he joined her.

"I . . ." She gasped for control, then said, "I don't know how we're going to explain that to Aunt Cassie!"

"We'll think of something." He sat down on the floor and cuddled her in his lap. "There. Now where were we?"

"I think it was your turn to say you love me."

He told her, and showed her, and by the time the shadows lengthened into darkness, she realized she had definitely underestimated the danger of being in the darkness with Jake Cameron.